Nothing is sweeter
than surrender...

"Seducing me won't change my mind," she said.

"Won't it?" Reynaud sounded unconcerned. "That remains to be seen."

Beatrice watched him a moment as he stripped off his stockings, breeches, and smallclothes. When she raised her eyes to his, he was watching her. He nodded and cupped himself.

"This is for you. Look your fill."

"What if I don't want it?"

"Then you lie."

That sent a spurt of anger through her. "I think I have the ability to know when I want something or not."

He shook his head. "Not in this case. You haven't experienced a fraction of what can be between a man and a woman."

She was warm now—and wet—but she still addressed him with sarcasm. "And if you show me all that can be, and I'm still not interested, will you desist then?"

"No." He strolled toward her, implacably confident. "You belong to me, and I intend to demonstrate that fact to you."

"Elizabeth Hoyt writes with flair, sophistication, and unstoppable passion."

—Julianne MacLean, author of *Portrait of a Lover*

Please turn this page for more praise for Elizabeth Hoyt . . .

PRAISE FOR
ELIZABETH HOYT'S NOVELS

To Beguile a Beast

"Hoyt works her own brand of literary magic . . . in the exquisitely romantic, superbly sensual third addition to her extraordinary Georgian-set Legend of the Four Soldiers series."

—***Booklist***

"4½ Stars! Top Pick! A magical love story that reads like a mystical fable and a very real and highly passionate romance. Hoyt has found a unique niche that highlights both her storytelling abilities and her considerable talents for depth of character and emotion."

—***Romantic Times BOOKreviews Magazine***

"Desert Isle Keeper! Books such as this one are the reason I read romance . . . Just about as good as it can get."

—**LikesBooks.com**

"Fascinating . . . A heady mix . . . part love story, part history, and part fairy tale . . . I recommend it and cannot wait for the final book in the series."

—***Historical Novels Review***

"5 Stars! An amazing novel . . . Extraordinarily touching and noteworthy . . . Hoyt did an exceptional job."

—**CoffeeTimeRomance.com**

"Everything a historical romance should be . . . Every aspect of this tale is first-rate. The characters come alive, the plot moves along at breakneck speed, and the images and details are so vivid the reader feels totally immersed in the words that spring to life. I loved this book from beginning to end . . . definitely one for the keeper shelf!"

—RomanceReaderatHeart.com

"Another scorching hot historical romance by one of the best . . . I thoroughly enjoyed Elizabeth Hoyt's story of mystery and sensual romance filled with suspense."

—FreshFiction.com

"Elizabeth Hoyt is three for three with a beguiling tale . . . and never misses a beat."

—Midwest Book Review

"Spins a web of pure delight . . . another sparkling diamond for the author's crown. Nothing less than magnificent!"

—HuntressReviews.com

To Seduce a Sinner

"Superbly nuanced historical romance."

—Chicago Tribune

more . . .

"4½ Stars! TOP PICK! Hoyt's magical fairy-tale romances have won the hearts of readers who adore sizzling sensuality perfectly merged with poignancy. Her latest showcases her talent for creating remarkable characters and cherished stories that make us believe in the miracle of love."

—Romantic Times BOOKreviews Magazine

"Hoyt expertly sifts a generous measure of danger into the latest intriguing addition to her Four Soldiers, Georgian-era series. Her ability to fuse wicked wittiness with sinfully sensual romance is stunning."

—Booklist

"I thoroughly enjoyed this story of action, mystery, and hot, hot romance. Be prepared to sizzle through this sensuous and exciting story that's impossible to put down until the last page is finished."

—FreshFiction.com

To Taste Temptation

"Hoyt . . . is firmly in control of her craft with engaging characters, gripping plot, and clever dialogue."

—Publishers Weekly

"4½ Stars! Hoyt's new series . . . begins with destruction and ends with glorious love. She begins each chapter with a snippet of a legend that beautifully dovetails with the plot and creates a distinct love story that will thrill readers."

—Romantic Times BOOKreviews Magazine

"4½ Stars! There's an interesting suspense embedded in this book . . . The sensuality is breathtaking and the reader is carried into the headiness of growing love . . . I loved this book, the high quality of the writing, the engaging plot, and, most of all, the character development. A terrific novel . . . highly recommended."

—TheRomanceReadersConnection.com

The Serpent Prince

"Exquisite romance . . . mesmerizing storytelling . . . incredibly vivid lead characters, earthy writing, and an intense love story."

—Publishers Weekly

"Wonderfully satisfying . . . delightfully witty . . . with just a touch of suspense. Set in a lush regency background, Elizabeth spins a story of treachery, murder, suspense, and love with her usual aplomb."

—RomanceatHeart.com

"Delectably clever writing, deliciously complex characters, and a delightfully sexy romance between perfectly matched protagonists are the key ingredients in the third book in Hoyt's superbly crafted, loosely connected Georgian-era Prince trilogy."

—Booklist

more . . .

The Leopard Prince

"4½ Stars! TOP PICK! An unforgettable love story that ignites the pages not only with heated love scenes but also with a mystery that holds your attention and your heart with searing emotions and dark desire."

—Romantic Times BOOKreviews Magazine

"The new master of the historical romance genre."

—HistoricalRomanceWriters.com

"An exhilarating historical romance."

—Midwest Book Review

The Raven Prince

"A sexy, steamy treat! A spicy broth of pride, passion, and temptation."

—Connie Brockway, *USA Today* bestselling author

"Hoyt expertly spices this stunning debut novel with a sharp sense of wit and then sweetens her lusciously dark, lushly sensual historical romance with a generous sprinkling of fairy-tale charm."

—Chicago Tribune

"Will leave you breathless."

—Julianne MacLean, author of *Portrait of a Lover*

To Desire A Devil

Other titles by Elizabeth Hoyt

The Raven Prince

The Leopard Prince

The Serpent Prince

To Taste Temptation

To Seduce a Sinner

To Beguile a Beast

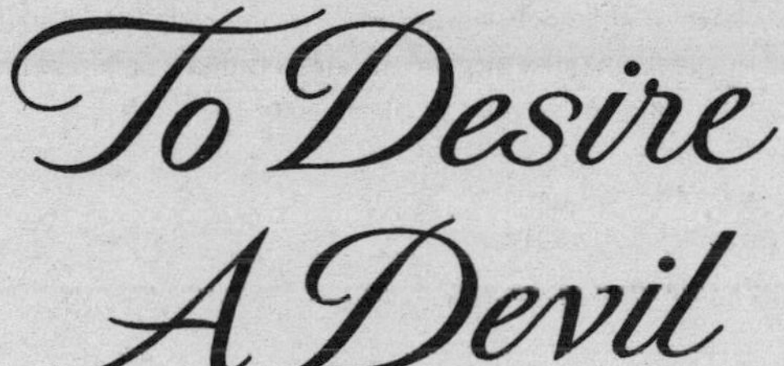

VISION

NEW YORK BOSTON

Cover design by Diane Luger
Cover illustration by Alan Ayer
Handlettering by Ron Zinn

Vision
Hachette Book Group
237 Park Avenue
New York, NY 10017
Visit our website at www.HachetteBookGroup.com.

Vision is an imprint of Grand Central Publishing.
The Vision name and logo is a trademark of Hachette Book Group, Inc.

Printed in the United States of America

First Printing: November 2009

10 9 8 7 6 5 4 3 2 1

*For my editor, **Amy Pierpont**, whose insight and patience made this book immeasurably better.*

Acknowledgments

Thank you to my aunt, **Kay Kerr,** for her help with French phrases—any mistakes are my own; to my agent, **Susannah Taylor**, for her good humor; to my editor, **Amy Pierpont**, for bringing this book together; to the super GCP sales team, including **Bob Levine**; to the wonderful GCP publicity department, including **Melissa Bullock, Anna Balasi,** and **Tanisha Christie**; to the amazing GCP art department, particularly **Diane Luger**; and to my fantastic copy editor, **Carrie Andrews**, for spotting my more embarrassing grammatical whoppers.

Thank you all!

To Desire A Devil

Prologue

Once upon a time, in a country without a name, a soldier was traveling home from war. He'd marched many miles with three friends, but at a crossroads, each had chosen a different way and continued on while our soldier had stopped to pick a pebble from his shoe. Now he sat alone.

The soldier put his shoe back on, but he was not yet interested in continuing his journey. He'd been many years away at war, and he knew no one waited for him at home. Those who might've welcomed his return had long ago died. And if they hadn't, he wasn't sure they would recognize the man he'd become over the years. When a man goes away to war, he never returns the same. Fear and want, courage and loss, killing and tedium all work on him subtly, minute by minute, day by day, year by year, until in the end he is entirely changed, a distortion for good or bad of the man he once was.

So our soldier sat on a rock and contemplated these things as the breeze blew coolly against his cheeks. By his side lay a great sword, and it was in honor of this sword that he was named.

For he was called Longsword. . . .

—from *Longsword*

Chapter One

Longsword's sword was quite extraordinary, for not only was it heavy, sharp, and deadly, but also it could be wielded only by Longsword himself. . . .
—from *Longsword*

London, England
October 1765

Few events are as boring as a political tea. The hostess of such a social affair is often wildly desirous for something—*anything*—to occur at her party so as to make it more exciting.

Although, perhaps a dead man staggering into the tea was a little *too* exciting, Beatrice Corning reflected later.

Up until the dead-man-staggering-in bit, things had gone as usual with the tea party. Which was to say it was crashingly dull. Beatrice had chosen the blue salon, which was, unsurprisingly, blue. A quiet, restful, *dull* blue. White pilasters lined the walls, rising to the ceiling with discreet little curlicues at their tops. Tables and chairs were scattered here and there, and an oval table stood at the center of the room with a vase of late Michaelmas daisies. The refreshments included thinly sliced bread with butter and small, pale pink cakes. Beatrice had argued for the inclusion of raspberry tarts, thinking that they at least might be *colorful,* but Uncle Reggie—the Earl of Blanchard to everyone else—had balked at the idea.

Beatrice sighed. Uncle Reggie was an old darling, but he did like to pinch pennies. Which was also why the wine had been watered down to an anemic rose color, and the tea was so weak one could make out the tiny blue pagoda at the bottom of each teacup. She glanced across the room to where her uncle stood, his plump bandy legs braced and hands on hips, arguing heatedly with Lord Hasselthorpe. At least he wasn't sampling the cakes, and she'd watched carefully to make sure his wineglass was filled only once. The force of Uncle Reggie's ire had made his wig slip askew. Beatrice felt a fond smile tug at her lips. Oh, dear. She gestured to one of the footmen, gave him her plate, and began slowly winding her way across the room to put her uncle to rights.

Only, a quarter of the way to her goal she was stopped by a light touch at her elbow and a conspiratorial whisper. "Don't look now, but His Grace is performing his famous imitation of an angry codfish."

Beatrice turned and looked into twinkling sherry-brown eyes. Lottie Graham was only a smidgen over five feet, plump, and dark-haired, and the innocence of her round, freckled face was entirely belied by the sharpness of her wit.

"He isn't," Beatrice murmured, and then winced as she casually glanced over. Lottie was quite correct, as usual—the Duke of Lister did indeed look like an enraged fish. "Besides, what does a codfish have to get angry about anyway?"

"Exactly," Lottie replied, as if having made her point. "I don't like that man—I never have—and that's entirely aside from his politics."

"Shh," Beatrice hissed. They stood by themselves, but there were several groups of gentlemen nearby who could overhear if they'd wished. Since every man in the room was a staunch Tory, it behooved the ladies to hide their Whig leanings.

"Oh, pish, Beatrice, dear," Lottie said. "Even if one of these fine learned gentlemen heard what I'm saying, none of them have the imagination to realize we might have a thought or two in our pretty heads—especially if that thought doesn't agree with theirs."

"Not even Mr. Graham?"

Both ladies turned to look at a handsome young man in a snowy white wig in the corner of the room. His cheeks were pink, his eyes bright, and he stood straight and strong as he regaled the men about him with a story.

"Especially not Nate," Lottie said, frowning at her husband.

Beatrice tilted her head toward her friend. "But I thought you were making headway in bringing him to our side?"

"I was mistaken," Lottie said lightly. "Where the

other Tories go, there goest Nate as well, whether he agrees with their views or no. He's as steadfast as a titmouse in a high wind. No, I'm very much afraid he'll be voting against Mr. Wheaton's bill to provide for retired soldiers of His Majesty's army."

Beatrice bit her lip. Lottie's tone was nearly flippant, but she knew the other woman was disappointed. "I'm sorry."

Lottie shrugged one shoulder. "It's strange, but I find myself more disillusioned by a husband who has such easily persuaded views than I would be by one whose views were entirely opposite but passionately held. Isn't that quixotic of me?"

"No, it only shows your own strong feeling." Beatrice linked her arm with Lottie's. "Besides, I wouldn't give up on Mr. Graham yet. He does love you, you know."

"Oh, I do know." Lottie examined a tray of pink cakes on the nearby table. "That's what makes the whole thing so very tragic." She popped a cake into her mouth. "Mmm. These are much better than they look."

"Lottie!" Beatrice protested, half laughing.

"Well, it's true. They're such proper little Tory cakes that I'd've thought they'd taste like dust, but they have a lovely hint of rose." She took another cake and ate it. "You realize that Lord Blanchard's wig is crooked, don't you?"

"Yes." Beatrice sighed. "I was on my way to setting it right when you waylaid me."

"Mmm. You'll have to brave Old Fishy, then."

Beatrice saw that the Duke of Lister had joined her uncle and Lord Hasselthorpe. "Lovely. But I still need to save poor Uncle Reggie's wig."

"You courageous soul, you," Lottie said. "I'll stay here and guard the cakes."

"Coward," Beatrice murmured.

She had a smile on her lips as she started again for her uncle's circle. Lottie was right, of course. The gentlemen who gathered in her uncle's salon were the leading lights of the Tory Party. Most sat in the House of Lords, but there were commoners here as well, such as Nathan Graham. They would all be outraged if they found out that she held any political thoughts at all, let alone ones that ran counter to her uncle's. Generally she kept these thoughts to herself, but the matter of a fair pension for veteran soldiers was too important an issue to neglect. Beatrice had seen firsthand what a war wound could do to a man—and how it might affect him for years after he left His Majesty's army. No, it was simply—

The door to the blue salon was flung savagely open, cracking against the wall. Every head in the room swiveled to look at the man who stood there. He was tall, with impossibly wide shoulders that filled the doorway. He wore some type of dull leather leggings and shirt under a bright blue coat. Long black hair straggled wildly down his back, and an overgrown beard nearly covered his gaunt cheeks. An iron cross dangled from one ear, and an enormous unsheathed knife hung from a string at his waist.

He had the eyes of a man long dead.

"Who the hell're—" Uncle Reggie began.

But the man spoke over him, his voice deep and rusty. *"Où est mon père?"*

He was staring right at Beatrice, as if no one else in

the room existed. She was frozen, mesmerized and confused, one hand on the oval table. It couldn't be . . .

He started for her, his stride firm, arrogant, and impatient. *"J'insiste sur le fait de voir mon père!"*

"I . . . I don't know where your father is," Beatrice stuttered. His long stride was eating up the space between them. He was almost to her. No one was doing anything, and she'd forgotten all her schoolroom French. "Please, I don't know—"

But he was already on her, his big, rough hands reaching for her. Beatrice flinched; she couldn't help it. It was as if the devil himself had come for her, here in her own home, at this boring tea of all places.

And then he staggered. One brown hand grasped the table as if to steady himself, but the little table wasn't up for the task. He took it with him as he collapsed to his knees. The vase of flowers crashed to the floor beside him in a mess of petals, water, and glass shards. His angry gaze was still locked with hers, even as he sank to the carpet. Then his black eyes rolled back in his head, and he fell over.

Someone screamed.

"Good God! Beatrice, are you all right, my dear? Where in blazes is my butler?"

Beatrice heard Uncle Reggie behind her, but she was already on her knees beside the fallen man, unmindful of the spilled water from the vase. Hesitantly, she touched his lips and felt the brush of his breath. Still alive, then. Thank God! She took his heavy head between her palms and placed it on her lap so that she might look at his face more closely.

She caught her breath.

The man had been *tattooed*. Three stylized birds of prey flew about his right eye, savage and wild. His commanding black eyes were closed, but his brows were heavy and slightly knit as if he disapproved of her even when unconscious. His beard was untrimmed and at least two inches long, but she made out the mouth beneath, incongruously elegant. The lips were firm, the upper one a wide, sensuous bow.

"My dear, please move away from that . . . that *thing*," Uncle Reggie said. He had his hand on her arm, urging her to get up. "The footmen can't remove him from the house until you move."

"They can't take him," Beatrice said, still staring at the impossible face.

"My dear girl . . ."

She looked up. Uncle Reggie was such a darling, even when red-faced with impatience. This might very well kill him. And her—what did this mean for her? "It's Viscount Hope."

Uncle Reggie blinked. "What?"

"Viscount Hope."

And they both turned to look at the portrait near the door. It was of a young, handsome man, the former heir to the earldom. The man whose death had made it possible for Uncle Reggie to become the Earl of Blanchard.

Black, heavy-lidded eyes stared from the portrait.

She looked back down at the living man. His eyes were closed, but she remembered them well. Black, angry, and glittering, they were identical to the eyes in the portrait.

Beatrice's heart froze in wonder.

Reynaud St. Aubyn, Viscount Hope, the true Earl of Blanchard, was alive.

RICHARD MADDOCK, LORD Hasselthorpe, watched as the Earl of Blanchard's footmen lifted the unconscious lunatic from where he'd collapsed on the floor of the sitting room. How the man had gotten past the butler and footmen in the hall was anyone's guess. The earl should take better care of his guests—the room was filled with the Tory elite, for God's sake.

"Damned idiot," the Duke of Lister growled beside him, putting voice to his own thoughts. "Blanchard should've hired extra guards if the house wasn't safe."

Hasselthorpe grunted, sipping his abominably watered-down wine. The footmen were almost to the door now, obviously laboring under the weight of the savage madman. The earl and his niece were trailing the footmen, speaking in low tones. Blanchard darted a glance at him, and Hasselthorpe raised a disapproving eyebrow. The earl looked hastily away. Blanchard might be higher in rank, but Hasselthorpe's political influence was greater—a fact that Hasselthorpe usually took care to use lightly. Blanchard was, along with the Duke of Lister, his greatest ally in parliament. Hasselthorpe had his eye on the prime minister's seat, and with the backing of Lister and Blanchard, he hoped to make it within the next year.

If all went according to his plans.

The little procession exited the room, and Hasselthorpe returned his gaze to the guests, frowning slightly. The people nearest to where the man had fallen were in small knots, talking in low, excited murmurs. Something was afoot. One could watch the ripple of some news spreading outward through the crowd. As it reached each new knot of gentlemen, eyebrows shot up and bewigged heads leaned close together.

Young Nathan Graham was in a gossiping group nearby. Graham was newly elected to the House of Commons, an ambitious man with the wealth to back his aspiration and the makings of a great orator. He was a young man to watch and perhaps groom for one's own use.

Graham broke away from the circle and strode to where Hasselthorpe and Lister stood in a corner of the room. "They say it's Viscount Hope."

Hasselthorpe blinked, confused. "Who?"

"That man!" Graham gestured to the spot where a maid was cleaning up the broken vase.

Hasselthorpe's mind momentarily froze in shock.

"Impossible," Lister growled. "Hope has been dead for seven years."

"Why would they think it's Hope?" Hasselthorpe asked quietly.

Graham shrugged. "There was a resemblance, sir. I was close enough to study the man's face when he burst into the room. The eyes are . . . well, the only word is *extraordinary*."

"Eyes, extraordinary or not, are hardly proof enough to resurrect a dead man," Lister stated.

Lister had cause to speak with flat authority. He was a big man, tall with a sloping belly, and he had an undeniable presence. Lister was also one of the most powerful men in England. It was natural, then, that when he spoke, men took care to listen.

"Yes, Your Grace." Graham gave a small bow to the duke. "But he was asking after his father."

Graham had no need to add, *And we stand in the Earl of Blanchard's London residence.*

"Ridiculous." Lister hesitated, then said, lower, "If it is Hope, Blanchard's just lost his title."

He looked significantly at Hasselthorpe. If Blanchard lost the title, he would no longer sit in the House of Lords. They'd lose a crucial ally.

Hasselthorpe frowned, turning to the life-sized portrait hanging by the door. Hope had been a young man, perhaps only in his twentieth year, when he'd sat for it. The painting depicted a laughing youth, pink and white cheeks unblemished, black eyes merry and clear. If the madman had been Hope, he'd suffered a sea change of monumental proportions.

Hasselthorpe turned back to the other men and smiled grimly. "A lunatic cannot unseat Blanchard. And in any case, no one has proved he's Hope. There is no cause for alarm."

Hasselthorpe sipped his wine, outwardly cool and composed, while inside he acknowledged the unfinished end to his sentence.

There was no cause for alarm . . . yet.

IT HAD TAKEN four footmen to lift Viscount Hope, and even now they staggered under his weight. Beatrice watched the men carefully as she and her uncle trailed behind them, worried they might let him fall. She'd persuaded Uncle Reggie to take the unconscious man to an unused bedroom, although her uncle had been far from happy with the matter. Uncle Reggie had initially been of a mind to toss him into the street. She took a more cautious view, not only from Christian charity, but also from the niggling worry that if this was Lord Hope, they'd hardly help their case by throwing him out.

The footmen staggered into the hall with their burden. Hope was thinner than in his portrait, but he was still a very tall man—over six feet, Beatrice estimated. She shivered. Fortunately, he'd not regained consciousness after glaring at her so evilly. Otherwise she wasn't sure they would've been able to move him at all.

"Viscount Hope is dead," Uncle Reggie muttered as he trotted beside her. He didn't sound as if he believed his protest himself. "Dead these seven years!"

"Please, Uncle, don't let your temper fly," Beatrice said anxiously. He hated being reminded of it, but Uncle Reggie had had an attack of apoplexy just last month—an attack that had absolutely terrified her. "Remember what the doctor said."

"Oh, pshaw! I'm as fit as a fiddle, despite what that quack thinks," Uncle Reggie said stoutly. "I know you have a soft heart, m'dear, but this can't be Hope. Three men swore they saw him die, murdered by those savages in the American Colonies. One of them was Viscount Vale, his friend since childhood!"

"Well, they were obviously wrong," Beatrice murmured. She frowned as the panting footmen mounted the wide dark-oak stairs ahead of them. The bedrooms were all on the town house's third floor. "Mind his head!"

"Yes, miss," George, the eldest footman, replied.

"If that is Hope, then he's lost his mind," Uncle Reggie huffed as they made the upper hall. "He was raving in French, of all things. About his father! And I know absolutely that the last earl died five years ago. Attended his funeral m'self. You'll not convince me the old earl's alive, too."

"Yes, Uncle," Beatrice replied. "But I don't believe the viscount knows his father is dead."

She felt a pang for the unconscious man. Where had Lord Hope been all these years? How had he gotten those strange tattoos? And why didn't he know his father was dead? Dear God, maybe her uncle was right. Maybe the viscount's mind was broken.

Uncle Reggie gave voice to her awful thoughts. "The man is insane; that's clear. Raving. Attacking you. I say, shouldn't you lie down, m'dear? I can send for some of those lemon sweets you like so much, damn the cost."

"That's very kind of you, Uncle, but he didn't get close enough to lay a hand on me," Beatrice murmured.

"Wasn't for lack of trying!"

Uncle Reggie stared disapprovingly as the footmen bore the viscount into the scarlet bedroom. It was only the second-nicest guest bedroom, and for a moment Beatrice had a pang of doubt. If this was Viscount Hope, then surely he merited the first-nicest guest bedroom? Or was the point moot since if he was Lord Hope, then he really ought to be in the earl's bedroom, which, of course, Uncle Reggie slept in? Beatrice shook her head. The whole thing was too complicated for words, and, in any case, the scarlet bedroom would have to do for now.

"The man ought to be in a madhouse," Uncle Reggie was saying. "Might murder us all in our sleep when he wakes. *If* he wakes."

"I doubt he'll do any such thing," Beatrice said firmly,

ignoring both her uncle's hopeful tone in his last words and her own uneasiness. "Surely it's only the fever. He was burning up when I touched his face."

"S'pose I'll have to send for a physician." Uncle Reggie scowled at Lord Hope. "And pay for it m'self."

"It would be the Christian thing to do," Beatrice murmured. She watched anxiously as the footmen lowered Hope to the bed. He hadn't moved or made a sound since his collapse. Was he dying?

Uncle Reggie grunted. "And I'll have to explain this to my guests somehow. Bound to be gossiping about it this very moment. We'll be the talk of the town, take my word."

"Yes, Uncle," Beatrice said soothingly. "I can supervise here if you wish to attend to our guests."

"Don't take too long, and don't get too close to the blighter. No telling what he might do if he wakes." Uncle Reggie glared at the unconscious man before stumping out of the room.

"I won't." Beatrice turned to the waiting footmen. "George, please see that a physician is called in case the earl becomes distracted and forgets the matter." *Or thinks better of the cost,* she mentally added.

"Yes, miss." George started for the door.

"Oh, and send Mrs. Callahan up, will you, George?" Beatrice frowned at the pale, bearded man on the bed. He was moving restlessly, as if he might be waking. "Mrs. Callahan always seems to know what to do."

"Yes, miss." George hurried from the room.

Beatrice looked at the remaining three footmen. "One of you needs to go tell Cook to warm some water, brandy, and—"

But at that moment, Hope's black eyes flew open. The movement was so sudden, his glare so intense, that Beatrice squeaked like a ninny and jumped back. She straightened and, feeling a little embarrassed of her missishness, hurried forward as Lord Hope began to rise.

"No, no, my lord! You must remain in bed. You're ill." She touched his shoulder, lightly but firmly pushing him back.

And suddenly she was seized by a whirlwind. Lord Hope violently grabbed her, shoved her down on the bed, and fell atop her. He might be thin, but Beatrice felt as if a sack of bricks had landed on her chest. She gasped for air and looked up into black eyes glaring at her malevolently from only inches away. He was so close she could count each individual sooty eyelash.

So close she felt the painful press of that horrid knife in her side.

She tried to press her hand against his chest—she couldn't breathe!—but he caught it, crushing it in his own as he growled, *"J'insiste sur le fait—"*

He was cut off as Henry, one of the footmen, bashed him over the head with a bed warmer. Lord Hope slumped, his heavy head thumping onto Beatrice's breast. For a moment, she was in fear of suffocating altogether. Then Henry pulled him off her. She took a shuddering breath and stood on shaky legs, turning to look at her unconscious patient in the bed. His head lolled, his piercing black eyes veiled now. Would he have really hurt her? He'd looked so evil—*demented,* even. What in God's name had happened to him? She rubbed her sore hand, swallowing hard as she regained her composure.

George returned and looked shocked when Henry explained what had happened.

"Even so, you shouldn't have hit him so hard," Beatrice scolded Henry.

"'E was hurting you, miss." Henry sounded mulish.

She brushed a trembling hand over her hair, checking that her coiffure was still in place. "Yes, well, it didn't actually come to that, although I admit for a moment I was fearful. Thank you, Henry. I'm sorry; I'm still a bit discomposed." She bit her lip, eyeing Lord Hope again. "George, I think it wise to place a guard at the viscount's door. Day and night, mind you."

"Yes, miss," George replied sturdily.

"It's for his own sake as well as ours," Beatrice murmured. "And I'm sure he'll be fine once he recovers from this illness."

The footmen exchanged uncertain glances.

Beatrice put a bit more steel in her voice to cover her own worry. "I would be obliged if Lord Blanchard didn't hear of this incident."

"Yes, ma'am," George answered for all the footmen, although he still looked dubious.

Mrs. Callahan arrived at that moment, bustling into the room. "What's all the bother, then, miss? Hurley's said there's a gentleman who's collapsed."

"Mr. Hurley is correct." Beatrice gestured to the man on the bed. She turned to the housekeeper eagerly as a thought occurred to her. "Do you recognize him?"

"Him?" Mrs. Callahan wrinkled her nose. "Can't say as I do, miss. Very hairy gentleman, isn't he?"

"Says 'e's Viscount Hope," Henry stated with satisfaction.

"Who?" Mrs. Callahan stared.

"Bloke in the painting," Henry clarified. "Pardon me, miss."

"Not at all, Henry," Beatrice replied. "Did you know Lord Hope before the old earl's death?"

"I'm sorry, no, miss," Mrs. Callahan said. "Came on fresh when your uncle was made the earl, if you remember."

"Oh, that's right," Beatrice said in disappointment.

"Practically the whole staff was," Mrs. Callahan continued, "and them that had stayed . . . Well, they're gone now. It's been five years, after all, since the old earl passed."

"Yes, I know, but I had hoped." How could they say for certain who the man was until someone who'd actually known Hope identified him? Beatrice shook her head. "Well, it doesn't matter at the moment anyway. No matter who he is, it's our duty to care for this man."

Beatrice ordered her troops and gave out assignments. By the time she'd consulted with the physician—Uncle Reggie hadn't forgotten to send for him after all—supervised Cook making gruel, and planned for a nursing regimen, the political tea was long over with. Beatrice left Lord Hope—if that was indeed who he was—under the eagle eye of Henry and drifted down the stairs to the blue sitting room.

It was empty now. Only the damp stain on the carpet gave any evidence of the dramatic events of several hours before. Beatrice stared at the stain for a moment before turning and inevitably facing the portrait of Viscount Hope.

He looked so young, so carefree! She stepped closer,

pulled as always by some attracting force she couldn't resist. She'd been nineteen when she'd first seen the portrait. The night she'd arrived at Blanchard House with her uncle, the new Earl of Blanchard, it had been very late. She'd been shown a room, but the excitement of a new house, the long carriage ride, and London itself had caused sleep to escape her. She'd lain wide awake for half an hour or more before pulling on a wrapper and padding down the stairs.

She remembered peeking into the library, examining the study, creeping through the halls, and somehow, inevitably—fatefully, it seemed—she'd ended up here. Here where she stood right now, only a pace before the portrait of Viscount Hope. Then, as now, it was his laughing eyes that had drawn her gaze first. Slightly crinkled, full of mischief and wicked humor. His mouth next, wide, with that slow, sensual curve on the upper lip. His hair was inky black, drawn straight back from a wide brow. He lounged in a relaxed pose against a tree, a fowling gun held casually through the crook of one arm, two spaniels panting adoringly up at that face.

Who could blame them? She'd probably worn the same expression when she'd first seen him. Maybe she still did. She'd spent innumerable nights gazing at him just like this, dreaming of a man who would see inside her and love her only for herself. On the night of her twentieth birthday, she'd crept down here, feeling excited and on the verge of something wonderful. The first time she'd ever been kissed, she'd come here to contemplate her feelings. Funny how now she couldn't quite remember the face of the boy whose lips had so inexpertly met her own. And when Jeremy had returned, broken from the war, she'd come here.

Beatrice took one last look at those wicked ebony eyes and turned aside. For five long years, she'd mooned over a painted man, a thing of dreams and fantasy. And now the flesh-and-blood man lay only two floors above her.

The question was, beneath the hair and beard, under the dirt and madness, was he the same man who'd sat for this portrait so long ago?

Chapter Two

Now, the Goblin King had long envied Longsword his magical sword, for goblins are never content with what they already have. As dusk began to fall, the Goblin King appeared before Longsword, wrapped in a rich velvet cloak.

He bowed and said, "Good sir, I have thirty gold coins in this purse that I will give to you in exchange for your sword."

"I do not wish to offend, sir, but I will not part with my sword," Longsword replied.

And the Goblin King narrowed his eyes. . . .

—from *Longsword*

Her brown eyes stared up through a mask of blood, dull and lifeless. He was too late.

Reynaud St. Aubyn, Viscount Hope, woke with his heart pounding hard and fast, but he made no movement, no outward sign that he was aware. He lay still, continuing to breathe quietly as he assessed his surroundings.

His arms were by his side, so they'd left off the rope that usually staked his hands to the ground. A mistake on their part. He'd wait silently until they were asleep, and then he'd gather his knife, the tattered blanket, and the dried meat he'd hoarded and buried beneath the side of the wigwam. This time he'd be far away when they woke. This time . . .

But something wasn't right.

He inhaled carefully and smelled . . . *bread*? He opened scratchy eyes and his world swung dizzily, caught between the past and the present. For a moment, he thought he'd cast up his accounts and then everything steadied.

He recognized the room.

Reynaud blinked in bemusement. The scarlet room. In his father's house. There was the tall casement window, draped in faded scarlet velvet and letting in bright sunshine. The walls were paneled in dark wood, and a single small painting of overblown pink roses ornamented the wall near the window. Below stood the overstuffed Tudor armchair, which his mother had hated but which his father had forbidden her to throw out, because old Henry VIII was said to have sat in it. Mater had banished it here the year before she died, and Father had never had the heart to move it after. Reynaud's blue coat lay across the chair, carefully folded. And beside the bed, on a small table, were two buns and a glass of water.

He stared hard at the food for a moment, waiting for it to disappear. He'd dreamed too many dreams of bread and wine and meat, dreams that vanished on waking, for him to take this abundance at face value right away. When the buns were still there a moment later, he lunged for them, his skeletal fingers scrabbling at the plate. He grasped one of the buns and tore it in pieces, shoving them into his mouth. Chewing drily, he looked around.

He lay in an antique bed made for some short ancestor. His feet hung off the end, tangled in the scarlet bedclothes, but it was a bed. He touched the embroidered coverlet over his chest, half expecting it to dissolve into delirium. He hadn't slept on a bed in over seven years, and the sensation was foreign. He was used to furs and a dirt-packed floor. Dried grass if he was lucky. The silk coverlet was smooth beneath his fingers, the fine cloth catching on rough skin and calluses. He must believe the evidence.

He was *home*.

Triumph surged through him. Months of dogged traveling, most of it afoot, without money, friends, or influence. These last weeks of wretched fever and purging, the fear that he'd be defeated so close to the goal. All over. Finally. He'd made it home.

Reynaud stretched for the water glass, wincing. Every muscle in his body ached. His hand trembled so badly that some of the water spilled on his shirt, but he still swallowed enough to wash down the bun. He twitched at the coverlet, pulling it back like an old man, and found that he was dressed in his leggings and shirt. Someone had taken off his moccasins, though. He looked about for them, panicked—they were his only shoes—and saw them under the Tudor chair where his coat lay.

Carefully he inched his way to the edge of the bed and stood, panting. Dammit! Where was his knife? He was too weak to defend himself without it. He found and used the chamber pot, then made his way to the Tudor chair. Under the blue coat was his knife. He held it in his right hand, and the familiar worn horn handle made him instantly calmer. Barefoot, he padded back to the bedside table and pocketed the remaining bun; then he went to the door, moving soundlessly, though the extra effort caused sweat to break out along his hairline. Seven years of captivity had taught him to take nothing for granted.

So he was not surprised to find a liveried footman stationed in the hall outside his room. He was, however, somewhat startled when the man moved to bar his exit.

Reynaud cocked an eyebrow and gave the footman a look that for the last seven years had made other men reach for a weapon. This boy had never had to fight for food or life, though. He did not recognize danger even when it stared him in the face.

"Yer not supposed to leave, sir," the footman said.

"Sors de mon chemin," Reynaud snapped.

The footman goggled at him, and it took a moment for Reynaud to realize he'd spoken in French, the language he'd used for most of the last seven years. "Ridiculous," he rasped, the English words strange on his tongue. "I'm Lord Hope. Let me pass."

"Miss Corning says as how yer to stay right there," the footman replied, eyeing the knife. The boy swallowed. "She gave me strict orders."

Reynaud clenched his knife and started for the footman, intending to move him bodily. "Who the hell is Miss Corning?"

"Me," came a feminine voice from beyond the footman. Reynaud paused. The voice was low and sweet and terribly cultured. He hadn't heard English spoken in such tones in a very, very long time. And the voice . . . He might move mountains and kill men for such a voice.

Might forget what he'd fought so long for. It was more than attractive, that voice.

It was life itself.

A slip of a girl peered around the footman. "Or is it 'I'? I can never remember, can you?"

Reynaud scowled. She wasn't what he'd expected somehow. She was of average height, with gold hair and fair skin and a pleasant expression. Her eyes were wide and gray. She was very English-looking, which made her exotic. No, that wasn't right. He swayed where he stood, trying to clear his mind. It was just that he still wasn't used to the sight of a blond woman. An *English* woman.

"Who are you?" he demanded.

Her pale brown eyebrows flew up. "I thought I'd explained. Pardon me. I'm Beatrice Corning. How do you do?"

And she curtsied as if they stood in the most formal ballroom.

Damned if he'd bow; he was unsteady on his feet as it was. He started forward again, intending to bypass the chit. "I'm Hope. Where's my—"

But she touched his arm, and the contact froze him. A wild image of her rounded form lying beneath him as he pressed his length into her softness filled his head. That couldn't be a true memory, he knew. Was he still delirious? His body seemed to *know* hers.

"You've been ill," she was saying, speaking slowly and firmly as if to a small child or a village idiot.

"I—" he began, but she was crowding him, moving him inexorably backward, and the only way to continue forward would be to push past her and perhaps hurt her.

His entire being recoiled at the thought.

So, slowly, gently, she maneuvered him into the scarlet room until he was staring down at her bemusedly by the bed again.

Who was this female?

"Who are you?" he repeated.

Her brows knit. "Can't you remember? I've already told you. I'm Beatrice—"

"Corning," he finished for her impatiently. "Yes, that I understand. What I don't understand is why you're in my father's house."

A wary expression crossed her face, so quickly he almost thought he'd imagined it. But he hadn't. She was hiding something from him, and his senses were put on the alert. He glanced uneasily around the room. He was cornered here if an enemy attacked. He'd have to fight his way to the door, and there wasn't much room to maneuver.

"I live here with my uncle," she said soothingly, as if she sensed his thoughts. "Can you tell me where you've been? What has happened to you?"

"No." *Brown eyes stared up through a mask of blood, dull and lifeless.* He shook his head violently, banishing the phantom. "No!"

"It's all right." Her gray eyes had widened in alarm. "You don't have to tell me. Now, if you'll just lie down again—"

"Who is your uncle?" He could feel some imminent danger raising the hairs on the back of his neck.

She closed her eyes and then looked at him frankly. "My uncle is Reginald St. Aubyn, the Earl of Blanchard."

He gripped his knife harder. "What?"

"I'm so sorry," she said. "You need to lie down."

He grasped her arm. "What did you say?"

Her pink tongue darted out to lick her lips, and he realized, incongruously, that she smelled of flowers.

"Your father died five years ago," she said. "You were thought dead, so my uncle claimed the title."

Not home, then, he thought bitterly. *Not home at all.*

"WELL, THAT MUST'VE been awkward," Lottie said with her usual bluntness the next afternoon.

"It was simply terrible." Beatrice sighed. "He had no idea, of course, that his father was dead, and there he was holding that huge knife. I was quite nervous, half expecting him to do something violent, but instead he became very, very quiet, which was almost worse."

Beatrice frowned, remembering the pang of sympathy that'd shot through her at Lord Hope's stillness. She shouldn't feel sympathy for a man who might strip Uncle Reggie of his title and their home, but there it was. She couldn't help but ache for his loss.

She took a sip of tea. Lottie always had such good tea—nice and strong—which was perhaps why she'd fallen into the habit of calling round the Graham town house every Tuesday afternoon for tea and gossip. Lottie's private sitting room was so elegant, decorated in deep rose and a grayish sort of green one might think was dull but was actually the perfect complement for the rose. Lottie was extraordinarily good with colors and always looked so smart that sometimes Beatrice wondered if she'd bought Pan, her little white Pomeranian, just because he looked so smart as well.

Beatrice eyed the little dog, lying like a miniature

fur rug at their feet, alert to the possibility of biscuit crumbs.

"The quiet gentlemen are the ones you have to watch out for," Lottie stated as she judiciously added a small lump of sugar to her tea.

It took a second for Beatrice to remember the thread of their conversation. Then she said, "Well, he wasn't very quiet when he first appeared."

"No, indeed," Lottie said contentedly. "I thought he'd strangle you."

"You sound rather thrilled by the prospect," Beatrice said severely.

"It would give me a tale to dine out on for a year or more, you must admit," Lottie replied with no trace of shame. She sipped her tea, wrinkled her nose, and added another tiny lump of sugar. "No, it's been three days, and I've heard nothing else but the story of the lost earl bursting into your little political tea."

"Uncle Reggie said we'd be the talk of the town," Beatrice said dolefully.

"And for once he's right." Lottie tried her tea again and must've found it palatable, because she smiled and set aside her cup. "Now tell me: is he or is he not truly Lord Hope?"

"I think he must be," Beatrice said slowly, choosing a biscuit from the tray on the tiny table between them. Pan raised his head and followed her hand as she transferred the pastry to her plate. "But so far no one who actually knew him from before the war has seen him."

Lottie looked up from selecting her own biscuit. "What, no one? He has a sister, doesn't he?"

"In the Colonies." Beatrice bit into her biscuit and said

somewhat indistinctly, "There's an aunt as well, but she's somewhere abroad. Her butler was rather vague. And Uncle Reggie said he'd met Hope, but the viscount had been a boy of ten or so at the time, so it doesn't help."

"Well, then, what about friends?" Lottie asked.

"He's too ill to go out yet." Beatrice bit her lip. It had taken all her powers of persuasion to keep Lord Hope in the scarlet bedroom this morning. "We have sent word to the man who said he witnessed Hope's death—Viscount Vale."

"And?"

Beatrice shrugged. "He's at his country estate. It may be days before he can come."

"Well! Then you shall simply have to play nurse to a wickedly handsome man—even if he has far too much hair at the moment—who is either a long-lost earl or a black scoundrel who might imperil your virtue. I must say I'm terribly jealous."

Beatrice glanced down at Pan, who had discovered a fallen lump of sugar near her chair. Lottie's words made her think of the viscount's body on hers and how very heavy it had been. How she had, for a small second, almost feared for her life.

"Beatrice?"

Oh, dear. Lottie was sitting bolt upright, her nose practically twitching.

Beatrice affected an unconcerned look. "Yes?"

"Don't you *yes* me, Beatrice Rosemary Corning. You sound as if butter wouldn't melt in your mouth! What happened?"

Beatrice winced. "Well, he was somewhat delirious that first afternoon . . ."

"Ye-es?"

"And when we took him to a bedroom—"

"Something happened in a *bedroom*?"

"It really wasn't his fault—"

"Oh, my goodness!"

"But somehow he pulled me down on the bed and he fell, too." Beatrice glanced at Lottie's excited face and closed her eyes very tightly to say, "On top of me."

There was a small silence.

Beatrice peeked.

Lottie was goggling at her and seemed—miraculously—speechless.

"Nothing happened, really," Beatrice said somewhat weakly.

"Nothing!" Lottie found her power of speech to nearly shout. "You were compromised."

"No, I wasn't. The footmen were there."

"Footmen don't count," Lottie said, and rose to yank vigorously on the bellpull.

"Of course footmen count," Beatrice said. "There were three of them. What are you doing?"

"Ringing for more tea." Lottie looked critically at the demolished tea tray. "We'll need another pot and a new plate of biscuits, too, I think."

Beatrice looked down at her hands. "The thing is . . ."

"Yes?"

Beatrice took a breath and looked at her suddenly sober friend. "He was rather frightening, Lottie."

Lottie sat down, her pretty lips tightening. "Did he hurt you?"

"No. At least"—Beatrice shook her head—"for a moment I couldn't breathe. But that was nothing. It was the look in his eyes. As if he wouldn't mind killing me." She scrunched her nose. "You must think me a fool."

"Of course not, dear." Lottie bit her lip. "Are you sure he's safe to have in your uncle's house?"

"I don't know," Beatrice admitted. "But what else are we to do? If we throw him into the street and he *is* the earl, we'll be judged most harshly. He might bring criminal proceedings against my uncle. I have taken the precaution of posting guards at his door."

"That sounds wise." Lottie still looked troubled. "Have you thought what you'll do if he is the earl?"

The maid trotted in at that moment, distracting Lottie and saving Beatrice from having to answer her friend. The truth was that her chest began to tighten in a panicked sort of way when she thought of what the future might bring. If the man in the scarlet bedroom was Viscount Hope and if he succeeded in taking back the title, both she and Uncle Reggie would be out of their home. They'd lose the estates and monies they'd become used to in the last five years, and that would aggravate Uncle Reggie terribly. What would such a situation do to him? He might protest that the apoplexy attack he'd had was nothing, but she'd seen his white, sweaty face and the way he'd gasped for breath. Just the memory made her press her hand to her chest. Dear God, she couldn't lose Uncle Reggie, too.

And she truly didn't want to discuss the matter at the moment.

So when Lottie plopped back down on her exquisite white and rose striped settee and looked at her expectantly, Beatrice smiled and said, "I thought we were to discuss Mr. Graham and the veteran's bill today. I've had word that Mr. Wheaton would like to have another secret meeting before—"

"Oh, pooh on Nate and the veteran's bill." Lottie pulled a tasseled gold silk cushion on her lap and hugged it. "I'm sick to death of politics and husbands as well."

The maid bustled back in with a laden tray at that minute. Beatrice watched her friend as the fresh tea things were arranged. Lottie always spoke carelessly, but Beatrice was beginning to worry that something was really wrong between her and Mr. Graham. They'd had a fashionable marriage, of course. Nathan Graham was the scion of a rather new wealthy family, while Lottie came from an old but impoverished name. Theirs had been an eminently practical union, but Beatrice thought it had been a love match as well—at least on Lottie's part. Had she been wrong?

The maid bustled out again, and Beatrice said softly, "Lottie . . ."

Her friend was pouring the tea, her gaze resolutely fixed on the teapot in her hand. "Did you hear that Lady Hasselthorpe cut Mrs. Hunt dead at the Fothering's musicale yesterday? I've heard wild speculation that it signals Lord Hasselthorpe's disapproval of Mr. Hunt, but one can't help wonder if Lady Hasselthorpe did it entirely accidentally. She is such a ninny."

Lottie held out a full teacup, and maybe it was her imagination, but Beatrice thought she saw pleading in her friend's eyes. And what could she do? She was a maiden who'd reached the overripe age of four and twenty without ever receiving an offer. What did she know about matters of the heart anyway?

Beatrice sighed silently and took the teacup. "And how did Mrs. Hunt respond?"

The problem with marriage, Lottie Graham reflected, was that there was such a difference between what one dreamed the matrimonial state would be like and, well, the *reality*.

Lottie sat back down on her settee—Wallace and Sons, bought just last year for a truly scandalous sum—and stared at the cooling tea things. She'd seen Beatrice to the door after babbling at her dearest friend in the world for a solid half hour. Poor Beatrice must heartily regret coming over for their weekly tea.

Lottie sighed and plucked the last biscuit from the plate, crumbling it between her fingers. Darling Pan came to sit beside her skirts, his foxy little face grinning up at her.

"It's not good for you, so many sweets," Lottie murmured, but she gave a bit of the biscuit to him anyway. He delicately took the treat between his sharp little teeth and retired with his prize beneath the gilded French armchair.

Lottie slumped into the settee, laying her arm wearily along the back. Perhaps she expected too much. Perhaps it was girlish fantasies that she should've outgrown long ago. Perhaps all marriages, even the very best like her own mama and papa's, ultimately settled into dreary indifference, and she was simply being a ninny like Lady Hasselthorpe.

Annie, the head downstairs maid, came in to gather up the tea things. She glanced at Lottie and said hesitantly, "Will there be anything else, ma'am?"

Oh, God, even the servants sensed it.

Lottie straightened a little, trying to look serene. "No, that'll be all."

"Yes, ma'am." Annie curtsied. "Cook was wanting to know if there'll be one or two for supper tonight?"

"Just one," Lottie muttered, and turned her face away.

Annie left the room quietly.

She sat there, draped on the settee, for some time, thinking wild thoughts until the door opened again a bit later.

Nate strolled in and then stopped. "Oh, sorry! Didn't mean to disturb you. I didn't know anyone was in here."

At Nate's voice, Pan emerged from under the armchair and pranced over to be patted. Pan had adored Nate from the very beginning.

Lottie wrinkled her nose at her pet and then said rather carelessly to Nate, "I didn't know you'd be home for dinner. I just told Cook there'd be only one."

"That's all right." Nate straightened from Pan and gave her one of his wide, easy smiles—the smile that had first made her heart quicken. "I'm dining with Collins and Rupert tonight. I just stopped in to see if I'd left that Whig pamphlet here. Rupert's interested in seeing it. Ah. There 'tis."

Nate crossed to a table in the corner, where a messy pile of papers lay, snatching up the pamphlet in evident satisfaction. He returned to the door, engrossed in the pamphlet, and only as an afterthought did he look up as he was about to leave.

He frowned rather vaguely at Lottie. "I say, that's all right, isn't it? I mean, me dining out with Collins and

Rupert? I thought you were attending some other social event when I made the plan."

Lottie lifted her brow and said loftily, "Oh, don't mind me. I'm—"

But she was talking to his back.

"Good, good. Knew you'd understand." And he was out the door, his nose buried in that wretched pamphlet.

Lottie blew out a breath and threw a small cushion at the door, making Pan start and yip.

"Married two years and he's more interested in dinner with a couple of boring old men than me!"

Pan jumped onto the settee beside her—which he was strictly forbidden to do—and licked her on the nose.

Whereupon Lottie burst into tears.

FOUR AND TWENTY and never even an offer.

The thought repeated in Beatrice's head all the way home, a nasty little chant. She'd never put her unmarried state into such blunt terms before. Where had the time gone? It wasn't as if she spent her days mooning about, waiting to start a life when the right gentleman finally presented himself. No, she led a busy life, a full life, she reminded herself, albeit somewhat defensively. Because Uncle Reggie had been widowed the last ten years, she'd practically grown up learning to hostess for him. And while political teas, dinners, house parties, and the yearly ball might be a tad dull, they were quite a job to manage.

To be fair, she *had* been courted. Just last spring, Mr. Matthew Horn had seemed quite interested—before he'd shot himself in the head, poor man. And she'd once come very close to an offer of marriage. Mr. Freddy Finch—

the second son of an earl, no less—had been dashing and funny and had kissed her so sweetly. He'd escorted her for the better part of a season several years ago. She had enjoyed their outings—had enjoyed Freddy—but not, as she finally realized, in any special way. She was happy to go with him on a carriage ride, but if he had to call off for some reason, she was only a little disappointed. Her own complacency she might've lived with, but she'd suspected that Freddy's emotions were no more entangled than her own, and she couldn't live with that in a marriage. When she married—*if* she married—she wanted a gentleman who was wildly, *passionately* in love with her.

A man who would never abandon her.

So she'd broken it off with Freddy, not in any dramatic way, but simply by seeing him less and less often, eventually drifting away from him. She'd been correct in her assessment of his emotional attachment, too, because not once had Freddy protested her drawing away. A year later, he'd married Guinevere Crestwood, a rather plain lady who ran a tea party like an army campaign.

Was she jealous? Beatrice stared out the carriage window while she examined her feelings, taking care to be quite honest with herself, for she despised self-deception. She shook her head. No, she could honestly say that she was not jealous of the new Mrs. Finch, even if her toddlers were quite adorable. The adorable toddlers might grow up to have Guinevere's enormous canine teeth for one thing, and for another, well, Freddy was funny and charming and quite nice-looking, but he hadn't been in love with Beatrice. Perhaps Freddy had fallen passionately in love with Guinevere, but Beatrice rather doubted it.

And that was the crux of the matter, was it not? None of the gentlemen whom she'd driven in carriages with and danced with and strolled with had been interested in her with any real depth of feeling. They complimented her gowns, smiled as they danced with her, but never truly saw her—the woman behind the facade. Perhaps a marriage without passion was enough for Guinevere Crestwood, but it wasn't enough for her.

She remembered now coming home from a ball, a year or more ago, and strolling into the blue sitting room and just gazing at Lord Hope's portrait. He'd seemed alive with passion. Next to him—even as a flat, painted image—all the other gentlemen she knew faded into the background like transparent ghosts. He was more real, even then when she'd thought him long dead, than those flesh-and-blood gentlemen who'd squired her only hours before.

Perhaps that was the real reason she was still a maiden at four and twenty: she'd been waiting for a man as passionate as she'd dreamed Lord Hope was.

But was he that man?

The carriage stopped before the Blanchard town house, and Beatrice descended the steps with the help of a footman. Usually at this time she met with Cook for their weekly consultation about menus. But today she went straight to the kitchen and asked to have a tray prepared and apprised Cook of her change of plans. Then she mounted the stairs to the third floor and the scarlet room, the tray in her hands.

George, the footman stationed outside the scarlet room, nodded at her as she neared. "Can I carry that tray for you, miss?"

"Thank you, George, but I believe I can handle it." She glanced worriedly at the door. "How is he?"

George scratched his head. "Ornery, miss, if you don't mind me saying so. Didn't like the maid coming in to tend his fire. 'E was yelling at her something awful in that Frenchie language—or so I think. Don't speak the lingo myself."

Beatrice pursed her lips and nodded. "Can you knock for me?"

"Certainly, miss." George rapped on the door.

"Come," Hope said.

George held the door open and Beatrice peeked in. The viscount was sitting up in the big bed wearing a loose nightshirt and writing in a notebook on his lap. His knife lay outside the covers by his right hip. He seemed composed enough now at least, and she exhaled a grateful breath. His cheeks no longer held the hectic flush they'd had the last two days, though his face was still gaunt. His long hair had been braided into a tight queue, but his jaw was still covered by his thick black beard. The top two buttons of his nightshirt had been left undone, and a few strands of dark hair were revealed, curling against the snowy cloth. For a moment, Beatrice found her gaze fixed on the sight.

"Come to tend to me, Cousin Beatrice?" he murmured, and she jerked her gaze up. Knowing black eyes met hers.

"I've brought some tea and muffins," she said tartly. "And you needn't sound so snide. You've scared most of the maids, and George said you yelled at one just this morning."

"She didn't knock." He watched as she came in and placed the tray on a table by the bed.

"That's hardly a reason to frighten her."

He looked away irritably. "I don't like people in my rooms. She should not have come in without leave."

She eyed him, her voice softening. "The servants are trained not to knock. I think you'll have to become used to it. But until you do, I'll warn them to knock at your door."

He shrugged, reaching for a muffin on the tray. He shoved half of it into his mouth rudely.

She sighed and pulled a chair near the bed, sitting in it. "You seem ravenous."

He paused in the act of grabbing another muffin. "You've obviously never had to eat wormy biscuits and watered ale on board a ship." He bit into the muffin, his black eyes watching her defiantly.

She stared back calmly, hiding the tremor of unease at his look. His eyes were feral, like a starving wolf. "No, I've never been on board a ship. Did you sail home recently?"

He looked away, silently eating the rest of the second muffin. For a moment, she thought he wouldn't answer her. Then he said bitterly, "I took a position as a cook's assistant. Not that there was much food to cook."

She looked at him wonderingly. What straits had made the son of an earl take such mean labor? "Where did you sail from?"

He grimaced and then glanced up at her slyly through black eyelashes. "Do you know, I don't recall having a cousin Beatrice."

Obviously he had no intention of answering her. Beatrice stifled a sigh of frustration. "That's because I'm not your cousin. At least not by blood."

He might've meant his question as a diversion, but now he cocked his head in interest. "Explain."

He'd set aside his notebook, and his whole attention was concentrated on her, making her feel rather self-conscious. Beatrice rose and busied herself pouring the tea as she talked. "My mother was sister to Uncle Reggie's wife, my aunt Mary. Mother died when I was born, and I was five when my father died. Aunt Mary and Uncle Reggie took me in."

"A sad story," he said mockingly.

"No." Beatrice shook her head, handing him a cup of tea with no milk but with lots of sugar. "Not really. I've always been loved, always been cared for, first by my father and then by Uncle Reggie and Aunt Mary. They had no children of their own, so they treated me just as they would a daughter, perhaps even better. Uncle Reggie has been wonderful to me." She looked at him earnestly. "He's a good man."

"Then perhaps I should relinquish my title and let Uncle Reggie keep it." His voice was sardonic.

"You needn't be mean," she replied with dignity.

"Shouldn't I?" He studied her as if he couldn't quite make her out.

"No. There's no need. It's just that this is our house now—"

"And I'm supposed to take pity on you for that? Lay down my arms and make peace?"

She inhaled to control her temper. "My uncle is old. He doesn't—"

"My title, my lands, my monies, my goddamned life

have been stolen from me, madam," he said, his voice rising with each word. "Think you I care a whit for your *uncle*?"

She stared. He was so angry, so determined. Where was the laughing boy in the painting? Had he entirely disappeared? "You were thought dead. No one meant to steal your title from you."

"Their intention is of no matter to me," he said. "I care only about the result. I've been deprived of what is rightfully mine. I have no home."

"But Uncle Reggie isn't to blame!" she cried, losing her self-possession at last. "I'm just trying to explain to you that this isn't a war. We can be civilized about—"

He flung the teacup against the wall and then swept his arm in an abrupt, violent gesture across the table. Beatrice was forced to hop out of the way as the tray, plate, and teapot—filled with hot tea—all crashed to the floor where'd she been standing.

"How dare you?" she demanded, staring first at the mess on the floor and then at the savage in the bed. "How *dare* you?"

His black eyes burned so fiercely she felt her skin heat. "If you don't think this a war, madam," he said softly, "then you are even more naive than I thought."

Beatrice set her hands on her hips and leaned forward, her voice shaking with rage. "Perhaps I am naive. Perhaps it is silly and girlish and . . . and *foolish* to think that one can settle even difficult matters in a civilized fashion. But I'd rather be a complete ninny than a nasty sarcastic man so lost to bitterness that he's forgotten his own humanity!"

She turned to sweep from the room, but her dramatic

exit was destroyed when he caught her wrist. He yanked, and, caught off balance, she fell back against the bed, across his lap. She gasped and looked up.

Into blazing black eyes.

He leaned so close she felt his breath across her lips. The muscles of his leg shifted under her hip, reminding her of her precarious position. His hands tightened around her upper arms, holding her prisoner. "I may indeed be a nasty, bitter, and sarcastic man, madam, but let me assure you that my *humanity* is more than intact."

Beatrice's breath stopped like a rabbit caught in the open before a wolf. She could feel the heat of his body coming off him in waves. Her bosom was nearly pressed to his chest, and to make matters worse, that sparkling black gaze fell to her mouth.

As she watched, his lips parted and his eyelids drooped as he growled softly, "And I will use any means at my disposal to win this war."

So mesmerized was she by the wicked intent in his eyes that she started when the door to the bedroom opened. Lord Hope abruptly released her arms. He was staring behind her at the intruder. For a fleeting second, she thought she saw something like joy cross his face, but so suddenly did it disappear that perhaps she was mistaken.

In any case, both his countenance and his voice were stony when he spoke.

"Renshaw."

Chapter Three

"Come, sir," cried the Goblin King, "I'll give you fifty gold coins for that sword. Tell me you'll agree."

"I fear I cannot," Longsword replied.

"Then surely you'll part with it for one hundred gold coins? It is but an old and rusting sword, and you can buy twenty more the same or better for that price."

At this Longsword laughed. "Sir, I'll not sell you my sword for any price you name, and I'll tell you why: to relinquish this sword would cost me my very life, for it and I are bound together magically."

"Ah, if that is the case," the Goblin King said craftily, "will you sell me a lock of your hair for one penny?"

—from *Longsword*

For seven years, Reynaud had thought about what he would say and how he would feel when he saw Jasper

Renshaw again. The questions he would ask, the explanations he would demand. And now, now that the moment was here, he searched within himself and felt . . . nothing.

"It's Vale now," the man standing by the door said. His face was a little more lined, his eyes slightly more sad, but otherwise he was the same man Reynaud had played with as a boy. The same man he'd bought a commission with. The same man he'd considered his best friend.

The man who'd left him for dead in a savage foreign land.

"You attained the title, then?" Reynaud asked.

Vale nodded. He still stood just inside the door, hat in hand. He stared at Reynaud as if trying to decipher the thoughts of a wild beast.

Miss Corning straightened from where he'd pulled her across his lap. So intent was he on Vale that he'd almost forgotten her presence. He made a belated grab for her hand but was too late. She'd moved away from the bed and was beyond his reach. He'd have to wait for another time when she might step unwarily close again.

She cleared her throat. "I believe we met once at one of your mother's garden parties, Lord Vale."

Vale's gaze jerked to her, and he blinked before a wide smile spread across his face. He bowed extravagantly. "Forgive me, gentle lady. You are?"

"My cousin, Miss Corning," Reynaud growled. No need to tell Vale the connection was not a blood one—he'd make what claim he could.

Vale's thick eyebrows rose. "I never knew you had a female cousin."

Reynaud smiled thinly. "She's newly discovered."

Miss Corning looked between the men, her brows knitted, clearly confused. "Shall I send for tea?"

"Yes, please," Vale said, while at the same time Reynaud shook his head. "No."

Vale looked at him, his smile gone.

Miss Corning cleared her throat again. "Well, I think, ah, yes, I think I'll leave you two to yourselves. There must be many things you'd like to catch up on."

She walked to the door where Vale still stood and whispered to him, "Just don't stay too long. He's been very ill."

Vale nodded, holding the door for her and then shutting it gently after she'd left. He turned to look at Reynaud.

Who snapped, "I'm not an invalid."

"You've been ill?"

"I took a fever on the ship over. It's nothing."

Vale raised his eyebrows but didn't comment on that. Instead he asked, "What happened?"

Reynaud smiled sardonically. "I think I should be asking that of you."

Vale looked away, his face paling. "I thought—we all thought—that you were dead."

"I wasn't." Reynaud bit off the words, his incisors closing with sharp finality.

He remembered the stink of burning flesh. The binds cutting into his arms. Of marching naked through new snowfall. *Her brown eyes stared up through a mask of blood. . . .* He shook his head once, sharply, chasing the ghosts from his mind, focusing on the living man before him. His hand moved to the hilt of his knife.

Vale watched his movement warily. "I would never have left you had I known you lived."

"Yet the fact remains that I was alive and you did leave me."

"I'm sorry. I . . ." Vale's mouth flattened. He stared at the carpet between his feet. "I saw you die, Reynaud."

For a moment, demons chattered in Reynaud's brain, whispering of treachery. He saw clearly the grimace a dying man made while being burned alive. Then, with an effort, he pushed back the image and the mad voices.

"What happened at the Wyandot camp?" he asked.

"After they took you away, you mean?" Vale didn't wait for the reply but sighed heavily. "They tied us to stakes and tortured the other men—Munroe, Horn, Growe, and Coleman. They killed Coleman."

Reynaud nodded. He'd seen how the enemies—both white and native—were treated by the Indians who captured them.

Vale inhaled, as if bracing himself. "Then, after Coleman's death on the second day, the Indians took us to where they were burning a man at the stake. They told us it was you. He wore your coat, had black hair. I thought he was you. We all thought he was you." Vale looked up, meeting Reynaud's gaze with haunted turquoise eyes. "His face was already gone. Blackened and burned by the flames."

Reynaud looked away. The reasonable part of his mind knew that Vale and the others had had no choice. They'd believed him dead because of overwhelming evidence. Any sane man would believe the same when faced with what they'd seen and been told.

And yet . . .

And yet the beast at his core refused the explanation. He'd been abandoned, left by those he'd risked life and limb for. Left by those he'd called his friends.

"It was almost another fortnight before Sam Hartley brought back a rescue party to ransom us," Vale said quietly. "Were you in the Indian camp that entire time?"

Reynaud shook his head, watching his left hand flatten against the counterpane, noting absently the contrast of his brown skin against the white fabric. His hand was thin, the tendons standing out clearly on the back. "How is my sister, Emeline?"

He heard Vale sigh as if frustrated. "Emeline. Emeline is just fine. She's remarried now, you know. To Samuel Hartley."

Reynaud's head jerked up, his eyes narrowing. "Corporal Hartley? The ranger?"

Vale smirked. "The same, although he's no longer a lowly corporal. He's made his fortune importing and exporting goods from the Colonies."

"Miss Corning told me that she married a colonial, but I hadn't realized it was Hartley." Even if Hartley was wealthy now, Emeline had married beneath her station. She was the daughter of an *earl*. What had possessed her?

"He came to London a year ago for business and for other matters and quite stole your sister's heart, I think."

Reynaud contemplated that information, his mind spinning in confusion and anger. Had Emeline changed so much in seven years? Or were his memories tainted? Warped by time and all that had been done to him?

"What happened, Reynaud?" Vale asked softly. "How did you escape death at the Indian camp?"

Reynaud's head jerked up. He glared at his former friend. "Do you really care?"

"Yes." Vale looked bewildered. "Yes, of course."

Vale stared at him as if waiting for the story, but Reynaud was damned if he'd rip open his soul for him.

Finally Vale looked away. "Ah. Well, I'm glad—very glad—that you're back safe and sound."

Reynaud nodded. "Is that it?"

"What?"

"Is that it?" Reynaud enunciated. He was tired and needed sleep, dammit, though he wouldn't let the other man know it. "Have you finished whatever you came for?"

Vale's head snapped back as if he'd been clipped in the chin. Then he widened his stance, squared his shoulders, and leveled his head. A wide, unamused smile spread across his lips. "Not quite."

Reynaud raised his eyebrows.

"I also wanted to talk to you about the traitor," Vale said silkily.

Reynaud shook his head. "Traitor . . . ?"

"The man who betrayed us to the Indians at Spinner's Falls," Vale said as a roaring began in Reynaud's ears that almost drowned his last words. "A traitor with a French mother."

BEATRICE HEARD THE crash as she mounted the stairs with another tray of tea and biscuits. She paused on the grand staircase, gazing blindly upward at the floor above. Had it been an accident? A China figurine or a clock falling off the mantel? The thought was hopeful, but she sped her steps, rounding into the upper hallway as the second crash hit. Oh, dear. It sounded rather as if Lord Hope and Lord Vale might be murdering each other.

Down the hall, the door to Lord Hope's room burst open and Viscount Vale stomped out, angry but blessedly still intact.

"Don't think this is over, Reynaud," he called. "Damn you, I'll be back."

He jammed his tricorne on his head and turned and saw Beatrice. A sheepish look momentarily crossed his face.

Then he nodded curtly. "Your pardon, ma'am. You might not want to go in there at the moment. He's not fit for civilized company."

She glanced at the door to the scarlet room and then back to Lord Vale. As he neared, she saw with horror that a red mark marred his chin.

As if someone had struck him.

"What happened?" she asked.

He shook his head. "He's not the man I once knew. His emotions are . . . extreme. Savage. Please, be careful."

Lord Vale bowed gracefully and then strode past her and down the stairs.

Beatrice watched him disappear before glancing at the tray still in her hands. The tea had spilled a bit, staining the linen cloth covering the bottom of the tray. She could go back to the kitchens and have one of the maids lay a new tray—and perhaps have the girl deliver it as well. Except that would be cowardly. It wasn't her duty to send servant girls into places she herself was afraid to venture.

She looked down the hall. The door to Lord Hope's room still stood open. He was in there all alone.

She squared her shoulders and marched to the open door. "I've brought some more tea and biscuits," she announced briskly as she sailed into the room. "I thought you might actually drink it this time."

Hope was lying in the bed, turned toward the wall, and at first she thought he might be asleep, silly as that notion was after the commotion of before.

He didn't turn. "Get out."

"You seem to be under a misapprehension," she said conversationally.

She started to set the tray on the little table beside the bed, but there were shards scattered in an arc away from the table, comprised of what had once been an ugly china clock and a matching pair of ceramic pugs. Added as it was to the previous tea things she'd brought up before Lord Vale's visit, it was beginning to be quite a pile.

She turned to a table near the window—well out of reach of the bed.

"What are you babbling about?" Hope muttered.

"Hmm?" The table was already occupied by a vase and a brass candelabra, and Beatrice had to maneuver the tea tray carefully to avoid yet another spill.

"The misapprehension you said I was under," Hope growled in a testy voice.

"Oh." The tray settled, Beatrice looked over at him and smiled, even though he still had his back to her. "You seem to think I'm one of the servants."

There was a silence from the bed as Beatrice poured

the tea. Perhaps he was covered in shame at her mild set-down.

"You do keep bringing me tea."

Or perhaps not.

"Tea is very fortifying, I find, especially when one feels under the weather." She added sugar to the tea—she'd noticed he seemed to like his tea very sweet—and brought the teacup to the bed. "But that does not mean I enjoy being addressed in such sour tones."

He still faced the wall. She hesitated a moment, the cup held uncertainly in her hand; then she placed it carefully on the table. It was an ugly cup with an orange and black decoration depicting a rather lopsided bridge, but still. One didn't like to see the china smashed.

"Would you like some tea?" she asked.

One large shoulder shrugged, but otherwise he didn't move. What had happened between him and Lord Vale?

"It'll warm your spirits," she whispered.

He snorted. "I doubt that."

"Well." She smoothed her skirts. "I'll leave you, then."

"Don't."

The single word was so low she almost missed it. She looked at him. He hadn't moved, and she wasn't sure what to do. What he wanted.

His upper arm lay outside the coverlet, and she took a step forward and reached out a hand. It was entirely improper, but for some reason, it seemed right. She touched his hand, large and warm. Slowly she burrowed her fingers under his hand until she grasped it in her own. He squeezed her fingers gently. She felt a point of warmth start in her breast, spreading gradually like a widening pool of warm water until her entire body was lit from within and she identified the feeling. Happiness. He made her wildly, inappropriately happy with just the squeeze of his fingers, and she knew she should be wary of this feeling. Be wary of him.

And then he spoke, low. "He thinks me a traitor."

Her heart stopped. "What do you mean?"

He turned then, finally, his face a mask, his eyes shadowed, but he did not let go of her hand. "You know our regiment, the Twenty-eighth of Foot, was massacred in the Colonies?"

"Yes." The massacre was common knowledge—one of the worst tragedies of the war.

"Vale says that someone gave away our position. That we were betrayed to the French and their Indian allies by a man within the ranks of our own regiment."

Beatrice swallowed. How terrible to know that so many had died because of one person's perfidy. And the knowledge of a traitor would be even more terrible for Lord Hope. Somehow, she still wasn't sure how—and really she was just about dying to ask—his seven lost years were connected to Spinner's Falls and the tragedy there.

All this went through her mind, but Beatrice merely said, "I'm sorry."

"You don't understand." He tugged her hand for emphasis. "The traitor had a French mother. Vale thinks I am the traitor."

"But . . . but that's silly," Beatrice exclaimed without thought. "I mean, not the French mother part—that makes sense, I suppose—but that anyone would think you a traitor . . . that . . . that isn't right at all."

He didn't say anything, merely squeezed her hand again.

"I thought," Beatrice said cautiously, "that Lord Vale was your friend?"

"As did I. But that was seven years ago, and I fear I no longer know the man."

"Is that why you struck him?" she asked.

He shrugged.

Beatrice shivered at the confirmation of her fears. She remembered Lord Vale's warning in the hall: *Be careful.* Still, she wet her lips and said, "I think anyone who truly knows you would realize that you don't have it in you to be a traitor."

"But then you don't know me." At last he let her hand drop, and the warmth began to leak from her body with the loss of contact. "You don't know me at all."

Beatrice inhaled slowly. "You are correct. I do not know you." She went to take the tea tray. "But then perhaps the fault for that is not wholly mine."

She closed the door gently behind her.

Even though Beatrice visited Jeremy Oates at least once a week—and more often two or three times—his butler, Putley, always pretended he did not know her.

"Who shall I say is calling?" Putley asked early the next afternoon, his pop eyes staring at her in what looked like appalled surprise.

"Miss Beatrice Corning," Beatrice replied as she always did, suppressing an urge to make up a name.

Putley was only doing his job. Well, at least that was

the most charitable explanation, and Beatrice did try to be charitable when she could.

"Very well, miss," Putley intoned. "Will you wait in the sitting room whilst I ascertain if Mr. Oates is at home?"

Charity was one thing, ridiculous adherence to form was another. "Mr." Oates was never anywhere but home. Beatrice rolled her eyes. "Yes, Putley."

He showed her to the second-best sitting room, a musty room with very little light and an overabundance of heavy, dark furniture. She used the time waiting for Putley's return to compose herself. Beatrice was still a little warm from her discussion with Lord Hope, and she'd felt ever so slightly guilty after she'd left his room. After all, should a lady set a gentleman down so thoroughly when he was bedridden and had just had a falling out with his best friend whom he'd not seen in nearly seven years? Wasn't she being just a tad mean? But then again, he'd been so very nasty with her. She knew he must be frustrated—enraged, even—by everything that'd happened since his return to England, but really, must he use her as his whipping boy?

Putley returned at that moment with the news that Jeremy would indeed see her, and Beatrice followed the butler's disapproving back up the two flights of stairs to Jeremy's room.

"Miss Beatrice Corning to see you, sir," Putley droned.

Beatrice pushed past the butler and into the room. Enough was enough. She turned a dazzling smile on Putley and said firmly, "That will be all."

The butler rumbled under his breath but left the room, closing the door behind him.

"He's getting worse, you know." Beatrice strode to the window and shoved back one side of the curtains. The light sometimes hurt Jeremy's eyes, but it couldn't be good for him to lie in a dark room in the middle of the day, either.

"I try to think of it as a compliment," Jeremy drawled from the bed.

His voice was weaker than the last time she'd visited. She took a deep breath and pasted on a wide smile before turning back around. The bed dominated the area, surrounded by the debris of a sickroom. Two tables stood within reach of the bed, their surfaces covered with small bottles, boxes of ointment, books, pens and ink, bandages, and glasses. An old wooden chair was to one side, a silk cord wound around the back, the ends tossed on the seat. Sometimes Jeremy found it easier for the footmen to tie him to the chair when they moved him before the fireplace.

"After all," Jeremy said, "Putley must have some confidence in my ability to ravish you if he disapproves so much of your visits."

"Or perhaps he's simply an idiot," Beatrice said as she pulled a stuffed chair closer to the bed.

There was an acrid smell; this near the bed—a combination of urine and other noxious bodily emissions—but she took care to keep her face pleasant. When Jeremy had first come home from the war on the Continent five years ago, he'd been horrified at the sickroom smells. She wasn't sure now if he'd become used to the odors and ignored them or if he simply no longer smelled them, but in any case, she wouldn't hurt his feelings by drawing attention to them.

"I've brought you the news sheets and some pamphlets my footman procured for me," Beatrice began as she drew the papers from a soft bag.

"Oh, no, you don't," Jeremy said. His voice was teasing, even in his weakened state.

She looked up to meet his clear blue eyes. Jeremy had the most beautiful eyes of anyone she knew, either woman or man. They were a true light blue, the color of the sky in spring. No other color muddied their depths. He was—or had been—a very handsome man. His hair was a golden brown, his face open and cheerful, but the ravages of his illness had incised lines of pain around his mouth and eyes.

Jeremy's mother had been a lifelong friend of Beatrice's aunt Mary, so Beatrice and Jeremy had practically grown up in each other's pockets. He knew her as no one else did—not even Lottie. When she looked into Jeremy's eyes, sometimes she felt that those blue orbs saw right past the cheerful mask she put on in his presence, straight to the well of sorrow for him at her middle.

She glanced away, down at the coverlet of his bed. To the place, in fact, where his legs should've been. "What—?"

"Don't pretend innocence with me, Beatrice Corning," he said with the same grin he'd had at eight years of age. "I may be an invalid, but I still have my sources of gossip, and they are abuzz with the news of your viscount's return."

Beatrice wrinkled her nose. "He's not *my* viscount."

Jeremy cocked his head against the pillows. Usually he was sitting erect by this time in the afternoon, but today he was lying on his back. Beatrice felt a frisson of fear bolt through her vitals. Was he worse?

"I can't think who else's viscount he might be if not yours," he teased. "Isn't this the same man as the pretty youth in that portrait in your sitting room? I've watched you moon over that thing for years."

Beatrice twisted her fingers guiltily. "Was I so obvious as all that?"

"Only to me, darling," Jeremy replied fondly. "Only to me."

"Oh, Jeremy, I'm such a wigeon!"

"Well, yes, but an adorable one, you must admit."

Beatrice sighed forlornly. "It's just that he's not at all what I thought he'd be like. Well, if I thought about him still being alive, which of course I didn't, because we all thought him dead."

"What? He's ugly?" Jeremy contorted his features into a grotesque scowl.

"Nooo, although he has a beard and terribly long hair at the moment."

"Beards are disgusting."

"Not on ship captains," Beatrice objected.

"Especially on ship captains," Jeremy said sternly. "There's no point in trying to make exceptions. One must be firm on the subject."

"Granted." Beatrice waved a hand. "But believe me, the beard is the least of it in Viscount Hope's case. He's been tattooed."

"Scandalous," Jeremy breathed in delight. Flags of high color were flaming on his cheeks.

"I'm overexciting you." Beatrice frowned.

"Not at all," he replied. "But even if you were, I'd beg you to go on. I'm here every day, all day and night, Bea, dear. I need the excitement. So, tell me. What is the real problem with Lord Hope? He may have a bushy beard and tattooed himself with anchors and snakes, but I don't think that's what's troubling you."

"Triangular birds," Beatrice said absently.

"What?"

"The tattoos are strange little birds, three of them, around his right eye. What could've possessed him to have them placed there?"

"I haven't the faintest."

"It's just that he's so bitter, Jeremy!" she burst out. "He's . . . he's positively hateful sometimes, as if whatever happened to him seared his very soul."

Jeremy was silent a moment; then he said, "I'm sorry. He was in the war, wasn't he? In the Colonies?"

Beatrice nodded.

He sighed and said slowly, "It's hard to explain to someone who has never experienced it, but war and the things that happen in war, the things one is forced to do and see sometimes . . . well, they change a man. Make him harsher, if he has any sensitivity at all."

"You're right, of course," she said, twisting her hands. "But it seems more than that somehow. Oh, I wish I knew what he's been doing for the last seven years!"

Jeremy half smiled. "Whatever it was, I doubt your knowing his history will change anything about him now."

Beatrice looked at him, into his dear, much too perceptive eyes. "I'm an idiot, aren't I? Expecting a romantic prince, from a man I knew only from a portrait."

"Perhaps," he conceded. "But if it were not for romantic dreams, life would be terribly dull, don't you think?"

She wrinkled her nose at him. "You always know exactly what to say, Jeremy, dear."

"Yes, I know," he said complacently. "Now, tell me. Will he take your uncle's title from him?"

"I think he must." Beatrice frowned down at her clasped hands, feeling her chest tighten. "Just this morning, Viscount Vale came to visit him, and although they argued, I don't think there can be any more doubt that he is, indeed, Viscount Hope."

"And if he is?"

She glanced at him, wondering if he knew how panicked the prospect made her. "We'll lose the house."

"You can always come live with me," he teased.

She smiled, but her lips trembled. "Uncle Reggie might just have another attack of apoplexy."

"He's tougher than you give him credit for," he said gently.

She bit her lip, not even pretending to smile now. "But if he does become ill, if anything happened to him . . . Oh, Jeremy, I just don't know what I'd do."

She pressed her hand to her chest, rubbing at the constriction.

"It'll come right in the end, Bea, dear," Jeremy said soothingly. "There's no use worrying."

"I know," she sighed, and tried to look cheerful for him. "Uncle Reggie had an appointment this morning with his solicitors. He came back just before I left."

"Hmm. That'll be a mess. If your uncle doesn't just hand over the title, I expect they'll have to present their case to parliament." Jeremy looked cheerful. "I wonder if there'll be fisticuffs at Westminster?"

"You needn't sound so happy at the prospect," Beatrice scolded.

"Oh, I don't see why not. It's things like this that make the English aristocracy so very entertaining." Despite his words, Jeremy ended with a gasp. His hand on top of the coverlet balled into a tight fist, his knuckles white.

Beatrice started up from her chair. "Are you in pain?"

"No, no. Don't fuss, Bea, dear." Jeremy took a breath, and she knew that he was in pain even though he denied it. His face had gone a little gray, save for those ever-present flags of color on his cheeks.

"Here, let me help you sit up so you can take some water."

"Dammit, Bea."

"Now, don't you fuss, Jeremy, dear," she said softly but firmly as she took his shoulders and helped him to sit. Heat radiated off him in waves. "I've earned this right, I think."

"So you have," he gasped.

She poured water into a small cup and held it out to him.

He sipped some and gave her back the cup. "Have you thought what it would mean if Hope becomes the Earl of Blanchard?"

She set the cup on one of the crowded tables, frowning. "I just told you, Uncle Reggie and I will have to move out of the town house—"

"Yes, but beyond that, Bea." Jeremy waved aside her loss of a home. "He would replace your uncle Reggie in the House of Lords."

Beatrice slowly sank back into her seat. "Lord Hasselthorpe would lose a vote."

"And, more importantly, we might gain one," Jeremy said with significance. "Do you know what Hope's political leanings are?"

"I haven't the faintest."

"His father was a Tory," Jeremy mused.

"Oh, then he probably is, too," Beatrice said, disappointed.

"Sons don't always follow in their father's political footsteps. If Hope votes in favor of Mr. Wheaton's bill, we may win at last." The high color had spread over Jeremy's face in his excitement, so now he glowed as if he were being consumed by a fire within. "My men—the soldiers who served and fought so valiantly under me—would get the pension they deserve."

"I'll find out which way he leans politically. Perhaps I can convince him to our side." Beatrice smiled, trying to share Jeremy's enthusiasm, but inside she was doubtful. Lord Hope seemed solely focused on his own affairs. She'd seen nothing so far to make her think he would care one way or the other about common soldiers.

Five days of a sickbed had made Reynaud damnably restless. Annoying as Miss Corning's regular visits to his room were—she seemed to think it normal to simply swan in without inquiring first if he wanted her company—the fact was that he'd grown used to her. Used to teasing her and arguing with her. And where was the woman today? He'd seen neither hide nor hair of her.

Reynaud dragged himself from the bed, pulled on his old blue coat, and snatched up his knife before throwing open the door to his room. A young footman was stationed outside his room—presumably to keep him from running amok in his own house.

Reynaud glared at the fellow. "Tell Miss Corning I'd like a word with her."

He started to close the door, but the man said, "Can't."

Reynaud paused. "What?"

"Can't," the footman said. "She's not here."

"Then when is she expected back?"

The footman stepped back nervously before catching himself and straightening. "Not too long, I expect, but I can't say for sure. She's visitin' Mr. Oates, and sometimes she stays there a fair while."

"Who," Reynaud inquired gently, "is Mr. Oates?"

"Mr. Jeremy Oates, that is," the man said, becoming chatty. "Of the Suffolk Oates. Family with quite a bit of money, or so I'm told. 'E and Miss Corning have known each other a long, long time, and she likes to visit 'im three or four times a week."

"Then he's an aging gentleman?" Reynaud asked.

The footman scratched his head. "Don't think so. A young, 'andsome gentleman, so I hear."

It occurred to Reynaud at this point that although he'd seen Miss Corning every day since his return to England, he didn't actually know much about the woman. Was this Oates—this proper English gentleman—a beau? Or a fiancé? The thought spurred a primitive part of him, and he blurted the next question.

"Is she engaged to him?"

"Not yet," the footman replied, winking cheerfully. "But can't be long, can it, if she visits 'im so often? 'Course, there is the matter of 'is—"

But Reynaud wasn't listening anymore. He pushed past the ass and started for the stairs.

"Oy!" the footman called from behind him. "Where're you goin'?"

"To meet Miss Corning at the door," Reynaud growled. His legs were shakier than he'd realized, and it only made him more irritable. He gripped the banister with one hand as he descended slowly. He moved like a goddamned old man.

"I'm not supposed to let you leave your room," the footman said, suddenly beside him. He took Reynaud's elbow to help him, and so weak was Reynaud that he didn't even protest the familiarity.

"Who ordered you to keep me in my room?" Reynaud demanded.

"Miss Corning. She was worried you might injure yourself." The footman glanced at him sideways. "Don't suppose I can get you to go back, m'lord?"

"No," Reynaud replied shortly. He was panting, dammit. Only a month ago, he'd walked all day without wearying, and now he panted descending a damned staircase!

"Didn't think so," the man said matter-of-factly. He didn't say anything else until they made the entrance hall. "Would you like some water, m'lord, while you wait?"

"Please." Reynaud leaned against the wall until the man disappeared in the direction of the kitchens. Then he went to the front doors and pulled them open.

The wind caught his breath as he went out on the step. The day was gray and cold, winter spreading her wings on London. There'd be snow on the ground north of Lake Michigan now, and the bears would be fat and slow, preparing for their winter sleep. He remembered how Gaho had loved to eat bear meat fried in its own fat. She would smile when he brought her a freshly killed sow or boar, the wrinkles in her brown cheeks deepening, her eyes nearly disappearing in her happiness. For a moment, his former life and his present merged and wavered in front of his eyes, and he forgot where he was. Who he was.

Then the Blanchard carriage pulled up in front of the town house.

The footman jumped down and set the step. Reynaud straightened and started for the carriage. The door opened and Miss Corning descended the steps.

Her brows snapped together when she saw him. "What are you doing out of bed?"

"I've come to meet you," Reynaud said, his voice hard. "Where have you been?"

She ignored his question. "I can't believe you're so silly as to stand outside in the cold. You must go in at once. Arthur"—she beckoned to the carriage footman—"please take Lord Hope in—"

"I'm not going to be taken anywhere," Reynaud said with deadly calm. The carriage footman took one look at him and found a consuming interest in putting away the step. "I'm not a child or half-wit to be taken care of. I repeat, where have you been?"

"Then you must allow me to help you inside." Miss Corning dismissed his growing anger with a wave of her hand.

He gripped her arms, making her end her sentence on a squeak. "Answer me."

Something green flared within her eyes, a surprising spark of iron will. "Why should I answer to you?"

"Because." His entire vision was filled with her eyes, sparkling gray and meadow green intermixed. The combination was absolutely fascinating.

She stared back at him and said, low, "And, anyway, why do you care where I've been?"

He'd faced capture and torture and the imminent prospect of his own death for years on end, but for the life of him, he hadn't a clue how to reply to this small slip of a girl.

So it was perhaps just as well that the shot rang out at that moment.

Chapter Four

Longsword could find no reason this stranger might want a lock of his hair, even for a penny, but he could see no risk to himself, either. So thinking to humor the other man, he took his great sword, cut off a lock of hair, and gave it to the Goblin King. The Goblin King smiled and held out the penny. But the moment Longsword grasped the coin, the ground opened in an enormous crack beneath him. The earth swallowed both Longsword and his sword, and he fell far, far below until he landed in the Goblin Kingdom.

There he looked up and saw the Goblin King throw off his velvet cloak. Now were revealed his orange glowing eyes, lank green hair, and yellow fangs.

"Who are you?" Longsword cried.

"I am the Goblin King," replied the other. "When you accepted my coin for your lock of hair, you sold yourself into my power. For if I cannot have the sword alone, then I will have both you and the sword. . . ."

—from *Longsword*

Surrounded. The enemy on both sides, shooting from hidden positions, his men screaming as they were picked off. He couldn't form a line of defense, couldn't rally his troops. They were all going to die if he—

The second shot rang out. Reynaud found himself on the ground against a carriage, Miss Corning's sweet, warm body under him. Her gray eyes stared up into his, no longer green with anger but only terrified.

And the screams—the screams were all around him.

"Descendez!" Reynaud roared to a soldier sitting in the carriage box looking stupidly around. "Form a line of defense!"

"What—" Miss Corning began.

But he ignored her. A man had been hit and was writhing on the top steps of the town house, his blood staining the white stone. It was the young soldier, the one who'd been walking with him. Dammit. It was *his* man.

And he was still exposed.

"Stay with Miss Corning," he ordered a nearby soldier.

The soldier in the box had finally dropped down and lay beside them as well. Where was the sergeant? Where were the other officers? They'd all be killed here in the open, caught between the cross fire. Reynaud's temples throbbed with pain; his heart thundered. He had to save his men.

"Do you understand?" he yelled at the soldier near him.

The soldier blinked at him, dazed.

Reynaud took the man by the shoulder and shook him. "Stay with Miss Corning. I'm counting on you."

Something in the soldier's face cleared. His gaze

locked on Reynaud's, just as they always did, and he nodded. "Yes, my lord."

"Good man." Reynaud eyed the soldier on the steps, judging the distance. It had been at least a minute since the last shot. Were the Indians still lurking in the woods? Or had they crept away again, silent as ghosts?

"What are you going to do?" Miss Corning asked.

Reynaud looked into her clear gray eyes. "Get my man. Stay here. Take this." He pressed the hilt of his knife into her palm. "Don't move until I tell you."

And he kissed her hard, feeling life—his and hers—coursing through his veins. Dear God, he had to get her away from here.

He got up before she could voice her protest and ran to the steps, keeping his upper body low. He paused by the moaning soldier only long enough to grab the man under the arms. The boy screamed as Reynaud pulled him to the front door, the sound high and animal, a cry of primeval agony. So many were in agony. So many were dead. And all so young.

The third bullet hit the door frame as Reynaud yanked his man through, splinters of wood exploding against his cheek.

Reynaud was panting, but the boy was out of the line of fire at least. The bastard couldn't shoot him again, couldn't scalp him as he lay dying. *Her brown eyes stared up through a mask of blood, dull and lifeless.* Reynaud shook his head, wishing he could think through the blinding pain. Something . . . something wasn't right.

"What is this?" Reginald St. Aubyn, the earldom thief, cried, his face red. He started for the door.

Reynaud shot out his arm, barring the way. "Snipers in the woods. Don't go out."

St. Aubyn jerked back his head, staring at him as if he were insane. "What are you babbling about?"

"I haven't time for this," Reynaud growled. "There's a shooter, man."

"But . . . but, my niece is out there!"

"She's safe at the moment, sheltered by the carriage."

Reynaud assessed the crowd of soldiers gathered by the commotion in the entry hall. Except . . . except they didn't look like soldiers. Something was wrong. His head was splitting with pain, and he hadn't the time to figure it out now. His back crawled with the knowledge that the Indians were still out there, waiting. The lad moaned at his feet.

"You." He pointed at the oldest. "Are there any guns in the house? Dueling pistols, birding pieces, hunting rifles?"

The man blinked and came to attention. "There's a pair of dueling pistols in his lordship's study."

"Good. Get them."

The man whirled and ran down the back passage.

"You two"—Reynaud indicated two practical-looking women—"fetch some clean cloth, linens, anything we can use for bandages."

"Yes, sir." They went without a word.

Reynaud turned to the boy but was stayed by a hand on his arm.

"Now, see here," St. Aubyn said. "I won't let my servants be ordered about by a raving lunatic. This is my house. You can't just—"

Reynaud spun and in the same motion took the older man by the throat and shoved him into the wall. He looked into watery brown eyes, suddenly widened, and leaned close.

"*My* house, *my* men," he breathed into the other man's face. "Help me or get out of my way, I care not, but never question my authority again—and don't *ever* lay a hand on me." There was no question in his tone.

St. Aubyn swallowed and nodded his head.

"Good." Reynaud let him go and glanced at the sergeant. "Look out the door—quickly—and check that Miss Corning and the others are still by the carriage."

"Yes, my lord."

Reynaud knelt by the wounded man. The boy's face was greasy with sweat, his eyes narrowed in pain. The wound was on his left hip. Reynaud took off his coat and found the small thin knife he kept in a pocket. Then he bundled the coat and placed it beneath the boy's head.

"Am I dying, my lord?" the lad whispered.

"No, not at all." Reynaud sliced open the boy's breeches from waist to knee and spread the bloody fabric. "What's your name?"

"Henry, my lord." The lad swallowed. "Henry Carter."

"I don't like my men dying, Henry," Reynaud said. There was no exit wound. The bullet would need to be dug out of the boy's hip—a tricky operation, as sometimes the hip bled badly. "Do you understand?"

"Yes, my lord." The boy's eyebrows rose questioningly.

"So you're not to die," Reynaud stated with finality.

The boy nodded, his face smoothing. "Yes, my lord."

"The pistols, sir." The older soldier was back, panting, with a flat box in his hands.

Reynaud rose. "Good man."

The women had returned as well with the linens, and one immediately knelt and began bandaging Henry. "I had Cook send for a doctor, my lord. I hope that was right."

Cook? That feeling that something wasn't right made his head spin again, but Reynaud kept his face calm. An officer never showed fear in battle.

"Very smart." Reynaud nodded at the woman, and a flush of pleasure spread over her plain face. He turned to the sergeant. "What's happening outside?"

The sergeant straightened from the door crack. "Miss Corning is still by the carriage, my lord, along with the coachman and two footmen. A small crowd has gathered across the street, but other than that, it seems just as usual."

"Good. And your name?"

The sergeant threw back his shoulders. "Hurley, my lord."

Reynaud nodded. He placed the dueling-pistols box on a side table and opened it. The pistols within looked like they might be from his grandfather's time, but they had been properly oiled and maintained. Reynaud took them out, checked to see if they were loaded, and stepped to the door.

"Keep away from the doorway," he instructed the sergeant. "The Indians might still be out there."

"Dear God, he's insane," St. Aubyn muttered.

Reynaud ignored him and ducked out the door.

The street was strangely quiet—or perhaps it just seemed so after the chaos of the shooting. Reynaud didn't pause but ran swiftly down the steps and dropped to the ground by Miss Corning, who was nearly underneath the carriage.

"Are you all right?" he asked.

"Yes. Quite." She frowned and touched a finger to his cheek. "You're bleeding."

"Doesn't matter." He took her hand and licked his blood from her fingertip, making her gray eyes widen. "You still have my knife?"

"Yes." She showed him his knife, hidden among her skirts.

"Good girl." He looked at the soldiers . . . except now they were a coachman and two footmen. Reynaud blinked fiercely. *Concentrate.* "Did you see where the shots were coming from?"

The coachman shook his head, but one of the footmen, a tall fellow with a missing front tooth, said, "A black carriage pulled away very fast just after you dragged Henry into the house, my lord. I think the shots may've come from inside the carriage."

Reynaud nodded. "That makes sense. But we'll take Miss Corning in with all precaution just in case. Mr. Coachman, please go first. I'll follow with Miss Corning while the footmen come behind." He handed one of the pistols to the footman who had spoken. "Don't shoot, but make sure anyone watching can see that you're armed."

The men nodded, and Reynaud rose with his little company. He wrapped one arm about Miss Corning, covering as much of her body with his as he could. "Go."

The coachman ran to the steps, and Reynaud followed with Miss Corning, damnably aware of how exposed they were. Her form was warm next to his, small and delicate. It seemed to take minutes, but they were within the house again in seconds. No more shots rang out, and Reynaud slammed the door behind him.

"Dear God." Miss Corning was looking at Henry, the wounded soldier.

But he wasn't a soldier, Reynaud realized all at once. Henry was the footman who'd been guarding his bedroom door. His head spun as burning bile backed up into his throat. The sergeant was the butler, the women the maids, and there were no soldiers, only footmen staring at him warily. And the Indians? In *London*? Reynaud shook his head, feeling as if his brain would explode from the pain.

Dear God, maybe he *was* mad.

Beatrice bent over a small prayer book, picking apart the binding. She found it easier to think when her hands were busy. So after Henry had been seen to, after Lord Hope had retired to his room, after she'd calmed the servants and sent them back to work, after all had been restored to order in her home, she'd retreated here to her own rooms to contemplate the events of this afternoon.

Although, she'd not come to any firm conclusions when a knock sounded at her door. She sighed and looked up at a second tap.

"Beatrice?"

It was Uncle Reggie's voice, which was odd, because he hardly ever visited her in her rooms, but then this had been a very odd day. She set the book down on the little table she worked at and rose from her chair to let him in.

"I wanted to make sure that you were unharmed, m'dear," he said once he'd entered. He glanced vaguely around the room.

Beatrice felt a pang of remorse. In all the excitement of the shooting, she'd not had a chance to talk to her uncle. "I'm quite all right—not even a scratch. And you? How do you feel?"

"Oh, nothing can hurt an old man like me," he blustered. " 'Course, that impostor did knock me against the wall a bit." He peered at her from under his bushy eyebrows as if waiting for a reaction.

Beatrice frowned. "He did? But why?"

"Bloody arrogance, if you ask me," her uncle replied heatedly. "He was raving about Indians in the woods. Started ordering the servants about and told me to get out of the way. I think the man is mad."

"He did save me." Beatrice looked down at her slippers. Lord Hope's sanity was the very subject she'd been grappling with when Uncle Reggie had interrupted her. "Perhaps he was merely confused by the suddenness of the events. Perhaps he spoke in haste when he talked of Indians."

"Or perhaps he's mad." Uncle Reggie's voice softened at her look. "I know he saved your life, and don't think I'm not grateful the bastard risked his life for you. But is it safe to have him in the house? What if he wakes one morning and decides *I'm* an Indian—or you?"

"He seems sane otherwise."

"Does he, Bea?"

"Yes. Mostly anyway." Beatrice sat in the chair before her worktable and bit her lip. "I don't think he'd ever hurt me or you, Uncle, truly, no matter his state of mind."

"Humph. I don't know if I share your optimism." Uncle Reggie wandered over and peered at her work. "Ah, you've started a new project. What is it?"

"Aunt Mary's old prayer book."

He gently touched a finger to the disassembled book. "I well remember how she used to carry it to church in the country. It belonged to her great-great-grandmother, you know."

"I remember her telling me," Beatrice said softly. "The cover was quite worn through, the spine had cracked, and the pages were coming loose from the stitching. I thought to restitch it and then rebind it in a blue calfskin. It'll be good as new."

He nodded. "She would've liked that. It's good of you to take such care of her things."

Beatrice looked at her hands, remembering Aunt Mary's kind blue eyes, the softness of her cheeks, and the way she used to laugh full-throatedly. Their household had never been the same without her. Since Aunt Mary's death, Uncle Reggie had become a less-humorous man, more prone to quick judgments, less able to understand or sympathize with other people's intentions.

"I enjoy it," she said. "I only wish she were here to see the result."

"As do I, m'dear, as do I." He patted the pages once more and then moved away from her table. "I think I must send him away, Bea, for your safety."

She sighed, knowing they'd returned to the subject of Lord Hope. "He doesn't present any danger to me."

"Bea," Uncle Reggie said gently, "I know you like to

put things to rights, but some things can't be fixed, and I'm afraid a man this wild is one of them."

Beatrice set her lips stubbornly. "I think we must consider how it'll appear if we toss him out of Blanchard House and he regains the title. He won't look favorably on us."

Uncle Reggie stiffened. "He won't get the title—I won't let him."

"But, Uncle—"

"No, I'm firm on this, Bea," he said with the sternness he rarely showed her. "I'll not let that madman take our home from us. I vowed to your aunt Mary that I'd provide for you properly, and I intend to do so. I'll agree to let him stay here, but only so I can keep an eye on him and gather proof that he's not fit for the title."

And with that, he closed the door to her room firmly.

Beatrice looked down at Aunt Mary's prayer book. If she didn't do something, there soon would be bloodshed in her house. Uncle Reggie was adamant, but perhaps she could make Lord Hope see that her uncle was only a stubborn old man.

"UNCLE REGGIE COULDN'T possibly have sent someone to kill you," Miss Corning said for the third or possibly fourth time. "I'm telling you that you don't know him. He's really the sweetest thing imaginable."

"Maybe to you," Reynaud replied as he sharpened his long knife, "but you're not the one displacing him from a title—and monies—he thought were his."

He examined her from under his eyebrows. Did she think him a madman? Was she afraid to be in his company? What had she thought of his actions just hours before?

But despite his watchfulness, all he saw was irritation on Miss Corning's face.

"You're not listening to me." She paced from the window of his bedroom to where he sat on the edge of the bed and stood before him, arms akimbo like a cook scolding the butcher's boy. "Even if Uncle Reggie *wanted* to kill you—which, as I keep telling you, he never would—he'd not be stupid enough to stage an assassination in front of his own house."

"*My* house," Reynaud growled. She'd been haranguing him for the last half hour and showed no signs of stopping.

"You," Miss Corning stated through gritted teeth, "are impossible."

"No, I am correct," he answered. "And you simply don't want to acknowledge the fact that your uncle may not be nearly as sweet as you think."

"I—" she began again, her tone indicating she might very well continue the argument until doomsday.

But Reynaud had had enough. He threw aside the knife and whetstone and rose from the bed, nearly in her face. "Besides, if you really did consider me impossible, you would never have kissed me."

She skittered back, and he felt a spear of rage shoot through him. She should not fear him. It wasn't right.

Then her lush mouth parted in what looked like outrage. For a moment she couldn't speak, and then she burst out, "It was *you* who kissed *me*!"

He took a step toward her. She took a step back. He stalked her silently across the room, waiting for fear to turn her eyes dark. Hadn't she realized what he'd shouted, out there by the carriage?

Didn't she know he was mad?

He bent over her, leaning down until the wisps of hair near her ear brushed his lips, inhaling the scent of sweet English flowers. "You returned the kiss; don't think I didn't notice."

And he had. Her soft lips had opened beneath his for just a fraction of a second before he'd turned and run toward the wounded footman. That kiss would be burned in his memory forever. He angled his head and looked into her eyes.

Instead of going dark with fear, they were snapping with green sparks. "I thought you were about to die!"

Foolish girl.

"Tell yourself that if it assuages your delicate sensibilities," he murmured, "but the fact remains that you. Kissed. Me."

"What an arrogant thing to say," she whispered.

"Granted." He inhaled. Her skin smelled clean and womanly, with that hint of a flowery soap that Indian women never had. It was a nostalgic scent for him, conjuring the memory of other civilized women he'd once known—his mother, his sister, forgotten young girls he'd squired to balls long ago. She smelled of England itself, and for some reason he found the thought unbearably arousing and at the same time utterly frightening. She had no defenses against him.

He no longer belonged in her world. "But did you enjoy the kiss?"

"And if I did?" she whispered.

He brushed his lips—softly, delicately—against her

jaw. "Then I pity you. You should run screaming from me. Can't you see the monster I am?"

She looked up at him with brave clear gray eyes. "You're not a monster."

He closed his eyes, not wanting to see her face, not wanting to take advantage of that purity. "You don't know me. You don't know what I've done."

"Then tell me," she said urgently. "What happened in the Colonies? Where have you been for seven years?"

"No." *Brown eyes stared up through a mask of blood. He was too late.* He pushed away from her, afraid she'd see the demons laughing behind his eyes.

"Why not?" she called. "Why can't you tell me? I can never understand you until I've heard what happened to you."

"Don't be ridiculous," he snapped. "There's no need for you to understand me."

She threw her hands in the air. "You're impossible!"

"And we are back where we started." He sighed.

She frowned at him, her gray eyes sparking with displeasure as she tapped one small foot. "Very well," she said at last, "I'll lay aside the matter of your past for now, but you can't ignore the fact that someone tried to kill you today."

"I'm not." He turned and gathered the knife, whetstone, and the piece of leather he'd been using to sharpen the knife. "I don't think it's any of your concern."

"How can it not be my concern?" she demanded. "I was there. I saw that third shot. The first two might have been random, but the third was most definitely aimed at you."

"And again, I say that this is none of your business."

He stowed the whetstone and leather in the top of a chest of drawers, but he hung the knife at his waist. He'd had it for seven long years, used it to butcher deer and bear, and once, years ago now, he'd killed a man with it. The knife wasn't a friend—he had no emotional attachment to it—but it had served him well, and he felt safer, more whole, with it at his side.

He looked curiously at Miss Corning, still standing by the bed across the room. "Why do you persist?"

"Because I *care,*" she said, "no matter how much you try to hold me at arm's length, I still can't help but care. And because I am the only one who might get you to understand that Uncle Reggie had nothing to do with the shooting. Think: If it wasn't Uncle Reggie, then someone else has tried to kill you."

"And who do you think that might be?"

"I don't know." She hugged her waist and shivered. "Do you?"

He frowned down at the top of the chest of drawers. It held only a basin and a pitcher of water—nothing like the furniture that'd been in his old rooms in this house. But then again it was richly appointed compared to the wigwams he'd lived in for many years. For a brief moment, he felt dizzy with displacement. Did he belong anywhere anymore? The demons surged forward to take control.

Then he shook his head, shoving them back. "Vale said he'd been looking for the traitor for a year now. He's obsessed with the search. And he said the traitor had a French mother. My mother was French."

"Would Lord Vale have you killed if he thought you the traitor?"

Reynaud remembered the man he'd known, a laughing man, a friend to everyone he met. That Vale would never have done such a thing, but then again, that Vale was from the past. Would Vale kill him if he thought he'd betrayed the regiment at Spinner's Falls? A man might change in many ways in seven years, but could Vale turn into a killer of friends?

"No." He answered his own silent question. "No, Jasper would never do that."

"Then who would?" she asked quietly. "If another of the survivors of the massacre thought you were the traitor, would they kill you?"

"I don't know." He frowned, thinking, and then shook his head in frustration. "I don't even know who survived the massacre besides Vale and a man called Samuel Hartley." *Dammit!* He wished he could call on Vale for help, but after yesterday afternoon, it seemed impossible. "I don't know who to trust."

He looked at her, the full realization dawning on him. "I'm not sure there *is* anyone I can trust."

"They say the bullet came within inches of his face," the Duke of Lister drawled, cradling a goblet of wine between his large pale hands.

"At least that close." Blanchard frowned. "There was blood on his cheek. Although I think that was from a splinter striking him."

"Pity it wasn't closer," Hasselthorpe said as he swirled the wine in his glass. The burgundy liquid was so dark it was nearly black. Like a glass of blood. He set it down on the table beside his chair in sudden distaste. "Had the bullet smashed his skull, you, Lord Blanchard, would have no fear for your title."

Blanchard, predictably, choked on his wine.

Hasselthorpe watched him, a faint smile playing around his mouth. They sat at his dining table, the ladies having retired to the sitting room for their tea. Soon they'd have to join them, and he'd have to put up with Adriana and her incredibly foolish conversation. His wife of twenty-some years had been regarded as a great beauty when she'd come out, and the years had done very little to dim her lovely form. Unfortunately, they'd done nothing to brighten her mind, either. Adriana was the one emotional decision he'd made in a life of calculated gamesmanship, and he'd been paying for it ever since.

"He was brave enough," Blanchard muttered grudgingly. "Got my niece off the street at the risk of his own life. But the feller thought he was fighting Indians."

Lister stirred. "Indians? What, the savages in the Colonies?"

"That's what he was raving about," Blanchard said. He looked from Hasselthorpe to Lister, his eyes calculating. "I think he's mad."

"Mad," Hasselthorpe murmured. "And if he's mad, he certainly can't gain the title. Is that what you plan?"

Blanchard jerked a single nod.

"That's not bad," Hasselthorpe said. "And it saves you from having to kill the man, too."

"Are you insinuating that I was behind the attempt on Lord Hope's life?" Blanchard sputtered.

"Not at all," Hasselthorpe said smoothly. He was aware that Lister watched them under hooded eyes. "Just pointing out a fact. One that every intelligent man in London will be thinking—no doubt including Lord Hope himself."

"Damn your eyes," Blanchard whispered. His face had gone white.

Lister laughed. "Don't worry yourself over it, my lord. After all, the gunman missed. Thus, it hardly matters who tried to kill the lost Lord Hope."

Hasselthorpe raised his glass to his lips, murmuring softly, "Not unless they try again."

"I DON'T UNDERSTAND gentlemen," Beatrice announced a day later as she and Lottie strolled about the vast warehouse showroom of Godfrey and Sons furniture makers. She squinted in disapproval at several gentlemen across the room who seemed to be vying for the attentions of a pretty redheaded girl by demonstrating who could lift a heavy-looking stuffed chair above their head the highest. "I cannot understand why Lord Hope kissed me yesterday and then accused *me* of kissing *him*."

"Gentlemen are an enigma," Lottie replied gravely.

"They are." Beatrice hesitated, then said quietly, "He seemed . . . confused during the shooting incident."

Lottie glanced at her. "Confused?"

Beatrice grimaced. "He was talking about Indians and forming a line of defense."

"Good Lord." Lottie looked troubled. "Did he know where he was?"

"I don't know." Beatrice frowned, remembering those minutes huddled next to the carriage. Her heart had stopped when she'd realized that Lord Hope was about to run into the open to go to Henry the footman. "I . . . I don't think so."

"But that's madness," Lottie whispered in horror.

"I know," Beatrice murmured. "And I'm afraid that Uncle Reggie will use it against Lord Hope to keep the title."

Lottie looked at her. "But if he is mad . . . Bea, dear, surely it's better that he not inherit the title?"

"The matter is more complicated than that." Beatrice closed her eyes for a moment. "Lord Hope seems perfectly fine—if hostile—most of the time. Should a man be deprived of his title because of one moment of confusion?"

Lottie cocked her head, looking skeptical.

Beatrice hurried on. "And there's more to consider. If Lord Hope attains the title, he might take his vote in parliament and cast it for Mr. Wheaton's bill."

"I'm as much in favor of Mr. Wheaton's bill as you," Lottie said, "but I don't know if I want it passed at your expense."

"If it was just me, I don't think I'd mind," Beatrice said. "I know it would be hard to live in reduced circumstances in the country after being in London all these years, but I think it wouldn't be so bad. It's Uncle Reggie I worry about. I'm truly afraid that losing the earldom might kill him." She pressed her hand to her chest to ease the ache there.

"There is no way for everyone to win, is there?" Lottie said somberly.

"I'm afraid not," Beatrice replied. They strolled in silence for a moment before she said, "The whole thing was terrible, Lottie. Poor Henry was quite soaked in his own blood, Uncle Reggie was shouting, the servants were in an uproar, and Lord Hope was striding about with a dueling pistol, looking like he wanted to kill someone. Then, two hours later, he says I kissed him when clearly he kissed me. And until that point, I didn't even think he *liked* me."

Lottie cleared her throat delicately. "Well, to be absolutely correct, he doesn't have to *like* you to want to kiss you."

Beatrice looked at her, appalled.

"I'm sorry, but there it is." Lottie shrugged and then said entirely too innocently, "Of course, generally speaking, the lady does like the gentleman when they kiss."

Beatrice pressed her lips together, though she knew her face was warming.

Lottie cleared her throat. "Do you? Like Lord Hope, that is?"

"How could I like him?" Beatrice asked. "He's surly and sarcastic and quite possibly mad."

"And yet you kissed him," Lottie reminded her.

"*He* kissed *me,*" Beatrice said automatically. "It's just that he has such an intense way of looking at one, as if I'm the only other human in the world. He's so full of passion."

Lottie raised her eyebrows.

"I'm explaining it badly," Beatrice said. She thought a moment. "It's as if the only music one had ever heard was a penny whistle. One would probably think it was quite all right, that music was a rather nice thing but nothing very special. But what if one then attended one of Mr. Handel's symphonies? Do you see? It would be overwhelming, beautiful and strange and complex, and so utterly compelling."

"I think I understand," Lottie murmured. Her brows knit.

Across the room, one of the gentlemen misjudged the chair's weight and dropped it. The chair smashed to the ground, the other gentlemen doubled over in laughter, and the young lady's chaperone escorted her from the showroom, scolding her all the way. The proprietor hurried over to the scene of his wrecked merchandise.

Beatrice shook her head. "I'll never understand men."

"Listen, dear," Lottie said. "Do you know what my husband did this morning?"

"No." Beatrice shook her head. "But I don't really—"

"I'll tell you," Lottie said without regard for her friend's answer. "He came down to breakfast, ate three eggs, half a gammon steak, four pieces of toast, and a pot of tea."

Beatrice blinked. "That seems like quite a lot of food."

Lottie waved her hand irritably. "His usual breakfast."

"Oh." Beatrice frowned. "Then why—?"

"He said not a word to me the entire time! Instead, he busied himself reading his correspondence and muttering over the scandal sheets. And mark this—he left the room without bidding me good-bye. And when he came back in a minute later, do you know what he did?"

"I haven't a clue."

"He walked to the sideboard, picked up another piece of toast, and strode right by me again without speaking!"

"Ah." Beatrice winced. "Perhaps he had important business on his mind."

Lottie arched one eyebrow. "Or perhaps he's simply a fool."

Beatrice wasn't certain what to say to that, so for a moment she was silent. Both ladies perambulated slowly through the crowded room and stopped with silent consensus before a side table entirely covered in gilded putti.

"That," Lottie said with consideration, "is the ugliest thing I've ever seen."

" 'Tis, isn't it? It's almost as if the maker had a morbid dislike of side tables." Beatrice tilted her head, examining the table. "I went to visit Jeremy yesterday."

"How is he?"

"Not well." She felt Lottie's swift glance. "It's very important that we pass Mr. Wheaton's bill. The soldiers who would benefit from this bill are many—perhaps thousands of men, and some of those men served under Jeremy. He cares so passionately about the bill. I know that it would do him immeasurable good if the veterans got a better pension."

"I'm sure it would, dear. I'm sure it would," Lottie said gently.

"He simply . . ." Beatrice had to pause a moment and swallow before she could continue; then she said more steadily, "He simply needs a reason to . . . to live, Lottie. I worry for him, I do."

"Of course you do."

"Mr. and Mrs. Oates leave him in that room by himself for far too long at a time." Beatrice shook her head. The Oateses' reaction to their son's horrific injuries when he returned home had long been a source of concern for her. "They've given up on him, I think."

"I'm sorry, dear."

"They looked at him when he returned," Beatrice

whispered, "and it was as if he were already dead. As if he meant nothing to them unless he was entirely whole and well. They've now turned to Jeremy's brother, Alfred, and treat him as if he is the heir instead of Jeremy."

Beatrice looked at her friend, and this time she couldn't keep the tears from swimming in her eyes. "And that horrible Frances Cunningham! I still get angry when I think how she threw him over when he returned. It's so shameful."

"Pity, isn't it, that no one condemned her for her heartlessness," Lottie said thoughtfully. "But then he had lost his legs and wasn't expected to live."

"She could've at least waited until he was out of the sickroom," Beatrice muttered darkly. "And she's married now. Did you know? To a baronet."

"A fat, old baronet," Lottie said with satisfaction. "Or so I've heard. Perhaps she got her just deserts after all."

"Humph." Beatrice stared a moment at the putti. The one on the corner of the table nearest her looked remarkably like a fat old man with digestive troubles. Perhaps Frances Cunningham *had* gotten what she'd deserved. "But you understand, don't you, how important it is that this bill is passed *now*—not a year or two hence?"

"Yes, I do." Lottie linked her arm with Beatrice's, and they began to stroll again. "You are so good. Much better than me."

"You want this bill passed as well."

"But my interest is theoretical." A faint smile curved Lottie's wide mouth. "I think it only just that men who have served for years in sometimes deplorable conditions have a fair compensation. You, dear Beatrice, believe with a passion. You feel for those wretched creatures, almost as much as you feel for Jeremy."

"Perhaps," Beatrice said. "But in the end, it's Jeremy that I feel the most for."

"Exactly. Which is why I am so concerned."

"Whatever about?"

Lottie halted and took her hands. "I don't want you to be disappointed . . ."

Beatrice turned her face to the side, but even so, she could not escape the end of Lottie's sentence.

". . . if the bill is not passed in time."

Chapter Five

Well, Longsword did not like this turn of events one wit, but a bargain once struck with the Goblin King is very hard to break. Thus he was compelled to work for the Goblin King, and that is a dirty job, indeed; I can tell you! He never saw the sun, he never heard laughter, and he never felt a cool breeze against his cheek, for the Goblin Kingdom, as you may have heard, is a horrible place. But the worst part for Longsword was the knowledge that the master he served and the things he did were an affront to God and Heaven itself.

Because of this, every year Longsword would go to his master, lower himself to one knee, and beg to be relieved of his horrible servitude.

And every year the Goblin King refused to let Longsword go. . . .

—from *Longsword*

"Ridiculous that I can't touch any of the Blanchard monies," Reynaud growled a day later. He paced the little sitting room from fireplace to window, feeling like a wild wolf caged. "How am I to pay my lawyers without funds?"

"You can hardly blame Uncle Reggie for being reluctant to pay for his own ouster," Miss Corning said. She sat serenely by the small fire, sipping some of her infernal tea.

"Ha! If he thinks that'll stop me, he'll be sorely disappointed," Reynaud retorted. "I have a petition before parliament to form a special committee to look into my case."

Miss Corning set her teacup down carefully. "Already? I had no idea."

Reynaud snorted. "If it were tomorrow, it'd not be soon enough for me. Once I prove my identity, they cannot keep the title from me."

Miss Corning frowned, fiddling with her teacup.

Reynaud's brows snapped together. "You don't believe me?"

"It's just . . . What if . . ." She shook her head slowly.

"What if *what*?"

"What if he says that you are mad?" she asked all in a rush, and looked up at him.

Reynaud stared. Insanity was one of the few reasons a man might be passed over for a title. "Do you have information that he will?"

"It was just something he said in passing." She ducked her head, hiding her gray eyes from him.

Reynaud scowled, wondering what her uncle had actually said. He felt cold sweat start at the small of his back. *You'll never be a proper Englishman again,* the goblins in his mind chittered. *You'll never belong.* Reynaud balled his hands, fighting the voices.

"Do you feel well?" Miss Corning asked.

"Fine," Reynaud snapped. "I'm fine."

Her gray eyes looked troubled. "Perhaps if I talk to Uncle Reggie, he'd be willing to lend you some of his money for new clothes and such."

"*My* money," Reynaud growled.

She was throwing him a bone, and they both knew it. Damn her uncle to hell. He parted the curtain to peer out. Three stories below, a carriage lurked in front of the town house. Probably one of St. Aubyn's political allies come to call.

"Yes, well, your money or Uncle Reggie's money, the fact remains that he is the one in control of it," Miss Corning observed. "It wouldn't hurt your case to be more civil to him, especially since you're staying in his house."

"*My* house. I have every right to live in my house, and I'll be damned before I crawl to that man." Reynaud let the curtain drop.

Miss Corning rolled her eyes. "I didn't say *crawl,* I said be more—"

"Civil, I know." He stalked toward her. She was looking remarkably pretty this morning in a green frock that offset the pale rose of her cheeks and made her eyes sparkle like diamonds. "The only one I'm interested in being 'civil' to is you."

She paused, her tea dish halfway to her lips, and eyed him warily. Good. She took him far too much for granted as it was. They were in a room alone, for God's sake, and he'd spent the last seven years in a society where the relations between a man and a woman were much more fundamental. In fact—

But his thoughts were interrupted by a footman appearing at the door. "You have a visitor, my lord."

And the man stepped aside to reveal a vision. An elderly lady stood there, her back ramrod straight, her snowy white hair pulled into a severe knot at the crown of her head, her piercing blue eyes already narrowed in disapproval. Reynaud hadn't seen her in seven years, and for a moment he feared he would lose his self-possession. He knew tears—awful unmanly tears—were near the surface.

Then she spoke. "*Tiens!* Such an 'orrible growth of 'air upon your face, nephew! I am quite repulsed. Is this, then, what gentlemen in the Colonies wear? I do not believe it; no, I do not!"

He went to her and took her hands, kissing her tenderly on the cheek despite her mutter of disgust. "I am glad to see you, Tante Cristelle."

"Tcha! I do not think you can see at all with this 'air." She reached a blue-veined hand to brush the hair falling into his face. Her touch, unlike her words, was gentle. Then her hand dropped. "And who is this child here? Have you lost so much of civilization that you closet yourself alone with a female in a respectable house?"

Reynaud turned, amused, to see that Miss Corning had jumped up from her chair and was eyeing Tante Cristelle warily. "This is a cousin of mine, Miss Beatrice Corning. Miss Corning, my aunt, Miss Cristelle Molyneux."

Miss Corning curtsied as Tante Cristelle employed

her looking glass and said, "I do not remember a cousin called Corning in my sister's family."

"I'm Lord Blanchard's niece," Miss Corning said.

Tante Cristelle's eyes darkened. "*C'est ridicule!* My nephew doesn't have a niece, only a nephew, and he not yet ten years of age."

Reynaud cleared his throat, feeling like laughing for the first time since he'd set foot on English soil. "She means the present Earl of Blanchard, Tante."

The old lady sniffed. "The *pretender* to the title. I see."

Miss Corning looked cautious. "Um . . . perhaps I can bring up some tea?"

Reynaud would've preferred coffee or brandy, but since Miss Corning seemed to be fixated on tea, he merely nodded. She glided from the room, and he watched her go.

"That one is very pretty," Tante Cristelle observed. "Not beautiful, but she 'as an air of grace about her."

"Indeed." Reynaud looked at his aunt. "You mentioned my sister. Is she well?"

"You don't know?" Her brows snapped together in disapproval. "Did you not ask?"

"I have asked," Reynaud replied as he ushered her to a chair. "But no one knows her as well as you do, Tante."

"Humph," said Tante Cristelle as she primly lowered herself to a chair. "Then I will tell you. You know your sister was widowed shortly after your . . . disappearance."

Reynaud nodded. "So Miss Corning has told me." He'd gone to look out the window again. London hadn't changed much since his absence, but everything else had.

Everything.

"*Bon,*" Tante Cristelle said. "Then last year she married a rustic, a man from the Colony of New England. His name is Samuel Hartley."

"That I'd heard as well," he replied.

Strange to think that Emeline was now married to a man Reynaud had known in the army—a Colonial. Once again he felt that nauseating sense that his world was in motion, past and present conflicting, warring for his soul.

Tante Cristelle continued. "She 'as taken herself to live with her husband far, far overseas in the city of Boston. I do not know if such an action was wise on her part, but you know your sister. She can be quite the stubborn mule when she wishes."

"And my nephew, Daniel?"

"Petite Daniel is fine and strong. Naturally his mother took him to live with her in America."

Reynaud contemplated that. Ironic that he was now farther from his sister than he'd been before he'd sailed for England. Would he have delayed his return had he known she was in New England? He wasn't sure. The need to regain his former life—his lands and title—had driven him for seven long years. Had in fact kept him alive and sane during the endless days and nights of his captivity. Nothing, not even the love for a sister, could keep him from his goal.

"Where have you been, Reynaud?" Tante Cristelle asked softly.

He shook his head, closing his eyes. How could he tell her, this gently bred aristocrat, what had been done to him?

After a moment he heard her sigh. "*Bien*. There is no need to speak of it if you do not wish."

At that, he turned around. Tante Cristelle was watching him patiently. She was the elder sister of his late mother. Both women had grown up in Paris and had immigrated to England on his mother's marriage. Tante Cristelle was in her seventh decade, but her snapping blue eyes were sharp, her mind one of the clearest he'd ever known.

"I intend to get my title back, Tante," he said.

She nodded once. "*Naturalement.*"

"I have petitioned parliament to form a special committee to hear my case. When it is convened, I will have to appear before the committee in Westminster and plead my case. The current earl will present his side at the same time."

Tante sniffed. "This usurper will not let go of his stolen title so easily, eh?"

"No," Reynaud said grimly. "He'll hold it for as long as he can, I'm sure. And he may ask to retain the title on the grounds that I'm mad."

"Mad?" The old lady's thin eyebrows rose.

Reynaud looked away. "I was delirious with fever when I arrived. I'm afraid there was a roomful of people to witness me raving like a lunatic."

"And is that all?"

Reynaud grimaced uncomfortably. "There was an . . . incident yesterday. I was shot at—"

"*Mon dieu!*"

He waved away her concern. "It was nothing terrible. But I forgot myself somehow. I thought I was on the battlefield again."

Silence.

Then Tante Cristelle drew breath. "Ah. Unfortunate. We will need good solicitors and men of business to combat the usurper."

Reynaud looked up, hope making him feel suddenly weak. "Then you'll help me."

"Mais oui." Tante Cristelle scowled. "And did you think otherwise?"

Reynaud helped her stand, feeling the fragile bones of her arm beneath his hand. "No, but it has been a very long time since I've had an ally."

She shook her skirts into order. "We must plan a campaign, I think. I shall seek out these men of law, for I have maintained the estate of le petite Daniel whilst he sojourned in the Colonies and thus have many contacts. And you, you shall shave."

"Shave?" Reynaud's eyebrows shot up in amusement.

Tante Cristelle nodded sharply. "But of course, *shave,* and also you will need the new clothing, the proper wig, and the elegant shoes. For you must regain the aspect of the so-boring English milord, must you not? Thusly we shall confound our enemies with your very placidity."

Reynaud clenched his jaw. He hated to ask, but he forced himself to. "I have no monies, Tante."

She nodded, unsurprised. "I will lend you what you need, and when you become the earl again, you shall pay me back, yes?"

"Yes. Of course." Reynaud bowed over her hand. "I cannot tell you, Tante, how relieved I am that you are on my side."

"Tcha!" The old woman made a dismissive sound. "You have not lost your charm, I see, underneath that forest upon your face. But mark you this, nephew: a shave and a haircut are only part of what you'll need to transform yourself into the respectable English gentleman."

Reynaud frowned. "What else do you think I need? Name it and I'll buy it."

"Ah, but this is a thing not to be bought. For this you will need all your charm." She turned at the door and looked him in the eye, her gaze level and solemn. "A wife is what you need. An *English* wife of good family. For what man can be mad with a sweet, not-too-pretty wife by his side? Obtain a chit such as this and you will be halfway to regaining your title."

THE NEXT MORNING dawned bright and sunny. After making her toilet, Beatrice decided to consult with Cook. She was descending the stairs to the front hall when she heard male voices.

Beatrice halted at the landing and looked over the rail to the hall below. There stood the butler, two footmen, and a gentleman she did not know but who looked—at least from the back—somehow familiar. She continued down the stairs slowly, eyeing the man. He wore a freshly powdered white wig and a black coat of a very fine cut, embroidered about the cuffs in silver and green thread. The butler was saying something to him, but the stranger must've sensed her stare. He turned.

And she froze on the stairs.

It was Lord Hope—but a Lord Hope transformed. Gone was the thick beard. His jaw was freshly shaven, revealing his square chin and the hard planes of his cheeks. He must've cut his hair very close to his head, for the wig he wore was beautifully curled and powdered and fit him excellently. Beneath the black velvet of his coat, his waistcoat was silver and green brocade, and lace fell at his wrists. He was the very epitome of a fine London gentleman, and Beatrice might have felt a pang of regret for the man she'd nursed for the last week had it not been for two things. First, from his left ear, the black iron cross still dangled, primitive and uncivilized next to the perfection of his white wig. And second, the three tattooed birds still circled his right eye, as permanent as the ebony color of the eye itself.

He wore the trappings of civilization, but no one but a fool would mistake them for anything but a thin veneer covering the savage beneath.

He bowed to her, one leg extended, his arm sweeping down sardonically. "Miss Corning."

"Lord Hope." She'd regained some of her self-possession and now finished her descent of the stairs. "You've undergone a most remarkable change."

He shrugged. "To fight demons, one must assume the guise of a demon."

She looked at him. "I'm not sure I understand what that means."

"No matter." He glanced away, and with any other man, she might've thought him uncertain. "I go to visit my aunt this morn. Would you care to accompany me?"

It was a civilized invitation, and she rather wanted to know what he was about with this sudden transformation, but she bit her lip. Was it safe?

Her hesitation had lasted a fraction of a second too long. His pleasant expression turned to a scowl. "Are you afraid of me, Miss Corning?"

"Not at all." She tilted her chin, daring him to call her on the fib.

"Then you won't mind a simple drive in the city."

Why did he want her to accompany him? She stared at him, trying to decipher his motivations.

"Come, Miss Corning," he rumbled softly, "a simple yes or no will do."

"Yes, thank you," she said. "On one condition."

"And that is?" His eyes had narrowed ominously at her words.

She took a breath. "I'll come if you'll tell me something about where you've been for the last seven years."

His face darkened, and for a moment she thought he would turn and leave her in the hall. Then he nodded once, sharply. "Done. Go get your wrap."

She ran up the stairs before he could change his mind.

But when she returned to the hallway, Lord Hope was not there. For a moment, disappointment swept through her. Had he only been playing with her?

Then George the footman said, " 'E's gone back to see Henry, miss. Said 'e wouldn't be but a minute."

"Oh." Beatrice drew a breath, steadying her nerves. "Oh, well, in that case, I'll call on Henry myself."

The servants slept under the eaves, of course, way at the top of the town house. But because Henry was a big strong lad, and because he needed nursing, a pallet had been laid for him in a corner of the town-house kitchens. An old screen had been found to place in front of Henry's pallet when he wanted privacy, but when she entered the kitchen, Beatrice saw that it had been put aside. Lord

Hope squatted by the pallet, talking in a low tone to the footman lying there.

Beatrice halted just inside the kitchen door. She couldn't see Lord Hope's face—his back was to her—but Henry's countenance was as brightly lit as if a god had come to visit him. It seemed an intimate moment somehow—even though the principals were surrounded by the bustle of the kitchen—and she didn't want to intrude. So she stood and watched.

Lord Hope spoke as Henry regarded him intently. She remembered now how Lord Hope had called to the footmen, mistaking them for soldiers. Even then, even when she'd known he was in the midst of some strange delirium, she'd seen his worry. His real care for "his" men. She pressed her trembling fingers to her lips silently. Just when she decided he was entirely self-centered, just when she feared he was nothing but a madman, now he must show this noble side of himself? Dear God, how could she side with her uncle against such a man?

The viscount murmured something more, leaned a little closer to the footman, and placed his hand on Henry's shoulder. With a final nod, he stood.

He turned and saw her.

Beatrice dropped her hand, smiling brightly.

"I'm sorry, I only meant to be a moment," he said as he neared. He eyed her curiously.

"It's no trouble at all." She tilted her head to look up at him, still dazzled by the whiteness of his wig, the harshness of his tattoos. "Henry seemed pleased to see you."

He frowned, glancing back toward Henry's pallet. "I

noticed in my army days that it sometimes made a great difference."

"What did?"

"Visiting the wounded." He held his arm for her, and she placed her fingertips on his black sleeve as they left the kitchen, very aware of the hard muscle beneath the fabric. "Sitting and chatting with a man laid low. It cheers the man's spirit, I think. Makes him realize that he is needed in this world. That others wait for his recovery."

"Did the other officers visit with their wounded men as well?" she asked as they came to the front hall.

"Some did. Not many." He handed her into the waiting carriage and then climbed in to sit opposite her. "I always thought it a pity more officers did not realize the effectiveness of visiting their wounded men."

He knocked on the roof to signal the driver that they were ready.

"Perhaps they weren't as compassionate as you," she said softly.

He seemed irritated. "Compassion has nothing to do with it. It's an officer's duty to look after his men. They are in his charge."

Beatrice looked at him wonderingly. Duty might be a different motive than compassion, yet the outcome was the same. There'd been a look of awe in Henry's face when Lord Hope had talked to him. Then, too, if Lord Hope cared so much for a footman he hardly knew but whom he considered one of "his" men, would he not care equally for men who'd actually served in His Majesty's army?

She licked her lips. "I've heard that many men who've

served in His Majesty's army become quite destitute when they leave."

He glanced at her curiously. "Where have you heard that? I wouldn't think it a lady's daily conversation."

"Oh, here and there." She shrugged, trying to look unconcerned. "I've also heard that some members of parliament are thinking of presenting a bill that would ensure veterans a fair pension."

He snorted. "That'll die a quick death. There're too many who would rather see the country's funds go elsewhere."

"But if enough members back it—"

"They won't." He shook his head. "No one cares about the common soldier. Why d'you think they're paid so poorly?"

Beatrice bit her lip, unsure how to convince him to her cause. "If you become the earl, you'll sit in the House of Lords and—"

"I haven't the time to think of sitting in the House of Lords right now." He grimaced and shook his head. "I must focus all of my mind, my time, my energy in obtaining my title. Once that bridge is crossed, then I'll contemplate the tangled web of politics, not before then."

Beatrice's heart sank. By the time he decided to involve himself in politics, it might be too late for Mr. Wheaton's bill. Too late for Jeremy.

She bit her lip, glancing out the carriage window as they rumbled along. How, then, could she convince Lord Hope that Mr. Wheaton needed his help to pass the bill now? If only she knew why he made the decisions he did—why he was so obsessed with regaining his title.

She straightened and turned to him with determination. It was even more important than ever to find out what had happened to him in the last seven years.

What had turned him into the man he was today.

REYNAUD WATCHED Miss Corning from beneath lowered eyelids. She sat primly on the seat across from him, nibbling at her full bottom lip. What was going through her quick little mind? And why had she brought up parliament of all things? Her uncle was a keen politician. Perhaps she merely wanted to know if he'd become interested in politics once he attained the title. Become like her uncle.

He frowned. *That* wasn't likely to happen. He might be wearing a proper wig and clothing, but he'd never settle into complacent English life entirely. His time in the Colonies had changed him, warped him. He was no longer the proper English aristocrat who'd left London seven years ago. Perhaps that was what bothered her now. Perhaps she saw through the trappings of civilization to the man he really was. Sometimes he caught her staring at him with a curious uneasiness, like a deer scenting the air, aware of danger but with no knowledge of the wolf hiding in the trees behind her.

He turned his head to gaze blindly out the carriage window. His aunt had counseled him to find an English wife of good family. Well, wasn't that exactly what Miss Corning was? Above reproach, a maiden of his enemy's family? She was perfect for the role of wife. He pushed aside that primitive part of himself that exulted at the thought of this particular woman belonging to him. Instead, he began laying plans. A year ago he would've simply carried her off in a raid. Now he must court in the English ways, which meant gaining the lady's favor.

Across from him, she cleared her throat with a delicate little sound.

He looked up at her.

She smiled, determined and beautiful, from beneath a ridiculously wide-brimmed hat. "I believe you made a promise, my lord?"

He inclined his head, though his pulse picked up. Of course she wouldn't forget their bargain.

And indeed her next words solidified his thought. "I know 'tisn't any of my business, but could you tell me where you were all these years?"

He looked at her silently, struggling not to bat her down with harsh, dismissive words.

The color rose in her cheeks, but she held his gaze even as she tilted her chin up. "Please."

Courage would be an asset in the mother of his children.

"It is your business," he said. "I was in the American Colonies."

"Yes, I know," she said gently, "but where? And why? Did you lose your memory? Who you were? I've heard strange cases of injured men forgetting who and what they were."

"No. I always knew who I was." He looked at her, so sheltered from the world. Would such a tale shock her? Repulse her? But she had asked. "I was captured by Indians."

"Indeed." Her gray eyes widened. "But surely you haven't been with them for seven years?"

"I was." He hesitated. The subject wasn't one he ever

wanted to visit again in this lifetime, but the expression on Miss Corning's face was rapt. Had not Othello wooed his Desdemona thus? If telling her his bloody war tales would win her, he'd do it, no matter the pain to himself. *Brown eyes stared up through a mask of blood.*

Even if it tore his soul in two.

"I had no choice. I was enslaved."

BEATRICE DREW IN her breath at the word *enslaved*. The carriage bumped around a corner, jostling her against the side, but she paid little mind, caught up as she was with the thought of proud Lord Hope in slavery. The very thought was an abomination.

"Is that where you got those?" She nodded at the bird tattoos.

He raised a hand to trace them. "Aye."

"Tell me," she said simply.

His hand dropped. "You've heard about the massacre at Spinner's Falls."

It wasn't a question, but she answered it anyway. "There was an ambush. Most of the regiment were killed."

He nodded, his face turned toward the window, though she somehow knew he saw nothing of what passed outside. "We were marching through the woods from Quebec to Fort Edward. The trail was narrow, and the men were forced to walk in single file. The regiment became strung out. Too damned strung out."

She watched as a muscle ticked in his jaw. He didn't like telling her this story, but he was doing it anyway.

He inhaled. "I was riding to tell our colonel that I

thought we should stop and let the tail catch up to the head of the line when the Indians attacked."

His lips set firmly, and for a moment she thought he wouldn't go on, but then he looked at her, his black eyes desperate.

"We couldn't form a line of defense. My men were being picked off before they could rally. The Indians shot from both sides of the trail, hidden in the trees. My men were screaming and falling, and then my colonel was pulled from his horse."

He looked blindly at his hands. "They scalped him. My men were dying all about me, screaming and being scalped." His fingers flexed into fists. "My horse caught a bullet and went down. I managed to jump free, but I was surrounded. I don't remember what happened then—I think I was struck on the head—but when I became aware of my surroundings again, we were being marched to the Indian camp. The French had given us to their allies as war booty."

"Dear God," Beatrice breathed, feeling sick to her stomach. How terrible for Lord Hope to lose his men thusly. How impotent he must've felt.

He was gazing out the window again and made no indication that he'd heard her. "After we made the camp, I was separated from the others by the Indian who had captured me. His name was Sastaretsi. He stripped me naked, took my clothes away, and gave me only a thin, flea-infested blanket to cover myself with. Then Sastaretsi marched me through the woods for six weeks. By the time we'd made his village, I was walking in bare feet through grass crusted with frost."

He paused, remembering that awful time, and Beatrice was silent, waiting.

"All that time," he whispered. "All that time, I schemed on how to kill Sastaretsi. But my hands were bound so tightly in front of me that the flesh had swollen into the leather thongs. He'd pulled my fingernails from my hands so I could not use even their feeble strength to scratch my bonds loose. And at night he tied my bound hands to a stake driven deep in the ground. I was weakened from the cold and lack of nourishment. I think I might've died in that endless wood if we hadn't happened upon a French trapper and his son. The man spoke some Wyandot and seemed to take pity on me, for he gave me an old shirt and a pair of leggings. Those leggings and shirt saved me."

He was silent again, and this time Beatrice knew he didn't mean to go on.

"But why?" she finally blurted. "Why did Sastaretsi do all this to you?"

He looked at her then, and his eyes were blank—flat as if he were dead. "Because he meant to burn me at the stake when we reached his village."

Chapter Six

Now, a giant hourglass sits in the throne room of the Goblin King, its sands endlessly flowing until time itself shall stop. By this means, the goblins mark time in their sunless land deep beneath the earth. It happened that one year when Longsword went to plea for his freedom, the Goblin King was in a particularly good mood, having just that day defeated a great prince in battle.

The Goblin King glanced at his hourglass and then said to Longsword, "You've served me well for seven years, my slave. Because of this, I shall make you a bargain."

Longsword bowed his head, for he knew well that a bargain with the Goblin King suits only the Goblin King.

"You may walk the earth above for one year," the Goblin King said. "Mark you, one year only. At the end of that time, if you have found one Christian soul to voluntarily take your place in the land of the goblins, then you shall be free and I shall trouble you no more."

"And if I do not?" Longsword asked.
The Goblin King grinned. "Then you shall serve me for all eternity. . . ."
—from *Longsword*

Lottie Graham sipped her wine, peering at her husband over the edge of the glass. Nathan was absorbed in thought tonight, his broad brow slightly knit, his blue eyes vague and unfocused.

She set down the wineglass precisely and said, "We received an invitation to a ball hosted by Miss Molyneux today."

There was a pause that stretched so long that for a moment she thought he wouldn't answer her at all.

Then Nate blinked. "Who?"

"Miss Cristelle Molyneux." Lottie cut into the roast duck on her plate. "She's Reynaud St. Aubyn's aunt on his mother's side. I think she plans to reintroduce him to society. In any case, the invitation was sent on scandalously short notice—she plans it for this Thursday."

"Seems silly to plan it on so little notice," Nate said. "Will anyone show, I wonder?"

"Oh, she'll have no problem filling her ballroom." Lottie speared a piece of duck, but then set it back on the plate. Her appetite seemed nonexistent tonight. "Everyone will be wanting to see the mysterious mad earl."

Nate frowned. "He's not an earl yet."

"But surely it's only a matter of time?" Lottie twirled her wineglass stem.

"Only a fool would think that."

Lottie felt tears spring to her eyes. She looked down at her lap. "I'm sorry you think me a fool."

"You know that's not what I meant." His voice was brisk, impatient.

There'd been a time back before they'd married when her slightest frown would cause him to offer profuse apologies. Once, he'd sent her an arrangement of flowers so big it'd taken two footmen to bring it into the house. All because he'd not been able to take her driving on a day it'd rained.

Now he thought her a fool.

"It'll take a special parliamentary committee, I believe," Nate was saying as she thought these gloomy things, "to decide if this man is indeed St. Aubyn, and if he is, who the proper Earl of Blanchard is. That, at least, is the opinion of many of the learned parliamentarians. There hasn't been a case such as this one in living memory, and many are quite interested in the legal implications."

"Are they?" Lottie murmured. She'd lost interest in the conversation while her husband had finally become engaged in it. Had her marriage always been thus? "In any case, I thought it would be nice to attend the ball. It's bound to have all the best gossip of the year."

She glanced up in time to catch the look of irritation that crossed his face.

"I know that keeping up with the latest scandal is vital to you, dearest," he said. "But there are actually other things of import in the world, you know."

There was a short, awful silence.

"First I'm a fool and now I'm interested only in gossip," Lottie said very clearly, because she was holding back the tears with all her will. "I begin to wonder, sir, why you married me at all."

"Now, Lottie, you know I didn't mean it that way," he replied, and didn't even bother trying to hide the edge of exasperation in his voice.

"In what way did you mean it, Nathan?"

He shook his head, a reasonable man beset by a mad wife. "You're overwrought."

"I am not," Lottie said, the tears beginning to overflow, "overwrought."

He sighed, pushed his chair back from the table, and stood. "This conversation is pointless. I'll leave you to yourself until you've once again regained your senses. Good night, madam."

And he left. She sat there in the dining room, gasping and trembling and thoroughly humiliated.

It was the last straw.

"HE'S VERY HURT, Jeremy," Beatrice said as she paced from Jeremy's heavily draped window to his bed. "You have no idea. He told me just a fraction of what he'd experienced in the Colonies, and it was all I could do not to scream aloud. How could he survive such horrors? And yet he's incredibly strong, incredibly determined. It's as if he's driven out of his soul whatever softness he may've once felt. He's been fire-hardened."

"He sounds very interesting," Jeremy said.

Beatrice looked at him. "I've never met a gentleman like him in all my life."

"What does Lord Hope look like now that he's transformed himself?"

"He's tall with very wide shoulders and wears a sort

of aloof glare most of the time. He's quite intimidating and rather savage-looking, actually."

"But you said he'd cut his hair and donned a wig and other civilized accoutrements. He sounds quite normal to me," Jeremy said from the bed. That was the best part about Jeremy—he always took an interest in one's thoughts and troubles, no matter how trivial.

"He may wear the same sort of clothes as other gentlemen, but they fit him differently somehow." Beatrice picked up a tall green bottle from Jeremy's cache of medicines and peered at the dark liquid inside before returning it to its brethren. "And he's still wearing that earring I told you about. The tattoos he can't remove, but why do you think he hasn't taken off the earring?"

"I haven't the faintest," Jeremy replied with evident delight. "I do wish I were able to meet him, though."

Beatrice turned and glanced at him. Jeremy was sitting up in bed today. She'd plumped the pillows for him and helped him sit higher. His cheeks were still flushed, his eyes too bright, but she fancied he was a little better than the last time she'd seen him.

At least she hoped so.

"Perhaps I can bring him around someday," she said.

He glanced away. "Don't, Bea."

She blinked. "Why ever not?"

His eyes met hers, and for a moment all amusement left his face. His extraordinary blue eyes were stern, almost cold, and she wondered in a flash of insight if this was what he'd looked like on the battlefield when he'd led his men.

Then his expression softened a little. "You know why."

She grimaced because she did know why. "You're too sensitive to your injury. Many men come home without an arm or a leg or even an eye, and one continues to see them at balls and events. No one singles them out except to say how brave they were."

"That's not what Frances said." Jeremy's eyes were old and sad.

She bit her lip. "Frances was a complete and utter ninny, and frankly I think you were saved years of insipid conversation over your morning tea when she called off your engagement."

He laughed, thankfully, but it turned to a cough, and she had to hurry over and pour him a cup of water.

"In any case," he gasped when he could draw breath again, "I'll not be going out in public again. You know that."

"But why?" She knelt by his bed on a little cushioned stool so that her face was closer to his on the pillow. "I know you fear the stares of others, Jeremy dear, but you must get out of this room. You live as if you're already deep beneath the ground in a coffin. You're not. You live and breathe and laugh, and I want you to be happy."

He caught her hand in his, and it was like being gripped by flames. "It takes two footmen just to lift me into that chair so I can sit by the fire. The last time they tried to carry me down the stairs, one of the footmen tripped and nearly dropped me." He closed his bright blue eyes, wincing as if in pain. "I know you think me a coward, but I can't face that again."

She closed her eyes as well, because she felt as if she were losing him, her oldest and dearest friend. For the last five years, ever since his return from the war on the Continent, she'd known that he was slowly slipping away from her. Every time she saw him, he was a little more distant, a little more beyond her reach. Soon she wouldn't be able to touch him at all.

"Let us be married." Beatrice tightened her hands around his, pushing aside her own desires in her desperate fear for him. "Jeremy dear, why don't we? Then we could buy a little house and live together, you and I. We wouldn't need that many servants—just a cook and some maids and footmen, and no haughty butler to bother with. Wouldn't that be lovely?"

"Oh, it would indeed, darling Bea." Jeremy's eyes were very gentle now. "But I'm afraid it wouldn't work. You'd want children one day, and I've set my heart on marrying a black-haired lass, perhaps with green eyes."

"You'd break my heart for a green-eyed lady you don't even know?" Beatrice half laughed, choking back tears. "I never knew I ranked so low in your estimation, sir."

"You rank above the angels themselves, my darling Bea." Jeremy laughed back. "But we all must have dreams. And my dream is that one day you'll be surrounded by a family of your own."

She bowed her head at that, for what could she reply? In her mind's eye, Beatrice, too, saw herself sitting among a crowd of children. But when she imagined their father, it wasn't Jeremy's face she saw but Viscount Hope's.

"WILL YOU TELL me what happened when you reached Sastaretsi's camp?" Beatrice asked late the next morning.

She'd accompanied Lord Hope on a shopping expedition to Bond Street, hoping for an opportunity to ask about his past again. His aunt was planning a grand ball on the morrow to reintroduce him to society, and there were many last-minute items to purchase, including dancing slippers for him. But more importantly—at least to her—she wanted to hear the rest of his story.

"I'd've thought you'd forget the matter by now," he replied.

It had been almost a week since he'd told her the story of the march to the Indian camp. During that time, she'd hardly seen him, he'd been so busy conferring with his aunt and doing other more mysterious things. He'd disappear before she rose for breakfast and sometimes didn't reappear back at Blanchard House until after dinner or later. This meant that his and Uncle Reggie's paths rarely crossed—which was good—but it also meant that she'd rather missed his sarcastic company over the last week.

"No," she murmured softly. "I doubt I'll ever forget what you've told me."

"Then why make me continue?" he asked almost angrily. "Is it not enough that I have to bear those images in my mind? Why should you share them, too?"

"Because I want to," she said simply. She couldn't explain it better than that. She wanted to know what he'd gone through; the need was more than simple curiosity.

He looked at her quizzically. "I don't understand you."

"Good," she said with satisfaction.

He grunted on what might've been a laugh. She turned to stare at him suspiciously, but his face became grave as he inhaled.

"When we came to the Indian camp, Sastaretsi blacked my face with charcoal to signify that I was to die. He tied a rope about my neck and led me into the village in triumph. He whooped as we came to let the others know that he'd brought home a captive."

"How terrifying." Beatrice shivered.

"Yes. It's intended to be terrifying to the captive. I was made to run the gauntlet," Lord Hope said as they came to a rather foul-looking puddle in the street. It was quite wide, and Beatrice was eyeing it uncertainly when he grasped her by the waist and simply lifted her over it.

"Oh," she squeaked. He stood for a moment on the other side of the puddle, holding her in the air without any visible sign of strain. "My lord!"

He cocked his head, studying her face just slightly above his. "Yes?"

She felt her breath come short, very aware of his large hands at her waist and the gleam in his black eyes.

"You should put me down," Beatrice hissed. "People are staring."

And indeed they were. A group of ladies giggled nervously behind gloved hands, and a cart driver leered as he passed.

"Are they?" he asked absently.

"Lord Hope—"

But he was lowering her to the ground as if nothing had happened. Really! He hadn't given her any warning at all. Did he *want* to be thought mad?

She peeked up at him and cleared her throat. "What's the gauntlet?"

"A nasty way to welcome captives to an Indian camp." He held out his arm for her, and she placed her gloved fingers primly on his sleeve. "All the inhabitants in the village form two lines, and the captive must run between them."

"That doesn't sound too bad."

He looked down at her, the bird tattoos decorating his swarthy skin, the iron cross swinging from his ear. He looked like a pirate. "They hit and kick the captive as he runs."

"Oh." She swallowed. "And when he reaches the end of the line, what happens then?"

"It depends," he said, guiding her around a clump of ladies eagerly peering in a shop window. "If the captive is a child or young boy, sometimes he is adopted into the Indian tribe."

"And if he is older?" she whispered, dreading the answer.

"Then most often he is tortured and killed."

She inhaled sharply. He said it so matter-of-factly.

"Were you . . ." She swallowed. How could she ask? But she had to know. The experience no matter how terrible was part of who he was. "Were you—"

"I wasn't tortured." His lips tightened as he looked straight ahead. "Not then anyway."

Sudden tears rushed to her eyes. *No,* part of her wailed inside. *Not him. Not this man.* She'd known it had to have happened, but to hear it from his lips was devastating. For them to have hurt—*shamed*—this man ripped apart a portion of her soul. She felt suddenly older. Weary with the knowledge.

"What happened instead?" she asked quietly.

"Gaho saved me," he said.

"Who is Gaho? And how did he save you?"

"She."

She stopped and looked up at him, ignoring the mutters of the other pedestrians who were forced to go around them. "A lady Indian saved you?"

He smiled down into her face, making the birds crinkle as if they'd taken flight. "Yes. A powerful lady Indian saved me. She owned more furs, more pots, and more slaves than any other in that village. You might even call her a princess."

"Humph." She faced forward and began to walk, but she was unable to keep the question from leaving her lips. "Was she pretty?"

"Very." She felt the whisper of his breath against her ear as he leaned down to tease her. "For a woman in her sixth decade."

"Oh." She tilted her nose in the air, feeling irrationally relieved. "Well, how did Gaho save you?"

"Sastaretsi had a rather bad reputation it seems. A year before, he'd killed one of Gaho's favorite slaves in an argument. Gaho was a wise woman. She knew that Sastaretsi had very little to his name, so she'd bided her time until he acquired something that she might demand in repayment for the loss of her slave—me."

"And what did she do with you?"

"What do you think, Miss Corning?" His wide, sensuous mouth twisted, curving down sardonically. "I was the son of an earl, a captain in His Majesty's army, and I became the slave of an old Indian woman. Is that what you wanted to hear? That I was reduced to the lowest of the low in that Indian camp?"

He'd stopped in the street, but no one muttered as the crowd gave them a wide berth. Lord Hope might be attired like an aristocrat, but his expression was savage at the moment.

Beatrice had a cowardly urge to flee, but she stood her ground, tilting her chin up at him, holding his wild black eyes as she said, "No. No, I never wanted to hear that you were humiliated."

He leaned over her, large and intimidating. "Then why persist in asking?"

"Because I need to know," she said low and rapidly. "I need to know everything that happened to you, everything you experienced in that place. I need to know why you are the man you've become."

"Why?" His black eyes widened with confusion. "Why?"

And all she could whisper was, "I just do."

Because she couldn't admit, even to herself, why.

REYNAUD HAD LED men into battle, had faced an Indian gauntlet without flinching, had endured seven years as the slave of his enemy and survived. All this he had done without a breath of fear. Therefore, it was simply impossible that he'd feel missish nerves at the thought of a ball.

Yet, impossible as it seemed, here he was pacing the hallway as he waited for Miss Corning to descend the stairs.

Reynaud halted and took a deep breath. He was the son of an earl. He'd attended innumerable balls before his capture in the Colonies. This creeping feeling he had—that he no longer belonged in London society, that he'd be denounced and repudiated—was ridiculous. He shrugged his shoulders in his new coat, twisting his head about to loosen the muscles of his neck. His new wig was impeccable, he knew—he'd hired a competent valet with the monies lent by his aunt—but it still felt foreign on his head. When he'd lived with the Indians, the only thing he'd covered his head with was a blanket, and then only when the winters were especially cold. He'd worn a long tail of braided hair, and his clothes had been a shirt, breechcloth, leggings, and moccasins—all soft materials, well worn and comfortable. Now he had a scratchy wig on his newly shorn head, a neck cloth half strangling him, and his new dancing slippers felt tight. Why so-called civilized men should choose to wear—

"Thought you'd be gone to that damned ball by now," a male voice said from behind him.

Reynaud whirled, crouching low, his knife already in his right hand. St. Aubyn started back.

"Have a care," the usurper cried. "Could hurt someone with that knife."

"Not unless I wished to," Reynaud said as he straightened. His heart pounded erratically. He slid his knife back inside the sheath he'd had specially made and glanced up the staircase. Miss Corning was late. "And I'm waiting for your niece if you must know."

"What d'you mean, waiting?" St. Aubyn's face darkened.

"I mean," Reynaud enunciated clearly, "that I intend to escort Miss Corning to the ball given by my aunt."

"Nonsense!" the old man sputtered. "If anyone's escorting Beatrice, 'twill be me."

Reynaud arched an eyebrow. "I wasn't aware you were attending the ball." St. Aubyn had been invited, of course, but from his lack of comment in the last week, Reynaud had rather thought the other man had thrown the invitation away.

Apparently not.

"Of course I'll be attending. Think I'd let a popinjay such as you chase me away?"

Reynaud took a step closer to the other man so that he loomed over him. "When I'm in possession of my title, I shall take great pleasure in personally throwing you from this house."

St. Aubyn's face was nearly apoplectic. "Your title! Your title! You'll never see it, sir!"

"I've already set the date to appeal my case before the parliamentary committee." Reynaud slowly grinned as he watched all color drain from the older man's face.

St. Aubyn's mouth twisted. "They'll take one look at you and deny you the title. You're insane, and everyone in London knows it. One only has to see those tattoos and—"

But something had snapped in Reynaud. He surged forward, gripping the older man's neck and slamming him against the wall. The usurper's face turned purple, the sour smell of fear rolling off him, and then St. Aubyn's gooseberry eyes suddenly shifted, looking behind Reynaud.

At the same time, small fists pounded his back.

"Let go of him! Let go of him!" Miss Corning cried.

Reynaud bared his teeth at St. Aubyn and then backed away, freeing the man.

Immediately Miss Corning flew to her uncle. "Are you all right?"

"I'm fine—" the old man started.

But she swung on Reynaud like an avenging fury. "How *dare* you? What could possibly possess you to manhandle him so?"

Reynaud raised his hands in surrender. He knew

better than to try to talk his way out of this. But then he really looked at Miss Corning. She wore a blazing bronze gown that made her creamy skin positively glow. The bodice was low and square, and her breasts were pressed into two tempting mounds.

"Ahem."

His gaze snapped up at her pointed murmur.

Miss Corning's bosom might be inviting, but her expression was anything but. "You had no right to lay hands on Uncle Reggie. He's ill—"

"Beatrice!" her uncle protested, looking embarrassed.

"It's true and he needs to know it." She stood with arms akimbo and glared at Reynaud. "Uncle Reggie had an attack of apoplexy a little more than a month ago. You could've killed him just now. Promise me you'll never lay hands on him again."

Reynaud eyed the older man, who wasn't looking particularly grateful for his niece's interference.

"Lord Hope." She stepped closer and laid one gloved hand on his chest, looking up into his face. "Promise me, my lord."

He took her hand and, holding her gaze, slowly raised it to his lips. "As you wish," he breathed over her knuckles.

She blushed and snatched back her hand. Reynaud grinned.

But St. Aubyn was not as interested in avoiding discord. "Surely you don't mean to accompany this . . . this jackanapes to the ball, Beatrice?"

Miss Corning hesitated, but then she threw back her shoulders and turned to her uncle. "I'm afraid I do."

"But, m'dear, had I known you wished to go to this ball, I could've escorted you."

"I know, Uncle Reggie, dear." She laid a hand on the old man's arm. "You've always been most attentive in taking me to whatever amusements I fancied. But you see, Lord Hope asked me to this ball, and I want to go with him."

St. Aubyn shook off her hand rudely. "Is that your choice, then, girl? Him? Because I tell you right now, there'll be a choice to be made: him or me. You can't have it both ways."

Miss Corning's hand fell to her side, but her gaze was steady and unwavering on her uncle. For the first time, Reynaud realized that there was a kind of strength there beneath her sweet manner. "Perhaps I will have to make a choice someday. But that is not my wish, truly. Can't you see that?"

"Your wishes don't come into it, lass. Remember that." He shook a finger in her face. "And don't forget who's kept a roof over your head these nineteen years. If I'd known how ungrateful you'd be for the care I've shown you—"

"Enough." Reynaud stepped toward the man.

"No." Miss Corning laid her hand on Reynaud's arm now, but unlike her uncle, he wasn't going to hurt her feelings by shaking her off.

St. Aubyn eyed her hand, and his lips twisted. Then he turned abruptly and stomped up the stairs.

"He hasn't the right to talk to you so," Reynaud growled softly.

"He has every right." She turned to look at him, but though her gaze was steady, her gray eyes sparkled with tears. "He's perfectly correct; he has provided a home—and love—for me for nineteen years. And I've hurt his feelings."

Reynaud took her hand and moved it farther up his arm so that he could escort her to the waiting carriage. "Nonetheless, I don't want him acting toward you the way he just did. Do you need a wrap?"

"I had my maid put a wrap in the carriage, and don't try to change the subject. It's not your duty to defend me from my uncle."

He stopped beside the carriage steps, forcing her to halt as well. "If I choose to defend you from your uncle—or anyone else—I damned well will with or without your permission, madam."

"Goodness, how very primitive of you," she said. "Are you going to help me into the carriage, or will you keep me out here, proclaiming your right to safeguard me until I freeze?"

He frowned down at her, but every reply he could think of made him look an ass, so he simply handed her into the carriage without a word. The door was shut behind him, and in a moment the horses started forward.

He looked across at Miss Corning, who'd pulled a thin wrap about her shoulders. "That gown becomes you."

She smiled, quick and brilliant. "Why, thank you, my lord."

He cast about for something else to say but couldn't think of a thing. He was out of practice in the art of light conversation, after all. Most of his discussion of the last seven years had been filled with the topic of food—where there might be game and if there was enough meat to feed Gaho's small band for the winter.

Miss Corning was the one who broke the silence.

"Are you going to tell me about your experiences in the Indian camp?"

He was silent a moment, reluctant to continue the story. It was all in his past anyway. Wasn't it better forgotten? To bring up starvation and torture, nights of lying awake far from home and family, fearful that he'd never see England again . . . surely there was no need to make that all come alive again?

"Please?" she whispered, and he caught the scent of English flowers—her scent.

Why did she demand this of him? She didn't even seem to know herself. And yet he felt compelled to answer her demand.

Even if it meant tearing open a still-fresh wound.

"Later." The glow from the carriage lantern illuminated her face and shoulders but left the rest of the lady in darkness, giving her an air of mystery. Reynaud felt a stirring low in his belly at the sight. If telling her his wretched story brought her closer, it was well worth it.

He stretched his legs so that they brushed against the voluminous skirts of her gown. "I'll tell you all about living in an Indian village, about hunting deer and raccoon, and even about the time I battled a full-grown bear."

"Oh!" Her lovely gray eyes widened in excitement.

He smiled. "But not tonight. There's too little time before we arrive at my aunt's house."

"Oh." Her lower lip thrust out just a little in a charming pout. He eyed that lip, full and shining in the carriage light. He wanted to bite it.

"You tease me so, my lord," she said softly, and her voice seemed to catch.

He looked into her eyes, wide and innocent, but with

a feminine spark that wasn't innocent at all. "Do I? And do you like to be teased, Miss Corning?"

Her eyelashes lowered. "I think . . . Yes, I do like the teasing. As long as it isn't too prolonged."

His smile widened, becoming wolfish. "Is that a challenge?"

She peeked up at him. "Perhaps."

Reynaud sat forward, reaching across the swaying carriage, and brushed his knuckles against her cheek. So soft. So warm. She sat very still.

He inhaled and sat back again. "I've lived a very long time away from civilization. I'm afraid I've forgotten the niceties of flirtation. I don't want to scare you."

She licked her lips, and his eyes dropped to her mouth. He watched it move, lush and beckoning, as she said, "I . . . I don't scare so easily as all that, my lord. And I've never been particularly fond of the artifice of flirtation."

His heartbeat quickened at her whispered words, his muscles tensing to leap on prey. *Mine,* a part of him far removed from civilization cried. *Mine.* What he might've done next he wasn't sure, but the carriage shuddered to a halt. He drew in a breath and straightened, easing his bunched shoulders. Glancing outside, he could see they were in front of his aunt's house.

He turned back to Miss Corning and held out his hand. "Shall we?"

She eyed his hand a split second before taking it.

And he hid a smile. Soon, very soon, he'd take what was his, but right now he had to face the horrors of a London ball.

Chapter Seven

Well, this was a terrible bargain, indeed! But Longsword looked into the Goblin King's glowing orange eyes and knew that if he were ever to see the sun again, he had no choice. He nodded once. At his assent, a great wind lifted him, whirling and sweeping him high, high, until he was suddenly dumped on hard, dusty earth. Longsword opened his eyes and saw the sun for the first time in seven years. The breeze brushed his cheek. He had just risen and grasped his sword when he heard a roar from behind him.

Longsword turned and beheld the most beautiful lady in the world . . . in the grasp of a giant dragon. . . .

—from *Longsword*

Mademoiselle Molyneux had had only a little more than a week to plan the ball in honor of Lord Hope, but in that time she'd created a wonder. Beatrice was hard-pressed not to stare as the viscount ushered her into the great ballroom. Three huge chandeliers hung from the ceiling, sparkling like miniature stars. All along one wall, tall mirrors were draped with garlands of flowers and gold silk, and a great pyramid of flowers hid the musicians in one corner.

"How splendid!" Beatrice exclaimed. "Your aunt must be a magician to have effected such a delightfully decorated room so soon."

"I wouldn't be surprised," Lord Hope muttered. "I've always thought Tante Cristelle had powers beyond a mere mortal's."

Beatrice glanced up at him in amusement. His body had stiffened beside hers when they'd entered the magnificent ballroom, and heads had turned toward them. People were staring and whispering behind fans. Even so, he seemed to be relaxing a bit, though he fingered the knife at his waist.

"Has she always lived in this town house by herself?" she asked.

"What?" His voice was distracted as he looked across the room, but then he glanced down at her. "No. Actually, this house belongs to my sister—or rather her son."

"Her son?"

"Yes. He's Lord Eddings—inherited the title from his father. When my sister, Emeline, married again and settled in the Colonies with her new husband, Tante Cristelle agreed to stay here and help manage the estate."

Beatrice laid her hand on his sleeve. "You must miss your sister so."

"I think of her every day."

An expression of sudden sorrow crossed his features,

sharp and fleeting and all the more breathtaking because he so rarely showed any of the softer emotions. She leaned closer to him, drawn by his emotion despite the crowd surrounding them.

"Hope," a male voice drawled from behind them.

Beatrice looked up to see Viscount Vale's turquoise eyes watching her curiously. He had a bluish bruise on his jaw. Beside him was his wife, a tall, thin lady with a calm, slightly amused face.

She felt the muscle of Lord Hope's arm flex beneath her fingers, but his face revealed nothing. "Vale."

Lord Vale cocked his head. "Pity you've shaved off all those whiskers. They gave you a rather Biblical air."

Lord Hope's lips twitched.

"Sorry to disappoint."

"Not at all," Lord Vale said carelessly. "I suppose you must don the local costume like the rest of us."

The lady beside him sighed. "Vale," she said, "are you going to introduce me, or will you continue to trade insults with Lord Hope for the rest of the night?"

"I do beg your pardon, my lady wife." Lord Vale turned and held out his hand to the lady, who placed her fingers in his. "May I introduce you to Reynaud St. Aubyn, Viscount Hope and no doubt soon to be the true Earl of Blanchard? Hope, this is my lady wife, Melisande Renshaw, Viscountess Vale."

The lady made a stately curtsy as Lord Hope bowed over her hand. "An honor, my lady, but we've already met, I think. Were you not a dear friend and neighbor of my sister, Emeline?"

Lady Vale's pale cheeks pinkened delicately. "Indeed, my lord. I spent many a happy afternoon at the

Blanchard estate in Suffolk. I know your sister will be very pleased to hear that you are well. The news of your death was a terrible blow to her."

Lord Hope stiffened, but he only nodded to Lady Vale.

"And this," continued Lord Vale, "is Hope's cousin, Miss Corning, whom we met last spring at Mother's garden party."

"How do you do, ma'am?" Beatrice murmured as she sank into a curtsy.

When she rose, she saw that the lady and her husband seemed to be exchanging some kind of silent communication.

Lady Vale smiled and turned to Beatrice. "Would you care to stroll with me, Miss Corning, and admire Miss Molyneux's fine decorations? Vale says we must hold a ball of our own soon, and I would be grateful for your opinion."

"Of course," Beatrice said. The gentlemen were outwardly polite, but there was a tension in their stances. Obviously Lord Vale wished to talk with Lord Hope alone.

Lady Vale linked her arm with Beatrice's, and they began a slow perambulation of the room.

"Do you make your home in London always, Miss Corning?" Lady Vale asked.

"I live with my uncle, ma'am, in Blanchard House." Beatrice darted a quick look over her shoulder. Lord Vale was talking intently with Lord Hope, but at least they hadn't come to fisticuffs. She faced forward again. "That is where Lord Hope is staying at the moment as well."

"Oh. That must be . . . interesting," Lady Vale murmured.

"Yes, it certainly is. I believe Lord Hope stays out of pure contrariness." Beatrice glanced at her companion. "You knew him when he was a boy?"

"He was away at school generally when I visited the Blanchard country estate, but, yes, he was a young boy, not quite a man. I remember that Emeline and I had not yet come out when he bought his commission in the army."

"What was he like?"

Lady Vale was silent a moment as they made a wide arc. They came to a side hall, and she asked, "Do you mind? I rather dislike crowds."

"Not at all," Beatrice replied.

After the brightness of the ballroom, the hallway's lighting was muted. Tall portraits lined the walls. A few other guests drifted here and there, but they were distant enough not to overhear their conversation.

"You asked about Lord Hope," Lady Vale began. "I did not see him often when I was young, but I remember being rather in awe of him."

"Really?"

Lady Vale nodded. "He was so very handsome, even then. But there was more. He was the young heir to the throne, as it were. He almost seemed to have a golden glow about him."

Beatrice bowed her head, contemplating this information as they walked. What a downfall it must've been for a man with a "golden glow" to have been made a slave. How much more humiliating it must've been for proud Lord Hope to sink so low. They came to a tall portrait of a man in armor in the style of the last century, and Lady Vale stopped.

She tilted her head, studying the painting. "His hair is quite extravagant, isn't it?"

Beatrice looked at the painting and smiled. The gentleman had abundant dark curls hanging on either side of his face. "And he's proud of it, isn't he?"

"Indeed."

They were silent for a moment.

Then Beatrice said, "There's a portrait of Lord Hope that hangs in the sitting room of Blanchard House. It's always been there, ever since I arrived when I was nineteen. I think it must've been painted when he was about the age you speak of. He's so handsome and looks so lighthearted. I used to think he was hiding a mischievous thought when he was painted. I confess I've spent hours staring at that painting. It rather fascinated me." She felt Lady Vale turn and look at her and knew she was blushing. "You must think me a fool."

"Not at all," the other lady said gently. "Merely a romantic."

"But you see, since Lord Hope's return . . ." She had to pause and swallow because her throat had tightened. "He was captured and held by Indians. Did you know?"

"No, I did not," the other woman murmured.

Beatrice nodded, taking a deep breath. "I don't see anything of that young boy in him anymore—the laughing boy in the painting. The things that happened to him in the Colonies were so very terrible that they changed him. He's grim now. Intent only on regaining his title. It's as if he's forgotten what he was before, as if he's forgotten how to enjoy life."

Lady Vale sighed. "My husband was in that war as well. He is quite merry on the outside, but inside there are wounds, believe me."

Beatrice thought about that. "But Lord Vale seems more free somehow. He is happy, isn't he?"

"I think so." Lady Vale smiled a secret smile. "But you comprehend that Lord Vale returned from the Colonies nearly seven years ago, while Lord Hope has only now come home. You must allow him time, I think."

"I suppose so," Beatrice said doubtfully. It was true that Lord Hope was still adjusting to his return, but would time truly heal him? Would he become more lighthearted, or had his experience seared him so deeply he was changed forever? She thought of something else. "Does Lord Vale truly think Lord Hope betrayed their regiment?"

"What?"

Beatrice turned to look at Lady Vale. The hallway was dim, but the lady's eyes seemed puzzled. "Lord Hope said that when your husband came to visit him last week, Lord Vale accused him of being the traitor who betrayed their regiment at Spinner's Falls."

"Surely not!"

"I do assure you."

Lady Vale sighed. "Gentlemen sometimes do not seem able to express themselves properly, and I must admit that my husband, though he loves to talk, is not always effective in communicating. He's never thought Lord Hope could be the traitor."

"Really?" Relief swept through her.

"Yes," Lady Vale said with certainty. "But the problem is, if Lord Hope has gotten the notion that my husband distrusts him, it may be rather hard to dispel the thought."

"Oh, dear," Beatrice murmured. "Gentlemen can be so boneheaded sometimes, can't they? What if they can't work it out?"

The other lady looked grave. "Then I fear it may be the end of their long friendship."

"And Lord Hope needs a friend very much right now," Beatrice whispered.

"Beware," Reynaud growled. "I've lived too long away from society. I no longer bother calling out a man who insults me."

"When have I insulted you?" Vale hissed. "'Twas you who hit me, man!"

They still stood almost in the middle of the damned ballroom, and if they talked too loud, they risked causing a scene. He was already the object of curious scrutiny. If he lost control here, in the midst of his aunt's ball, it would do irreparable harm to his cause.

Cold sweat slid down his back, but Reynaud still bared his teeth in a parody of a grin. "I struck you because you had the damnable gall to accuse me of betraying our regiment."

"I did not."

"You most certainly did."

"I did—" Vale cut himself off to breathe forcefully through his nostrils. "We sound like lads nearly come to blows over sweetmeats."

"Huh," Reynaud grunted, looking away. He felt an unaccountable urge to shuffle his feet.

For a moment, both men stood silent, the chatter of the crowd rising around them.

Vale laughed under his breath. "Remember when we stole those strawberry tarts from the cook at my father's house?"

Reynaud raised an eyebrow. "I do. We were caught and whipped."

"Which never would've happened had you not decided we should hide in the dovecote."

"Nonsense." Reynaud's lips twitched. "It would've been a perfect hiding place had you not laughed and scared all the doves, which gave away our position to those outside."

"At least we gobbled the tarts before they discovered us." Vale sighed. "I never meant to accuse you, Reynaud."

Reynaud nodded once, curtly. "What did you mean to say, then?"

"Walk with me."

Reynaud raised an eyebrow at the order but fell into step with his boyhood friend without protest.

"I hear there was an attempt on your life last week," Vale said in a low voice.

"Someone shot at me, certainly." Reynaud frowned. "Miss Corning was in the line of fire."

"Careless."

"Foolish," Reynaud corrected grimly. "When I find him, I'll kill him."

"Miss Corning means so much to you?" He felt Vale's curious glance.

"Yes." The knowledge solidified as he said it. Beatrice Corning did mean a lot to him—how much he wasn't sure. But he knew he wanted to keep her close. Wanted to keep her safe.

"Indeed?" Vale said thoughtfully. "And does the lady know this?"

"Is that any of your business?"

Vale coughed as if covering a laugh, and Reynaud turned to glare at him.

The viscount held up a conciliatory hand. "I mean no offense, but the lady is exceedingly proper and you . . . well."

Reynaud frowned down at the floor. Vale was right. Miss Corning was all that was proper in an English lady. Everything, in fact, that he no longer was. Perhaps that was why his voice was sharp when he said, "I'll let you know when I want your opinion."

"No doubt." Vale's voice was dry. "And I look forward to the day, but in the meantime, we have other matters to discuss. Did you know Hasselthorpe was shot at last summer?"

"No, I didn't." Reynaud glanced to the side of the room, where Lord Hasselthorpe stood with his usual cohorts. The Duke of Lister, Nathan Graham, and, of course, St. Aubyn the pretender were about him, all of them looking rather sour. "You think it's related?"

"I don't know," Vale mused. "Hasselthorpe was winged in the arm—not a grave wound as I understand. He seems to've recovered entirely. He was riding in Hyde Park when he was shot. The shooter was never found. It does seem odd."

"Hasselthorpe has aspirations to be prime minister," Reynaud pointed out. "It may've simply been a political assassination gone awry."

"Of course, of course," Vale murmured. "But I can't help noting that he was shot shortly after I tried talking to him about Spinner's Falls."

Reynaud halted and stared at Vale. "Really?"

"Yes." Vale glanced about the ballroom. "I say, do you know where my lady wife and your Miss Corning have got to?"

"They went into the portrait gallery." Reynaud nodded toward the hall leading off the ballroom. "Do you think Hasselthorpe knows something about this business?"

"Perhaps." Vale started walking again, and Reynaud fell into step. "Or perhaps someone else merely thinks he does. Or the thing isn't related at all and I'm merely chasing unicorns."

Reynaud grunted. Vale might like to play the simpleton, but he'd known the man since childhood and wasn't fooled. Vale was one of the most clever men he knew. "I thought at first that the attempt on me must've been Reginald St. Aubyn's doing."

"And now?"

"Miss Corning pointed out that he'd have to be a half-wit to try and kill me on his own front step."

"Ah."

"If the attempt against me is linked to the shooting of Lord Hasselthorpe, then it's got something to do with Spinner's Falls," Reynaud said thoughtfully. "But what?"

"I think you know something," Vale said.

Reynaud stopped, eyeing the other man narrowly. "What do you mean?"

Vale held up his palms. "I'm not accusing you. I just

think you must have some information about the traitor that we haven't considered."

Reynaud frowned. "I separated from you at the Indian camp and never saw you again until the other day. What could I possibly know that you don't?"

"I don't know." Vale shrugged. "But I think we should meet with Munroe and pool our individual recollections."

"Munroe survived the camp?" Reynaud's eyebrows rose. He hadn't thought of the naturalist in years.

"Aye, but he's scarred." Vale looked away. "He lost an eye in that camp, Reynaud."

Reynaud grimaced. He knew well what fate befell Indian captives. Seven years of his life had been lost, and now it seemed it was all because someone—one of their own—had betrayed them at Spinner's Falls.

"Then let's meet with Munroe and figure this thing out," he said with decision. "Let's find the bastard and make sure he hangs."

"He's set a date to plead his case before the parliamentary committee." Lord Blanchard whispered the news as if the potted plant behind them might have ears.

Lister raised an eyebrow, looking bored as always as he surveyed the crowded ballroom. "Are you surprised?"

Blanchard's face reddened. "You needn't sound so unaffected. If St. Aubyn gets my title, your political career will be a toss-up as well."

Lister shrugged, though his face had turned stony.

"Come, gentlemen," Hasselthorpe said softly. "Fighting among ourselves does not serve our cause."

"Well, then what does?" Blanchard was looking sullen. "None of you have offered your support to me. I am alone—even my niece has turned against me. Hope is courting her, the bastard."

"Is he?" Hasselthorpe turned to glance at Hope, who was walking with Vale about the perimeter of the ballroom. "A clever stratagem. If he has a wife, he can dispel these rumors of insanity. A man always looks more settled with a wife by his side."

"Indeed," Lister drawled. "Wouldn't you agree, Graham?"

Nathan Graham blinked. He'd been staring at his feet as if lost in thought. "What?"

"I say, a wife makes the man's career," Lister said. "Don't you agree?"

Graham's handsome face flushed. There were rumors flying about the ballroom tonight that he'd argued with his wife. He answered steadily enough, though. "Naturally."

Lister's eyes narrowed as if he scented blood.

Hasselthorpe pursed his lips. "I haven't seen an event filled with such luminaries of our society in quite some time."

Lister turned to him, a puzzled question in his eyes.

Hasselthorpe smiled. "I confess, I admire Miss Molyneux's courage."

"What do you mean?" Blanchard asked.

Hasselthorpe shrugged. "Only that if her nephew has an attack of madness in such a venue, all of society will see."

Young Graham was the first to understand. His face went blank as he darted a look at Lord Hope across the room.

Lister opened his mouth to say something, but he was interrupted by Adriana, who came fluttering over to land at Hasselthorpe's side. She wore a pale yellow and lavender gown and looked like nothing so much as a particularly frivolous butterfly.

"Darling!" she crowed. "Oh, do come leave your stuffy political discussions and dance with me. I'm sure these gentlemen won't mind if you pay a tiny bit of attention to your wife."

And she batted her eyes at Lister, Blanchard, and Graham.

Lister, who'd been eyeing the soft expanse of her exposed bosom, bowed. "Not at all, ma'am."

"There, you see! His Grace has given his kind permission." Adriana curtsied flirtatiously.

Hasselthorpe sighed. If he protested, Adriana would only cajole and flatter in ever more irritating ways until he was forced to give in or make a scene. "Very well. If you'll excuse me, gentlemen?"

The others bowed as his wife latched on to him and dragged him toward the dance floor.

"I thought young Bankforth was squiring you about the dance tonight," he muttered.

She giggled, as gay as a girl in the schoolroom instead of a woman in her fortieth year. "I wore him out, poor thing. Besides"—she maneuvered him into the proper position—"you know how you love to dance!"

Hasselthorpe sighed again. He loathed dancing, and he'd told Adriana so on many an occasion. For some reason, she chose to think he was teasing when he protested. Or perhaps her brain was too small to keep track of the information for any length of time.

Hasselthorpe looked over his wife's head as he waited for the music to start and saw Blanchard staring daggers across the room. It wasn't hard to find the object of his gaze—Lord Hope was making his way to Miss Corning, who sat in a corner with Mrs. Graham. He looked back at Blanchard. If looks could kill, Lord Hope would be lying bleeding on the floor. Interesting. It seemed Blanchard's hatred of Hope was personal.

It made one wonder what such an intense animosity would drive a man to do.

"Now tell me," Beatrice said a little later. "What's so urgent that you needs must pull me away from Lady Vale?"

"I wanted you to hear it from me," Lottie said solemnly. They sat together at the side of the ballroom on a gold silk settee. A statue of a Greek god to one side and a potted plant to the other gave them a measure of privacy.

"Your manner is terribly secretive," Beatrice said. Her eyes drifted to her friend's belly. Could it be . . . ?

"I've left Nathan."

Beatrice's gaze snapped up. "But why?" She stared at Lottie in bewildered concern. "I thought you loved Mr. Graham."

"I do," Lottie said. "Of course I do. But that just makes it so much worse."

"I don't see how."

Lottie sighed, and for the first time, Beatrice saw that her friend was truly weary. There were faint mauve half circles beneath her eyes, and she squeezed her hands together as if to control a tremor. "I love him, and I think he still loves me, but he no longer cares. I . . . I'm a thing to him, Bea."

"I'm not sure I understand what you mean, dear. Can you explain it to me?"

"Oh!" Lottie lifted her hands from her lap and balled them into fists. "Oh, it's so very difficult to articulate."

Beatrice placed her hand around one of Lottie's fists. "I'm listening."

Lottie inhaled and closed her eyes. "It's as if I'm one of the things he owns or possesses. He has a carriage, he has a butler, he has a town house, and he has a wife. I fill a position, as it were, and he might love me, somewhere deep underneath his everyday exterior, but I could be anyone, Bea." She opened her eyes and stared at her friend with something very like despair. "I could be Regina Rockford or Pamela Thistlewaite or that girl who married the Italian count."

"Meredith Brightwell," Beatrice murmured. She'd always had a better memory for names than Lottie.

"Yes," Lottie said. "Any of them. I fulfill a . . . a space in his life, nothing more. If I died, he'd mourn and then go out and find another to fill that space again."

"Surely not," Beatrice murmured, not a little shocked. Was this truly what marriage was like? Did the love and compliments and courting really not last?

"Believe me, it's all true." Lottie wiped her eyes with one wrist. "I couldn't take that anymore. I may be naive, but I want to be loved—loved for myself, not the position I hold—so I left."

Beatrice swallowed, looking down at her hand still clasped with Lottie's. "Where are you staying?"

"At Papa's house," Lottie said. "He isn't pleased, and

Mama's worried about the scandal, but they'll let me stay."

"But . . ." Beatrice frowned. "What will you do?"

"I don't know." Lottie laughed, but the sound caught and she quieted. "Perhaps I'll be scandalous and take a lover."

She didn't look particularly excited at the thought.

Beatrice glanced across the ballroom. A minuet had started, and couples were pacing gracefully on the dance floor. She could see Lord Hope making his way toward them, and her heart gave a kind of skip in her chest. And beyond him, suddenly clear, was Mr. Graham—Nate—staring rather wistfully at them.

"Perhaps you can try talking to him." Even as she said it, she knew the suggestion was hopelessly inadequate.

Lottie smiled wearily. "I've tried. It hasn't worked."

"I'm sorry," Beatrice said helplessly. "I am so sorry."

She sat with Lottie, saying nothing and watching as Lord Hope approached them. She felt guilty because even knowing that Lottie's whole life was in turmoil and that her friend was deeply hurt, she still rejoiced at the sight of him. Lord Hope looked so strong, stood so straight. He was still too thin, but his face had begun to fill out a bit, his cheeks and eyes no longer so hollow. He was handsome in a daunting sort of way, even with the grim expression he habitually wore, and she couldn't help the gladness she felt at the sight of him.

He continued cleaving relentlessly through the crowd until he stood before them. He bowed. "Ladies."

"My lord," Beatrice said rather breathlessly.

He glanced at the dancers. "This dance is ending

soon, I think. Might I have the honor of the next one, Miss Corning?"

"I . . . I'm flattered, of course." Beatrice bit her lip. "But I really think not."

"Go ahead, Bea." Lottie had straightened with Lord Hope's approach, and now she smiled widely. "Really. I do so wish to see you dance."

Beatrice turned to look in her friend's eyes. Sorrow still lurked there, though Lottie was determined to appear as if nothing were wrong. "You're sure?"

Lottie nodded firmly. "Yes, certainly."

Beatrice held out her hand, and Lord Hope took it. He glanced at Lottie and said with a crooked smile, "Thank you."

Then he was leading Beatrice through the crowd, his shoulders wide and strong beside her. They came to the dance floor and paused as the music ended with a flourish. The dancers curtsied and bowed to their partners and then drifted from the dance floor. Beatrice and Lord Hope took their positions, waiting patiently for the music to begin again. She snuck a look at him, standing beside her. He seemed preoccupied.

She cleared her throat. "Did your discussion with Lord Vale go well?"

"Yes." The music began and the figures of the dance took them away from each other a moment. Lord Hope was frowning fiercely when they drew near again. "Why do you ask?"

"He is your friend," she replied, and then said, lower, "I worry about you."

They paced away. A gentleman nearby tripped and

jostled against Lord Hope. He froze and glared at the man but then seemed to recover himself.

When they came together again, she whispered, "Are you feeling well?"

"Of course," he snapped, a little too loud.

Heads turned.

He paced about her as she stood, and even though it was part of the dance, she felt as if a great predator prowled around her.

Then something awful happened.

The same man who had jostled Lord Hope before tripped and bumped into him again, this time much harder, shoving Lord Hope a step. Lord Hope whirled on the man, drawing out his huge knife from under his coat. The dancers nearby stumbled to a halt. A woman screamed.

The man turned white, backing up with his hands raised. "I . . . I say, I'm dreadfully sorry!"

"What do you mean by it?" Lord Hope demanded. "You deliberately ran into me."

Beatrice started forward. "My lord—"

But Lord Hope grabbed the other man by the neck. "Answer me!"

Dear God, had he gone mad again? Gentlemen were shoving their ladies behind them, and the crowd was backing away, leaving a wide cleared space in the middle of the dance floor.

"Reynaud," Beatrice said softly. She touched the arm that held his raised knife. "Reynaud, let the man go."

He'd paused at the sound of his name on her lips, and now he turned his head, his black eyes blank and frightening.

Beatrice swallowed and whispered, "Reynaud, please."

Lord Hope let the man go so abruptly he staggered.

"We're leaving." With his free hand, Lord Hope grabbed Beatrice's arm and began towing her through the crowd. He still gripped the bare knife in his other hand.

And as they went, the mass of people parted before them, some half falling in their haste to get away from Lord Hope. On every face they passed, Beatrice saw the same expression.

Fear.

Chapter Eight

Longsword raised his mighty sword. The dragon roared again and blew searing flames at him. But Longsword had lived seven long years in the kingdom of the goblins, and fire was no longer a thing he feared. He jumped through the blast and swung his sword hard, driving it between the dragon's eyes. The great beast staggered and fell dead, but as it did so, it dropped the most beautiful lady in the world. Longsword saw that the lady would be smashed on the rocks beneath her, and he ran to catch her in his strong arms.

The lady clutched at his broad shoulders and looked at him with eyes the color of the sea. "You have saved my life, kind knight, and for this I give you my gratitude. But if you will save the life of my father the king, I will give you my hand in marriage. . . ."

—from *Longsword*

Beatrice rose early the next morning, summoning her maid and dressing quickly in a simple blue and white striped gown. She breakfasted by herself—both Uncle Reggie and Lord Hope appeared to be still abed—and then on impulse she asked for the carriage. It was much too early to be making social calls, but she knew that Jeremy often had trouble sleeping, and he liked to have company when he was awake in the morning. And besides, she needed to talk to someone about the events of the night before.

So it was that a half hour later, after arguing her way past the odious Putley, Beatrice was pouring tea for Jeremy and herself.

"What did you wear?" he asked as she carefully placed the teacup in his hands. She'd filled it only partially full—he was sitting against two pillows, but his fingers trembled, and she was worried he might spill the hot tea on himself.

"My bronze," she replied, stirring rich cream into her cup. "Remember, I showed you the pattern and a swatch of the material last summer before I had it made?"

"The silk that had a kind of iridescence?" At her nod he smiled. "Reminded me of the way brandy sparkles in a glass when you hold it to the light." He sipped his tea and laid his head back against the pillows, his eyes closed. "You must've been beautiful."

She laughed. "I think I looked quite well."

He cracked one eye. "As modest as ever. What did Lord Hope think?"

She looked down at her cup, too self-conscious to meet his knowing gaze. "He said the gown became me."

"Not an overly eloquent man, then," Jeremy said drily.

"Perhaps not, but I liked the compliment."

"Ah."

She set her cup carefully back on the saucer in her lap. "There was a bit of a . . . a scene at the ball."

Jeremy straightened. "And?"

Beatrice wrinkled her nose, still looking at her cup of tea. "A gentleman bumped into Lord Hope on the dance floor and he reacted badly."

"Who was Lord Hope dancing with?"

She huffed out a sigh. "Me, if you must know."

"Oh, I must," Jeremy said with delight. "And what exactly do you mean by *badly*?"

"He took out his knife—he always carries a very long knife with him—and he, um, waved it about, I'm afraid. While holding the other gentleman's throat." Beatrice squeezed her eyes shut at the memory.

There was a pause, and then Jeremy said, "Oh, I wish I'd been there."

Beatrice's eyes flew open. "Jeremy!"

"Well, I do," he said without a trace of remorse. "Sounds like a jolly good to-do. And did Lord Hope get thrown out of the ballroom?"

"It was his aunt's ball," Beatrice reminded him. "So I don't think he would've actually been ejected from the house, but it doesn't matter much since we left after that."

"Ah, he took you with him, did he?"

"He did." She hesitated, then said in a low voice, "He didn't speak at all the entire way home. You should have seen the way everyone stared at him, Jeremy. As if Lord Hope was a dangerous beast."

"Is he?" Jeremy asked quietly. "Dangerous, I mean?"

"No." She shook her head and then admitted, "Well, not dangerous to me, I think."

"Are you sure, Bea?"

She bit her lip, looking at Jeremy helplessly. "He wouldn't hurt me. Truly he wouldn't."

"I hope not, Beatrice, dear." Jeremy laid his head back against his pillow, looking tired. "I would hate for him to hurt you in any way."

There was a question in Jeremy's voice. She could feel his eyes on her as she sipped her tea, but she didn't want to share this, not even with Jeremy. Her emotions were something special, something soft within her, too delicate for the light of day.

She got up and took his empty teacup from his hands, setting it aside when he indicated he wanted no more. When she sat back down again, she said, "Lottie told me last night that she'd left Mr. Graham."

"Probably a lover's spat. She'll be back within the week, mark my words."

"I don't think so," Beatrice said slowly. "She seemed subdued somehow, not at all her usual cheerful self."

She glanced up to see Jeremy's eyes closed, his face drawn. She set down her cup to rise, but as if he knew she was looking, he opened his eyes.

He blinked and frowned. "I hadn't thought Nate Graham such a bad sort. Has he taken a mistress and flaunted her?"

Beatrice hesitated but then decided to play along and pretend she hadn't seen that moment of weakness. "Lottie didn't say there was another woman. I don't think there is one, actually. She said Mr. Graham took her for granted, that any lady would do as well as her for his wife. I confess I'm . . ."

"Disillusioned?" Jeremy asked softly.

She nodded, mute.

"Men can be very disillusioning, I'm afraid," Jeremy said. "We're but things of clay, bumbling about, stumbling over the feelings of those dearest to us. That is why we rely so heavily on the compassion of you ladies, for if you ever lost your pity, took offense, and abandoned us en masse, we would be quite lost, you know."

Beatrice smiled at his play. "You're not like that, dear Jeremy."

"Ah, but we both know I am not much like other men, either, dear Bea," he retorted lightly. Before she could reply, he continued. "Have you discussed the veteran's bill with Lord Hope?"

"Well, I started to," she said slowly.

"And?"

She shook her head. "He's intent on regaining the title and cannot consider other matters at the moment."

"Ah." Jeremy looked down at his teacup, frowning.

Beatrice hurried to say, "He did speak highly of his men—the soldiers he led in battle—and that makes me a little optimistic that he might be sympathetic to our cause. The problem is convincing him to act, I think. I still haven't figured out how exactly to do that."

"He sounds rather selfish," Jeremy murmured.

"I don't think he is," Beatrice said slowly. "Not truly. It's just that he's so focused on regaining what he's lost, there doesn't seem to be room for anything else right now."

"Hmm. I think we all try to get back the life that we've left behind when we return home, we old soldiers." Jeremy's voice was growing weaker. "The problem is, some things can't be regained once lost. I wonder if he's realized that yet?"

"I don't know."

"In any case, you should speak to him soon. The bill will come up before parliament within the next month. Our time is growing short—so short." Jeremy closed his eyes again as he leaned against the pillows.

She bit her lip. "You're tired. I should go."

"No, don't." He opened his eyes, so blue and clear against the white of his pillow. "I adore your company, you know."

"Oh, Jeremy," she said, touched enough that her throat swelled. "I—"

Something thumped loudly in the downstairs hall.

She looked at the bedroom's shut door. "What—?"

Shouting came from below, advancing closer as a male voice bellowed, "I'll see her, damn your eyes! Get out of my way!"

It sounded very like Lord Hope. Beatrice half rose from her chair. "I can't believe he would—"

The voices were rapidly advancing closer. If she didn't do something, he was going to burst into the room. Beatrice ran out into the hallway, closing Jeremy's bedroom door firmly behind her. Coming up the stairs, looking like a charging bull, Lord Hope's face was grim. Putley trailed him, several steps behind, his wig lost, his face frightened as he pleaded with the viscount.

"What do you think you're doing?" she demanded.

"Discovering your lover," he growled as he strode toward her.

"I don't have a lover!"

He stepped to the side to go around her to the door, and she mirrored his movement.

"Go home!" she hissed. "You're making a frightful ass out of yourself."

"Brought it on yourself, miss," Putley crowed somewhere behind Lord Hope.

"Do shut up, Putley!" Beatrice cried, and then squeaked because Lord Hope had eliminated her barrier by simply picking her up and moving her to the side. "Oh, don't!"

But it was too late. He'd opened the door, barged into the room, and then stopped dead, blocking her view.

She heard a breathless laugh from Jeremy. "Lord Hope, I presume?"

"Goddamn," the viscount said.

"Oh, get out of the way!" Beatrice shoved hard at his great big stupid back.

He moved obligingly to the side.

She hurried past him. "Jeremy, are you all right?"

"Quite all right," he said, his color high and hectic. "Haven't had this much excitement in years."

"And it isn't good for you." She took his hand and turned to glare at Lord Hope, still standing by the door. The man didn't even have the grace to look embarrassed. "What do you think you're doing here?"

"I told you"—he casually kicked the door closed behind him—"discovering you in a lover's nest. It seems I might be mistaken."

"*Might* be?" She balled her free hand and set it on her hip. "You've been a complete and utter idiot and have insulted both me and Jeremy. *Obviously* we aren't lovers—"

"There's nothing obvious about it," he growled, eyeing the remains of Jeremy's legs beneath the covers. "I've known men who've lost their legs but not their—"

"*Don't* be disgusting!" She was shouting now, but it was completely out of her control. How dare he? What kind of woman did he think her? He'd humiliated her!

Behind her, Jeremy was making choking sounds, and she turned swiftly, alarmed.

He was trying to hold back big belly laughs and not succeeding very well.

"Oh, not you, too," she said, thoroughly exasperated, even as she poured him a glass of water.

"Thank you, dear," Jeremy said. "And I'm sorry. At this moment, I feel that I should apologize for my entire sex."

"You should," she grumbled. "You're rotten to the core, all of you."

"Yes, I know," he said humbly. "You're simply a saint to put up with us at all. But I have a boon to ask of you, dearest."

"What is it?" she asked, not very graciously.

"Would you mind terribly going and seeing to Putley's ruffled feathers? I know it's a tiresome chore, but I'd rather not have him tattling to my parents about this matter."

"Oh, all right." She glared at Lord Hope. "But I'll have to leave you here with *him*."

"I know." Jeremy adopted an angelic expression that

didn't fool her for a moment. "I'd rather hoped to have a chat with the viscount."

"Humph," she said. She stepped up to Lord Hope until they were nearly chin to chin—although she had to tilt hers quite far up—and poked him in the chest with her forefinger.

"Ow," said Lord Hope.

"If you lay a single finger on him," she hissed into his face, "or overexcite him in any way, I'll tear that silly earring right out of your ear."

Behind her, Jeremy went into peals of laughter, but she didn't bother glancing at him again. She slammed the door behind her and stomped off in search of Putley.

Men!

REYNAUD RUBBED THE spot where Miss Corning had attempted to drill her forefinger through his breastbone. "I apologize."

"'Tisn't me who needs the apology," the man in the bed said, still laughing. "I'll give you a hint—her favorite flowers are lily of the valley."

"Are they?" Reynaud eyed the door speculatively. He hadn't brought a woman flowers in eons, but the situation might very well call for the formal English method of suing for peace from a lady. At the moment, though, he had other matters to settle. He turned back to the man in the bed. "Battle wounds?"

"Blown off by cannon fire at Emsdorf on the Continent," Oates said. His color was unnaturally high, as if he was feverish. "Back in sixty."

Reynaud nodded. He strolled to the table littered with

medicine bottles of all shapes and sizes. There wasn't a medicine in the world that could put a man's legs back on once lost. "Did she tell you I was with the Twenty-eighth Regiment of Foot in the Colonies?"

"She did." He laid his head back against the pillow as if exhausted. "I was in the Fifteenth Light Dragoons. Much more dashing than a foot soldier—until, of course, one gets shot off one's horse."

"Battle is never as romantic as one thinks," Reynaud said.

He remembered well his boyish romanticism of the army. It had died fast on the reality of rotten food, incompetent officers, and boredom. His first skirmish had destroyed what little illusion still survived.

"Our regiment was newly formed," Oates said, "and we hadn't yet seen action. Many of the men were London tailors who'd been on strike and had to join. We never stood a chance."

"You were defeated there?"

Oates smiled bitterly. "Oh, no. We won the day. One hundred and twenty-five men killed in my regiment alone, over a hundred horses dead, but we won the battle. I went down in our second charge."

"I'm sorry."

Oates shrugged. "You know as well as I the wages of war—perhaps more so than I."

"I won't debate the matter. I came for something else entirely." Reynaud sat in the chair that was beside the bed. "What are you to her?"

The other man arched his brows as if amused. "I'm Jeremy Oates, by the way."

There was nothing for it but to stick out his hand. "Reynaud St. Aubyn."

Oates took his hand and shook it, looking in his eyes as if searching for something. His fingers were as thin as twigs. "Pleased to meet you." The odd thing was he sounded sincere.

Reynaud took back his hand. "My question?"

Oates half smiled, his eyes closing as he lay against the pillows. "Childhood friends. I played hide-and-seek with her in my family's sitting room, helped her with her geography lessons, escorted her to her first ball."

Reynaud felt a jolt somewhere in the region of his breastbone at the other man's words. Perhaps it was the lingering aftereffects of that sharp poke, but he rather thought it might be jealousy instead.

Jealousy. He'd never felt the emotion before.

True, he'd been enraged this morning to learn that Miss Corning had already left to visit her mysterious beau. He'd come here at once with the intent to confront them and thrash the other man if necessary, but he hadn't stopped to examine his emotions. *Mine,* his instinct had said, and so he'd acted on it without thought. The realization now that his reaction was emotional was an unwelcome shock.

"Do you love her?" he asked.

"Yes," Oates said simply. "With all my heart. But not, I believe, in the way you mean."

Reynaud shifted in the chair, uncomfortable with his need to know exactly what the other man meant. "Explain."

Oates smiled and Reynaud saw that he'd once been a handsome man before illness had carved lines of suffering into his face. "Beatrice is dearer than any blood sister could ever be to me."

Reynaud narrowed his eyes. The man might say his relationship with Miss Corning was fraternal, but she wasn't in fact related. How, then, could their friendship be as innocent as he claimed?

"So you wouldn't have married her even if that hadn't happened." He jerked his chin at the other man's missing legs.

Most would have taken offense, but Oates merely grinned. "No. Although Beatrice has brought up the idea of marriage to me more than once."

That was an unpleasant jolt. Reynaud straightened. "What?"

And Oates's grin widened, making him realize he'd risen to the bait.

"What game are you playing?" Reynaud growled.

"A game of life and death and love and hate," Oates replied softly.

"You're babbling."

"No." The grin abruptly vanished. "I'm completely serious. You'll take care of her."

"What?" Reynaud frowned. Sometimes invalids became confused from the pain and the drugs they took to mask it. Was Oates floating in some drug-induced haze?

"Promise you'll take care of her," the other man said, and although his voice was weak, his tone held the ghost of a good officer's command. "Beatrice is a special woman, someone to be cherished for herself. She wears a mask of practicality, but underneath she's a romantic and prone to heartbreak. Don't break her heart. I won't ask if you love her—I doubt you know yourself—but promise me you'll take care of her. See to it she's happy every day of her life. Lay down your own life for her if need be. Promise."

And suddenly Reynaud understood. His emotions had blinded him to the reality that lay in front of him. He'd seen this look in other men's eyes before, and he knew damned well what it meant.

So he said simply and sincerely, "I swear on everything I hold dear that I'll take care of her, keep her safe, and do my damnedest to make her happy."

Oates nodded. "I can ask for nothing more. Thank you."

HOW DARE HE?

Beatrice opened the front door of Jeremy's town house and went outside for a badly needed breath of fresh air. She'd already browbeaten Putley into keeping quiet about Lord Hope's violent invasion of the house, but she was still dealing with her own reaction to his suspicions. And what terrible suspicions they were! Insulting both to Jeremy and herself. When had she ever given him cause to think her a wanton? And how he thought he could just barge in and dictate to her, she did not know.

Beatrice stamped her feet, both to keep warm and to emphasize her own anger.

There were three men loitering in the street below—two scrawny fellows in ragged brown coats and a taller man in black. The taller man turned to look at the sound of her stamping. His right eye rolled to the corner of the socket, revealing rather horribly the white membrane of the eyeball. She glanced quickly away from the poor man. She should go back inside, but she was still angry. She wanted to be composed when next she saw Lord Hope—the better to tell him exactly what she thought of him.

A brewer's cart went by, rattling on the cobblestones, and one of the loitering men shouted something to the driver.

Behind her, the door opened so quickly she almost fell back in the house. Instead, strong hands caught her.

"I've been looking all over the house for you," Lord Hope said. "What are you doing out here?"

She tried to pull away, but he held fast to her upper arms. "I wanted some air."

He looked down at her disbelievingly, and she couldn't help but notice how thickly his eyelashes rimmed his black eyes.

"In the cold?"

"I find it very *refreshing,*" she said, pulling at her arms again. "*Might* I have my person back?"

"No," he muttered, turning to guide her down the steps, his hand still gripping one of her arms.

"What?" she demanded.

"I'm not letting you go," he said. "Ever."

"That's not funny."

"It's not meant to be," he said maddeningly as they came to the street. "Where's the damned carriage?"

"Around the corner; there's no room for it to stop here. Are you bamming me about not letting me go?"

"I don't make jokes."

"That's the silliest thing I've ever heard," she said, rather too loudly. "Everyone makes jokes, even people with no sense of humor like you."

He yanked the arm he still held, making her bump into his chest. Hard.

"I assure you," he snarled into her face, "that—"

But something odd happened then. She felt a shove from behind her, a sharp hit at her side. Lord Hope's hands tightened painfully on her arms, and she saw that he was glaring murderously over her shoulder.

"What—?" she began.

But he pushed her back and behind him, toward the house's steps as he took his big knife out from under his coat. "Get inside!"

And she saw, horribly, that the three loitering men were advancing on him. Their leader—the man with the walleye—had a knife in his hand, and there was blood on the blade.

Beatrice screamed.

"Get inside!" Lord Hope shouted again, and launched himself at the leader.

The big man lifted his bloody knife to strike the viscount. But Lord Hope caught his wrist, halting the blow, even as he slashed at the man's belly. The leader sucked in his belly and skipped back, his shirt and waistcoat in ribbons. A second man, hatless and balding, wrapped his arms about Lord Hope from behind, imprisoning his upper arms. The walleyed man grinned and advanced to strike again. The viscount grunted and wrenched his left arm free just in time, blocking the knife with his arm. The knife blade sliced through his sleeve, and blood sprayed in a thin arc across the street.

Beatrice covered her mouth and sat suddenly on the town-house steps. Black dots swam in front of her eyes.

A man screamed and she looked up.

The balding man had fallen to the ground and was clutching his bloody side. Lord Hope was grappling with the leader again while the third man raised his dagger behind the viscount's back.

Beatrice tried to scream a warning but couldn't. It was as if she were in a nightmare. Her throat worked, but no sound came. She could only stare in horror.

The knife descended, but the leader stumbled back under Lord Hope's ferocious attack, bringing the viscount with him, and the knife missed. Lord Hope suddenly whirled, dragging the leader with him, and shoved the man into the attacker behind him. Both men fell to the ground in a tangle of legs and arms. The leader was bleeding from a terrible cut to his head, and his ear appeared to be dangling.

Lord Hope straightened and advanced on the fallen men with an intent, deadly stride, like a wolf sighting a wounded hare. He wore a warlike grin as he came, savage and gleeful. His great knife was raised, its blade bloody now, too. His bared teeth were white against his swarthy skin. The men on the ground looked more civilized than he.

And then as suddenly as it'd begun, it was over. The walleyed man and his cohort scrambled to their feet, caught the third man with the bleeding side under his arms, and ducked across the street, nearly under the noses of a team of horses pulling a heavy cart. The driver yelled abuse. Lord Hope took one running step as if tempted to give chase, but then he stopped himself. He sheathed his knife with a disgusted look.

He turned to her, his expression still savage, but all Beatrice could see was his left hand, dripping blood to the ground.

"Why didn't you go in the house?" he demanded.

She looked up dazedly. "What?"

"I gave you an order. Why the hell didn't you follow it?"

His wound was all she could think about. She raised her own right hand to catch his. But something was wrong. Her hand was already bloody.

"Beatrice!"

She frowned at her hand, confused. "Oh, blood."

And then the world did a dizzying spin, and she knew no more.

Chapter Nine

"I am the Princess Serenity," the lady said as Longsword set her on her feet. "My father is the king of this land, but there is an evil witch who lives in the mountains near here. The witch told my father that if he did not pay her a yearly tribute, she would destroy him and this kingdom. My father paid the tribute last year, but this year he refused. The witch sent that dragon to steal my father and bring him to her. When I rode out with a party of knights to rescue my father, the dragon came and killed all save myself."

Princess Serenity laid a small white hand on Longsword's arm. "The witch will kill my father on the morrow if I do not rescue him. Will you help me?"

Longsword looked at the dead dragon, at the white hand on his sleeve, and into Princess Serenity's sea-blue eyes, but he had decided on his answer before she had ever spoken. "I will help you. . . ."

—from *Longsword*

"Beatrice!" Reynaud yelled again, though he knew she couldn't hear.

She'd fainted, slumping to her left side on the steps. A palm-sized bloodstain on her right side and back was revealed, and the sight filled him with irrational terror. He'd seen far more blood in battle—had seen horrific wounds, men without arms or legs, bodies blown apart—and not lost his composure. Yet his hands shook as he reached for her. She was as light as a child as he lifted her in his arms. He felt the wet fabric against his fingers; the blood was soaked into her skirts as well, and for a moment he froze, afraid she was dying. *Her brown eyes stared up through a mask of blood, dull and lifeless. He was too late.*

No. No, this woman could not die. He would not allow it.

He gripped her against his chest and turned to where she'd said the carriage was waiting. He didn't trust this area; the attackers, whoever they were, knew he'd be here. He needed to get her away. Needed to get her to his own home. There he could guard her and tend to her, and she would be safe. He sprinted past houses, his heart thumping in his chest. She moaned and clutched his waistcoat but did not open her eyes.

There! He saw the Blanchard carriage as he turned the corner and ran toward it, yelling an order to the coachman. He saw the man's wide eyes, the footman's startled face, and leaped into the carriage without waiting for the steps.

"Go!" he bellowed, and the carriage lurched into motion, the coachman swearing at the horses.

He held her across his lap and looked into her face. It

was flour-white, so pale that tiny freckles he'd never noticed before stood out on her cheeks. Oh, God, he would not let this happen. He brushed a lock of hair from her eyes, but his hand was bloody, and he only smeared crimson across her temple. Dammit. He needed to see how bad the wound was.

Reynaud reached under his coat and drew out his knife. The carriage swayed as they rounded a corner, and he braced himself with feet and elbows. Carefully he sliced through gown, stays, and chemise, from low on her hip to the top of the bodice, both in back and in front. He pulled the fabric away and saw the wound. It was a two-inch cut at her side just to her back, raw and ugly against the expanse of her smooth pale skin. The assassins had been aiming for him and had caught her instead as he held her in front of himself, an inadvertent shield. Fresh blood flowed clear and bright red from the wound. The fabric had stuck, and he'd reopened the wound when he'd pulled it away.

He swore softly and cut a swath from her underskirts, wadding it and pressing it against the wound. He wrapped his other arm about her shoulders and held her close to himself, her head under his chin. She was so soft, so small in his arms, and he could feel the blood soaking the wadded bandage, wetting his fingers.

"Come on," he whispered.

Outside, houses and shops flashed by. They were making good time, but they still weren't at his town house yet. The coachman shouted something, and the entire carriage lurched heavily. Reynaud slid across the seat, crashing into the coach's side painfully, trying to cushion the movement with his body.

Beatrice moaned.

"Dammit. Dammit. Dammit." He stroked her fair hair back with the hand that held her and pressed his open mouth against her forehead, whispering, "Hold on. Just hold on."

The carriage halted, and he was standing with Beatrice in his arms before the footman had the door all the way open.

"Turn your back!" he snapped to the gawking man.

Reynaud climbed from the carriage, conscious that Beatrice was almost nude to the waist. He leaped up the town-house stairs just as the butler opened the door.

"Send for a doctor," he told the gaping butler. "And I'll need hot water and cloths in Miss Corning's room at once."

He started up the stairs but was blocked by St. Aubyn coming down.

"Beatrice!" The older man's naturally red face paled. "What have you done to my niece?"

"She was stabbed," Reynaud replied curtly. Only the concern in the other man's voice kept him from knocking him aside. "Not by me."

"Dear God!"

"Let me pass."

St. Aubyn fell back, and Reynaud surged past him, mounting the steps as quickly as possible. Beatrice's bedroom was two floors above. He could hear her uncle panting behind him. By the time he reached her room, the door was open and her maid was turning back the bed.

"Lord have mercy," the woman murmured. She was a capable-looking sort, short, red-haired, and sturdy.

"Your mistress has been stabbed," Reynaud said to her. "Help me get her gown off."

"Now, see here!" St. Aubyn sputtered from the door. "You can't do that!"

"She's bleeding," Reynaud said, low and intense. "I can hold the bandage as the maid works. Or would you rather preserve your niece's modesty and let her bleed to death?"

St. Aubyn gulped but said nothing, his eyes fixed on Beatrice's face.

Reynaud nodded at the maid, and St. Aubyn turned away with a mutter and closed the door as she began pulling Beatrice's gown off. A gentleman would've averted his eyes, but Reynaud hadn't been a gentleman for some time now. He watched as the maid undressed Beatrice. Her breasts were high and round, the nipples a pretty pink. The maid pulled the gown from her legs, and he stared with possession at her feminine triangle, so vulnerable, so sweet, scattered with dark gold hair. This was his woman, and he'd failed to protect her. The maid pulled the covers up over Beatrice's breasts and one arm, leaving her right side bare so he could press the now-sodden cloth against the wound.

"Where's the damned doctor?" he growled.

No sound had come from Beatrice's lips as the maid had moved her. She slept deeply.

"Build the fire in the fireplace," he ordered the maid.

"Yes, my lord." She hurried to the fireplace and heaped coals on the embers there.

"What's your name?" he asked her when she returned to the bed, as much to distract himself as anything else.

"Quick, my lord," she said.

"How long have you been with your mistress?" His mind was running in circles, like a mouse trapped in a glass jar. Where was the doctor? How much blood had she lost? Was the bleeding stopped?

"Eight years, my lord," Quick replied. "I've been with Miss Corning since she came out."

"A long time, then," he said absently. He laid the back of his hand against Beatrice's cheek. Still warm. Still alive.

"Yes, my lord," the maid whispered. "She's such a gentle mistress."

The door opened and several footmen came in with cloths and hot water. One of them was Henry, looking grave at the sight of his unconscious mistress.

"Has the doctor been sent for?" Reynaud asked him.

"Yes, my lord," he replied. "Right away 'e was sent for, and Lord Blanchard has gone down to wait for 'im."

Reynaud nodded. "Bring a new cloth here."

"Will she be all right, m'lord?" Henry asked as he gave him the cloth.

"God, I hope so," Reynaud replied.

He replaced the torn piece of underskirt with the clean cloth. The wound was merely oozing now. That at least was good. He closed his eyes. If he still believed in praying, he'd be on his knees right now.

A commotion on the stairs made him raise his head. A tall thin man in a gray bob wig strode into the room, closely followed by St. Aubyn. The doctor took one all-encompassing look at Beatrice and then turned to Reynaud.

"How is she?"

"She hasn't woken from her faint," Reynaud said. "But the bleeding is slowing."

"Good. Good. A stab wound, I was told?" The doctor stepped close. "May I?"

Reynaud relinquished the bandage, and the doctor raised it, making approving murmurs. "Yes. Yes, I see. Only a few inches and not deep, I think. Good. We'll close it while she still sleeps. Bring me the water."

This last was said to Henry, who brought a basin over.

Reynaud stood to give the doctor room, feeling uncommonly useless.

The doctor splashed water on the wound and wiped at the blood. "Need to see to sew." He took an already-threaded needle from his bag. "Can you hold the edges together?" he asked the maid.

She paled.

"I'll do it," Reynaud muttered. He gently pinched the wound closed.

"Ah. Good." The doctor inserted the needle into Beatrice's flesh.

Reynaud winced as the blood welled fresh around the needle prick. Beatrice moaned.

"Hurry," he whispered to the doctor. To see her in pain would undo him now.

"Haste makes waste," murmured the doctor, carefully pulling the bloody thread through. He placed the second stitch, moving deliberately.

"Christ," St. Aubyn muttered.

Reynaud glanced up. The usurper's face was pasty, and for once he felt pity for the man—St. Aubyn looked sick with worry for his niece.

Reynaud looked down again to where the doctor's needle was poking into tender flesh. "There is no need for so many in here. All of you go, except for the earl and Quick."

Feet shuffled to the door.

"One more to close it completely," the doctor said.

Beatrice moaned again.

"Can you hold her shoulders?" Reynaud said tightly to the maid. "Don't let her move."

"Yes, my lord." She went to the head of the bed.

The doctor tied a knot, slowly and carefully. Reynaud frowned at his hands, silently urging him to hurry.

"That's got it," the doctor finally said, and snipped the thread.

"Thank God." Reynaud felt a bead of sweat slide down his face.

"We'll bandage her," the doctor said briskly, "and then it's in the hands of God."

Reynaud nodded and stood, watching closely as the doctor did just that. He produced a bottle of some potion from his bag, gave instructions to administer the medicine when the patient woke, and then left just as abruptly as he'd come. The usurper followed him out of the room, presumably to see him to the door, and Reynaud turned to Quick.

"Let's make her comfortable."

The maid nodded and brought over a fresh basin of water. She sponged and patted dry the area around the bandage while Reynaud gently wiped Beatrice's face clean. She still had not woken, and he frowned at her as he took the pins from her hair and combed flaxen locks over the pillow. At least she did not look as if she was in any pain.

"She's as settled as she's going to be, my lord," Quick said. "I'll just stay here if—"

"No," he said swiftly, interrupting her. "I'll stay. Leave us, please."

The maid looked uncertain for a moment, but when Reynaud stared at her, she bobbed a curtsy and left the room, closing the door behind her.

Reynaud unsheathed his knife and laid it on the bedside table. He took off his wig and set it on a chair. Then he pulled off his boots and climbed into the bed. Carefully, tenderly, he gathered Beatrice to him, her uninjured side against him as he lay.

He brushed the hair from her face, feeling helpless. All his strength, all his determination, mattered not a whit here. It was up to Beatrice and what strength she had.

"Wake up, sweetheart," he whispered into her hair. "God, please wake up."

THERE WAS SOMETHING warm against her side. Big and warm and, oh! so very nice to lie next to. Beatrice shifted a little, intending to burrow her nose into the warmth, but something cut into her side. "Ouch."

"Don't move."

Her eyes flew open at the deep voice, and for a moment she simply stared up at black eyes framed in thick black eyelashes. He did have such pretty eyelashes; it almost made her jealous. Why a *man* should have . . .

Her mind ground to a halt over the thought and then carefully retraced her steps. A *man* . . .

Beatrice blinked up at Lord Hope. "What are you doing in my bed?"

"Taking care of you."

The words were soft, but his face wasn't. She studied him lazily, too tired somehow to get up. He'd left off his wig, and the hair on his shorn head was barely longer than the stubble on his chin. It lay sleek and flat against his head. She wanted to touch it, to see if his hair was soft or prickly. The three birds flew about his right eye, all of them similar but all slightly different. And his midnight eyes watched her back, his brows knit as if with concern.

"Why do you need to take care of me?" she whispered.

"You were hurt," he said, "and it was my fault."

"How?"

"There were three assassins outside of Jeremy Oates's town house."

She remembered now—the man with the walleye and the other two smaller men, loitering. "Why? Why were they there?"

"To kill me," he said grimly.

She reached up a hand and traced one of the bird tattoos near his eye. "Why is someone trying to kill you? Do you know?"

He closed his eyes at her touch. "No, I don't know. Vale thinks it's someone from our past."

"I don't understand." Her hand dropped.

"I don't either." He opened his eyes, which were blazing black. "All I know is that it's my fault that you're hurt."

She frowned, still confused. "But why is that your fault?"

"I failed to protect you," he said.

She raised her eyebrows bemusedly. "Is that your job? To protect me?"

"Yes," he said. "It is."

And he bent his head very slowly toward her. She watched him nearing, the birds getting ever closer, and she thought, *He's going to kiss me.*

And then he was.

His lips were far softer than she would've thought—and they moved over hers gently but firmly. He'd kissed her once before, but that time it'd been so swift she'd hardly had time to assimilate the sensations. This time she could. His bristly cheeks scratched hers, but she didn't mind. She was caught up in the sensation of his mouth, the smell of his neck—warm and masculine—and the sound of his breathing coming faster as he kissed her. He ran his tongue lazily over her lips, and she was so enchanted that she parted them, letting him in. He surged into her mouth, tasting of man, and she moaned, softly, just a little, but it was enough for him to pull back.

"I'm hurting you," he said, scowling.

"No," she replied, but it was already too late.

He rolled off the bed, taking with him all his glorious warmth and his magical mouth.

Beatrice pouted.

"I'll send for your maid," he said as he pulled on his boots. "Would you like anything? Tea? Some broth?"

"I'd like some tea," she replied. She squinted at the window, but the curtains were pulled. "What time is it?"

"Almost night," he said. "You've slept all day."

"Did I?" How strange to remember morning and then

nothing at all until after dark. The thought jogged her brain. "You were hurt!"

He turned to look at her. "What?"

"Your arm. I saw one of the men cut your arm."

"This?" He pushed back the sleeve of his coat to reveal a torn and rust-stained shirt.

"Yes, that!" She was struggling to sit up now. "Why haven't you had it seen to?"

He pressed her gently back down. "Because it isn't of any concern."

"Maybe not for you—"

"Hush." His gaze was quite fierce. "You've had a stressful day, and your wound must ache. Rest now and I'll come and see you when you're properly attired."

He strode from the room masterfully.

Properly attired? Beatrice frowned and only then realized that she hadn't a stitch of clothing on under the covers.

Oh, my.

IT WAS AFTER ten by the time Reynaud got to Vale's house and started banging on the door. Too early for Vale to have returned if he was out at a social event, too late for him to be receiving if he was spending a rare evening at home. Reynaud banged anyway. Vale was his only ally as far as he could see, and at the moment he needed an ally.

The door opened to reveal the face of a disapproving butler, whose expression modified only a little when he saw it was a gentleman knocking.

"Sir?"

Reynaud shouldered past the man. Damned if he'd stand on the step like a beggar. "Is the viscount home?"

The butler's brows lowered. "Lord and Lady Vale are not receiving this evening. Perhaps if you—"

"I'm not coming back tomorrow," Reynaud interrupted. "Either you go rouse him from wherever he is, or I'll get him myself."

The butler drew himself up and sniffed. "If you'll wait in the sitting room, my lord."

Reynaud stalked into the indicated room and spent the next ten minutes pacing from one end to the other. He was just about to give it up and go find Vale himself when the door opened.

Vale strolled in, yawning and wrapping a banyan about his middle. "Much as I'm glad that you've returned from the dead, old man, I really must insist that I reserve my evenings at home for my wife."

"This is important."

"So is marital harmony." Vale went to a tray with a decanter and glasses. He held up the bottle. "Brandy?"

"Beatrice was stabbed this morning."

Vale paused, decanter still in his hand. "Beatrice?"

Reynaud waved an impatient hand. "Miss Corning. She got in the way of an assassination attempt on me."

"Good God," Vale said softly. "Is she all right?"

"She fainted and bled quite profusely," Reynaud muttered, the image of Beatrice's soft skin violated still fresh in his mind. "But she woke just an hour ago and seemed in her right mind."

"Thank God." Vale splashed some brandy into a glass and took a gulp. "And how closely related to you is Cousin Beatrice?"

Reynaud gave him a look. "Not that close."

"Glad to hear it." Vale dropped into a cushioned chair. "I hope she recovers fully so that you can then propose to her. Because I tell you now, matrimony truly is a blessed state, enjoyed by all men of good sense and halfway adequate bedroom skills."

"Thank you for that edifying thought," Reynaud growled.

Vale waved his glass. "Think nothing of it. I say, you haven't forgotten how to treat a lady in the bedroom, have you?"

"Oh, for God's sake!"

"You've been out of refined society for years and years now. I could give you some pointers, should you need them."

Reynaud's eyes narrowed. "This from the man I had to save from an irate whore when we were seventeen?"

"Good God, I'd forgotten that incident."

"I haven't," Reynaud muttered. "She had a big bruiser for a pimp."

"Yes, well, her argument was with the fact that I refused to pay triple her price when her pimp showed up, not with my bed skills," Vale pointed out. "Even at seventeen, I could've shown you a trick or two—"

"Jasper," Reynaud growled in warning.

Vale hid a grin in his glass and then sobered as he lowered it. "Who were the assassins?"

Reynaud threw himself into a chair. "Three ruffians, not very skilled at it, I think. They were led by a man with a pronounced walleye."

"Indeed?" Vale tilted back his head to stare at the

ceiling. "Did he have any other interesting characteristics that might make him recognizable?"

"Tall, quick, knew how to use a knife." Reynaud shrugged. "Not much else, I'm afraid."

"The color of his hair?"

"Brown."

"Ah." Vale considered for a moment. "I'll send another letter to Munroe. We need him here."

Reynaud frowned. "You think the attack on me is somehow related to what happened seven years ago?"

"I do."

"Why?"

"Look here." Vale sat forward in his chair, no longer the lazy aristocrat but a man of intense intelligence. "I'd thought we'd hit a dead end in finding the Spinner's Falls traitor. And then you arrive home, and in the space of little more than a week, two attempts have been made against your life. This is extraordinary!"

"Glad to bring you some joy," Reynaud muttered.

Vale ignored the sarcasm. "I'm more convinced than ever that you have important information that will either expose the traitor or make him vulnerable in some way."

"Then you've entirely cast off the idea that St. Aubyn was behind the attacks?" Reynaud had already come to this conclusion, but he wanted to hear Vale's thoughts.

The other man shook his head. "Blanchard is a pompous blowhard, but he has enough brains not to make an attempt against your life. Besides, I know you dislike the man, but he's never struck me as so thoroughly lacking in morals as to hire an assassin."

Reynaud scowled. "That's—"

"Besides, why would Blanchard risk killing you when you gave the gossips such lovely fodder the other night?"

Reynaud swung to glare at his friend.

"I sympathize." Vale shrugged. "But you must admit your antics on the dance floor did nothing to help your cause."

"We're talking about Blanchard—"

Vale waved a hand, interrupting him. "Blanchard's not the point. We're getting closer to the Spinner's Falls traitor. How I'm not sure, but we must be, judging by these attacks on you. If we can get Munroe down here and put our heads together, maybe we can figure this thing out, once and for all."

"Very well," Reynaud said slowly. "But perhaps we should send a messenger. A rider would get to Scotland before the mail. Or would you rather go yourself?"

"We'll send a messenger with a letter." Vale jumped up and went to rummage in a desk as if intending to write the letter that very moment. "As it happens, I don't want to leave London at the moment."

Reynaud looked at him inquiringly and was astonished to see a flush climbing his old friend's cheeks.

"My wife is, ah, expecting the sixth Viscount Vale," the other man muttered. "Or perhaps merely an honorable miss—not that I care a whit in either case. I just want a babe with all its toes and not looking too much like its pater."

Reynaud grinned. "Congratulations, man!"

"Yes, well." Vale cleared his throat. "She's a bit nervous about the whole thing, so we're keeping the matter quiet while we can. You understand?"

"Of course." Reynaud frowned. Melisande looked healthy enough, but so many things could go wrong in a pregnancy.

"And in the meantime," Vale said as if happy to drop the subject, "while we wait for Munroe, I think it prudent to make some inquiries regarding your attackers. London is an enormous place, but there can't be *that* many walleyed assassins for hire."

"Thank you," Reynaud said, and for the first time in many, many, years, he felt like a friend had his back.

Now if he could only keep Beatrice safe.

"Tell me a story," Beatrice said. She was in bed—the fourth day of lying abed to "rest"—and she was bored beyond reason. She wore a comfortable day dress and sat up against her pillows, but she was definitely confined to her bed.

"What sort of story?" Lord Hope said rather distractedly. He was in a chair by the bed, supposedly to keep her company, but he had a stack of papers from his solicitors, and he was reading them instead.

"You could tell me about the first time you made love to a woman," she said conversationally.

There was a pause during which she was certain that he hadn't heard her, and then he looked up. His black eyes were gleaming, and now she knew he *had* heard her. "You're still recovering, so I think we might want to save that particular story for another time."

"How disappointing," she said, looking down demurely.

He cleared his throat. "Perhaps something else might amuse you."

"Such as?"

He shrugged. "Would you like to hear about army life? Or what Vale and I did in the schoolroom?"

She cocked her head. "I'd love to hear about those stories sometime. But now I'm wondering about your time with the Indians."

He looked back at his papers, a small frown between his brows. "I've already told you: I was captured and made a slave. There isn't much else to talk about."

She studied him, aware that it would be polite to drop the subject. The story of how he was captured and brought to the Indian camp was harrowing. He obviously didn't want to talk about his captivity. But she also knew—somehow, without logical explanation—that he was lying. There was more, much more, to his story. Seven whole years' worth. The time during which he'd transformed from the laughing boy in the portrait to the hard man before her. She needed to hear how that had happened, and perhaps he needed in some way to tell her.

"Please?" she asked softly.

For a moment, she was sure he'd deny her. Then he flung the papers down. "Very well."

"Thank you."

He stared into space for a time. Then he blinked and said, "Yes, well. Gaho wanted me because she needed another hunter for her family. I should explain that some Indians have an interesting tradition. They take captives of war or raids and place them ceremonially in their family. So I took the position that a son would've filled in Gaho's family."

"Then she was your adoptive mother?"

"In theory only." Reynaud's mouth twisted. "I was, for all practical purposes, a slave."

"Oh." Again she thought that must've been a terrible blow to his pride—to go from being a viscount and an officer in His Majesty's army to being regarded as a slave.

"She treated me well enough." He was gazing sightlessly out her bedroom window. "Certainly better than we sometimes treat our prisoners of war. And, of course, I was glad not to've been executed. But, in the end, I was a slave, without control over my own life."

For a moment he was quiet.

"What were your duties?" she asked.

"Hunting." He looked at her, his mouth twisting. "I found out after a while that at one time the village had been much bigger, but the tribe had been decimated by disease some years before. Where once there had been many able-bodied men to provide meat during the winter, now there were only a handful. I went out with Gaho's husband, another older man who we called Uncle, and Sastaretsi."

She shivered. "That must've been awful—to have to hunt with the man who had intended to kill you."

"I watched my back at all times."

"And did you try to escape?"

He looked down at his papers. "I thought of escaping constantly. Every night as they bound my hands and staked me to the ground, I thought of ways I could unwork the knots. My fingernails grew back in, but I soon realized that I wouldn't be able to survive for long on my own. Not in the dead of winter when meat was scarce and the whole village was in danger of starving. That country is vast and savage. The snow can reach as deep as a man's chest. I was hundreds of miles into French-held territory."

Beatrice shivered. "It sounds brutal."

He nodded. "It was so cold that my eyelashes froze when we went hunting."

"What did you hunt?"

"Whatever we could find," he said. "Deer, raccoon, squirrels, bear—"

"Bear!" She wrinkled her nose. "You didn't eat it, did you?"

He laughed. "It takes some getting used to, but, yes—"

The door opened, interrupting him. Quick came in with a tray of tea. "Here's something for you, miss." She set down the tray. "Oh, and a note for you, my lord."

She handed a folded scrap of paper to Lord Hope.

Beatrice watched him as she took a dish of tea from Quick. Lord Hope knit his brows as he read, and then he crumpled the paper and threw it into the fire.

"Not bad news, I hope," she said lightly.

"No. Nothing for you to worry about." He got up from his chair. "In fact, you should be resting now. I'm off to see about some business."

"I've been resting for four days," she called to his broad back.

He merely smiled over his shoulder and shut the door behind him.

"I'm tired of lying abed," she complained to Quick.

"Yes, miss, but Lord Hope says as you're to stay there another day or so."

"When did everyone start listening to him?" Beatrice muttered childishly.

But Quick considered the question solemnly. "I think 'twas when he took charge of Henry after he was wounded, miss. And then he seemed to know just what to do when you were hurt." The maid shrugged. "I know he 'tisn't officially the earl yet, miss, but it's hard not to treat him that way."

"He does seem to've fallen naturally into the role," Beatrice murmured.

In the last week, Lord Hope had overseen her medical care. In addition, from what she could tell by the letters he read and the conversations she overheard with the servants, he seemed to be receiving reports from the various Blanchard estates and holdings. Reports that normally would go to her uncle.

She hadn't seen Uncle Reggie since the morning after she'd been attacked, and now she wondered—rather guiltily—how he was getting on. No matter how Uncle Reggie protested, everything was changing about him. It must be hard for him. Harder still since he seemed to have the idea that she was only on Lord Hope's side. If it were up to her, she'd be on *both* their sides . . . if only they'd let her.

Beatrice sighed. She was tired of lying abed, tired of only hearing about news and events instead of experiencing them. "I'm getting up."

Quick looked alarmed. "Lord Hope said—"

"Lord Hope is not my master," Beatrice said loftily, and threw back the covers. "Have the carriage brought round."

Forty-five minutes later, she was rolling through London on the way to Jeremy's house. She hadn't seen him since the attack, and she was beginning to get rather worried. Lottie had sent a note every day and a lovely little bunch of flowers, but Beatrice had received no word from Jeremy. Had he even heard that she'd been hurt?

By the time the carriage pulled up in front of Jeremy's town house, the sky had darkened, threatening rain. Beatrice climbed out of the carriage and ran up the steps of the town house to knock at the door. She glanced at the black clouds overhead while she waited, wishing Putley would hurry.

When at last he opened the door, she made to walk past him, saying, "Good afternoon, Putley. I won't be staying long."

"A moment, miss," the butler gasped.

"Oh, really, Putley, after all this time, can't you at least pretend you know me?" She smiled up at him, but then her smile fell from her face as completely as if it'd never been there.

The butler's face was gray.

"What is it?" she whispered.

"I'm sorry," he said, and for once he did sound sorry.

Which only made panic rise in her chest. "No. Let me in. Let me see him."

"I can't, miss," the old butler said. "Mr. Oates is dead. Dead and buried."

Chapter Ten

Princess Serenity's horse had been killed, and Longsword had none, so they were forced to set off for the witch's lair on foot. All that day they walked, and though the princess was small and slight, never did she falter. At nightfall, they came to the foot of the mountain where the witch lived. In the dark, guided only by the light of the pale moon, they climbed the great black mountain. Strange beasts stirred in the shadows, and mournful birds cried in the dark, but Longsword and the princess pressed on. And as the first light of dawn crested the peak of the mountain, they stood before the witch's castle. . . .

—from *Longsword*

"What do you mean, she's gone out?" Reynaud grated at the butler. He stood in the front hall, having just returned from his business meeting.

The man cringed but stood his ground bravely enough.

"Miss Corning said she was going to visit Mr. Oates, my lord."

"Dammit!" Reynaud turned and ran to the front door, throwing it open. The stable boy was just leading his horse to the corner. "Oy! Bring him back here!"

The boy looked up, startled, but led the big bay around. Reynaud leaped down the steps and mounted the horse, nudging the gelding into a trot. He'd seen the note just this afternoon while sitting with her in her bedroom. Jeremy Oates had died two days before. Why it had taken Oates's parents that long to write the terse note, he had no idea. He knew he should feel shame for reading Beatrice's letters, but he'd wanted to protect her while she was recovering from that terrible stab wound. He'd intended to break the news of her friend's death gently. Hold her while she wept. Dammit! Now his plan to cushion the blow was in shambles. He urged the horse into a canter, riding dangerously fast past carts and pedestrians.

Five minutes later, when he rounded the corner onto Oates's street, the first thing he saw was Beatrice, standing at the top of the town-house steps, looking like a forlorn waif. He jumped down from the horse and threw the reins to one of the footmen attending her carriage. Then he slowly mounted the stairs. One fat raindrop fell, then two, then a deluge let down.

They were instantly drenched.

He took her arm gently. "Come home, Beatrice."

She looked up at him, the water running down her face like tears. "He's dead."

"I know," he murmured.

"How?" she asked. "How could he be dead? I just saw him the other day, and he was fine."

"Come home." He started leading her down the steps. "You're still ill."

"No!" She yanked her arm suddenly and surprised him enough to pull it from his grasp. "No! I want to see him. Maybe they're wrong. They hardly look in on him at all. Maybe he's just . . . just . . ." She trailed away, looking around wildly. "I want to see him."

She started back up the stairs.

He came up swiftly behind her and picked her up. "You need to go home."

"No!" She flailed her arms and hit him—whether on purpose or accidently, it was hard to tell. "Let me go! Let me see him!"

He no longer tried arguing with her. Instead he ran down the rain-slicked steps and took her to the carriage.

"Home!" he yelled to the coachman before ducking into the vehicle.

The footman slammed the door behind them, and the carriage bumped into motion.

He wrapped his arms about her to contain her movements so she wouldn't pull the stitches out of her wound, but she'd stopped struggling. Deep, heaving sobs shook her frame.

He laid his cheek against her wet hair. "I'm sorry."

"It isn't fair," she choked.

"No, 'tisn't."

"He was so young."

"Yes."

He murmured into her hair, gently stroking her cheek, her shoulder, and let her sob against him. Her grief was uncontrolled, childish and wild and without grace, and such raw emotion stirred something within him. This woman was real. He might never again be the sort of civilized English gentleman she deserved, but she was exactly what he wanted. What he needed. She was warm and caring, and she was *home.*

He wanted her.

So when the carriage at last pulled up in front of Blanchard House—*his* house—he took her in his arms and carried her up the steps and into the house as and his ancestors with their brides. He passed the butler, the footmen, and the maids, and all fell back, making way for him and his prize.

"No one disturbs us," he said, and then mounted the stairs to her room. The master bedroom—the one used by his father and all the Earls of Blanchard before him—would've been better for what he intended, but the usurper was using it, and it didn't matter anyway. This was between only the two of them and no one else.

He made her room and walked in. The maid was there, dithering by the wardrobe.

"Leave us," he said, and she did.

He set Beatrice down gently by the bed. She had her face still buried in his shoulder and was as limp as a rag doll.

"No," she said feebly, though what she still protested he had no idea. She probably didn't, either.

"You're wet," he said gently. "I need to dry you."

She stood without protest as he unlaced her bodice and stays, stripping the wet fabric from her body. He did it dispassionately. It was important to get her warm and to make sure she hadn't reopened the wound. When she was nude, he took a cloth from the wardrobe and rubbed her all over, drying what wet there was. Her skin was white and peach, a smooth, beautiful expanse. He took the pins from her hair and dried them with the towel, watching as the silky gold strands curled against his fingers. When that was done, he wet a corner of the cloth at the basin on the dresser and washed her face. Her cheeks were reddened, her eyelids and lips swollen, and he knew she didn't look her prettiest, but his cock didn't care. He'd been erect since he'd walked into the room.

Finally, he pulled back the coverlet on her bed and, picking her up, laid her on the bed and tugged the sheets over her to keep her warm.

It was only after he'd taken off his coat and begun unbuttoning his waistcoat that her eyebrows knit.

"What," she said softly, "are you doing?"

HER CHEST HURT. Her heart and lungs and breasts, they all hurt with every breath she took. She felt as if part of her world had broken off and fallen, never to be reclaimed again. Jeremy was dead. Dead, and she'd not even known it until Putley had blurted the news. Shouldn't she have known? Shouldn't she have felt his passing in some fundamental portion of herself?

She shied from the thought, from the bone-crushing hurt, and looked at Lord Hope. Somehow he'd taken her to her rooms and undressed her. She should be scandalized, but she just hadn't the will to be. And now . . . and now he appeared to be taking off his own clothing.

She peered at him, only a little bit curious. "What are you doing?"

"Undressing," he said, and that certainly made sense because he was.

He took off his waistcoat and shirt, and she watched, detached. His arms were strong and brown from the sun. Had he worn a shirt when he'd lived with the Indians? He unbuttoned the fall of his breeches, and she watched him strip those off as well. His smallclothes were tented over his masculine parts, and at any other time she would be very interested at the sight, but at the moment she felt . . . nothing.

Or at least almost nothing.

"But why?" she asked, and even in her sad state, she knew her voice sounded like a small child's.

"Why what?" he asked as he removed his shoes and stockings.

"Why are you undressing?"

"Because I intend to lie with you," he said, and took off his smallclothes.

Well, that certainly was something she'd not seen before. His cock stood up as proudly as a soldier, thick and round and almost a purplish red, particularly at the head. She blinked at the sight. Then he was walking toward her, that part of himself bobbing with each step, and he got into the bed with her. He gathered her close and he felt so hot. So hot he was like a furnace and she sighed a little at how nice his hard, hot body felt against her cold skin.

She looked up at him, so close, his black eyes only inches from her own, and said, "He's dead and I'll never forget him."

"Yes, I know," he replied.

"I want to die, too."

His eyes hardened. "I won't let you."

And he kissed her. His mouth was hot, too, and this time he didn't wait but thrust his tongue into her mouth. She moaned a little at the sensation. He tasted of rain-water and salt, and suddenly she couldn't think of anything better to taste. She grasped at his shoulder and felt bare, masculine skin, and she dug her fingernails in. If she wasn't allowed to die, then she would live and forget the rest of the world for right now.

At this moment, there was only the two of them, together in this cozy bed.

He pushed his fingers through her hair, gripping the back of her head, holding her as he explored her mouth with his tongue. He darted in and then out until she caught him and sucked on him, and he made an approving sound. He rolled then, climbing atop her, and she felt the brush of his chest hair against her breasts, tickling and arousing.

She made a sound deep in her throat, and he raised his head. "Am I hurting you?"

"No." She tried to pull him back down to kiss her, but he held still, resisting her.

"Are you sure?"

"Yes." She said it irritably, because she missed his kisses. It seemed to her that he was simply teasing her.

Then he moved, shifting so that one of his legs began to part hers. Her eyes flew to his, and she saw the corner of his mouth quirk.

"You're sure?"

"Ye-es," she said, but she was distracted, feeling the slow insertion of his thigh between hers. Her legs fell open, admitting him, but he didn't stop there. He continued pressing down until his thigh had thrust to the very apex of her thighs, until he had burrowed against her feminine flesh, and she was parted, open against him.

Her eyes widened.

His eyes drooped, the tattooed birds looking wild and pagan.

"It doesn't hurt?" he asked gently.

"No . . . oh!" She gasped because he'd shifted and pressed, and somehow the combination was simply divine. "Do that again," she demanded.

He grinned, his teeth white against his brown skin. "As my lady commands."

And he kissed her as he pressed with his thigh. She opened her mouth wide, wanting to taste all of him, wanting to experience everything he might show her. When next he pressed down, she shoved up, rubbing herself against him, twisting and thrusting. She wanted . . . *more*. Much more.

She tore her mouth from his and looked him in the face. "Put it in me."

He didn't pretend shock. "Not yet."

"But why not?" She widened her legs in invitation. She could feel that part of him, pressing against her thigh. "Isn't that what comes next? Isn't that what you want?"

"Not yet," he said maddeningly, and placed his mouth against hers again. But this time he didn't stay there. He caressed her with his open mouth, with his soft lips, as he trailed downward over her throat. He licked the upper slope of her breast and then took the nipple in his mouth.

She gasped. That small point flamed with pleasure,

each strong suck a pull that tugged at her center. She arched, clutching at his head, feeling his shorn bristles beneath her palms.

He shifted, licking his way to her other breast, and tasted that nipple as well. At the same time, his thigh still pressed against her.

She arched up. "Oh, please, now."

"Not yet," he whispered, his breath blowing over her wet, sensitive nipple.

He raised himself on straight arms and brought both legs between hers. She was spread wide now, eager and waiting for the inevitable conclusion to this.

But it didn't come. He reached down to position himself, laying his penis against her wet folds. Then he bore down, pressing himself against her most sensitive point.

She twisted, panting, under him. "What are you doing?"

His face was grim, the cross earring shining dully at the corner of his jaw. "I'm preparing you."

She glared at him through slitted eyes. "I *am* prepared."

His lips curled, not quite smiling. "Not yet."

He bent and caught her lower lip between his teeth, gently biting as he rocked against her. And something combusted down there. A flame flickered and flared, growing steadily, spreading through her belly, threatening to burn out of control.

"Stop," she cried, but her voice was muffled beneath his lips. He opened his mouth over hers and swallowed whole her moan of ecstasy.

"Now," he said when he lifted his head. "Now it's time. Put me where you want me to be."

He caught her hand and brought it between their bodies, guiding her to his hard, slick flesh. He wrapped her fingers around his heat and then took his hand away. He looked at her. "It's up to you."

She blinked. "But I don't know—"

"Do you want it?" Beads of sweat stood out on his upper lip. She realized that he was holding himself very still.

She licked her lips. "Yes."

"Then"—he nudged her with his hips, his length sliding through her fingers, his eyes half closed—"do it."

So she guided him to where she thought he should be, feeling the width of his head slip through her folds, wondering if this was quite possible. She looked up at him, into black, intense eyes, and for a fraction of a second thought she must've lost her mind.

Then he leaned down and kissed her forehead. "Are you sure?"

And that small bit of tenderness decided her. "Yes."

He wasn't gentle. He didn't try to go slowly. He thrust himself inside her, quickly and violently, and her entire body arched with the pain. Burning. Tearing. Something wasn't right.

She pressed her palms against his chest. "No."

He looked down at her, his face drawn, the tattooed birds flying about his eye, wild and savage, and he no longer looked tender. He looked like a conqueror. "Too late. You're mine now."

And he withdrew his penis slowly, until only the head remained inside her, large and intrusive.

"You're so soft, so tight around me," he whispered like a demon incubus. His upper lip curled in erotic bliss. "I want to stay in you forever. I want to make love to you for an eternity."

He thrust back into her, and although it hurt, it wasn't as bad as the first time. He leaned down and touched the corner of her mouth with the tip of his tongue. "I can smell your sex, and it's hot around me. You make me tremble with want."

She touched his face, tracing the damp birds wonderingly. Was it true? Did he tremble for her? She'd never known, never dreamed she could affect him thus.

He closed his eyes as if in pain. "I'm trying to hold back, trying to go slow, but I can't." His head fell, his iron cross earring brushing her breast. "I can't."

And he thrust into her again, hard and fast. She gasped at the impact. It no longer hurt, but there wasn't the same pleasure as there had been before when he'd used his thigh on her. She watched his face, hard and intent above her, and felt the slide of his flesh in hers. He was on her and in her, physically dominating her, but he seemed the more vulnerable one, and it fascinated her. His breathing was rough, coming in quick gasps; his eyes were unfocused and desperate, his mouth drawn in a line of desire. His body seemed to act of its own volition, as if he no longer controlled his movements.

She reached up to caress his cheek.

His eyes closed. "Beatrice. Beatrice."

He bent and kissed her wildly, uncontrolled and desperate, and she returned the kiss, awed that she'd brought him to this extreme.

And suddenly he arched and shuddered, his big body convulsing. He buried his head in her breasts and muffled a shout, trembling all over.

Then the room was silent. She felt his heavy weight on her and listened to the patter of the rain hitting her window. She should move—make him move—get up and deal with tragedy and loss and her life.

Instead, she fell asleep.

HE WOKE TO the sound of thunder outside and the soft breath of a woman against his side. Every muscle in his body, every bone and sinew, was completely and utterly relaxed, and he smiled before he even opened his eyes. For the first time in seven long years, he felt . . . at peace. He turned his head to look at the woman beside him. The woman who had brought him such overwhelming contentment.

Beatrice lay sleeping. Her wheat-colored hair was tangled about her face. Her sweet lips were slightly parted, her lovely brows drawn together as if even in sleep she mourned her friend. He wanted to smooth that small indent between her eyebrows, wanted to take her pain from her, but that was impossible. He couldn't heal her grief, but he could make sure she was never harmed again. She was too important to him now. She made him feel whole. Sane and calm. He knew he'd have to work quickly to consolidate his position.

Quietly he drew back the coverlet and climbed from the bed. He stretched, feeling the pop of his spine, and then bent to retrieve his smallclothes from the floor. He must not've been as stealthy as he thought, for when he straightened, clear gray eyes met his own.

He dropped the smallclothes and went to her. "Are you all right?"

She blinked sleepily and then blushed enchantingly. "I'm . . . rather sore."

"I'm sorry." He sat on the bed and brushed the hair from her eyes. "Stay here and I'll send the maid up with a hot bath."

A corner of her mouth curved down sadly. "That would be nice."

"You can spend the rest of the day abed," he said softly.

Her eyes slid away from his. "But Jeremy . . ."

"I'll find out what arrangements his family made—where they buried him." He bent to kiss her gently on the cheek.

She caught his hand. "Thank you."

He nodded and straightened, picking up his small-clothes again. He drew them on and buttoned the flap.

Her brows knit. "What time is it? How long have you been closeted here with me?"

He glanced at the clock on the mantel. "A little over an hour and a half."

"Oh, my God!" She struggled to sit up in the bed. The sheets slid down to her lap, baring her sweet breasts. She snatched them up again. "What will Quick think—or my uncle?"

He stilled in the act of buttoning his breeches and looked at her. She seemed so young, lying against the white linens, her hair all about her, her wide gray eyes watching him seriously. She'd just lost her childhood friend. Perhaps she hadn't thought ahead as he had. "They'll think I've bedded you."

Her mouth fell open. "You must leave at once."

He set his jaw and picked up his shirt. "Beatrice—"

"Hurry! Quick and I can make something up if you just leave at once. I'm sure we can find a way around this. It can be as if it never happened."

Reynaud scowled, not liking the sound of that at all. Frankly, he didn't give a damn what anyone thought, including her uncle, but her cheeks had gone pale. Dammit, he didn't want to distress her.

He leaned over her, placing his hands on either side of her hips. "I'll leave, but I'm not a callow youth to be dismissed from your bed, madam."

And he kissed her before she could retort. Hard and hot, thrusting his tongue into her mouth without preamble. This woman was his, and damned if he was going to let her doubt it for even one second after he'd already laid claim.

He straightened and looked into her dazed gray eyes. "This matter is far from settled."

And scooping up the rest of his clothes, he left the room.

Chapter Eleven

From the castle gates poured one hundred fierce warriors. They were clad in armor so black it reflected no light, and they shouted their war cries so loudly the very air trembled. They charged at Longsword. You might think such a show of force would send a mere mortal running, but not he. Longsword stood firm and true and swung his heavy sword. His blade glinted in the sun, the sweat streamed from his broad brow, and the heads of the magical army fell like leaves in autumn. For an hour he fought, and at the end of that hour, not a black warrior still lived. . . .

—from *Longsword*

"And he actually threatened to bed you again?" Lottie asked the next afternoon, looking more animated than she had for some days now.

"Not in so many words," Beatrice said slowly. "But the implication was there, certainly."

Both ladies were in Lottie's carriage, riding toward a salon at Mrs. Postlethwaite's residence.

"How very thrilling!" Lottie exclaimed. "It's like an awful play."

"But it isn't an awful play," Beatrice replied morosely. "It's my life. Oh, what am I to do, Lottie? I *gave* myself to him."

"Oh, *gave*! How can one give oneself to a man, I ask you?"

Beatrice knit her brows. "I don't know what else to call it. I'm no longer a virgin."

"And what of it?" Lottie asked spiritedly. "It's only a bit of blood and an act of five minutes or so—"

"Rather more than five minutes," Beatrice muttered, blushing.

Lottie waved aside her friend's comment. "In *any* case, I don't think it ought to decide your entire life."

"But what if I'm pregnant?"

"Highly unlikely after just the one time."

"Yes, but—"

"And besides, he definitely took advantage of you. I mean, right after you'd learned about poor Jeremy! It wasn't at all sporting. I don't think it ought to count, really."

Beatrice frowned, unsure what Lottie meant by "count."

"See here," Lottie continued, oblivious. "It'll be at least a couple of months until you're certain. Although, I have heard of ladies who never knew until the moment they were holding a squirming baby in their arms."

Beatrice moaned.

"*But*, in any case," Lottie said hastily, "there's no need

to make a decision right now. Just because the man has taken your virginity doesn't mean he should own your entire life. What if you decide to take other lovers?"

"But I don't *want* other lovers."

"After all, why tie yourself to one man? You could be a dashing and scandalous courtesan!"

Beatrice sighed. Lottie seemed to be confusing Beatrice's predicament with her own life since she'd left Mr. Graham. Although Beatrice noticed that *Lottie* hadn't started taking lovers and living the life of a fast matron.

"I don't want to be a dashing and scandalous courtesan," Beatrice said quietly. "And I do have to make a decision, because Lord Hope isn't the sort of man who sits about waiting for others to make up their minds. He'll decide it for me if I don't do it soon."

"Hmm, that does pose a problem."

"Yes, it does." Beatrice looked at her hands in her lap, trying to sort through her feelings. "I wish I knew how he felt for me—or even if he *can* feel."

"What do you mean?"

"He's so cold sometimes, Lottie, as if whatever gentleness he once had, whatever capacity to love, was destroyed by his years in the Colonies." Beatrice looked at her friend to see if she understood.

"You don't know if he can love you."

Beatrice nodded miserably.

All of Lottie's animation seemed to leave her. "It's so hard to tell, isn't it? Gentlemen don't have the same thoughts and goals as we ladies." Lottie thought for a moment and then said, "I'm not even sure they know themselves when they love a lady or not."

And that was the problem, wasn't it? Beatrice thought

morosely. How was she to understand Lord Hope's motives when she didn't understand the man himself? Had he made love to her because he cared for her? Or for some other, more subtle male reason, perhaps even simply lust? Making the whole situation more difficult was her own desire. Deep inside, a part of her simply wanted him, whether or not he felt the same. And that, she knew, was dangerous. She risked dreadful hurt if all the emotion was only on her side.

At that moment, the carriage pulled up in front of Mrs. Postlethwaite's town house, and Beatrice's thoughts turned to other matters. "Do you see Mr. Wheaton's carriage?"

She glanced up and down the crowded street. Two more carriages were behind them, and a pair of burly men loitered by the house next door. Her eyes narrowed, but they looked nothing like the toughs who had attacked her and Lord Hope the other day. These men were much better dressed for one thing.

"No," Lottie replied. "But he will've entered through the mews so as not to draw attention to himself."

That certainly made sense. This was only the third clandestine meeting of Mr. Wheaton's Veteran's Friends Society. Had it not been a Society meeting, Beatrice probably wouldn't have gone out at all; Jeremy's death was too recent. But she was here for Jeremy in a way. He'd been the one to introduce her to Mr. Wheaton's thoughts on soldiers and what happened to them after they retired from His Majesty's army. Jeremy had cared deeply for the men who had served under him. He'd wanted them to retire with enough money that they wouldn't end up begging on the street. One so often saw those pitiful creatures, still in their red coats, missing limbs or an eye, sitting on corners with a tin cup in their hands. Beatrice shuddered. She felt sure Jeremy would understand her being here today.

She descended the carriage with Lottie and gave their names to the butler who answered the door. In a moment, they were being shown into a small but neat sitting room, and Mrs. Postlethwaite was greeting them.

"How kind of you to join us, Miss Corning, Mrs. Graham." Mrs. Postlethwaite took their hands and squeezed them gently before leading them to a settee.

She was a lady of middling years, dressed always in somber gray and black, her silver hair pulled away from her face into a simple knot and covered with a cap. Mrs. Postlethwaite had lost her husband, Colonel Postlethwaite, to action on the Continent some years ago. She'd been left with a comfortable annual income and time on her hands, which she'd decided to put to use helping the men her husband had led. The men she'd come to know over the years as she followed Colonel Postlethwaite on campaign.

Beatrice glanced about the room as their hostess led them in. Besides Mrs. Postlethwaite, there were perhaps half a dozen gentlemen of middling to elderly years. Beatrice and Lottie were the only other ladies in the room, and Beatrice was grateful that their hostess had made the case to include them in the society.

Mrs. Postlethwaite served tea and small, hard biscuits, and then Mr. Wheaton entered the room. He was a young man of average height, his light brown hair clubbed back simply without powder of any kind. As usual, he wore a preoccupied frown. Mrs. Postlethwaite had once confided that Mrs. Wheaton was in poor health and had been confined to bed for some years now. To have an ailing wife and to deal with all the business being a member of parliament entailed must be a weary burden for the poor man.

Mr. Wheaton had a sheaf of papers in his hand, and he set these down on a table before clearing his throat. The room grew quiet. He nodded in acknowledgment of their attention and said, "Thank you, friends, for coming today. I have some matters of import that I'd like to discuss regarding the bill and the members of parliament we think we can count on to vote in its favor. Now, then . . ."

Beatrice leaned forward as Mr. Wheaton outlined his plans, but a small part of her mind thought about how Jeremy would've loved to be here. She'd not fulfilled her promise to him. He'd died before Mr. Wheaton's bill could be passed. She'd failed in that, but she vowed to herself that she wouldn't fail the bill itself. She'd do everything in her power to help the bill and all the soldiers who'd fought for England. The bill *would* pass. She'd see to it.

For Jeremy.

"THE MAN WHO led the attack on you is named Joe Cork," Vale said as he threw himself into a chair.

Reynaud looked up from the solicitor's report he was reading and stared at his old friend. He was in a small sitting room to the back of Blanchard House, which he'd commandeered as his study. There was an official study for the earl, of course, but the usurper held it at the moment, and Reynaud's solicitors were counseling patience. Thus this temporary refuge for business. He'd be damned, though, if he'd give up residence in his own house.

"You found him, then?" he asked Vale.

Vale screwed up his mouth into a comical face. "Not exactly found, no. The blighter appears to have disappeared. But several lowlifes identified him from the description given by my man, Pynch."

"Pynch?"

"I say, you don't know Pynch, do you?" Vale scratched his nose. "I acquired him after, well, after Spinner's Falls. He was my batman in the army and now serves as a rather uppity valet."

"Ah." Reynaud tapped the paper in front of him with his pencil. "And how does this pertain to the assassin?"

Vale shrugged. "Well, Pynch was the one I sent to make inquiries. Amazin' what he can worm out of the most tight-lipped fellows. But it seems this Joe Cork has flown the coop. No one's seen him for several days."

Reynaud leaned back in his chair. "Dammit. I'd hoped to find out who had hired him."

"It's a setback, I agree." Vale pursed his lips and stared at the ceiling a moment. "Have you thought about hiring guards?"

"Already have." Reynaud sat forward. "But not for myself. For Miss Corning. They came too close to her last time. If the knife wound had been a little higher . . ." He trailed off, not liking to think about it. He'd dreamed about Beatrice's blood on his hands last night.

Vale's shaggy eyebrows arched up his forehead. "Do you think they'll target her as well as you? Surely if you simply stay away from the gel, she'll be safe?"

"But I don't propose to stay away from her," Reynaud said.

"Ah." Vale stared at him for a moment, and then a wide smile spread across his face. "Like that, is it?"

"That," Reynaud snarled, "is none of your business."

"Indeed?" Vale was grinning like an idiot now. "Well, well, well."

"What is that supposed to mean?"

"I have no idea. I just like saying it. Well, well, well. Makes one sound uncommonly insightful."

"Not you it doesn't," Reynaud muttered.

Vale ignored him. "Have you asked the question yet? I'm rather good at it, if I do say so myself. I got three different ladies to agree to marry me while you were gone. Did you know? Some didn't actually make it to the altar, but that's another problem altogether. Perhaps you'd like some pointers on—"

"I would *not* like any pointers from you, damn your hide," Reynaud growled.

"But are you sure the chit even cares for you?"

Reynaud thought back to Beatrice eagerly parting her legs for him, her eyelids lowered, her throat suffused in a blush of desire. "I don't believe that's a problem."

"You never know," Vale said chattily. "Emeline threw me over for Samuel Hartley, and the man's not nearly as handsome as I."

Reynaud blinked. "You were engaged to my sister?"

"Didn't I tell you?"

"No, you did not."

"Well, I was," Vale said airily. "Not that it lasted once Hartley put his fascinatin' hooks into her. Now, my second fiancée threw me over for a curate."

Reynaud looked at him.

"A butter-haired curate." Vale nodded. "I assure you. 'Course, that's how I came to be married to my own sweet wife, but at the time you could've knocked me over with a feather. I don't suppose Miss Corning knows any butter-haired curates, does she?"

"She had better not," Reynaud growled. And right then he determined that this thing would not drag on with Beatrice. He needed a wife. She'd already given herself to him. It was as simple as that.

And tonight he'd prove it to her.

IN THE MIDDLE of the night, Beatrice woke and opened her eyes to a single candle shining in her bedroom. It should've startled her—frightened her, even—but instead she lay quietly and watched as Lord Hope set the candle on a small table near the door.

"What are you doing?" Beatrice asked.

"Coming to see you," he said, equally matter-of-fact. He had on a red and black banyan, and his head was bare.

He took off the banyan.

"*See you* seems to be a euphemism," she observed.

He paused, his hands on the buttons of his shirt. "You're right." And he drew the shirt off over his head.

For the first time, she felt a flicker of fear. He hadn't smiled. He was serious and intent, as if he performed a grim duty.

"You don't have to do this," she whispered.

"It seems I do," he replied. He sat on a chair to remove his shoes. "You seem to be uncertain of me—of us together. I intend to make sure there are no uncertainties after tonight."

She noted that he made no mention of love, and she felt disappointment shoot through her.

"Seducing me won't prove anything," she said.

"Won't it?" He sounded unconcerned. "That remains to be seen."

She watched him a moment as he stripped off his stockings, breeches, and smallclothes. He seemed entirely comfortable with his own nudity, but she felt her breath quicken. When he'd bedded her the day before, she'd been in shock, only half aware of what was going on. Now she was wide awake, her senses almost too alert to him. He stood tall and proud, his skin an even light brown over his entire body. His arms and shoulders were leanly muscled, like a laborer's. She remembered that he'd told her he'd had to hunt for his food. There was black curling hair on his chest, but it wasn't thick, and she could see the dark brown points of his nipples.

Her gaze wandered downward, drawn inevitably to what lay between his thighs. The hair was thick and black there, as if to highlight his cock, standing boldly. He was hugely erect, the veins of his penis standing out, the head glistening with moisture. The whole was beautiful and at the same time intimidating in his obvious intent.

When she raised her eyes to his, he was watching her. He nodded and cupped himself. "This is for you. Look your fill."

"What if I don't want it?"

"Then you lie."

That sent a spurt of anger through her. "I think I have the ability to know when I *want* something or not."

He shook his head. "Not in this case. You're new to

lovemaking. You haven't experienced a fraction of what can be between a man and a woman."

She was warm now, and wet, but she still addressed him testily. "And if you show me all that can be and I'm still not interested, will you desist then?"

"No." He strolled toward her, implacably confident. "You've given yourself to me. That choice has already been made."

"But why me?" She truly didn't understand. Why now? Why *her*? "Do you love me?"

"Love has nothing to do with it," he said, and pulled the covers from her body. "This is much more basic than love. You belong to me, and I intend to demonstrate that fact to you."

"Reynaud," she said softly, using his name for the first time, hating the pleading in her voice. She was so disappointed that this wasn't love to him. She wasn't interested in his "more basic" feeling. She wanted his love.

He climbed into the bed and reached for her chemise. She didn't resist him, because the reality was that she couldn't. He was right and a part of her acknowledged it. She had given herself to him. She did belong to him on some basic level that seemed to bypass love altogether.

And maybe, just maybe, she wanted to watch his face as he lost control in her again.

Then it was too late for analyzing and worrying. He'd bared her body, and she lay before him like a feast for a starving man. He just looked for a moment, sitting beside her, not moving, only his eyes roaming over her. She felt her nipples crest as if displaying themselves for him. His face was grave. He reached out and touched her right nipple with only one finger.

Lightly. Delicately. Devastatingly.

She swallowed, feeling the heat build at her center.

"You are so pretty," he said, his voice deep and rough. He circled that one nipple with his finger, his touch so light it might have been a feather, and she shivered. "Your skin seems to glow from within, and it's soft, so soft."

His finger wandered down, lightly tracing the undercurve of her breast and then skimming over her skin to her other breast. She breathed shallowly, the very lightness of his touch making her tremble with need.

"Your nipples are pink," he whispered, brushing over the tip. Her nipples were so tight they ached. "But they deepen to rose as they come erect. I wonder if I sucked them if they would turn red like cherries?"

She closed her eyes, feeling that one point of contact, so slight and so erotic. This wasn't what she'd expected when he'd declared his intent. She thought he would act quickly, consummate his desire in fast, hard moves.

Instead this was a slow, unhurried seduction.

His finger was wandering down over her ribs, gliding over her belly, circling her navel. She sucked in her tummy; the touch was almost tickling.

"So soft," he crooned. "Like velvet."

He was trailing lower, and her whole attention was focused on that finger and where it was headed.

"Spread your legs," he murmured.

Her heart leaped in alarm. "I . . . I . . ."

"Beatrice," he said darkly, "spread your legs for me."

Maybe it was because her eyes were closed—if they'd been open, if she could see him looking at her so intimately, she wouldn't have been able to do it. But as it was, she widened her thighs.

His finger dipped into her maiden hair, stroking through it. "So pretty, so sweet. I wonder what you taste like."

And something touched her tenderly below her maiden hair, and it was soft and wet and most definitely not his finger.

"Reynaud!" she cried.

"Shh," he whispered, his breath blowing across damp, excited flesh. "Quiet, now."

She bit her lips, her hands clutching anxiously at the bedclothes.

His tongue probed her folds, stroking and licking. He was so close he must be able to smell her, to taste her, and she struggled between appalled horror and trembling delight.

"Do you like this?" he murmured. His lips brushed her with every word.

"I . . ."

He parted her with his thumbs and blew softly. "Do you, Beatrice?"

"Oh, God!"

He chuckled then, like an evil demon, and said, "I think you do."

Then he was flicking his tongue against her so rapidly she couldn't think, couldn't squirm away. Not that she wanted to. He was relentless, untiring and thorough, focused entirely on that one point. Just when she thought she couldn't take any more—when her breath was coming in short quick pants—he opened his mouth around her bud and sucked strongly.

Beatrice pressed the back of her head into the pillow, her lips opening on a soundless scream. He was pulling, tugging on that small bit of flesh, his broad hands pressed against her thighs, holding her firmly open, and she couldn't withstand the sensation. Stars imploded within her, sending flashes of delight throughout her entire body. She jerked and jerked again, and then her limbs sank, weighted with pleasurable relaxation.

She opened her eyes to see him crawling up her. First his chest and then his hips brushed against newly sensitized flesh, and then he settled his weight on her, flattening her breasts. He nudged her legs apart effortlessly.

"Reynaud," she breathed.

He looked into her eyes as he slid up a little, the broad head of his penis just kissing her entrance. He flexed his hips and began to breach her. Her eyes narrowed as she felt a pinch. It'd been only a day since she'd lost her virginity.

"Beatrice," he breathed.

"It hurts," she said, her voice small.

He nodded. "Keep your eyes on me."

She widened them, looking into his eyes. He had a tiny indent between his heavy eyebrows.

He shoved a little.

She felt the stretching of her inner muscles. He pressed steadily, widening her, burrowing into her flesh. Then he thrust suddenly and with definite force, and he was seated fully. She felt the pressure of his pubis against hers. His mouth thinned as if he controlled himself by only a tiny thread.

"Now," he said. "Now, I make love to you."

He bent and kissed her with his open mouth, his tongue conquering her lips as his penis conquered the quivering flesh between her legs. He withdrew and slid back into her, more easily this time, hitching himself up her body a little. He caught her beneath the knees and widened her legs, settling in, making himself comfortable in her body.

She moaned and moved beneath him. For, unlike the previous night, what he was doing to her now began to feel good. More than good.

She slid her hands to the back of his head, rubbing the bristling hair there. She felt full, heavy, as if waiting for something. He still kissed her, and she nipped at his lip, provoking a growl from him.

He quickened his thrusts.

She grasped his shoulders, slippery from sweat, and hung on, urging him with her mouth and hands. More. More. More.

Until she crested, suddenly and without warning, a blissful, glorious explosion of pleasure. She would've shouted had her mouth not been full of his tongue. He stiffened and lifted himself up, and she saw that he had reached his point as well. His nostrils were flared, his teeth gritted and bared. He thrust home one last time, shuddering, and then he let his head hang, his arms straight and holding up his upper body.

He inhaled deeply.

She kneaded the muscles of his back, wanting still to feel this connection.

He raised his head and she saw his face. Stark. Uncompromising. And without a trace of pity.

"You are mine," he said.

Chapter Twelve

Longsword and the princess entered the castle's gates together, but the minute their feet touched the ground, a thorny vine leaped up, faster than a bolt of lightning. Higher and thicker it grew until a giant, thorny hedge so entirely surrounded the castle's keep that not a stone could be seen. Longsword began to hack at the hedge, but as soon as he cut a branch, another one grew in its place.

"It is impossible!" the princess cried.

But Longsword took a deep breath and ran at the hedge, swinging his sword faster than the eye could see. He slashed so quickly that the blade of his sword glowed white-hot, and as it cut, it seared as well so that the branches could not grow again. In a minute more, Longsword had cut a path through the magical hedge. . . .

—from *Longsword*

"Did you know that Lottie Graham has left her husband?" Adriana asked as she forked up a piece of fish at dinner. She looked at it critically and said, "Do you think he's taken a mistress? Or two? Because most men do take a mistress at one time or another, and I think the practical wife just doesn't notice, don't you?"

Hasselthorpe took a drink of wine, boggling a bit at the thought of Adriana lumping herself together with "practical" wives. They sat in their town-house dining room tonight, a rather overdecorated room featuring gold putti and pink marble. He didn't bother answering the question, because she rarely needed anyone else's help in her conversations. This was handy, especially on the rare occasions when they dined just the two of them, for he had no need to follow the conversation.

And indeed she continued after swallowing. "I can't think of another reason for her to leave Mr. Graham. He is so handsome, and every time I see him, he compliments me on my appearance, and I do like a gentleman who can turn a pretty phrase."

She poked her fish and frowned. "I don't see why fish should have so many bones, do you?"

Hasselthorpe, who'd been contemplating Blanchard's lessening odds of keeping his title, looked up rather irritably. "What are you talking about, Adriana?"

"Fish," his wife said promptly. "And their bones. They have so many, and I really don't see why. They live in the water."

"All creatures have bones." Hasselthorpe sighed.

"Not worms," his wife said. "Nor jellyfish nor snails, although they do have shells, which I suppose are very like bones, on their outsides."

He winced. Why must she always blather about nonsense?

"But I'm not sure a shell is quite the same as a bone on the inside." She scowled quite adorably down at her haddock. "And, in any case, I still don't understand why they should have so many and they be always waiting to catch in one's throat."

"Quite." Hasselthorpe gave up trying to follow his wife's mind and instead drank some more wine. Sometimes it helped get him through these meals. How had Hope survived that second assassination attempt? Dammit, why the man should survive two attempts in as many weeks and not a scratch on him was—

"Do you suppose he doesn't wash?"

Hasselthorpe paused, his wineglass halfway to his lips. "The fish?"

"No, silly!" Adriana trilled gaily. "Mr. Graham. Some gentlemen seem to think washing their persons is merely a monthly or even yearly chore. Do you suppose Mr. Graham is one of them?"

Hasselthorpe blinked. "I—"

"Because I can't think why else Lottie would leave him." Adriana frowned. "He's quite handsome and rather charming, and I haven't heard any tales of him keeping one mistress, let alone two, so I think it must be the washing, or rather *not* washing, don't you?"

He sighed. "Adriana, my dear, as usual, you've quite lost me."

"Have I?" She smiled at him. "But I didn't mean to. And you considered one of the leading lights of the Tories, too!"

Her ripple of laughter was enough to send a less-strong man into raving fits. As it was, Hasselthorpe merely smiled tightly at his spouse. "Very amusing, my dear."

"Yes, aren't I?" she said complacently, and went back to poking at her fish. "I think it must be the reason you love me."

Hasselthorpe sighed. Because despite her lack of wits, her irritating conversation, and her execrable decorating style, Adriana was quite right about this one matter.

He did love her.

Beatrice should've been suspicious when Reynaud sat down to dine with her and her uncle that night. But alas, she was so caught up in keeping her expression bland that she didn't even think to wonder what he was doing there. So when he made his request over the fish, she nearly choked on her wine.

"What did you say?" Beatrice gasped when she'd caught her breath.

"I wasn't addressing you," the odious backstabber said.

"Well, you'll certainly have to consult with me about the matter eventually," she said tartly.

A muscle in Reynaud's jaw flexed. "I doubt—"

"No!" roared Uncle Reggie.

Beatrice's head swung toward her uncle in alarm. His face had gone the color of claret. "Please don't excite yourself—"

"It's not enough that you must have my title, but now you want to take my niece as well," Uncle Reggie bellowed. He thumped a fist on the table, making the silverware jump.

"I haven't accepted Lord Hope's proposal," Beatrice said soothingly.

"But you will," Reynaud said, crushing what little peace she might've gained.

"Don't you threaten my niece!" Uncle Reggie shouted.

Reynaud's lips thinned. "I don't threaten; I merely state a fact."

And they were off again. Really, she might not be in the room for all the attention they paid her. She was like an old bone for two dogs to fight over. Beatrice sighed and sipped her wine again, taking a surreptitious glance at Reynaud. He'd left her the night before, soon after their lovemaking, and she hadn't seen him all day. He wore the white wig tonight and a dark wine-red coat that made his tanned skin and dark brows and eyes exotically elegant. The iron cross earring swung against his jaw as he tilted his head mockingly at her uncle. It made him look a bit like a pirate, she decided.

He caught her eye and winked. The rest of his face was impassive, and it was done so quickly that she almost thought she imagined it. Did he really want to marry her? The notion sent an odd shaft of warmth to her center.

Until Uncle Reggie said, "You only want to marry my niece to bolster your claim that you aren't mad. It's another scheme to steal my house and title!"

Well, that was certainly dampening. Beatrice stared fixedly at her wineglass. She would not weep before these two buffoons.

Reynaud's upper lip curved in a sneer as he leaned toward her uncle. "It's my house. How many times must I repeat it? The title, the house, the monies, and, yes, now Beatrice. They're all mine. You hold them by the tips of your fingers, and they're all sliding away from you, old man. That's why you're so angry."

Beatrice cleared her throat. "I don't know if either of you are aware, but I *am* sitting right here."

Reynaud lifted an eyebrow at her, his black eyes glinting. "And would you care to join this conversation? Perhaps list one or two reasons a match between us is inevitable?"

How dare he? The threat was implicit that he'd inform Uncle Reggie that he'd bedded her if she balked at this proposal.

Beatrice lifted her chin, addressing her remarks to Uncle Reggie, although she still held Reynaud's gaze. "I'm sure Lord Hope would be amenable to some sort of compensation for your stewardship of the earldom, Uncle."

A corner of Reynaud's mouth quirked as he mouthed, "Touché."

But Uncle Reggie roared, "Be damned afore I accept help from this popinjay!"

Beatrice sighed. Gentlemen could be so extraordinarily pigheaded sometimes. "It wouldn't be help, Uncle; it would be compensation for years of service to the title. Really, it's only fitting."

Reynaud leaned back in his chair, watching her speculatively. "Whatever makes you think I'd give anything to this usurper of my title?"

"Well, fitting or not, I'll not accept it." Uncle Reggie pushed back his chair with a *thump*. "I'll leave you, Niece, to the company of this man you've chosen over me."

And with that, he left the room.

Beatrice looked down at her plate, trying to conceal the hurt she'd felt at her uncle's words.

"He's an old fool," Reynaud said softly.

"He's my uncle," Beatrice replied without looking up.

"And because of that, I should reward him for stealing my title?"

"No." She finally inhaled and met his eyes. "You should gift him with a small remuneration, because it would be the right and honorable thing to do."

"And if I don't give a damn about honor?" he asked softly.

She watched him, lounging in his seat, his hand on the stem of his wineglass, idly twirling it. But she knew he was far from idle. He'd maneuvered her here to this spot, this confrontation as deftly as a chess master cornering his opponent's queen. *And why not?* a small part of her whispered. If she was Reynaud's wife, she would be in a much better position to urge him to vote for Mr. Wheaton's bill.

And she could press for concessions before surrender.

Beatrice leaned back in her chair, mimicking his pose. "Then you might do it for me."

"Might I?" he said. He contemplated her, as if weighing her worth against that of his pride.

"Yes," she said firmly, "you might. You might also offer Uncle Reggie permanent residence here in this house should you regain your title."

"And what would be the benefit to me of this magnanimous gesture?"

"You know full well what the benefit would be," she said, tired suddenly of this game. "Don't play with me."

He took a sip of his wine and set down the glass with finality. "Come here."

She rose and circled the table to stand before him. Her heart was beating fast and hard, but she tried to regulate her breathing. Tried not to show how desperately he affected her.

He pushed his chair from the table and spread his legs. "Closer."

She stepped between his legs, almost touching him, the blood rushing in her ears.

He looked up at her, a conquering warrior. "Kiss me."

She inhaled and then bent, placing one hand on his shoulder. Her lips brushed his, and she could not control their trembling. She straightened and looked at him.

"More," he said.

She shook her head. "Not here. The servants will return soon to clear the meal."

"Then where?" His eyelids drooped lazily. "And when?"

In answer, she held out her hand, for she didn't trust her voice. Her action went against everything she'd ever been taught about how a lady should behave. She'd been told this was wrong. That it would only lead to sorrow and disgrace. But her heart seemed to be telling her otherwise, and she had no one else to turn to anymore. Jeremy was dead. Uncle Reggie had made clear his displeasure with her, and Lottie was too wrapped up in her own life right now.

Which left only herself to depend upon.

He placed his hand in hers, and she gave a gentle tug to make him stand up. She led him from the room without saying anything. The hall was deserted; Uncle Reggie didn't like servants hanging about during the evening meal. She went quickly up the stairs, aware of Lord Hope's footsteps, steady and almost ominous behind her, but she didn't look back. She took him to her own room and then paused beside the door.

"Wait here," she said, and slipped inside. Quick was in her room, as she was every night, waiting to help her ready for bed.

"That'll be all," she said to the maid. "And, Quick?"

The maid turned toward her. "Miss?"

"Be sure you don't see anything in the hall."

Quick's eyes widened but she was far too good a servant to comment. She merely curtsied and left the room.

Beatrice took a deep breath and went to the door, opening it. He was outside, leaning against the wall, waiting patiently.

"Come in," she said, and he straightened.

SHE STOOD TALL and prim and invited him into her room. He'd been there twice before, of course, but not at her invitation.

And that, it seemed, made all the difference.

He could feel his pulse pounding at his temple and lower down at the base of his cock. He was already erect, already ready for her, but he moved slowly. The wolf never wanted to frighten the deer until it was ready to pounce.

She turned and went to the fire, stirring it with a poker. "Will you undress?" Her hand might be steady, but her voice was high and thready.

"Why don't you?" he asked, his own voice deep.

"Oh." She set aside the poker and reached for the laces of her bodice.

"No." In two strides he was beside her, staying her hands. "Why don't you undress me?"

She looked at him, her face pinkening into a blush, her bottom lip caught between her teeth. He wanted to bite that lip himself, wanted to catch her in his arms and bear her to the bed, a warlord with a prize. But he needed to have her come to him of her own volition. True, he'd coerced her, but she'd led him here. He'd take that small bit of free will on her part.

Beatrice set her hands on his coat, slowly, carefully pushing it back over his shoulders. He moved his arms to help her take off the garment, but otherwise he simply watched her. As a young officer in His Majesty's army, he'd been to brothels in London and the New World. Had sampled the favors of accomplished courtesans. Yet the sight of this properly brought-up woman taking off his coat was far more erotic than anything he'd ever seen at a brothel.

She folded his coat and carefully set it aside. Then she stood on tiptoe and pulled off his wig. He ran his hands over his head, scrubbing at the stubble of his hair.

"I confess it made me sad the day you cut your hair," she said quietly.

A half smile curved his lips. "You'd rather I sport that wild mane?"

"No." She reached up to smooth her palms over his head. "But maybe a little more hair than this. Your long hair softened your aspect a bit. I never really realized until you cut it all off. Without it, you look so . . . ruthless."

But he was ruthless. Didn't she know that yet? He didn't say the words, merely watched her as she bent her head over the buttons of his waistcoat. The only sounds in the room were her breathing and the slide of fabric over the bone buttons. She reached the end and pushed the waistcoat off his shoulders. She laid the waistcoat aside and hesitated for a moment, staring at the expanse of his white shirt. Had her feet grown cold? Only two days before, this woman had been a virgin, and now he was demanding that she undress him. He should take pity on her.

He grasped her hand and brought it to his chest. "The shirt next, I think."

She began on the buttons without comment, though her breath was coming faster. The brush of her fingers, even with the fine linen in between his skin and hers, was a torture. She undid the last button, and he raised his arms so she might draw the shirt off over his head.

She licked her lips and glanced shyly at him from under her brows. "Everything?"

"Everything."

She nodded, inhaling as if bracing herself, then reached for the fall of his breeches. He placed his hands on her shoulders as she worked, watching the top of her head rather than where her hands were. She knelt to pull down his breeches, and he stepped out of his shoes and stockings as well. When she reached for his smallclothes, her hands shook.

"Are you frightened?" he murmured.

She paused and looked at him. "No."

And he had to clench his jaw. That frankness, those wide gray eyes above freckled cheeks, looking at him so innocently, without guile or disguise, nearly undid him.

She took off his smallclothes, and he kicked them aside, entirely nude now

"What do you want me to do?" she asked.

He looked at her, kneeling at his feet, her face so close to his crude erection, and several thoughts came to his mind, but in the end, he held out his hand to her. "Come here."

She rose, placing her hand in his, and he led her to the bed. He threw back the covers and laid himself down on his back, propped against several pillows. He pulled her down beside him so she was sitting on the bed, her gown bunched around her folded legs. "Make yourself comfortable."

"I am."

He wanted to smile but found that the rigidity of his muscles prevented him. "Then touch me."

"Here?" She placed her palm on his chest, trailing her fingers through his chest hair.

"Yes." He watched her face as she explored, circling a nipple. She looked intent, solemn like a little girl mastering a needlework stitch.

"Does it feel sensitive? Like mine?" she asked.

He half closed his eyes. "It's sensitive."

She nodded and stroked lower, following the trail of his body hair to below his navel. Here she hesitated again, looking uncertain.

He waited, not prompting her anymore. Slowly she ran her fingers through his pubic hair, drawing ever closer to his cock. When at last she touched him—too delicately, too softly—he let out a sigh.

Her eyes darted to his face, watching him as she traced up his shaft. He held her gaze, though he wanted to close his eyes at the sensation of her warm fingers on his flesh. When she reached the head of his cock, she looked down again, bending closer as if fascinated.

"It's so hard," she murmured, circling the helmet. "Does it hurt?"

"No." His mouth twisted. "Not as long as it's eventually assuaged."

Her eyes rounded. "You mean it stays like this until—"

He laughed rustily—it was that or howl. "No. It, ah, goes away after a bit if there's no stimulation."

"Stimulation." Her brows drew together as she watched her fingers wrap about his length.

"The sight of a pretty woman, the sound of her voice, the feel of her hand," he said.

"*Any* pretty woman?" She frowned.

Ah, it wasn't funny, not with his cock in her small, sweet hands, but his mouth quirked. "Some more than others."

"Hmm."

He cleared his throat. "You can stroke it."

She tentatively rubbed him with her fingers.

"More firmly," he murmured, and wrapped his hand about hers to show her. He brought both their hands up his cock, strongly enough to move his skin over the stony flesh beneath, and then down again. He let go of her hand.

She did it again.

"Ye-es," he hissed.

"You like that?"

"God, yes."

She worked him, and he lay like a pasha among the pillows, letting her pleasure him. He watched her through slitted eyes, her prim hair still in its bun, her serious expression, and the shockingly raw sight of his bare cock between her hands. And he might've let her complete him, but then she leaned closer and with one finger touched the tip of his prick, where the clear liquid had begun to leak. He was strong and had quite a bit of willpower, but he wasn't made of stone.

He jackknifed up, grabbed her about her middle—ignoring her startled squeak—and twisted to put her facing the headboard of the bed.

"Hold on there," he ordered in a guttural voice.

Thank God she obeyed without questioning what he was about, because he wasn't going to last long in any case. She was up on her knees, and he simply flipped her skirts up over her hips. He ran his hands over her sweet arse, reveling in the feel of silky flesh.

"Part your legs for me," he said, and she widened her stance with a gasp.

He touched her there, between her thighs where she was the softest, the most tender, and he parted the wet folds, revealing the gleaming center. He heard her whimper. That's what he wanted, his woman, bent over, wet and waiting for him. He took his cock in hand and guided himself to her. Christ! She was so tight, so slick. He felt sudden moisture in his eyes, and he closed them so she wouldn't see. This was mating, a good and proper fuck, nothing else.

But even as he worked his flesh into hers, he knew that he lied to himself. Everything about her—her scent, her feel, her warm body, and her small panting sounds—meant something more to him. *Home*. She was home and he'd returned to her.

He pushed the odd thought aside as he shoved the rest of his length into her. He grasped the headboard on either side of her arms and enclosed her within his embrace. She shivered, and somehow that little movement was the final straw. He began thrusting, hard and fast, the feel of her slippery flesh around him, holding him so tightly, sending him completely out of control. She arched her hips, pushing back at him, and he leaned forward, biting her nape to keep her steady. She gave a cry, high and helpless, and then her cunny was flexing about him, milking his cock as she came.

He growled deep in his throat and felt his balls draw up tight as he released himself within her. Even then he didn't stop but kept humping her as he filled her with his seed. When finally he fell to the side, every bone in his body was liquid. He had only enough presence of mind to clutch her to his chest as she snuggled against him.

And then he fell asleep.

HER BEDROOM WAS nearly black when Beatrice woke. Her stays were poking into her side. She'd fallen asleep fully dressed. She turned her head and saw the glow of the fireplace embers and then felt the shift as Reynaud moved beneath her hand. Carefully, quietly, she rose from the bed. He lay, sprawled nude, on her sheets as if he had every right. She smiled a little sadly. He'd probably say this room and this bed belonged to him, too.

Beatrice shook down her skirts and left the room. No doubt she was quite rumpled, and she wouldn't like to meet anyone in the hallways, but it must be past midnight by now, and she didn't think she would. Farther down the hall was Uncle Reggie's room, the crack beneath the door dark. She felt a pang of regret that they'd parted on such a sour note at dinner. Would he ever come to terms with Reynaud's reappearance? Would he forgive her for the choices she'd made—and would make in the future?

She'd lived in this house for years, and she had no need of a candle, even in the near total darkness. She felt her way to the main staircase and crept down like a mouse. On the main level, a footman passed in the hall below, making his way toward the kitchen and the servant's quarters. Beatrice stood still on the stairs, waiting patiently, and then descended silently once he'd disappeared into the depths of the house. She stopped in the dining room to light a candle from the embers in the fireplace, and then she took it to the blue sitting room. Here she set the single candlestick on a small table. She sank into a settee facing the door and curled her feet beneath her on the seat.

The portrait of Reynaud was directly in front of her. Beatrice rested her chin in her hand, looking at him. All those nights, sitting with him, dreaming of what the man behind the laughing eyes was really like. And now she knew. She knew him, had been his lover, and he was nothing like what she'd imagined in her girlish fantasies. He was hard, sometimes cruel, driven to obtain what he wanted; he was maddening and frustrating. He was also intelligent, caring of those he considered his own—like Henry—complex and baffling and an exquisite lover.

He was a passionate man.

Even if that passion wasn't for her, she admired it. Beatrice stared into those black eyes, so physically similar and so spiritually apart from the living, breathing man. Marriage to him would not be easy. There was a very good chance that it might turn into a disaster, in fact. But to save Uncle Reggie, she would take that chance.

The sitting room door opened and Reynaud stepped in, unconsciously standing next to his painted image. He wore his breeches and shirt. His gaze found her, and then he turned to see what she'd been looking at. He studied the portrait of himself for a long moment before looking back at her.

"Are you all right?"

She nodded.

He paced toward her, his eyes never leaving her form. When he was directly in front of her, he stopped and held out his hand. "Will you marry me, Beatrice?"

She placed her hand in his. "Yes."

Chapter Thirteen

Before Longsword and the princess stood a huge black tower—the castle's keep. Longsword advanced upon the tower warily, the princess behind him, but the tower remained ominously quiet. A single huge wooden door stood on the tower's facade, its surface scarred and charred as if it had withstood some terrible battle. Longsword pulled open the door, and beside him Princess Serenity gasped.

For inside the tower, her father the king lay bound in chains. Around the king flew three dragons, each larger than the last. And the smallest dragon was twice as big as the one Longsword had killed just the day before. . . .

—from *Longsword*

The freshly turned earth was already frosted over, hard, frozen, and final. Beatrice bent and placed her handful of Michaelmas daisies on the grave. There wasn't a stone yet, merely a wooden marker. The words JEREMY OATES had been crudely scrawled on it.

"I'm going to marry him," she whispered to the pitiful marker.

The words were carried away by the wind, whipping through the small graveyard. As if to emphasize her sorrow, the day was overcast and gray. Jeremy's parents had chosen to bury him in a little churchyard outside of London proper. It wasn't even a family plot. Perhaps they thought by hiding him so far out of the way, they could forget him altogether. Jeremy would've smiled and reminded her that a tiny graveyard was just as good as a cathedral when one was dead.

Beatrice shook her head and frowned fiercely to hold back the tears. Jeremy wouldn't have cared, but she did. This was no way to memorialize a good man. She closed her eyes for a moment, simply remembering him, and the tears came anyway, whether she wanted them to or not.

When she finally opened her eyes again, her face was cold and wet, and her head was beginning to ache, but oddly she felt better.

She wiped her cheeks and glanced at the churchyard gate. Reynaud leaned against the stone wall there, waiting patiently for her. The drive here had taken over an hour, and he hadn't made any complaints. Although he hadn't visited her room in the week since she'd agreed to marry him, Reynaud had made sure to attend her when he could. Of course, he was a busy man. He was in daily consultation with solicitors about the estate and his title, and he met with his friend Lord Vale very often as well. Beatrice frowned. She wasn't quite sure what they discussed, but she was glad that they seemed to have recovered from their initial animosity.

She knelt to touch the frozen earth over Jeremy's grave one last time, and then she stood and dusted her hands. In the spring she'd bring some lily-of-the-valley pips to plant here. That would keep him company. Beatrice began picking her way back to the carriage and Reynaud. The little churchyard was sadly neglected, the stone path overgrown with weeds. The wind blew her skirts against her legs, and she shivered as she neared Reynaud.

"Finished?" He put a hand under her elbow to steady her.

"Yes." She looked up into his stern face. "Thank you for bringing me."

He nodded. "He was a good man."

"Yes, he was," she murmured.

He handed her into the carriage and then climbed in after her, knocking against the ceiling to signal the coachman. She watched out the window as they pulled away from the cemetery, then looked at him. "You're still set on a marriage by special license?"

"I'd like to be already married by the time I go before parliament," he said. "If it bothers you, we can plan a celebratory ball in the new year."

She nodded. After the passion of his seduction, the practicality of his plans for their marriage was slightly dampening. She remembered Lottie's words about a gentleman filling a position with his choice of wife. Wasn't that what she herself was doing? Reynaud needed her as his wife so that he could convince others he was sane. Nathan needed Lottie as his wife to further his career.

The only difference was that Lottie had believed her husband loved her.

Beatrice had no such illusions.

She straightened a bit and cleared her throat. "You never told me how you eventually escaped the Indians. Did Sastaretsi give up his hatred of you?"

He flattened his mouth impatiently. "Do you really wish to hear this tale? It's boring, I assure you."

His stalling tactics only made her curiosity keener. "Please?"

"Very well." He looked away and was silent a moment.

"Sastaretsi?" she prompted softly.

"He never did give up his hatred of me." Reynaud was staring out the window, his long nose and strong chin in profile against the wine-red squabs behind him. "But that first winter was hard, and it was all we could do to simply find enough food to feed everyone. I was an able-bodied hunter, if not a very good one at first, so I think he laid aside his animosity for a little while. We were all weak from hunger anyway."

"How dreadful." She looked down at her lap, examining her fine kid gloves. She'd never wanted for food in her life, but she'd seen beggars on the street now and again. She tried to imagine Reynaud with that gaunt face, that glittering, desperate expression in his black eyes. She didn't like the thought of him suffering so terribly.

"It wasn't amusing, certainly," he said. "I remember once finding a she-bear. They crawl into the biggest trees, into holes in the wood, to sleep the winter away. Gaho's husband showed me how to look for the claw marks on tree trunks that meant a bear lay above. After we'd killed the bear, they skinned a part of it and ate the fat without waiting to light a fire and cook the meat."

"Dear God." Beatrice wrinkled her nose in disgust.

He looked at her. "I ate it as well. The flesh steamed in the cold winter air, and it tasted of blood, and I gulped it down anyway. It was life. We'd had no food for three days prior to that."

She bit her lip and nodded. "I'm sorry."

"Don't be," he said quietly. "I survived."

He folded his arms across his chest then and leaned his head against the squabs, his eyes closed as if he slept, though she doubted he did.

She bowed her head. He'd survived, and she was glad, truly, but at what cost? What he'd endured had changed him. It was as if he'd passed through a fiery furnace, burning away all the parts of him that had been soft or sentimental, leaving a fire-hardened inner core, impervious to pain or feeling, perhaps impervious to love as well.

She shivered at the thought. Surely he felt something for her?

They spent the rest of the carriage ride home in silence, and it was only when the carriage slowed before Blanchard House that she glanced out the window.

She leaned a little forward. "There's another carriage blocking the way."

"Is there?" Reynaud said absentmindedly, his eyes still closed.

"I wonder who it could be?" Beatrice mused. "Now a gentleman is getting out, and he's handing down a very elegantly dressed lady. Oh, and there's a small boy as well. Reynaud?"

She said the last because he'd suddenly sat up and twisted around to look out the window.

"Christ," he breathed.

"Do you know them?"

"It's Emeline," he said. "It's my sister."

HE'D DREAMED OF this moment for nights on end during his captivity: the day when he'd finally see his family again. The day when he'd see Emeline.

Reynaud climbed slowly down from his carriage, turning to help Beatrice alight. Her face was excited, beaming with curiosity, wonder, and joy, as if she reflected all the many emotions he ought to be feeling right now. He hooked her hand through his elbow and approached the small group of people gathered on the top step of Blanchard House. The man was turned toward them with a face that looked impassive from this distance, but it was the woman Reynaud focused on. She'd only just now noticed their presence and was turning quickly. Her face went blank, and then an expression of rapturous joy spread over it.

"Reynaud!" she cried, and started down the steps. The man—it must be Hartley—caught her under the arm, slowing her, and for a moment Reynaud felt anger rise in his breast.

Until he saw why Hartley urged her to slow down.

"Oh, my," Beatrice breathed.

Emeline was quite obviously enormously pregnant. Seven years ago, she'd been a young mother and a bride. Now she was married to a different man and was expecting her second child. He'd missed so much.

So much.

He and Beatrice reached the bottom of the steps just as Emeline and Hartley made the street. Emeline stopped suddenly, staring at him, then reached out a hand, touching his cheek in wonder.

"Reynaud," she breathed. "Reynaud, is it you?"

He covered her fingers with his hand, blinking back the moisture in his eyes. "Yes, it's me, Emmie."

"Oh, Reynaud!" And suddenly she was in his arms, and he was awkwardly hugging her close around the bulk of her belly. She felt so sweet, his little sister, and he closed his eyes, simply holding her for a moment.

She pulled away at last and smiled, the same smile she'd had since the age of ten, and then frowned. "Oh, fustian! I'm going to cry. Samuel, I need to go inside."

Hartley whisked her inside the town house, and Reynaud and Beatrice followed more sedately. The boy trailed his mother, but he darted glances over his shoulder at him. Reynaud remembered Daniel as an infant, hardly able to walk the last time he'd seen him. Now he was almost as tall as his mother.

Reynaud nodded at the boy. "I'm your uncle."

"I know," Daniel said, dropping back to walk beside them as they moved down the hall. "I've got a pair of your pistols."

Reynaud's eyebrows rose. "Do you?"

"Yes." The boy looked a bit worried. "I say, can I keep them?"

Beside him, Beatrice smothered a giggle. Reynaud turned a quelling look on her before addressing the boy. "Yes, you may."

They were in the sitting room now, and Beatrice left his side to order tea and some type of refreshments.

"Did the Indians draw those birds around your eye?" the boy asked.

"Daniel." Hartley spoke for the first time, his voice even. He said nothing more, but the boy ducked his head.

"Sorry," he mumbled.

Reynaud nodded and took a seat. "Yes, the Indians tattooed my face."

Beatrice returned at that moment and met his gaze. Her eyes were filled with sympathy, and the sight warmed his chest. She sat down next to him and tucked her hand under his.

She cleared her throat. "I'm Beatrice Corning."

He squeezed her hand in gratitude.

Emeline sat a little straighter, rather like a birding dog at the sight of a grouse. "Tante Cristelle said you were engaged to be married to my brother."

Beatrice glanced at him and then said brightly, "Yes. We hope to have a small wedding soon. Miss Molyneux didn't tell us you were coming. Were you expected?"

"Evidently not." Emeline pursed her lips. "I wrote, of course, to say that we'd be coming, but the letter must've gone astray. Samuel has business to attend to in England, and I'd hoped to visit with Tante. As it was, we quite surprised her with our arrival in London, and then she startled us with her news that Reynaud was alive."

"Wonderful news." Beatrice smiled.

"Yes." Emeline cast a quick, curious glance between him and Beatrice. "I'm sorry, but aren't you related to the present Earl of Blanchard?"

"The usurper," Reynaud growled.

"I'm his niece," Beatrice said.

"And my soon-to-be wife," he stated.

"Hmm. About that," Emeline murmured. "Tante said you'd only been home for less than a month."

Beatrice stirred beside him. "I'm afraid Reynaud swept me off my feet."

Emeline was frowning now, which irritated Reynaud. Seven years apart and his baby sister thought she could tell him how to live his life? He opened his mouth but felt a sharp elbow in his side. Surprised, he glanced down at Beatrice, who was looking quite sternly at him.

As if by some feminine cue, the talk turned to lighter matters then. Hartley explained his business dealings in Boston and London, and Emeline told the story of how they'd met and what had happened since Reynaud's absence, her news little different than that he'd heard from Tante Cristelle, but it was wonderful to hear her voice. Reynaud let the talk flow about him, content to simply sit and listen to his sister and Beatrice. This was his family now.

Finally, Emeline declared herself weary, and Hartley leaped to help her up from her seat.

As the ladies made their farewells, Hartley turned to Reynaud and said quietly, "I'm glad you made it home."

Reynaud nodded. He was home now, wasn't he? "I hear you ran through the woods to bring back the rescue party for those who were captured."

Hartley shrugged. "It was all I could do. Had I known they'd taken you alive, I would've searched until I'd found you."

It was an easy vow to make, seven years after the fact, but Hartley's face was grave, his eyes serious and intent, and Reynaud knew the other man meant it.

"You didn't know," he said, and held out his hand.

Hartley grasped his hand and shook it firmly. "Welcome home."

And Reynaud could only nod again and look away, lest he lose his composure entirely.

Reynaud escorted Emeline and her family to the front door, then returned to the sitting room to find Beatrice pouring herself another cup of tea. He paced to the mantel, paused to glance at a small shepherdess—had it been his mother's?—then went to the windows. All the while, he felt Beatrice's gaze on him.

She set her cup down on the table beside her and eyed him. "Are you feeling well?"

He scowled out the window. "Why do you think something is wrong?"

She raised her eyebrows. "Forgive me, but you seem restless."

He inhaled, watching a carriage rumble by below. "I don't know. I have Emeline back, my family back, but something's still missing."

"Perhaps you need time to adjust," she said quietly. "You've been seven years away, lived a very different lifestyle. Perhaps you simply need to settle."

"What I need is my title," he growled, turning to her.

She looked at him thoughtfully. "And when you have the title and all that goes with it, you'll be content?"

"Are you suggesting otherwise?"

She glanced down at her teacup. "I'm suggesting that you might need more than a title and money to be happy."

His head reared back as if struck. What was this? Why did she challenge him now? "You don't know me," he said as he strode to the door. "You don't know what I need, so please refrain from speculating, madam." And he left her there.

A week later, Beatrice hid her trembling hands in the folds of her wedding dress. It was quite a smart frock. Lottie had said that just because she was having a hurried wedding didn't mean she couldn't have a new dress for it. So she wore a lovely shot silk that changed from green to blue as she moved. But despite the beauty of her new gown, she couldn't control the trembling of her fingers.

Perhaps this was normal wedding-day nerves. She tried to pay attention to the bishop marrying her and Reynaud, but his words seemed to run together into a senseless stream of droning sound.

She very much hoped she wasn't about to faint.

Was she doing the right thing? She still didn't know even as she stood at the altar. Reynaud had promised to care for Uncle Reggie, had promised to let him live in Blanchard House no matter the outcome of the fight for the title. She'd made Uncle Reggie safe, and perhaps that was reason enough to marry this man, even if he didn't love her.

He didn't love her.

Beatrice frowned down at the posy of flowers in her hands. She'd wanted a man to love her for herself, but she was marrying a man out of cold calculation instead. Was that enough? She wasn't sure. Reynaud might never soften his heart sufficiently to love her. In the last few weeks, he'd seemed harder than ever, more focused on his goal of attaining his title and the power that went with it. If he never came to love her, could she endure this marriage?

But then Reynaud turned to her and placed a simple gold ring on her finger and kissed her gently on the cheek. Suddenly the whole thing was over, and it was too late for second thoughts or regrets. Beatrice drew a deep breath and placed her hand on Reynaud's elbow, holding more tightly than she normally might have.

He leaned his head closer to hers. "Are you all right?"

"Yes. Quite." A wide smile seemed to be frozen on her face.

He glanced at her dubiously as he led her through the small crowd of well-wishers. "We'll be home soon, and if you'd like, you can go lie down."

"Oh, but we have the wedding breakfast!"

"And the wedding night," he whispered in her ear. "I don't want you too ill to enjoy that."

She ducked her head at that to hide a pleased smile. The fact was, he hadn't done more than kiss her chastely on the lips since their engagement, and a small part of her had begun to wonder if he'd already lost interest.

Evidently not.

He handed her into the carriage to the cheers of the crowds and then hastily entered. He smiled at her as the carriage pulled away. "Does it feel different, being married?"

"No." She shook her head, then thought of something. "Although, I suppose I'll have to get used to being Lady Hope, won't I?"

He scowled. "It should be Lady Blanchard." He looked out the window. "And it will be soon, too."

There was nothing more to say to that, so they rode in silence until they came to the town house. Many of the guests had already arrived and were entering the town house as Beatrice descended the carriage. She mounted the steps of Blanchard House with Reynaud, feeling odd. This was still her uncle's home, but very soon it would be hers and Reynaud's only—if he won back his title. She would be reversing positions with Uncle Reggie, and the thought was not a comfortable one.

Inside, the dining room had been laid ready for a feast. Yards of frothy pink fabric lined the table, and for a moment Beatrice felt for how horrified Uncle Reggie would've been at the expense. He sat at the head of the table already, looking rather subdued and sad. He refused to meet her eyes.

Reynaud sat her next to Uncle Reggie as was proper and then was distracted by a guest. For a moment, Beatrice was quiet.

"It's done, then," Uncle Reggie said.

She looked up and smiled. "Yes."

"Can't back out now."

"No."

He sighed heavily. "I only want the best for you, m'dear. You know that."

"Yes, I do, Uncle," she said softly.

"The blighter seems to care for you." He placed his hands on the table and looked at them as if he'd never seen the like before. "I've noticed how he watches you sometimes, as if you're a jewel he's afraid of losing. I hope he treats you right. I hope you're very happy."

"Thank you." Beatrice felt silly tears—so close to the surface all day—start in her eyes.

"But if he doesn't," her uncle said, in a low voice, "you always have a place with me. We can move out of this damned house, find another by ourselves."

"Oh, Uncle Reggie." She caught her breath on a laugh that was almost a sob. Dear, dear Uncle Reggie, so disapproving of her choice yet unwilling to abandon her entirely.

She was dabbing at her eyes with a handkerchief when Reynaud took the chair next to her. He scowled at her. "What has he said to you?"

"Shh." Beatrice glanced at Uncle Reggie, but he was talking to Tante Cristelle. "He's been very nice."

Reynaud grunted, not looking particularly convinced. "He's an old blowhard."

"He's my uncle and I love him," Beatrice said firmly.

Her new husband merely grunted.

The breakfast was long and sumptuous, and when it was finally over, Beatrice was ready for a nap. But she rose and prepared to say farewell to her guests.

Near the end of the line were Lord and Lady Vale. The viscount started talking to Reynaud, and for a moment Beatrice and Lady Vale were together alone.

"He's very pleased with this union," Lady Vale said quietly.

Beatrice looked at her, surprised. "Viscount Vale?"

The other woman nodded. "He's been quite worried about Lord Hope. This whole business of your husband returning alive has been a shock to him—a good shock, of course, but a shock nonetheless."

Beatrice raised her eyebrows.

"He's worried about how Lord Hope has changed."

"He's darker," Beatrice murmured.

Lady Vale nodded. "So Vale tells me. In any case, he was very happy that you consented to marry Lord Hope."

Beatrice wasn't sure what to say to that, so she merely nodded.

The viscountess hesitated a moment. "I wonder . . ."

Beatrice looked at her. "Yes?"

The other woman seemed a tad embarrassed. "I wonder if I might give you a rather unusual wedding present?"

"What is it?"

"It's a job, actually, so if you don't want it, please do say so, and I won't be put out."

Beatrice was intrigued now. "Tell me, please."

"It's a book," Lady Vale replied. "I was told some time ago by a friend that you bound books as a hobby."

"Yes?"

"Well, this has been something of a project of mine," Lady Vale said almost shyly. "It's a book of fairy tales that originally belonged to Lady Emeline—and your husband."

Beatrice leaned forward. "It belonged to Reynaud?"

Lady Vale nodded. "Emeline found it last year, and she asked me to translate it—it was in German. Once I translated it, I had it transcribed by a friend, and I was wondering if you might like to bind it for me? Or rather for Emeline. I'd like to give it to her eventually so she can have it for her own children. Will you help me?"

"Of course," Beatrice murmured, taking the other woman's hands. She was filled with a kind of pleased delight, as if Lady Vale had somehow given her an entry into the St. Aubyn family. "I'll be happy to."

* * *

"BEATRICE LOOKS LOVELY," Nate said as he sidled up to Lottie after the wedding breakfast.

"Yes, she does," Lottie replied without looking in his direction. "I hadn't realized you were invited to the wedding."

She stood just inside the front doors of Blanchard House, waiting for her carriage to be brought round. Even though she made sure not to glance at him, she was vividly aware of his deep blue coat and breeches, the white of his wig and neck cloth making him look very nice indeed. She was probably the only one aware that the cuff of that particular coat was fraying and needed mending. She'd forgotten to point it out to his valet before she'd left, and apparently no one else in the house had noticed.

His handsome face darkened. "Didn't you? I could've sworn I saw you glancing my way at the church."

She smiled tightly. "Perhaps you thought everyone was watching you? You are such an ambitious young member of parliament."

Nathan's lips tightened but he merely said, "It's a good match. Beatrice seemed very happy."

"Hmm. But then it's only been three hours."

"Your cynicism ill becomes you."

"Oh, that's right. You prefer a lady to pretend happiness," she said sweetly.

"Actually, I prefer a lady who is happy in reality, not just pretense," he said.

"Then perhaps you should've paid more attention to your lady," she snapped.

"Is that it?" He moved closer to her, almost touching

her shoulder with his chest, speaking low and intensely. "Would you come back if I promise a trip to the theater or ballet? Perhaps bring you sweets and flowers?"

"Don't paint me a little child."

"Then tell me what you want," he hissed, his normally congenial face twisted with anger. "What did I do that was so wrong, Lottie? What'll make you come back? Because the gossips are in a frenzy over your defection. My reputation—my career—can't take much more of this."

"Oh, your career—" she started.

But he interrupted her, something he'd never done before. "Yes, my career! You knew when you married me that I was a career politician. Don't act the wounded innocent now."

"I knew you had a career," she said quietly. "What I didn't know was that it consumed your life—your heart—so much that you had no room for a wife."

He pulled back to eye her. "I don't know what you mean."

"Don't you?" Lottie shot back. "Well, perhaps you should think about it a bit, then."

And she walked out the door before he could reply—or before she could burst into tears.

Chapter Fourteen

At the sight of Longsword and the princess, the three dragons flew at them, enormous claws extended, fire roaring from their jaws. Longsword braced himself and swung his mighty sword. THWACK! The smallest dragon fell to the ground, screaming in pain from a mortal wound to its breast. But the remaining dragons separated and attacked him from both sides. Longsword slashed at the one before him even as he felt the rake of fiery claws on his back. He turned, falling to one knee. The remaining dragon—the biggest dragon—shrieked in triumph and swooped down to finish the kill. . . .

—from *Longsword*

By the time night fell, Beatrice was a bundle of nerves. She was no longer a virgin, so perhaps she shouldn't have been nervous—after all, what did she have to fear? But despite their physical familiarity, she felt in some ways that she knew her husband less now than she had weeks ago.

Perhaps one never really understood a man, even after one had accepted him into one's body. It was a gloomy thought to have on one's wedding night, and Beatrice frowned as she removed the pearl drops from her ears. The earrings had been Aunt Mary's, and she wondered what that imminently practical woman would've thought of her marriage. Would she have approved of Reynaud? She wouldn't have liked the high-handed way he'd treated Uncle Reggie; that was certain. Beatrice felt a twist of remorse. Had this day been one enormous mistake?

On that thought, Reynaud entered the room. Beatrice dismissed Quick with a soft word. She'd moved into the countess's rooms, unused since Reynaud's mother had occupied them. Uncle Reggie still had possession of the earl's room, at least in name—he'd left the house for the night. Beatrice had half expected Reynaud to take advantage of her uncle's absence to assume control of the master bedroom. But he hadn't.

Once again he'd surprised her.

He strolled toward her now wearing only his breeches and shirt under a deep gold banyan. That, together with the earring swinging near his jaw and the tattoos of the flying birds, made him look like some exotic prince. One that might lounge on mountains of silken pillows while he was administered to by a harem of dark beauties. Beatrice shied at the thought. She was no harem beauty.

Perhaps that was why her voice seemed a little high as she said, "There's some wine and biscuits and also some sweetmeats on the table there by the fire. Perhaps you'd like me to pour you a glass?"

"No." He slowly shook his head as he advanced on her. "I'm not thirsty for wine."

"Oh." *Oh, goodness.* She should make some sophisticated comment, something that would make him think her more than a rather naive lady of not very much experience.

A corner of his mouth twitched up, and now he looked like a rather dangerous exotic prince. Beatrice backed up a step, and her bottom hit the bed.

"Nervous?" he asked, sounding as if he were trying to be innocent and failing abysmally.

"No," she said, and then honesty compelled her to immediately amend her statement. "Well, yes. Yes, I am a bit nervous. I'm not really the seductive type."

"No?"

"No," she said almost tartly. "I'm practical and straightforward, and I've never had gentlemen crowding about me."

He cocked an eyebrow, which, what with the tattoos and all, made him look positively diabolical. "No admiring swains, no lovers prostrate with despair?"

She winced. "I'm afraid not. I'm just an ordinary English girl."

"Thank God," he said, and he was suddenly so close to her that she could feel the heat of his body, even through her chemise and his banyan. "I'm glad no other man saw your sweet inner core. I think I might have to kill him if there was another man."

He said it lightly, but Beatrice shivered at the dark undertone to his language. Was he merely seducing a new wife on their wedding night, or was he speaking some kind of truth?

Was he really attracted to her?

Oh, how she wished he was! To be wanted simply for herself and no other reason was a desperate desire within her. But she was distracted from the thought, for he'd bent his head, lowering it so that he could lay his lips just at the juncture of her shoulder and neck. The sensation was an odd one, part ticklish, part erotic. She actually felt the frisson spike from her shoulder to the juncture of her thighs. Dear God, if he could do this with only a kiss on her *shoulder,* for goodness' sake, she had no hope. How could she be an equal in this marriage if his mere touch turned her into a puddle of yearning?

She couldn't. She was going to have to take her ordinary English-girl ways in hand and turn them around somehow. She might not be able to tell him that she loved him, but she could certainly show him with her body.

With that thought in mind, she reached for her husband. Her hands slid along the silk of his banyan, feeling the heat of his body beneath. He'd ordered her to undress him that last time. This time she'd wait for no instructions. She peeled the banyan from his shoulders. He was still kissing her neck, but he made a small growling sound in his throat at her action.

She took that as encouragement.

Next she unbuttoned his shirt, glad to see again the expanse of his chest. He had a lovely chest, wide and muscled and still tanned a dark brown. She urged him to raise his arms and drew off the shirt. Perhaps it was because she was trying to go slow, to seduce, but this time she felt something on his back that she hadn't the last time. She threw his shirt down next to his banyan and ran her hands around his sides to his back. There were bumps there. How odd. She frowned, exploring them with her fingers. It was almost as if—

He took her hands away from his back, holding them between their bodies as he kissed her passionately. His tongue invaded her mouth, and she pursed her lips about it, sucking. He let go of her hands, and she slid them over his chest, glorying in the feel of his skin. Her hands wandered lower and reached the waistband of his breeches. Blindly she began searching for the buttons, a job made harder when he began caressing her breasts with his hands.

She tore her mouth away from his, panting. "You're distracting me, doing that."

"What, this?" he asked innocently, and then pinched her nipples.

"Oh!" She got the first two buttons opened on the fall of his breeches and inserted her fingers inside, brushing against hard flesh.

Reynaud muttered under his breath, then abruptly let her go to shuck his breeches and smallclothes. "Let's continue this on the bed."

He backed to the bed, pulling her with him, and then lay against the pillows. She climbed in beside him, sitting on her knees. He stretched, his arms curving over his head. The hair under his arms was black and thick, and his upper arms bulged with the flex of his muscles. Beatrice felt her belly warm at the sight. She lowered her eyes. His penis was straight now but not yet fully erect. The last time they'd made love, he'd directed her explorations. Right now, though, she wanted to do only what she wished.

She leaned a little forward and stroked over his cock,

and it bobbed in acknowledgment. She knew that he liked a firm touch—he'd shown her that before. She circled him, just under the swollen cap, measuring his width with her thumb and forefinger.

He shifted beneath her. "Come here."

She crawled up him then, this big man who belonged to her now, and when she reached his face, she cupped him between her palms and kissed him. His experiences might've made him hard, cruel even on occasion, but she rejoiced in them if they brought him home alive.

So she kissed him, deeply, moving against him, and he arranged her as he liked, pulling her legs over his hips on either side and drawing them up until she nearly sat on him. She pulled back to look a question at him and he nodded.

"Ride me."

She lifted herself up and drew off her chemise so that she might be as naked as he. This was the consummation of their marriage, and she wanted to meet him as an equal, bare before God. When she lowered herself, her wet folds met his hardness.

She looked at him. "You do it this time. Put it in me."

He met her eyes and reached down between them, his hand right there, brushing against her.

"Like this?" he asked, and she felt that first push, that stretching and yielding as his head breeched her.

"Yes, like that," she whispered, entirely enthralled by what he did.

His lips tightened.

She leaned a little forward, grasping his shoulders, and then he shoved up and suddenly was all the way in. They were joined together. Bound by their bodies and the vows they'd made. She trembled a little at the thought, and her eyes met his. Did he feel the importance of the occasion as well? She couldn't be sure; his eyes were black and fathomless, impossible to read.

"Ride me," he said again.

So she did. She rose up carefully, letting him slide from her depths and then shoved herself down, gasping as he refilled her. His eyes half lowered, his upper lip drawn back from his teeth. He palmed her breasts with his big hands, flicking over her nipples with his thumbs, and she fought the urge to close her eyes. This was important. This was an act of holy significance, and she wanted to be aware of every bit of it.

She leaned forward, grinding herself against him, and quickened her pace. It was coming soon now, that awful bliss. She could feel her body tightening as she rode toward her release. His cock was hard and slick, and she swiveled on it, grinding her folds against him, pleasuring herself even as she pleasured him. His head was arched back, his eyes slitted. She darted forward to lick his nipple and he moaned. She watched him as his clever black eyes unfocused. Watched him as he opened his mouth and shouted. He arched under her, his body a taut bow, and she clutched his shoulders to keep her seat even as she spasmed, sweet pleasure flooding her belly.

She fell against his heaving chest, openmouthed, and tasted the salt on his skin even as another wave hit her. She closed her eyes and buried her face against his strong neck.

It was almost perfect.

She lay against him, on him, and felt his chest rise and fall beneath her. She could stay here forever, lost in the blissful aftermath, but eventually the outer world would intrude. So she asked the question she'd been withholding since he took off his shirt.

"How did you get the scars on your back?"

He should've realized she'd seen through his prevarication, but her question came as a shock nonetheless. For a moment, he considered ignoring it or even pretending he didn't know what she was asking about. But they were married now. She'd see it soon enough—and for many years to come, God willing.

So he braced himself and said, "I'll tell you once, but I don't ever want to speak of it again. Is that understood?"

He thought she might pout—or worse, be hurt by his curt tone—but she simply looked at him with those wide gray eyes. "Very well. May I see?"

He scowled, looking away, but then abruptly rolled so that his back was to her. She gasped and then was silent.

He closed his eyes, imagining what she saw. He knew from looking in the mirror—once and only once—that his back was a mass of scars. Thin white ones carved through the tan of his skin. Thicker, reddened scars, the ones she'd felt before, roped from midback to his right hip.

She asked, "How did this happen?"

He turned back to her, his eyes still closed. "It was the second winter I was with Gaho's family."

"Tell me," she said simply, and he opened his eyes to see her watching him. Her face was unlined, pure and beautiful, her gold hair still pulled back. She'd covered her breasts with the sheets, but her white shoulders were still revealed.

"We had more food come spring." He tilted his head to focus on the bed curtains. "The bears and deer might be thin from the winter, but they were easier to hunt. And the women gathered berries and vegetables from the woods and fields once the green things began to grow."

"Things were better," she said quietly. There was no impatience in her voice, though he was avoiding the reason for this tale.

"They were better, yes," he said. "And I should've been, too. There was finally plenty to eat after a winter of starvation. But the summers can be very hot in that part of the world. Hot and damp and I think the combination crept into my lungs. I became very ill with fever and purging. Gaho and the other women of her family tended me, but there are days I don't remember."

"How horrible," Beatrice said, lacing her fingers with his. "But you survived."

"I survived, but I almost didn't," he said. "And then . . ." Odd, he could feel the sweat start at his back at just the memory. He breathed deeply, fighting down the nausea that climbed his throat. He was so ashamed of the event.

"What happened?"

He drew a breath. "Gaho left the camp to attend a ceremony. She took with her both daughters and their spouses and her husband. I was too ill to travel. Only I, a few old men, a female slave, and Sastaretsi stayed behind. He said he had had an argument with the chief of the tribe Gaho and her family were to visit, but I think he stayed behind solely to kill me."

Beatrice was silent, but she squeezed his fingers.

Reynaud closed his eyes, trying to keep his voice

steady, remembering the horror of being in another's power. "My being alive deeply wounded Sastaretsi's pride. He took it as a personal affront that I hadn't been tortured to death for his greater glory. When we were so close to death that winter, I think he bided his time because the band needed another able-bodied hunter. But when I grew ill that summer, he saw his chance."

"What did he do?" she asked.

"He came for me in the night. I was tied down and still weak from fever. I had no chance, but I fought anyway. I knew that to be in his clutches would be fatal."

"But he caught you despite your resistance?" she asked softly.

He nodded. The words seemed stuck in his throat, and his chest hurt as if he could not draw breath. The feel of another man's hands on his throat, the knowledge that he wasn't strong enough to dislodge him. Suddenly he smelled bear grease, hot and sour and strong. Impossible. He was imagining it. No one smeared themselves with bear grease in England. But Sastaretsi had in that land so far away. The stink had been thick in his nostrils that night.

"Reynaud?" he heard Beatrice call. "Reynaud, you need not go on."

"No," he gasped. "No. I'll tell it this once and never again."

He lay for a moment, just breathing, trying to get the smell of bear grease out of his nose. Then he said, "He took me and bound me to a stake, and he beat me. Over and over. He broke sticks against my back, carved long lines into my flesh, and when I'd pass out, he'd wake me to start it all over again."

She was silent, both of her hands wrapped around his now.

"He meant to kill me. To torture me until I begged and then burn me alive."

"But you didn't die," Beatrice said. She sounded urgent. "You survived."

"Yes, I survived," he said. "I survived by refusing to utter a sound. No matter what he did to me, no matter how he beat me or made my blood flow, I remained silent. And then a miracle occurred."

He looked at her, his sheltered wife. He should've never told her this story, never let her hear about the darkness he'd been through, the shame.

"What happened?"

"Gaho and her family returned," he said simply, the words in no way conveying the wonder he'd felt at the event. "She told me later that she'd had a dream. In the dream, a snake was wrestling with a wolf, and the snake had its fangs sunk into the wolf's neck. She said that the voice of her father told her that the snake must not win. When she woke, she cut short the festivities and came home."

"What did she do?" Beatrice asked.

Reynaud's mouth twisted. "She saved me from death. She freed me, gave me water, washed and bound my wounds, and on the morning of the next day, she gave me a knife and bid me to do what I must."

"What did you have to do?"

"Kill Sastaretsi," he said. "I was weak, suffering from the loss of my blood and the illness, but I had to kill him. He knew what I would do—even without Gaho's permission, I could not let him live—and he could've run in the night, but instead he stayed to fight me."

"And you won," she said.

"Yes, I won," he said, feeling no victory at all.

She sighed and settled against his shoulder. "I'm glad. I'm glad you killed Sastaretsi. I'm glad you survived."

"Yes," he said softly. "As am I."

If he hadn't survived, she wouldn't be in his arms right now. That at least was good. Reynaud closed his eyes and felt the warm softness of his wife, the scent of woman and flowers surrounding him. He listened as her breathing evened and deepened as she fell asleep, and he gave thanks that he could experience this moment, this woman.

Perhaps it made everything that had come before worth it.

"YOU RISE EARLY for a man newly married," Vale said cheerfully a week later. "Perhaps you got too much sleep last night."

Samuel Hartley, walking on the other side of Vale, snorted. All three men were strolling a fashionable London street to discourage eavesdroppers, their pace swift, for the wind was quite chilly.

Reynaud scowled at them both. It was a beautiful morning, and he'd left his new wife sleeping in their warm bed so he might come consult with these two jesters.

And they didn't even appreciate his sacrifice. "We can give you some help, if you need it," Vale continued, as mindless as a jackdaw, "on the wonders of marital bliss. At least I can."

He looked at Hartley in question.

"As can I," the Colonial replied. His wide mouth was

straight, but something about it made it seem like he was laughing.

"I'm glad to hear it considering that you're married to my sister," Reynaud replied with an edge to his voice.

Hartley's expression didn't change, but his body seemed to grow more tense. "You should have no worries that I'll take care of Emeline."

"Good to know."

"Now, now," Vale said in a sickeningly sweet voice reminiscent of a nursery nanny. "I already gave him a drubbing for courting Emmie."

Reynaud raised his eyebrows. "You did?"

"He did not," Hartley said even as Vale nodded happily. "I threw him down the stairs."

Vale pursed his lips and looked skyward. "Not my recollection, but I can see how your memory of the event may've become hazy."

"Now, look here," Hartley began quietly, a thread of amusement in his voice.

"Gentlemen," Reynaud said, "we need to come to the crux of the matter, for it is indeed only a week after my wedding, and my lovely wife will eventually expect me to wait attendance on her."

"Very well." Hartley nodded, serious now. "What have you discovered since I last saw you, Vale?"

"There are rumors both that the Spinner's Falls traitor was a nobleman and that his mother was French," Vale said promptly.

Hartley cocked his head. "And where did you get this information?"

"Munroe," Reynaud said, Vale having informed him

at their previous meeting. "The first bit of information he had from a colleague in France; the second—"

"He got it from Hasselthorpe," Vale said, "although he didn't deign to share the information with me until a month or so ago."

Hartley looked at him curiously. "Why ever not?"

Vale looked embarrassed.

"I expect because of me," Reynaud said. "My mother was French."

"Of course." Hartley nodded.

"No doubt he thought that if I was already dead, there was no point in casting doubt upon my name," Reynaud said drily. "But since it happens that I'm not dead . . ."

"Now we need to think of who else among the survivors had a French mother," Vale said grimly. "Because whoever it is must be the traitor."

"But there isn't anyone else," Hartley said.

Reynaud grimaced. "If you're suggesting it's me—"

"Don't be ridiculous," Hartley snapped. "Just listen. There's you, me, Vale here, Munroe, Wimbley, Barrows, Nate Growe, and Douglas—I've talked to them all."

"Yes." Vale said. "And all are from London and probably had ancestors running about in blue at the time of the Roman invasion."

"Thornton, Horn, Allen, and Craddock are dead," Hartley continued, "but we investigated them thoroughly. None of these men had French mothers. There simply isn't anyone else who survived who could be the man."

"Then perhaps it was someone killed," Reynaud said softly. "Though that doesn't make sense."

"Who else had a French mother?" Vale asked.

"Clemmons had a French sister-in-law," Hartley said thoughtfully.

"Did he?" Vale stared. "I had no idea."

Hartley nodded. "He mentioned it once. A younger brother's wife, but she is dead."

"It doesn't fit in any case," Reynaud said impatiently. "Not unless Munroe's source was inaccurate."

Hartley shook his head.

"We need to talk to Munroe, see if he has any recollection," Reynaud said.

"I sent a messenger to him some weeks ago," Vale said. "But the man hasn't responded."

Reynaud grunted. Munroe was well known as a recluse, but they needed his memories, too. Perhaps he'd have to take Beatrice on a trip to Scotland.

But first there were more pressing matters to attend to.

"I plan to plead my case before the special committee of parliament tomorrow," he said to the other two. "So that I can regain my title as the Earl of Blanchard. And I'd like your help."

Vale raised an eyebrow. "You have it, of course, but what do you have in mind?"

Reynaud glanced about them to make sure no one was paying special attention to their conversation, then said, "I have an idea . . ."

BEATRICE LAID OUT her bookbinding tools carefully. She was always excited to begin a new project. She liked the anticipation of taking either an old and falling-apart book and putting it in order or taking what was essentially a sheaf of papers and turning it into a lovely book. It was almost an art, really. And she liked her tools and materials to be just so. The different-sized bonefolders aligned perfectly, the needles in their little box, the spools of thread lined up along the upper edge of her worktable. Later she'd look through her supplies of pretty paper and calf's hide, but for the moment she was interested only in cutting, folding, and sewing.

She hummed softly to herself as she worked, quite content, and thus it was with some surprise that she heard the clock in the hall and realized that it was almost time for dinner. Footsteps and male voices sounded in the hall, and she cocked her head, listening for her husband's voice. She looked up when the door to her little sitting room opened.

"Ah, there you are," Reynaud said as he walked in.

She smiled because it seemed she could not help but smile like a fool when she saw her husband. Every day she was married to him, she became more enthralled with him—and the knowledge made her uneasy. He'd still not said that he loved her, and he rarely showed her affection except in the privacy of their bedroom. Perhaps that was normal in a society marriage. Perhaps most gentlemen had trouble expressing affection.

God, she hoped so.

Beatrice looked down blindly at her worktable. "Did you enjoy your visit with Lord Vale?"

"*Enjoyed* may not be exactly the right word." He came to stand beside her table. "What is this?"

"A book I'm binding for Lady Vale." She looked up at him. "It's for your sister. Apparently, your nanny read it to you both when you were children."

"Indeed?" He bent over her shoulder, studying the

pages she was sewing. "I'll be damned. It's the tale of Longsword." A wondering smile lit his face. "That was a favorite of mine."

"Perhaps I should make a book for us as well, then," Beatrice said lightly.

"Why?"

"Well . . ." She looked down at her hands, carefully drawing the thread. "For our children, naturally. I'm sure you'd like to read them the book you enjoyed as a child."

He shrugged. "If you wish."

Beatrice wrinkled her nose, frowning fiercely to keep back silly tears. Childish of her to feel hurt at his dismissive tone. She drew a breath. "What did you talk about with Lord Vale?"

"My title," he said. "I intend to get it back tomorrow, if you remember."

"Of course." She busied herself with her tools. He sounded so sure, but the rumors of his madness still swirled about the streets of London.

"And once I obtain it, this house will be mine alone."

"I hope you'll not mind Uncle Reggie and me staying here as well." She tried to say the words lightly.

"Don't be silly." He frowned.

"I'm not silly," she said, pulling her thread too tight. "It's just . . ."

"What?" he snapped.

She laid down her work and looked at him, drawing a deep breath. "You're obsessed with regaining your title, your monies, your lands, everything you lost, in fact, and I understand that, but there's more than that for you to think about."

"What do you mean?" he asked, his face sharp and lined.

Beatrice lifted her chin. "Have you thought about what you'll do once you become the earl?"

"I'll manage my estates, attend to my land and investments." He waved an impatient hand. "What else do you suggest I do?"

She laid a hand on her worktable, clutching the edge. He could be so intimidating when angered! "You could do so much good as the earl—"

"And I intend to," he said.

"Do you?" Her voice was sharp, and she no longer cared. He was dismissing her and her thoughts out of hand. "Do you? All I've heard you talk about is your house, your monies, your lands. Have you no thought of how you'll live your life once you already have all those things? You'll sit in the House of Lords. You'll be able to vote on bills before parliament, even champion your own if you wish."

"You talk to me like I'm an infant, Beatrice," he snapped. "What are you trying to get at?"

"There's a bill that'll be presented tomorrow," she said before she could lose courage. "Mr. Wheaton's veteran's pension bill. It would provide for soldiers who are no longer in His Majesty's army, give them a pension so they wouldn't have to beg on the street—"

He waved a dismissive hand. "I don't have the time right now to—"

She slammed her hand down on her desk, making the book slide to the floor. He turned, looking at her in astonishment.

Beatrice drew herself up. "When will you have the time, Reynaud? When?"

"I've told you," he said coldly. "After I am certain of my title."

"You'll just suddenly start caring for others then? Is that it?" She'd begun to shake. This discussion was no longer about Mr. Wheaton's bill. It'd become bigger somehow. "Tell me, Reynaud, do you love me?"

He cocked his head, eyeing her warily. "Why are you asking me now?"

Hot tears stung her eyes, but she kept them open, staring at him. "Becuase I think you've kept your emotions under such tight rein for so long that you no longer know how to let them loose. I don't think you can care for others at all."

And she walked from the sitting room.

Chapter Fifteen

The princess shrank in fear, but though he knelt on one knee, Longsword did not flinch. He met the dragon's charge with the steel of his blade. Once, twice, thrice, he swung his mighty sword, and when at last the dust had cleared and all was silent again, there lay the great dragon, dying at his feet. And as the beast died, its form changed until a horrid hag lay in its place, for it was the evil witch herself who had assumed the shape of a dragon. Well! The princess was quite pleased, I can tell you. She rushed to release her father the king. When it was made known to him that Longsword had by himself defeated the evil witch, the king was happy indeed to give his only child as a reward. And so it was that Longsword married a princess royal. . . .

—from *Longsword*

It was well after midnight by the time Reynaud joined her in their bed. Beatrice lay still, feigning sleep. It was her wifely duty to let him make love to her if he so desired, but she certainly had no desire at the moment. Not when they'd argued. He probably hated her now for the blunt things she'd said, but she'd had to say them.

She'd married a man who thought only of himself.

So she stared into the darkness and breathed evenly and slowly, in and out, without hitch, as if she was deep in slumber. She listened as he undressed—the rustle of fabric, a soft mutter when he bumped into something—and she'd never felt so lonely in her life.

He blew out his candle, and the bed dipped and shook as he climbed in. The bedclothes tightened on her shoulder as he pulled them over himself, and then he lay still. She stared into darkness. The minutes ticked by, and for a bit she thought he might've fallen asleep.

But then he said, "Beatrice."

She didn't move.

He sighed. "Beatrice, I know you're awake."

She bit her lip. It seemed rather silly to continue to pretend sleep, but if she acknowledged him now, it would be an admittance that she'd pretended in the first place.

"I know I've disappointed you," Reynaud said quietly. "I know I'm probably not the type of man you would've wanted for yourself, had you had the choice."

She curled her fingers into the coverlet but still didn't say a word.

"But I'm the man you have, and that's final. You'll just have to make the best of it." He was quiet a moment. "And if you can't be happy with me tonight, do you think you could at least come lie next to me? Dammit, I've grown used to holding you while I sleep."

As olive branches went, it wasn't the most eloquent she'd ever heard, but it tugged at her heart anyway. Besides, she'd been the one to start the argument earlier. She'd been the one who chose to marry a man she knew wasn't perfect. By rights, it should be her extending her hand in peace. Beatrice rolled over and came to rest against him.

"That's better." He yawned and wrapped his arm about her, pulling her close. "You're so soft and warm." He was silent a moment, his breathing growing deeper; then he added sleepily, "And I like the smell of your hair."

His breathing grew sonorous, and Beatrice knew he was asleep, but she was still awake. She listened to his heartbeat, slow and strong under her ear, and the reassuring sound of his breaths. And she knew, suddenly and completely, like the last brick sliding into a wall, that she loved him, this strange angry, exotic man. Was her love enough for the both of them?

She pondered the question for what seemed a long while, but she still had no answers when at last she fell asleep.

SHE WOKE TO the slide of warm hands on her back, strong and steady, moving down, reaching her bottom under her chemise. She lay on her side in the big bed, facing away from him, cocooned in the covers and him, still mostly asleep. She could feel his humid breath against her neck. One of his arms lay beneath her; the other stroked her bottom. All along her back, he was a large, hot presence, surrounding and protecting her. She was embraced by his heat and his scent.

In the world between dreams and waking, she felt him move against her, his hard erection insistent, demanding. She sighed a little, burrowing her face into the pillow. The room was gray with dawn's advent, and she wanted him—needed him—even if he only desired her. The thought made her sad, and she pushed it aside, wanting to feel only him, to no longer think and worry.

He hooked his hands under her knees, curling them forward, parting her legs, and he moved into the space he'd created. He was larger now, his erection pressing against her bottom, hot and insistent. He slid forward and then his penis lay against her feminine flesh. She was wet, and he seemed just right there. Perfect, as if he'd always meant to be in that part of her. His cock glided through her folds, the head bumping her clitoris. She panted, suddenly overwhelmed by sensation. If only he loved her, too, this would be perfect.

But she would not think about that.

His hand caressed her hip and slid around to her front, petting her curling hair, pressing her just there. From behind, he withdrew his cock in a slow, sensuous caress and notched himself in her, intruding.

She moaned, threading her fingers with the hand that lay next to her cheek. It was suddenly too much, the sharpness of her desire mingled with the newfound knowledge of her love for him. Bittersweet tears pricked at her eyes.

He squeezed her fingers and thrust a little, his breadth shockingly large in this position. Her mouth opened in a soundless gasp, and she arched her back a little, tasting the salt of her tears on her tongue. He was slow but insistent, steadily pushing, filling her in gradual, devastating increments. She lifted her upper leg a bit, hooking it over his calf, and suddenly he was all the way in, his length stretching her. She closed her eyes, tilting her head back toward him in submission. He kissed her neck, openmouthed, still and large within her.

Then his hand moved, his fingers spreading to hold her femininity, and his middle finger pressed with exquisite accuracy on her sensitive bud.

Her hips arched into him. "Reynaud."

"Hush," he murmured against her neck.

He withdrew his cock, his flesh pulling against the walls of her core, and thrust hard. She had to push one hand against the bed to keep from sliding. He withdrew and thrust again and she moaned.

"Hush," he whispered, seductive and invisible behind her. She felt the rough wet slide of his tongue on her neck.

He jolted into her again. Steady, relentless. Each movement shocking in its own way. She closed her eyes, biting her lip. She wanted to push back. Wanted to jerk against him and make him go faster until she exploded. She wanted to scream aloud her love. But that knowing hand buried in the juncture of her thighs held her, imprisoned her so that he might pleasure himself and her at his leisure.

He ground into her, pushing his hips until she felt the press of his balls against her wetness, until she was stretched wide open and waiting for his next movement.

"Please," she whispered brokenly.

"Hush." He took the lobe of her ear between his teeth

and bit in warning, just as he withdrew and slammed into her again.

Her breath caught, and her heart stopped—perhaps it broke.

He twisted into her, large, male, demanding, and he slid his finger against her engorged clitoris, rubbing, pressing.

She couldn't stand it. She was going to explode, fly apart into a thousand small pieces that would never be put back together in this lifetime. She'd never be the same again. She shook her head, sobbing into the pillow, pressing her cheek against their clenched hands.

"Beatrice," he crooned, deep and seductive in her ear. "Beatrice, come for me."

And she did, crying, shaking, her body hot and needing more. Needing him even if he didn't need her.

He used his cock on her like a battering ram. Thrusting, pounding hard, and sparks of pure delight went off in her body, traveling through her veins, illuminating her limbs, shining like a sun within her.

He bit her shoulder and shuddered heavily against her, and she felt his fire flood her, joining and mixing with her light, combining to become an inferno.

THE SUN SHONE through the windows when Beatrice next woke. She lay and watched as Reynaud washed his face in the basin on the dresser. He'd donned smallclothes but nothing else yet, and the muscles of his back flexed as he moved, making the scars ripple.

"You haven't told me how you managed to escape your captivity," she said quietly.

Did it matter anymore? She didn't know. Perhaps not, but she still needed to know.

He turned, unsurprised, at the sound of her voice. "You're awake."

"Yes." She drew the covers up over her chin. It was warm, and the bed smelled faintly of their combined intimate scents. She rather wished she could spend all day in it and never have to get up to face her realities. Right here, right now, she could pretend she had a loving marriage.

"Will you tell me?" she asked softly.

He faced the dresser again and she thought he'd refuse. He took up a razor and a strip of leather and began stropping it. She'd noticed that although he had a very competent valet, Reynaud liked to do most of his dressing himself. Perhaps he hadn't yet gotten used to a personal servant.

"Many Indian captives never go home again," he said quietly. "They die in captivity not because their masters are so strong but because the prisoners no longer try to escape."

"I don't understand," Beatrice said.

He nodded. "It doesn't make much sense unless you've experienced it firsthand. I told you before that the Indians in that part of the New World adopt their prisoners into their family to take the place of family members who have died."

"But you said they weren't truly regarded as family. That their role was symbolic."

"Mmm." He finished sharpening his razor and laid it aside. "That's more or less correct. The prisoner takes the place of a working member of the family—say a hunter—so those skills can be fulfilled."

"But there's more?" she asked.

"Sometimes." He lathered his face with some soap from a dish. "I suppose that it's only human nature to become fond of a person one lives with day in and day out. One hunts with members of the band or family, eats and sleeps with them. It's a very intimate living arrangement."

She was silent as she watched him pick up the razor and make the first pass through the foam on the side of his face.

"Sometimes," he said quietly, "the captive becomes a true member of the family. He may take a wife and even have children by her."

Beatrice stilled. "Did you take an Indian wife?"

He rinsed the razor in the basin of water and looked over at her. "No. But it wasn't because I couldn't have."

"Tell me," she whispered.

He tilted his head and shaved the area next to his ear in short, careful strokes. It might've been her imagination, but it seemed to Beatrice that he took overlong at it. "After Gaho spared my life for the second time, she became rather fond of me—whether because of myself or because of her dream, I'm not sure. But, in any case, she determined that I should be content living among them, and she knew that if I had a wife and family, I would have reason not to try and escape."

"She meant to tie you to herself," Beatrice said.

He nodded and tapped the razor slowly against the porcelain basin. "Exactly. But Gaho had a problem. Both her daughters were already married, and although sometimes men of their tribe would take a second wife, the women never take a second husband."

"How unfair," Beatrice said drily.

A smile flickered across his face and was gone. "It wasn't my idea."

"Humph."

He turned back to the mirror over the dresser and said, "I spent that next winter recovering from my illness and injuries. In the spring, Gaho took me and tattooed my face with the image of one of her gods. She pierced my ear and gave me one of her own earrings. In this way, she signified that I was a good hunter, part of her band, and that she valued me. Then she sent word to another band of Indians whom she wanted to befriend. She sought to arrange a marriage between me and the daughter of a warrior."

She saw the muscle in his jaw flex. "In this way, the two bands would make peace and become allies."

"Was the girl pretty?" Beatrice asked before she could stop herself.

"Pretty enough," he replied, "but she was very young, not yet sixteen, and I didn't want to marry her. I didn't want a wife and children who would bind me more firmly to Gaho and her band. I wanted to come home—it was the only thing I thought of."

"What did you do?"

"I found a way to talk to the girl myself. It was forbidden in theory, but since we were supposed to be courting, the elders looked the other way. I found that the girl already had a secret beau, a slave like myself but from another tribe. After that, it was simple. I gave the other man everything of value I had, what furs and little trinkets I had saved up in two years' captivity. The next night, my prospective bride disappeared with her lover."

"That was kind of you," Beatrice said.

"No." He splashed water on his face and wiped away the last of the suds. "Kindness had very little to do with it. I was determined to escape. Determined to come home and recover the life that should've been mine. Had I been forced to marry that girl, it would've been easy to relax into that life. To become a member of Gaho's family in truth. To never see England again."

He threw down the cloth he'd used to dry his face and looked at her. His eyes were black and stark. "In fact, it was because of me that Gaho and her entire band were slaughtered."

"What?" Beatrice whispered.

He nodded, his mouth twisting bitterly. "It took me five years to gather enough funds so that when the opportunity presented itself, I could escape. In my sixth year, a French trader began visiting the camp, and little by little, I persuaded him to help me flee, even though it meant risking his own life. We walked for three days through the woods until we came to his camp. And there I heard that Gaho's enemies were planning to attack her band. I was half-starved and weary, but I tell you I ran back to that village. Ran back to save the woman who had saved me."

He looked down at his hands, flexing his fingers.

"What did you find?" Beatrice asked, because he had to finish this awful story.

"I was too late," he said quietly. "They were all dead, young and old, the camp a smoking ruins. I looked for

Gaho. I turned over the bodies, looking into each bloody face."

"Did you find her?" she whispered.

He shook his head slowly and closed his eyes as if to blot out a sight. "When I came to Gaho, I only knew her by her dress. I turned her and her brown eyes were staring up at me through a mask of blood. They were dull and lifeless. She'd been scalped."

"I'm so sorry."

His head jerked up, his face hardening. "Don't be. She was an old Indian woman. She meant nothing to me."

"But, Reynaud"—Beatrice sat up—"you said she saved you, treated you as a son. I know you were fond of her."

"You don't understand." He picked up his knife and stared at it a moment—so long she thought he might never finish. Then he said softly, "The band that attacked Gaho and her family was the same one she'd tried to make peace with five years before. The one I was to marry into."

Beatrice inhaled, not saying anything, simply watching him.

"If I was fond of her, I would've made that marriage. I would've ensured her village's safety. I didn't. I had only one goal the entire time I spent in her family—to come home. Nothing was more important." He slid the knife into the sheath at his waist. "After I buried Gaho, I spent months tramping through the woods, evading Indians and Frenchmen alike until I reached British territory. And every step of the way, I reminded myself that I'd sacrificed Gaho and her family for this freedom."

"Reynaud—"

"No." He looked at her sharply. "You wanted to know, so let me finish. I had very little funds and no friends. When I reached a port, I signed on as a cook on a ship to pay my passage home."

"You were ill and feverish when you got here," she whispered.

He nodded. "I lived on dried meat and berries for months in the woods. By the time I made civilization, I was mostly skin and bones, and the fare on a ship isn't particularly nourishing. I contracted some illness from the sailors and was feverish when we docked in London."

"You're lucky to've survived," she said soberly.

"I was driven," he said. "I wasn't going to die without seeing home again. And I made a vow when I stepped foot on that ship: This was the last time I'd ever serve another man. I'll never let myself be captured again, never be imprisoned to another's will. I'll die before I let it happen again. Because if I do, I'll have let her die for nothing. Do you understand?"

She stared at him, standing so proud and tall. The scars of his captivity were etched upon his back, his years of imprisonment illustrated by the tattoos on his face. He'd always have them with him, no matter where he went, no matter what he did. There was no way he could ever forget his captivity or his vow to never submit to another's will. He was a hard man, and his will was iron.

He nodded. "Now you know."

She swallowed, feeling a little sick but not wanting to appear weak before him. "Yes, now I know."

He turned his back on her and left the room.

Beatrice looked about the room, dazed. His story had been worse even than she'd expected, because now she *did* know: Reynaud would never let himself love her.

WHAT HAD POSSESSED Beatrice to make him tell that story? Reynaud ran down the stairs to the front hall. What did she want of him? Had he not been an attentive husband and a sensitive lover? What more did she need?

And why bring all this up today? His belly felt twisted in knots, and he absently rubbed it as he strode through the front hall. He needed his mind sharp and clear, uncluttered by emotional upheaval. Tonight he'd make amends for his abrupt exit—bring her those flowers that Jeremy had said she'd like. But right now he had an appointment with his solicitors to go over his petition to the special committee, and that he couldn't miss.

Reynaud was descending the front steps of his town house, his mind still occupied with thoughts of Beatrice, when he heard his name called. He turned and saw a vision from his past.

Alistair Munroe walked toward him, bearing the scars of ritual Indian torture on his face.

Reynaud flinched.

"Horrible, aren't they?" Munroe rasped in a raw voice.

Reynaud studied him. Munroe's right cheek was marred by the scars of knife wounds and burning sticks. A black eye patch covered the socket of one eye. Reynaud had seen the captured killed by Indians twice—one right after Spinner's Falls and again in his fourth year with Gaho's band. Her husband had disappeared for a month one summer and then returned with an enemy warrior he'd captured on a raid. The man had taken two days to die.

"Did you scream?" he asked.

Munroe shook his head. "No."

"Then you were a worthy captive," Reynaud said. "Had you not been rescued, you would've been tortured to death eventually. Then the men of the tribe would have cut your heart from your body, and all would have eaten a small piece of it so that they might take your courage into their own bodies and use it when next they fought."

Munroe threw back his head and laughed, the sound harsh and rusty. "No one has ever talked about my scars so frankly to my face."

Reynaud gestured, unsmiling. "They're badges of honor. I have the same on my back."

"Do you now?" Munroe looked at him thoughtfully. "You must've been a stubborn bastard to survive seven years a captive."

"You might say that." Reynaud cocked his head. "Have you been to see Vale yet?"

"Indeed I have, and he says you might have a small chore for me."

"Good man." Reynaud grinned. "Actually, I have two favors to ask of you. Let me tell you what I need done. . . ."

LORD HASSELTHORPE CLIMBED into his carriage and pounded his stick against the roof to alert the driver. Then he sat back and withdrew a memorandum book from his greatcoat pocket. His majority was thin, but he had no doubt they would easily vote down Wheaton's ridiculous veteran's pension bill. The government could ill afford to pay drunks and riffraff to lie about all day just because they once took the king's shilling. Still, it never hurt to be careful. He licked his thumb and turned to the first page in the little book and began to study his speech against the bill.

So intent was he on the points he meant to argue, in fact, that it was some time before he noticed that the carriage was driving by Hyde Park.

Lord Hasselthorpe scowled and leaped to his feet, knocking against the carriage roof. "Stop the carriage! Stop the carriage, I say! You're going in the wrong damned direction."

The carriage pulled to the side of the road and halted. Hasselthorpe prepared to give the idiot coachman a tongue-lashing. But before he could reach the carriage door, it was jerked open and a familiar face filled the doorway.

"What the hell are you doing?" Hasselthorpe roared.

Chapter Sixteen

So Longsword lived with the princess and her father in the royal castle, and his days were filled with ease and joy. The food was rich and abundant, his clothing warm and soft; he didn't have to battle any imps or demons, and the princess was delightful company. In fact, the more time Longsword spent riding with the princess, dining with her, and strolling the castle gardens, the sweeter his pleasure became, until he longed to spend all his days and nights with her forever.

But he knew he could not. His year on earth was growing to a close, and the Goblin King would soon demand his return. . . .

—from *Longsword*

Westminster Hall's stern Gothic architecture gave it a conservative air much admired by the majority of the older members of parliament. A corner of Reynaud's mouth curled up as he neared the imposing doors. He'd come here often as a young man, accompanying his father when he sat in the House of Lords. It was strange to enter now, knowing that he came to defend a title held by his father—a title that should've passed to him without any dispute at all. He squared his shoulders and thrust his chin out as he entered the facade. It occurred to him they were the same movements he used to make right before battle.

This, too, was a battle, but one he must fight with his wits.

Reynaud strode through the great vaulted hall, passing under the watchful eyes of the angels that lined the eaves, and proceeded to a dark back passage. This led down a short flight of stairs and to a series of dark-paneled doors. Outside one was a somberly dressed servant.

The servant bowed to Reynaud. "They're waiting within, my lord."

Reynaud nodded. "Thank you."

The dark little room he entered was sparsely furnished. Four rows of wooden benches sat facing a large wood table. Beside the table was a single tall chair. The room was loud with the voices of men, for the benches were nearly full. There were twenty members of this Select Committee for Privileges, appointed from the House of Lords to decide the matter of his title. As Reynaud found a seat, the chairman of the committee, Lord Travers, got up from where he'd been sitting with Beatrice's uncle on the front bench. He saw Reynaud, nodded, and went to stand before the tall chair.

"My lords, shall we begin?"

The room gradually quieted, although total silence

was not achieved, because several members continued to murmur, and one elderly lord was cracking walnuts in the corner, apparently oblivious to the proceedings around him.

Lord Travers nodded, gave a brief, dry outline of the case before the committee, and then called on Reynaud.

Reynaud took a deep breath, his fingers moving to touch where his knife usually hung by his side before he remembered he'd left it at home. He stood and strode to the front of the room and faced his peers. The faces that looked back at him were mostly old. Would they understand? Did they still have pity?

He took a breath. "My lords, I stand before you and plead for the title my father, my grandfather, my great-grandfather, and his father before him held. I ask you for what is only mine by birth. You have papers attesting to my identity. That, I think, is not at issue." He paused and looked at the men sitting in judgment of him. Not a one looked particularly sympathetic. "What is at issue is what my opponent intends to claim: that I am mad."

That caused several lords to frown and put their heads together. Reynaud felt his shoulder blades twitch. The tack he was taking was a risk, but a calculated one.

He let the murmurs die and then lifted his chin. "I am not mad. What I am is an officer of His Majesty's army, one who has seen perhaps more than his fair share of combat and hardship. If I am mad, then every officer who ever saw battle, who ever came home missing limb or eye, who ever dreamed in the night of blood and war cries, is mad as well. Shame me and you shame every brave man who has fought for this country."

The voices had grown louder at his assertion, but

Reynaud raised his voice to be heard over the murmuring. "Grant me, then, my lords, what is mine and mine alone. The title that belonged to my father. The title that in time will descend to my son. The earldom of Blanchard. *My* earldom."

There were frowns and voices raised in argument as he made his way back to his seat. As Reynaud sat down he wondered if he'd just won back his title—or lost it forever.

Algernon Downey, the Duke of Lister, was on the way to the House of Lords, but he paused on the front steps of his town house to give his secretary some additional instructions. "I've run out of patience. Tell my aunt that if she cannot keep figures, then she should hire someone literate to do it for her. Until then, I do not intend to give her any further monies this quarter. A few refusals of service from tradesmen may help her to be more frugal with her allowance."

"Yes, Your Grace." The secretary made a low bow.

Lister turned to descend his steps to the waiting carriage.

Or at least that was what he intended. Instead he stopped so suddenly that he nearly lost his footing. Waiting for him at the bottom was a tiny, beautiful woman in a bright green frock.

Lister frowned. "Madeleine, what are you doing here?"

The woman thrust out her chest, imperiling the fine silk of her bodice. "What am I doing here?"

Behind him, Lister heard a dry cough. He turned to see his secretary goggling at his mistress.

"Go inside and make sure Her Grace doesn't take a notion to come out the front door," Lister ordered.

The secretary looked a bit disappointed, but he bowed and went inside.

Lister started down the steps. "You know better than to visit my family residence, Madeleine. If this is some attempt at blackmail—"

"Blackmail! Oh, I like that! I like that indeed," Madeleine rcplied somewhat obscurely. "And what about *her*?"

Lister followed her pointing finger to find . . . "Demeter? I don't understand."

The blond lady thus addressed cocked a magnificent hip and folded her arms across her ample bosom. "And you think I do? I received this letter"—she waved an elegant-looking missive—"saying you need me at once and please come here, of all places, if I had any affection for you at all."

Lister drew himself up. His ancestors had fought at the Battle of Hastings, he was the fifth-richest man in England, and he was known for his ill temper. Two of his mistresses appearing at one time on his very doorstep was, of course, disconcerting, but a man of his experience, stature, and—

"And what the blazes is this?" Evelyn, the most strident of his mistresses, exclaimed as she came around the corner. Tall, black-haired, and imposing, she looked at him with the same wild passion that usually turned his loins to iron. "If this is your way of giving me my congé, Algernon, you will regret it, mark my words."

Lister winced. He hated it when Evelyn called him by his Christian name. He opened his mouth and then wasn't entirely sure what to say, a thing that had never before happened to him in his life. This experience was ominously close to one of those awful dreams even a man of his stature had once in a while. The nightmares in which one stood up to address the House of Lords and looked down to see that one was wearing only one's smallclothes. Or the nightmare in which all of one's mistresses somehow managed to be in the same place at the same time—and at his house, no less.

Lister felt sweat slide greasily down his back.

Of course, this wasn't quite all of his mistresses. If it were, his newest light o' love would have been here, and she—

A dangerously high phaeton rounded the corner, scandalously driven by a sophisticated woman, a little boy in flamboyant purple and gold livery behind her. Everyone turned to look.

Lister watched the vision approach with the fatality of a man who stands before a firing squad. Francesca drew the horses to a halt with a flourish. Her pretty little rosebud mouth fell open.

"What eez theez?" she cried in an excruciating French accent. "Your Grace, 'r you having zee joke wit' your poor petite Francesca?"

There was a long and awful pause.

And then Evelyn pivoted and stared dangerously at him. "Why does *she* have a new phaeton?"

It was at this moment, as the shrill voices of four slighted women rose about him, that the Duke of Lister saw a man across the street tip his hat. The man wore an eye patch.

Lister blinked. Surely it couldn't be . . .

But that thought was driven from his mind as the women converged on him. The House of Lords would have to wait.

REYNAUD GLANCED ABOUT the room, trying to judge his standing, but it was near impossible. The lords still talked avidly among themselves, with one or two throwing him curious glances. No one smiled at him.

Reynaud balled his fists on his knees.

The usurper took his spot before the table and cleared his throat. He began speaking, but his voice was so low that several lords shouted for him to speak up. Reginald paused, visibly gulping, and began again in a louder but slightly unsteady voice.

And suddenly Reynaud felt sorry for the man. Reginald was in his sixth decade, a short, stout, red-faced man who wasn't a good speaker. Reynaud remembered very little of the man. Had he come to Christmas dinner with his wife once when Reynaud was down from Cambridge? He couldn't remember.

The fact was that Reginald simply hadn't been important. He'd been a distant relation unlikely to inherit the title, since Reynaud was young and healthy. What a surprise it must've been when he received news that he'd become the Earl of Blanchard. Had he celebrated Reynaud's supposed death? Reynaud wasn't even sure he could hold that against the man. Becoming the Earl of Blanchard had probably been the high point in his life.

Reginald had stuttered to a halt. He'd really not had that much to say to begin with, his basic plea being that he held the title and was therefore the earl. The chairman nodded, and Beatrice's uncle resumed his seat with evident relief.

Lord Travers stood and called for a vote.

Reynaud felt the blood rush in his ears, so loud that at first he didn't hear the verdict. Then he did and a wide grin split his face.

". . . this committee therefore will recommend to Our Sovereign King, His Majesty George the Third, that Reynaud Michael Paul St. Aubyn be given his rightful title as the Earl of Blanchard."

The chairman continued with the litany of Reynaud's other titles, but he no longer listened. Triumph was flooding his chest. The lord sitting beside him clapped him on the back, and the man behind him leaned over the bench saying, "Well done, Blanchard."

Dear God, it felt good to be addressed by his title finally. The chairman wound down and Reynaud stood. The men about him crowded close, offering congratulations, and Reynaud couldn't help but feel a bit of cynicism at his sudden popularity. He'd gone from being a madman to one of the most influential men in the kingdom. Beatrice had been right. He had great power now—power he could use to effect good if he wished.

Over the heads of the crowd, he saw Reginald standing by the door. He was alone now, his power gone. Reginald caught his eye and nodded. It was a graceful gesture, an acknowledgment of defeat, and Reynaud wanted to go to him, but he was prevented by the press of bodies. In another moment, Reginald had left the room.

The committee began filing out, and Lord Travers came to offer Reynaud his congratulations. "That's done, then, what? I'll have the secretary draw up the official committee recommendation to be sent to His Majesty."

"Ah. As to that," Reynaud began, but there was a commotion in the doorway. A tall, ruddy-faced young man with strikingly prominent blue eyes came into the room.

"Your Majesty!" Lord Travers exclaimed. "To what do we owe the honor of your visit?"

"Come to sign a paper, what?" King George replied. "What a dingy little room this is." He turned and examined Reynaud. "You're Blanchard?"

"I am." Reynaud bowed low. "It's an honor to meet you, Your Majesty."

"Captured by savages, or so we're told by Sir Alistair Munroe," the king said. "Bound to be a good tale in that, what? We would be most pleased if you'd come to tea and tell us the story. Bring your lady wife as well."

Reynaud fought back a grin and bowed again. "Thank you, Your Majesty."

"Now, where's that recommendation?" the king asked, looking around as if it might appear out of thin air.

"You've come to sign the recommendation?" Lord Travers asked in mild astonishment. He snapped his fingers urgently at the servant by the door. "Walters, fetch a pen and paper, if you will. We must prepare the committee's recommendation for His Majesty's signature."

The servant left the room at a dead run.

"And then there's the writ so you can sit in the House of Lords," the king said cheerfully. He motioned to an attendant. "We've had it already drawn up, just in case."

"Your Majesty is quite prepared, I see," Lord Travers said somewhat drily. "Had I known Your Majesty's plans, I would've had some papers already prepared. As it is, we'll have to work fast, I'm afraid."

"Oh, yes?" The king raised his eyebrows.

"Indeed, sire," Lord Travers said somberly. "The House of Lords is convening at this moment."

"What the hell're you doing?" Lord Hasselthorpe roared. It was the Colonial, Samuel Hartley, climbing into his carriage as if he had every right.

"Sorry," the other man said. "I thought you'd stop to give me a ride."

"What?" Hasselthorpe glanced out the window. They were almost on the outskirts of London. "Is this robbery? Have you commandeered my carriage?"

"Nothing of the sort." Hartley shrugged and crossed his arms over his chest, slumping a bit in the seat, his legs taking up too damned much of the room. "I merely saw your carriage stopped and thought I'd ask for a ride. You don't mind, do you?"

"I have a session of the House of Lords to attend at Westminster Palace. Of course I mind!"

"Then you'd better tell your coachman," Hartley said maddeningly. "We're driving in the opposite direction."

Once again, Hasselthorpe rose and pounded on the roof of the carriage.

Ten minutes later, after a ridiculous argument with his coachman, who seemed to've entirely lost his sense of direction, Hasselthorpe once again took his seat.

Hartley shook his head sadly. "Good help is hard to find. Do you think your driver's drunk?"

"That or mad," Hasselthorpe grumbled. At the rate they were going, the session might very well be over by the time they got to Westminster Palace. He clutched his memorandum book in sweaty hands. This vote was an important one—it would demonstrate his ability to lead and direct the party.

"I've been meaning to ask you," Hartley drawled, interrupting his thoughts. "Who were you referring to when you told Sir Alistair Munroe that the Spinner's Falls traitor had a French mother?"

Hasselthorpe's mind went entirely blank. "What?"

"Because I've been racking my brain, and the only veteran of Spinner's Falls who had a French mother that I remember is Reynaud St. Aubyn," Hartley said. "Of course, your brother was there as well, wasn't he? Lieutenant Thomas Maddock. A brave soldier as I remember. Perhaps he wrote you about another soldier who had a French mother?"

"I don't know what you're talking about," Hasselthorpe said. "I never told Munroe anything about soldiers with French mothers."

Hartley was silent a moment, staring at him.

Hasselthorpe felt sweat dampen his armpits.

Then Hartley said softly, "No? How strange. Munroe remembers the conversation vividly."

"Perhaps he'd been drinking," Hasselthorpe snapped.

The Colonial smiled as if he'd revealed something damning and said lightly, "Perhaps. You know, I hadn't thought about your brother Thomas for a very long while."

Hasselthorpe licked his lips. He was too hot. The carriage felt like a trap.

"He was your older brother, wasn't he?" Hartley asked softly.

Chapter Seventeen

As the end of his year on earth drew nearer, Longsword grew more and more despondent until Princess Serenity feared for his very life. Yet although he was distracted and moody, in his body he remained healthy and strong. She decided then that the problem must lie with his mind, and to find out the matter, she questioned him closely, both day and night. So vexed was her husband that in the end he could do naught but confess his story. How he had made a very bad bargain with the Goblin King. How he could remain on the earth for only one year unless he could find someone to take his place in the kingdom of the goblins of their own volition. And how if Longsword failed to find his replacement, he would be damned to labor for the Goblin King for all eternity. . . .

—from *Longsword*

"Westminster is so very masculine, isn't it?" Lottie mused as they stopped and glanced about the great hall.

"Masculine?" Beatrice stared at the high vaulted ceiling, nearly black with age. "I don't know what you mean by *masculine,* but I do think it could do with a good cleaning."

"What I mean by *masculine,*" Lottie said, linking her arm with Beatrice's, "is stodgy and self-important and much too serious to notice mere womenfolk."

Beatrice eyed her friend, who was looking elegant as usual in a deep purple and brown striped gown. She'd just taken off her fur hood, but her cheeks were rosy from the cold outside, and her eyes snapped with an aggression that Beatrice wasn't sure had anything to do with Westminster Palace's architecture.

"It's a building, Lottie."

"Exactly," Lottie said. "And all buildings—at least the great ones—have a sort of spiritual sense about them. Did I ever tell you about the chill I felt in St. Paul's last spring? Quite mysterious. It sent a shiver down my spine."

"Perhaps you were standing in a draft," Beatrice said practically. They'd reached the end of the hall and had come to a passage. "Which way now?"

"To the right," Lottie said decisively. "The left leads to the Commons' Strangers Gallery, so the right must be the way to the gallery for the lords."

"Hmm." This seemed rather haphazard, but as Beatrice had never visited parliament before and Lottie had, she followed her.

And as it turned out, whether by luck or accident, Lottie was exactly right. They turned right down a narrow passage that led to a set of double doors. To the side was a staircase that led upward. Once at the top, they each gave the waiting servant two shillings and were admitted to the ladies' side of the visitor gallery.

Below them was a hall with tiered benches arranged on either side rather like the choir in a cathedral. The benches were covered in red cushions. Between the rows of benches was a long wooden table, and at the end of the hall stood several single chairs. The gallery overhung the hall and ran around three sides.

"I thought they were in session," Beatrice whispered.

"They are," Lottie replied.

Beatrice examined the noble members of the House of Lords. "They don't look like they're doing very much."

And they didn't. Some men wandered the chamber or chatted together in small groups. Others lounged on the cushions, more than one dozing. A gentleman stood at the end and appeared to be talking, but the noise in the hall was so loud that Beatrice couldn't hear him. Some of the lords appeared to be heckling the poor man.

"The governing process can be obscure to the untrained eye," Lottie said loftily.

"Why, that's Lord Phipps," Beatrice exclaimed in dismay, having finally identified the speaker. "It doesn't look very good for Mr. Wheaton's bill."

For Lord Phipps was the champion of the veteran's bill in the House of Lords. He was a kindly man but was a bit dry and nondescript and, as it was obvious now, not a particularly good speaker.

"No, it doesn't," Lottie said, subdued. "He is so sweet

when he comes to the meetings. He sat and told me all about his ginger cat once."

"He got tears in his eyes when he talked about his late wife," Beatrice said.

"Such a nice man."

They both watched as a lord in a full-bottomed wig and black and gold robes at the end of the room vainly shouted for order. Someone threw an orange peel.

"Oh, dear," Lottie sighed.

There was a commotion by the doors, but since the gallery overhung the room, Beatrice couldn't at first see who had entered below them. Then Reynaud strode into the room, and her heart gave a sort of painful leap. He was so handsome, so commanding, and he seemed farther away from her than ever. Reynaud headed straight to the man in the chair as heads turned to follow his progress.

"What's he doing?" Lottie asked. "A peer has to have a writ of summons from the king to join parliament."

"He must've won the title back," Beatrice said softly. She rejoiced for Reynaud, but she worried about Uncle Reggie. He must be crushed. "Perhaps he got a special dispensation?"

"From the king himself," a male voice said from the aisle separating the ladies' section from the rest of the gallery.

"Nate!" Lottie cried.

Mr. Graham nodded at his wife. "Lottie." He came to stand by the rail near them. "It's all over Westminster. Reynaud has been given the title and the earldom by King George—he actually came to Westminster to do it."

"But how could he sit in the House of Lords today?" Lottie asked.

Mr. Graham shrugged. "The king issued his writ of summons at the same time."

"Goodness," Beatrice said. "Then he'll be able to vote on Mr. Wheaton's bill." Would his vote be for or against the bill?

The peer in the black and gold robes was calling for order. "The noble Earl of Blanchard will now speak on this matter."

Beatrice gasped and leaned forward.

Reynaud stood and placed one hand on the table in the middle of the room. He paused a moment as the House quieted and then said, "My lords, this bill has been explained to you at length by the noble Lord Phipps. It is to provide for the well-being of the gallant men who serve this country and His Majesty, King George, with their bravery, their labor, and sometimes their very lives. There are those who value this service lightly, who consider the soldiers of this green and glorious isle to be less than deserving of a decent pension in their old age."

A lord cried, "Hear him!"

"Perhaps these persons find mealy peasemeal and gruel a banquet. Perhaps these persons think marching for twenty miles through mud in pouring rain a stroll through a pleasure garden."

"Hear him! Hear him!" The calls were growing more frequent.

"Perhaps these persons find facing cannon fire relaxing. Enjoy meeting the charge of galloping cavalry. Find the screams of dying men music to their ears."

"Hear him! Hear him!"

"Perhaps," Reynaud shouted above the chant, "these persons love the agony of a severed limb, the loss of an eye, or the infliction of torture such as *this*."

And Beatrice covered her mouth in mingled horror and pride. For on his last word, Reynaud flung from his body his coat and waistcoat and pulled his shirt half down his arms, revealing his upper back. Sudden silence descended on the hall as Reynaud pivoted in place, the light reflecting off the ugly scars snaking through his tanned skin. In the quiet, the sound of linen ripping was loud as Reynaud tore off the remainder of the shirt and threw it to the floor.

He raised one hand, outstretched, commanding. "If such a person is in this room, let him vote against this bill."

The room erupted into cheers. Every peer was on his feet, many were still shouting, "Hear him! Hear him!"

"To order! To order!" the peer in the gold and black robes called to no avail.

Reynaud still stood, his chest bare, his back straight in the middle of the hall, proudly displaying the scars she knew had shamed him. He glanced up and caught her eye. Beatrice stood up, clapping, the tears standing in her eyes. He nodded imperceptibly and then was distracted by another peer.

"He's won it," Mr. Graham shouted. "They'll vote, but I think it a mere formality. Your uncle can no longer vote on the Lords, and Hasselthorpe and Lister haven't shown."

Lottie leaned toward him. "You must be disappointed."

Mr. Graham shook his head. "I've decided Hasselthorpe isn't a leader I want to be following." He looked sheepishly at Beatrice. "I'm almost certain he was behind that scene at Miss Molyneux's ball. In any event, I intend to vote for Mr. Wheaton's bill."

"Oh, Nate!" Lottie cried, and threw her arms most improperly about his neck.

Beatrice looked down, smiling as Lottie and Mr. Graham embraced.

"Sir! Sir!" a servant called. "Gentlemen are not allowed in the ladies' side of the gallery!"

Mr. Graham raised his head only fractionally. "She's my wife, dammit." And while gazing in a most romantic manner into Lottie's eyes, he added, "And my love."

And he kissed her again.

This was too much for Beatrice's already overwrought emotions. She found herself wiping tears from her cheeks. In order to give her friends more privacy and to compose herself, she slipped from the gallery, quietly descending the back stairs. In the dark passageway below, she stood by herself, leaning a little against the wall.

Why had he done it? Just last night he said he never wanted to talk of his scars again. Then why reveal them to a roomful of strangers? Did the bill mean so much to him—or, wonderful thought, had he done it for her after all? Beatrice felt selfish, wanting his reason to endorse the bill to be her. The lives of so many soldiers were at stake. Perhaps he'd done it simply of noble consideration for the veterans. But then there'd been that glance he'd given her . . . Oh, she must not read too much into a mere glance!

While she'd been silently contemplating all this, the lords had quieted, but now they roared again, and she could tell by the shouts of "Blanchard! Blanchard!" that Reynaud had carried the day for Mr. Wheaton's bill. Her heart was nearly overflowing. She turned blindly to return to the gallery, but in doing so bumped into a large male form.

Beatrice looked up with an apologetic smile on her face, but it died when she saw the man she'd run into. "Lord Hasselthorpe!"

The peer looked ghastly. His face was blanched a greenish white, and it shone with sweat. He'd been staring at the closed doors to the Lords, but at her voice, he turned to her and his eyes seemed to focus and then grow cold.

"Lady Blanchard."

"TO THE TRUE Earl of Blanchard!" Vale cried, not a little inebriated, as he held up a foaming tankard of ale.

"Blanchard! Blanchard!" Munroe, Hartley, and most of the rest of the rather seedy tavern they sat in cheered. Vale had stood the entire small, smoky room drinks twice already.

They were at a booth in the corner, the table scarred and pitted from numerous previous patrons. The barmaid was buxom and pretty and had at first obviously held high hopes for them. Now, however, after a half hour of concentrated effort, she'd turned her ample charms on a table of sailors sitting nearby. Reynaud couldn't help but think how different her seduction of Vale would've ended seven years ago.

"I thank you. I thank you all." Reynaud was on only

his second pint despite Vale's urging to drink more. He still had a niggling fear of not being completely alert—perhaps a leftover from his years of captivity. "Without your help today, gentlemen, this would've been a far more difficult endeavor. Therefore, to Munroe, who so ably diverted a certain duke and requested the presence of another gentleman of importance at Westminster."

"Huzzah!" shouted the tavern customers, most of whom had no idea what was being said. Even the barmaid waved her cloth.

Munroe merely smiled and inclined his head.

Reynaud turned to Vale. "To Jasper, who gave the deciding vote to pass Mr. Wheaton's veteran's bill!"

"Huzzah!"

Vale actually blushed, the color running high over his hangdog face. Of course, that might've been the ale as well.

"And to Hartley, who delayed the main opposition to the bill!"

Hartley also inclined his head to the cheers of the crowd, though his eyes were still grave. He waited until the surrounding tavern regulars had quieted and turned back to their own affairs and then said, "There's something you all ought to know about Hasselthorpe."

"What's that?" Suddenly Vale didn't look drunk at all.

"He denies telling Munroe that the traitor's mother was French."

Where another man might sputter into protestations, Munroe merely raised his eyebrows. "Indeed."

"Why would he lie about such a thing?" Reynaud set down his tankard of ale, wishing he'd not drunk even that. They were close to something here; he could feel it.

"Perhaps it was his first statement that was the lie," Hartley said softly.

"What d'you mean?" Vale asked.

"When he told Munroe that the traitor's mother was French, Reynaud was still thought dead. Hasselthorpe risked nothing by throwing suspicion on him. Further, he knew that there was a good chance that Munroe would never reveal his information—the news would be too harrowing for Vale to take. Why stir up trouble when the man who might be the traitor is dead?"

Munroe nodded. "That's true. I nearly never told Vale. But I began to think that the truth, even if bitter, was better than lies."

"And a good thing you did, too," Hartley said. "Because when Reynaud returned, Hasselthorpe was then backed into a corner. Should he continue his lie and implicate a now-live man? Or should he call Munroe the liar? Either way, he needed to draw suspicion away from himself fast."

"Then you think Hasselthorpe is the true traitor," Reynaud said quietly. "Why?"

"Think of it." Hartley leaned forward. "When Vale went to question Hasselthorpe, the man was shot—but not fatally. A glancing wound, as I understand it. He then left London altogether and sequestered himself at his estate near Portsmouth. When Munroe questioned him, he told a lie that prevented further interrogation. And remember this: Hasselthorpe's older brother was Thomas Maddock—Lieutenant Maddock of the Twenty-eighth of Foot."

"You think he killed so many to get the title?" Vale frowned.

Hartley shrugged. "It's certainly a reason to betray the regiment. Isn't that something we've been searching for all along—a motive to betray the Twenty-eighth? I asked around—Hasselthorpe was the younger brother. He came into the title shortly after Maddock's death. In fact, Maddock died after their father had passed away, but he seemed to've never heard the news that his father was dead. He was killed at Spinner's Falls before it could reach him."

"This is all well and good," Munroe cut in, his broken voice grating. "We've established why Hasselthorpe might've betrayed the regiment, but I still don't see how he could've done the deed. Only the officers who marched with the Twenty-eighth knew our destination. It was kept secret precisely so we wouldn't be ambushed."

Reynaud stirred. "Only the officers of the Twenty-eighth—and the superiors who ordered them on their route."

"What are you thinking?" Vale turned to him eagerly.

"Hasselthorpe was an aide-de-camp to General Elmsworth at Quebec," Reynaud said. "If Maddock didn't tell him the route—they were brothers, after all—then it wouldn't have been very hard to discover it. Elmsworth may've made him privy to it himself."

"He would've had to get the information to the French," Munroe pointed out.

Reynaud shrugged, pushing away his tankard of ale altogether. "He was in Quebec. Do you remember? It was swarming with the French troops we'd captured,

French citizens, and Indians who'd supported both sides. It was chaos."

"He could've done it easily," Hartley said. "The question now is did he indeed do it? We have supposition and conjecture but no real facts."

"Then we'll have to find the facts," Reynaud said grimly. "Agreed?"

The other men nodded. "Agreed," they said in unison.

"To discovering the truth," Vale said, and raised his tankard.

They all raised their tankards and knocked them together, solemnizing the toast.

Reynaud toasted the sentiment with the rest. He drained his tankard and slammed it down on the table. "And to seeing the traitor swing, goddamn his eyes."

"Hear, hear!"

"Another round on me," Reynaud called.

Vale leaned close, blasting Reynaud with the ale on his breath. "Shouldn't a newly wedded man such as yourself go home?"

Reynaud scowled. "I'll go home soon."

Vale wagged his shaggy eyebrows. "Had a falling-out with the missus?"

"None of your goddamned business!" Reynaud hid his face in his tankard of ale, but when he lowered it, Vale was still staring at him rather blearily. And had it not been for the ale, Reynaud probably wouldn't have said, "She thinks I don't know how to care, if you must know."

"Doesn't she know you care for her?" Hartley asked from across the table.

Wonderful. Both he and Munroe had been listening in like a pair of gossiping biddies.

Munroe stirred. "She needs to know, man."

"Go home," Vale said solemnly. "Go home and tell her you love her."

And for the very first time Reynaud began to think that Vale's romantic advice might—just might—be correct.

Chapter Eighteen

Now, although Princess Serenity had married Longsword as a reward for saving her father, she had, in the many months she had lived with him, come to love her husband deeply. Hearing his terrible fate, she became quiet and withdrawn, contemplating silently what this news meant to her. And, after many long walks in the castle garden, she came to a decision: she would offer herself to the Goblin King in Longsword's stead.

And so, on the night before Longsword was to return to the kingdom of the goblins, Princess Serenity drugged Longsword's wine. As her husband slept, she kissed him tenderly and then set out to meet the Goblin King. . . .

—from *Longsword*

Seven years of planning. Seven years of careful moves on a giant chessboard. Some of them so infinitesimally small that even his most intelligent enemies had been blind to their true meaning. Seven years that should have culminated in his becoming prime minister and the de facto leader of the most powerful country on earth. Seven years of patient waiting and secret lusting.

Seven years destroyed in one afternoon by one man—Reynaud St. Aubyn.

He'd seen the knowledge in Hartley's eyes when he'd mentioned Thomas. Poor, poor Thomas. His brother had never been cut out for greatness. Why should Thomas have the title when it would serve him so much better? But now that old decision had come back to haunt him. Vale, Blanchard, Hartley, and Munroe. All in London at once, all putting their heads together. Hasselthorpe could read the writing on the wall. It was only a matter of time before they had him arrested.

All because St. Aubyn had returned home. He glared across the carriage at his enemy's wife. Beatrice St. Aubyn, Countess of Blanchard now, née Corning. Little Beatrice Corning sat across from him bound and gagged. Her eyes were closed over the cloth tied across her mouth. Perhaps she slept, but he doubted it.

He'd never really paid much attention to her before, besides noting that she made a good hostess for her uncle's political parties. She was pleasant enough to look at, he supposed, but she was no immortal beauty. Hardly the type a man might choose to die for.

He grunted and glanced out the window. The night was black with barely any moonlight, and he couldn't make out where they might be. He let the curtain fall. However, he knew by the number of hours they'd traveled that they must be nearing his estate in Hampshire. He'd told Blanchard that he'd wait until dawn and he would; the boat he'd arranged to pick him up at Portsmouth wouldn't come until eight. He could wait until dawn and no longer before fleeing to the prearranged rendezvous spot. First to France and then perhaps Prussia or even the East Indies. A man could change his name and start a new life in the more remote corners of the world. And with enough capital, he might even make his fortune again.

If he had enough capital. Damnably stupid—he could see that now—tying up most of his monies in investments. Oh, they were good investments, solid investments that would yield a healthy return, but that wasn't much good to him at the moment, was it? He had a little cash, and he'd taken what jewelry Adriana had in the town house, but they weren't all that much.

Not enough to start again as he meant to.

He eyed the girl across from him, measuring her worth. She was his last gamble, his last chance to take with him a small fortune. Of course *he'd* never risk his life, his fortune, for any woman, let alone this pale child, but that really wasn't the gamble was it?

The real question was whether Blanchard had enough regard for his bride to ransom her for a small fortune . . . and lose his life as well.

IT WAS WELL after midnight by the time Reynaud returned home to Blanchard House. The celebration with Vale, Munroe, and Hartley had gone on for hours more and ended in a disreputable tavern that Vale swore brewed the best ale in London. So it was rather commendable that he saw the man lurking in the shadows by the stairs at all.

"What're you doing there?" Reynaud put his hand on his knife, ready to draw it if need be.

The shadow moved and coalesced into a boy, not more than twelve. " 'E said you'd give me a shilling."

Reynaud looked up and down the street in case the lad was a diversion. "Who did?"

"A toff, same as you." The boy held out a sealed letter.

Reynaud fished in his pocket and tossed the boy a shilling. The lad scampered off without another word. Reynaud held the letter up. The light was too dim to see much, but he did notice there was no inscription on the outside of the letter. He mounted the steps and went inside, nodding at the yawning footman in the hall. Beatrice was probably abed by now, and he yearned to lie beside her warm softness, but the oddity of the strange missive intrigued him. He went to the sitting room, lit a few candles from the fire, and tore open the letter.

The handwriting inside was scrawling and partially smeared as if sealed in haste:

I won't be hung.

Bring me the Blanchard jewels. Come alone to my country estate. Tell no one. Be here by the dawn's first light. If you come after light, if you come with friends, or if you come without the jewels, you'll find your wife dead.

I have her.

Richard Hasselthorpe

* * *

Reynaud had hardly gotten to the last line when he was running to the sitting room door. "You!" he shouted at the startled footman. "Where is your mistress?"

"My lady hasn't returned yet this evening."

But Reynaud was already leaping up the stairs. This thing was impossible. She must be here. Perhaps she'd slipped past the footman. The note was a joke. He reached her bedchamber and flung open the door.

Quick jumped to her feet from a chair by the fireplace. "Oh, my lord, what is it?"

"Is Lady Blanchard here?" he demanded, though he could see the bed was still made and empty.

"I'm sorry, my lord. She went out this afternoon, to visit parliament, and she hasn't returned."

Dear God. Reynaud stared down at the letter in his hand. *I have her.* Hasselthorpe's country estate was hours away, and the dawn would be coming soon.

THEY'D BEEN TRAVELING for hours. Beatrice stiffened her body, bracing as the carriage lumbered around a corner. She couldn't use her hands, which had long since fallen asleep because they were bound behind her back, and she was afraid that if she were thrown to the floor, she'd hit her face. She very much doubted that Lord Hasselthorpe would bother to catch her.

She twisted a bit, trying to work her fingers, but it was useless. She felt the pain from where the rope had cut her wrists, but nothing else. She remembered Reynaud telling her how he'd walked for days in the woods of the New World with his hands tied. How had he withstood such torment? The pain must've been intense, the fear that he'd lose his hands terrible. She wished now that she could've said something when he'd related his experiences, conveyed her sympathy more eloquently.

Told him that she loved him.

She closed her eyes, biting hard on the cloth gag stuffed in her mouth. She would not let this dreadful man see her fear, but she wished—oh, how she wished!—that she'd been able to tell Reynaud that she loved him. She wasn't sure why she needed to tell him. He might not even care—*probably* wouldn't care. He'd shown her affection and passion, but nothing more, nothing that could be called love. Perhaps he no longer had the ability to feel romantic love. It seemed to her that in order to feel true and lasting love, once-in-a-lifetime-if-one-were-lucky real love, one must be prepared to let oneself fall. To give oneself up utterly to the other person if need be. She knew that she could do just that, but Reynaud would not *let* himself love.

And still it didn't seem to matter. Beatrice had discovered that one's love needn't be reciprocated in order for it to thrive. It seemed her love was perfectly happy to grow and even bloom in the complete absence of his. There was no controlling it.

The carriage jolted, and Beatrice wasn't quite quick enough to brace herself entirely. Her shoulder hit the side painfully.

"Ah," said Lord Hasselthorpe. It was the first time he'd spoken in hours. "We're here."

Beatrice craned her neck, trying to see out the window, but what she could see was mostly black. They rounded a curve, and she braced her feet against the floorboards.

And then the carriage stopped.

The door was opened by a footman, and Beatrice tried to catch the man's eye to perhaps gain his sympathy. But he kept his gaze fixed downward, save for one darted glance at Lord Hasselthorpe. There would be no help from that quarter.

"Come, my lady," Lord Hasselthorpe said rather nastily, and yanked her to her feet.

He pushed her ahead of him, out of the carriage, and for a moment she feared she'd fall headlong down the steps. The footman caught her arm to steady her, though he just as hastily let her go. Beatrice looked at him again and saw a faint frown between his brows. Perhaps there was hope of help from him after all.

But she hadn't time to consider the matter further, for Lord Hasselthorpe was marching her toward a great mansion. Even in the dark she could see it was a huge building with but one light in one of the lower windows. As they neared the front doors, one was flung open and an ancient manservant stood to the side, holding a candelabra that looked too heavy for his thin wrist.

"My lord." He bowed his head, his expression serene enough to make Beatrice wonder if Lord Hasselthorpe often brought bound-and-gagged ladies to his doorstep.

Her captor made no acknowledgment of the butler but dragged her up the steps and into the hall.

It was only after they'd passed the old manservant that the man cleared his throat and said, "Her ladyship is in residence, my lord."

Lord Hasselthorpe stopped so suddenly that Beatrice stumbled over her own feet. He absently held her up as he glared at the butler. "What?"

The old man appeared unperturbed at his master's

ire. "Lady Hasselthorpe arrived yesterday evening and is even now upstairs asleep."

Lord Hasselthorpe scowled at the ceiling as if he could see his wife in bed several floors above. Obviously his wife's presence at his country estate was a surprise. Beatrice's heart leaped a little in cautious optimism. Lady Hasselthorpe was not known for her intelligence, but surely she'd protest her husband bringing home kidnapped countesses?

If Lady Hasselthorpe was ever allowed to see her, that is. For now Lord Hasselthorpe was trotting her quickly toward the back of the house. He turned down a dark passage so narrow that he had to push her ahead of himself, for they would not fit abreast. This ended in a steep flight of stairs that spiraled downward into the depths of the mansion. Beatrice felt sweat start at the small of her back as she descended. The steps were bare stone, well worn and slippery. A fall here might break her neck. Was that what Lord Hasselthorpe intended? Would he kill her out of some strange revenge for Reynaud's win on the parliament floor? But then why bring her all the way to his country estate merely to murder her? Surely that made no sense.

Beatrice clung to that minuscule hope as they descended farther into the depths of the mansion. They reached an uneven stone floor at last, and she saw that it was a kind of dungeon. The house above must be built on some type of older fortification. Hasselthorpe backed her into a stone wall. She heard the clank of chains and then felt cold metal against her wrists.

He stepped away and nodded. "That'll hold you until your bastard husband comes to take your place."

Beatrice strained, trying to say something, anything to get his attention, but he simply walked away, taking the light with him. She was left in cold, dank darkness. She pulled hard on the chain, hoping the anchor might've rotted, but it held fast. And then she could only stand and wait, for the chain would not let her sit. Would she die here, alone in the blackness? Or would Lord Hasselthorpe or one of his servants rescue her? She thought of Reynaud, his angry black eyes, his confident hands, his gentle mouth, and she wept a little, wondering if she'd ever see his dear face again. She knew he wouldn't come for her, though.

He'd told her already. He'd not put himself into the power of another ever again.

REYNAUD'S FISTS SLID against the horse's sweaty neck. He bent low over the animal, his hands on either side of the beast's neck, a rein in each hand. He'd traded in his own horse two hours ago when it'd begun to lag, throwing an exorbitant sum at a sleepy innkeeper for his best horse. The gelding was a great bony animal, not pretty, but he had stamina.

Stamina and speed were all that mattered now.

Bulging saddlebags were tied behind him. They held a small fortune—every bit of gold he could find in the house, as well as his mother's jewelry. He'd stuck a pistol in each coat pocket before he'd ridden out of London, though it was mainly his speed that deterred robbers.

The horse's gait jarred him with each leap of his great legs, but Reynaud no longer cared. His arms and legs and arse ached, his hands had gone numb, his fingers were stiff with cold, and still he urged the beast on. He rode through black night, hell-for-leather, not caring of potential holes or unseen barriers in the road, endangering both the horse's neck and his own.

It didn't matter. If he wasn't in Sussex at Hasselthorpe's door by dawn, that madman would kill Beatrice, and he wouldn't have a reason to live anyway. It was ironic, really. All this time he'd thought only of what he'd lost and never of what he'd gained. He'd wanted his title, his lands, his money, when all along they meant *nothing* without *her* by his side. Those calm gray eyes watching him curiously, showing no fear and no illusion as to who he was. That sweet, amused smile in an otherwise tart expression when she ticked him off for being an ass. The erotic surprise on her face when he entered her, her mouth opening in wonder.

God! Oh, God! He was going to lose her. Reynaud felt the burn of tears on his cheeks. The dawn was coming soon. He urged the gelding on, hearing the rasp of the horse's breath, the jingle of the tack, and his own desperate heartbeat in his ears, knowing it was too little, too late. He wasn't going to make it in time.

He'd kill the bastard, the murderer of his wife. He'd take his revenge in blood and pain, and then he'd end all this himself.

If she was dead, he'd have nothing to live for.

Chapter Nineteen

All night Princess Serenity journeyed. As the sun's first rays blessed the earth, she came to the place where a year ago she had met Longsword. It was a barren spot, devoid of trees or even grass. The princess looked about her but could see no other living thing. Just as she began to wonder if she'd come in vain, a crack appeared in the dry ground. Wider and wider it grew until the Goblin King rose from the depths of the earth.

His orange eyes glowed bright at the sight of her, and he smiled with yellow fangs as he said, "And who might you be?"

"I am Princess Serenity," she replied. "And I have come to take my husband's place in the kingdom of the goblins. . . ."

—from *Longsword*

It was dark, so dark, and she'd lost track of the time. She could've been standing here for minutes or hours, her arms wrenched painfully behind her, her eyes straining uselessly in the blackness. Every now and again she'd nod off despite the pain and fear, but as her body sagged forward, her shoulders would be yanked by the chain on her wrists, and she would startle awake. At first she'd thought the dungeon was silent as well, but as she stood there, she began to hear things. Small rustlings. The scrape of a tiny claw against stone. The slow drip of water somewhere. In the dark, all alone, the sounds should have frightened her more. Instead they were almost comforting. She wasn't sure she could've remained sane if her hearing had been taken away as well as her eyesight.

Finally she heard footsteps, distant but drawing nearer. She straightened, trying to look serene, trying to be brave. Reynaud had been brave in captivity and so could she. She was a countess. She wouldn't meet death weeping.

The door to the dungeon was thrown open, and she flinched away from the lantern light.

"Beatrice."

Oh, dear God, it couldn't be. She squinted and saw her husband's broad shoulders blocking the light from the lantern. He was hatless, his boots muddy and scuffed, and he carried a full saddlebag over one shoulder. She jerked forward, her throat working, trying to say something. To warn him. Lord Hasselthorpe had ranted for nearly an hour when first they entered the carriage about the revenge he would inflict on Reynaud.

"Don't touch her," Lord Hasselthorpe said, and Reynaud stepped aside. Behind him was Lord Hasselthorpe, a gun pointed firmly at Reynaud. "Here she is.

You can see that no harm has come to her. Now give me the money."

Reynaud didn't look at the other man. His eyes were on hers, blazing, black, and dangerous. "Take off her gag."

"You've already—"

Reynaud turned his head and hit Lord Hasselthorpe with a stare. "Take it off."

Lord Hasselthorpe frowned, but he stepped forward, keeping his eyes on Reynaud. He fumbled, one-handed, with the cloth tied at the back of her head, and then the binding fell.

Beatrice spat out the wadded cloth in her mouth. "Reynaud, he'll kill you!"

"Shut up," Lord Hasselthorpe said.

"Don't." Reynaud took a step toward the other man, seemingly oblivious to the raised gun between them. He stared at Lord Hasselthorpe a moment, then looked at Beatrice, a muscle flexing in his jaw. "Has he hurt you?"

"No," she whispered. "Reynaud, you *cannot*."

"Hush." He shook his head slightly and almost smiled. "You're alive. That's all that matters."

"She's alive and I want the money," Lord Hasselthorpe said impatiently.

"What guarantee can you give me that she'll go free?" Reynaud was staring at her, as if memorizing her features.

Beatrice felt ice begin to form at her center. "Reynaud," she whispered, pleading now.

"My wife is in residence," Lord Hasselthorpe said. "She has nothing to do with this. I'll put Lady Blanchard into her care and send the both of them to London. I've already sent a footman to bring Adriana here."

"You don't intend to take your wife with you?" Reynaud's eyes were horribly gentle, and though he spoke to the other man, his gaze never left her face.

"Why should I?" Lord Hasselthorpe replied impatiently.

The corner of Reynaud's mouth twitched. How could he find any of this amusing? "A certain sentimentality, perhaps?"

"I haven't time for sentimentality or your wit," Lord Hasselthorpe snapped. "If you want your wife to live to see the dawn—"

"Very well." Reynaud threw the saddlebag at Lord Hasselthorpe's feet just as Lady Hasselthorpe appeared in the doorway to the dungeon.

"Why, my lord, you didn't tell me we had guests," Lady Hasselthorpe exclaimed as if being woken before dawn to greet callers in the dungeon was perfectly normal. She seemed not to notice that her husband held a gun on one of her "guests."

She made to step into the dungeon, but the burly footman by her side prevented her. "Best not, my lady. 'Tis dirty down here."

Lord Hasselthorpe nodded to the man. Despite the footman's words, his real reason for stopping her must be so that she wouldn't get too near Reynaud.

"I'd like you to take Lady Blanchard to London, my dear," Lord Hasselthorpe said. "She's ill and Lord Blanchard and I have business to discuss." He reached behind Beatrice with one hand and unlocked the chains about her wrists.

Beatrice's heart sank. "Reynaud, I can't leave you here."

Lord Hasselthorpe gave Reynaud a hard look. "It matters not to me, but you know the alternative."

Reynaud's mouth thinned. "Let me talk to her."

"As you wish."

Reynaud bent to her ear, his face against hers. Beatrice's hands were still tied behind her back. She wished they were free so she might feel his dear face.

"You must leave with Lady Hasselthorpe," he whispered in her ear.

She felt hot tears overflow her eyes. "No. No, you said you would never put yourself in another man's power again."

"I was wrong." His breath caught on a quiet laugh that blew against her cheek. He smelled of horse and leather and her husband. "So very wrong. I was foolish and vain, and I nearly didn't realize it in time. I nearly lost you. But I didn't."

"Reynaud," she sobbed.

"Shh," he whispered. "You asked me if I loved you. I do. I love you more than life itself. Nothing matters in this world but that you live. Can you do that for me? Can you live?"

What could she say? He was sacrificing himself, she knew that. Sacrificing himself for her and he wanted her to just walk out of this room and leave him here. . . . She shook her head, her throat swollen shut with grief.

He took her face between his palms and looked at her, and for the first time since his return, she saw the laughing boy of the portrait in his black eyes. They stared at her, confident and whole, with the hint of a mischievous gleam.

"Yes, you can," he said in that low, deep voice she loved so much. "For me. Live for me."

"I love you," she whispered, and she saw gladness in his eyes.

She turned, stumbling, and walked from that hell-hole. Lord Hasselthorpe said something, and Lady Hasselthorpe babbled and chirped, but she heard none of it, because she was leaving Reynaud behind. She turned one last time at the door and looked over her shoulder.

Reynaud was kneeling next to the stone wall where she'd been chained. She saw that there were three iron rings set in the stone wall. She'd been chained to the middle one, but now iron links were threaded through the two outer rings. Reynaud's strong arms were out-stretched wide, and Lord Hasselthorpe was watching as the burly footman fastened chains to his wrists. The cold stone floor must've been hard against Reynaud's knees, and she knew the chains were painful, but he met her eyes and smiled at her.

Smiled as they chained his arms in a cross.

WHEN HE'D ESCAPED from captivity, so many months ago now, he'd vowed that he'd never let himself be caught alive again. He'd sworn to himself that he'd die before being taken by an enemy. And he'd meant that vow, truly.

But now Reynaud broke that vow. He kneeled at the feet of his foe, his arms stretched wide and chained to the wall, helpless, and he was glad. None of it mattered as long as Beatrice was alive. He could face this and worse as long as she lived.

Hasselthorpe bent and opened the saddlebags. Mater's sapphire necklace spilled into the lantern light. Hasselthorpe grunted and picked up the jewels.

"Very nice." The dark blue stones sparkled as he examined them. "The Blanchard jewels, if I'm not mistaken." He grinned at Reynaud.

Reynaud shrugged. "You're not."

"Very nice indeed." Hasselthorpe shoved the necklace back in the leather pouch and began tying the cords as he spoke to the brute of a footman. "See that my horse is ready and my bag brought down. The boat sails in two hours, and I must be away to meet it in time."

For the first time, the big servant showed signs of independent thought. He hesitated, glancing at Reynaud. "An' him?"

Hasselthorpe looked at the footman coldly. "That's none of your business."

The man shifted from one foot to the other. "But, see, they'll blame me."

"What?"

"For him." The footman jerked his chin in Reynaud's direction. "You'll be gone and I'll have a dead aristocrat on me hands, and the first one they'll be looking at will be me."

Reynaud grinned. The man had a point.

"Oh, for God's sake," Hasselthorpe burst out just as the door opened to the dungeon.

Lady Hasselthorpe entered with Beatrice behind her.

Christ! Reynaud lunged against his chains, but the

thick iron links held. Hasselthorpe swung toward the door, his gun pointed at Beatrice.

"Get out!" Reynaud ordered. Beatrice was looking at him, her sweet face set in mulish determination. He pulled at the chains with all his strength and felt a slight give.

Hasselthorpe turned toward him as the chains clanked. The lantern's light glinted off the barrel of the pistol in his hand. Hasselthorpe raised it as Reynaud bared his teeth in defiance.

"No!" Beatrice screamed.

Lady Hasselthorpe rushed toward her husband. "Richard! Have you lost your mind?"

"Beatrice!" Reynaud lunged again, and the iron ring holding his right wrist burst from the wall.

Hasselthorpe swung toward him with the gun, but Lady Hasselthorpe was there, and Beatrice, damn her, *Beatrice* threw herself against the man.

The gun exploded with a deafening thunderclap, echoing off the stone walls and ceiling. For a moment, everyone froze.

"Beatrice," Reynaud whispered.

She looked at him, her eyes puzzled, and raised a hand toward him.

Blood streaked her fingers.

SHE'D BEEN NEARLY deafened by the pistol's report, but Beatrice still heard Reynaud's angry roar. He sounded like an enraged lion, like some fiery archangel come from heaven to wreak vengeance on a mortal man. He leaped forward, his freed right hand outstretched toward Lord Hasselthorpe. The chain shrieked against the iron ring, and he jerked back, his fingertips brushing Lord Hasselthorpe's sleeve.

"Dear God!" Lord Hasselthorpe exclaimed. He fell against Beatrice, grasping at her arm.

It was the wrong thing to do.

Reynaud roared again and lunged. The other iron ring exploded from the wall. He was on Lord Hasselthorpe in one bound, tearing the man away from Beatrice.

Lady Hasselthorpe screamed.

Reynaud hit the other man in the face with a horrible smacking sound, and Lord Hasselthorpe fell to the ground. Reynaud followed him down to the stone floor, kneeling above him, his balled fist driving again and again into Lord Hasselthorpe's face.

"Stop him!" Lady Hasselthorpe clutched Beatrice's arm. "He'll kill Richard."

He would, too. Reynaud showed no signs of halting, though the other man had long since ceased resisting.

"Reynaud," she said. "Reynaud!"

He stopped abruptly, his chest heaving, his hands, bloody, hanging by his sides and the chains still dangling from his wrists.

Beatrice went to him and hesitantly touched his short, black hair. "Reynaud."

He turned suddenly and laid his face against her stomach, his big hands grasping her hips. "He hurt you."

"No," she said, stroking his dear head, feeling his warmth beneath her palms. "No. The blood was his. The bullet must've hit him somewhere. I am not hurt."

"I could not bear it," he said against her. "I couldn't bear it if you were hurt."

"I wasn't," she whispered. She took his hands, large

and bruised, in hers and drew him up. "I'm whole and safe. You've rescued me."

"No," he said as he stood. "I am the one who is rescued. I was lost and broken, and you saved me." He bent and whispered against her lips, "You have redeemed me."

He pulled her close, and she came willingly, happily, into the arms of the man she loved.

And who loved her in return.

Chapter Twenty

At the princess's words, the Goblin King threw back his head and laughed until his green hair waved all about his head. "You shall be a delightful addition to my menagerie, my dear."

He held out his horny hand. Princess Serenity laid her own small white hand in the Goblin King's palm. At that very moment, Longsword appeared at a dead run.

"Stop!" he cried when he saw them. "Stop this dreadful thing! I did not know what my wife meant to do, but when I woke in the dark and found her gone, I suspected the worst. I have run all this night to prevent this thing."

"Ah," sighed the Goblin King. "But you are still too late. The pact between your wife and I has already been agreed upon and sealed. There is naught you can do. She is forfeit to me. . . ."

—from *Longsword*

"What will happen to Lord Hasselthorpe?" Beatrice asked later—much later—that day. She sat at her dressing table in her chemise, brushing her hair.

She watched Reynaud in the mirror. He lounged on the bed, his banyan falling open to reveal his bare chest. He'd discarded shoes and stockings, but he still wore his breeches. She'd almost lost him today, and the horror was still close to the surface. If she'd had her way, she would've shadowed him all day, just to watch him breathe. But they'd had to part early this morning. Reynaud had been concerned with taking Lord Hasselthorpe to prison, and she'd made an exhausting journey back to London in the company of a distraught Lady Hasselthorpe. The poor woman had had no idea of her husband's murderous character, and moreover it seemed that she'd truly loved the awful man. Beatrice had spent the ride trying to comfort her.

As a result of all this, she'd only been reunited with Reynaud shortly after dinner, when he'd embraced her hurriedly and excused himself to bathe. His hair was still damp from that bath, she could see, and she wanted to touch it, but she restrained herself, feeling unaccountably shy.

"He'll be charged with treason and murder," he said. "And when he's found guilty, he'll be hanged."

"How awful for Lady Hasselthorpe." Beatrice shivered a little, placing her brush carefully on the dressing table. "Did he really inform the French of your regiment's movements solely to kill his brother?"

Reynaud shrugged, causing his banyan to fall farther open. "He was probably paid as well, but I think the main reason was so he could steal his brother's title."

"What a terrible man."

"Indeed."

Beatrice swiveled on her stool to look at him fully. "I never thanked you for what you did to help pass Mr. Wheaton's bill."

"You don't have to thank me," he replied quietly. "The men the bill benefits are soldiers. My men. I should've been more interested in the bill all along, instead of worrying solely about myself."

She stood, walking toward him. "You'd lost everything. There was a reason you were focused on what you needed to have again."

"No." He shook his head and looked away, a muscle tightening in his jaw. "I thought only of money and lands and my title. I didn't consider what was truly important until it was almost too late."

She felt her throat tighten. She climbed into the bed to sit beside him and trailed her fingers down his chest. "And what is that?"

He turned and seized her hand, making her start.

"You." He kissed the tips of her fingers, watching her with black eyes so serious they nearly frightened her. "You. Only you. I realized it on the ride to Hasselthorpe's estate—realized it and knew I was too late. God, Beatrice. I rode for hours thinking that you would be dead before I got there."

"I thought you might not come," she admitted.

He closed his eyes as if in agony. "You must've been terrified. You must hate me."

"No." She drew their joined hands toward her mouth and kissed his knuckles. "I could never hate you. I love you."

He grabbed her and rolled her under himself in a sudden movement. His position was dominating and aggressive. She should've been wary, but she had no fear of him at all.

Reynaud leaned close to her, nearly nose to nose. "Don't say it unless you mean it. There'll be no going back—no *holding* back—once you're truly mine. I do not have it in me to let go once I have what I desire in my grasp. Tread softly."

She framed his face with her palms. "I won't tread softly. I want to go running and leaping. I'll shout it from the rooftops. I love you. I've loved you since you came crashing into my tea party. Before that, really—ever since I was a young girl and saw that roguish portrait of you in the blue sitting room. I love you, Reynaud. I love—"

He covered her mouth with his, swallowing her words. She slid her hands up, reveling in the smooth feel of his hair beneath her hands. He was alive. She was alive. Joy flashed through her, and she widened her legs beneath him in invitation.

Fortunately, he seemed to have the same idea.

He tore his mouth from hers, gasping as he fumbled between their bodies. "You are mine. Forever, Beatrice."

He levered himself up and pulled at the skirts of her chemise. Something ripped and then she felt his hot penis against her folds. He thrust into her, once, twice, and was fully seated, but he froze then.

His head dropped and he shuddered. "Beatrice."

She stretched slowly, sensuously.

"God, don't," he muttered. "Beatrice . . ."

She wrapped one leg over his calves and the other high over his hips. "Hmm?"

She clenched internally.

His flesh leaped within her. "Christ."

"Do that again," she murmured, tilting her hips against his. He was heavy on her—she couldn't displace him—but she could sort of undulate, which she did.

"You're going to kill me," he whispered, lowering his forehead to hers.

"Really?" She slid her hands inside his banyan, kneading his bare back.

"Yes," he groaned. "And I'll die a happy man."

"Then let us die together," she whispered against his lips.

She kissed him then, a tender caress, light and sweet, her lips slightly parted, trying to show him how much she loved him, for she truly had no words to tell him.

And perhaps he understood. He gasped a little, moving his hands to frame her face, raising his own to watch her as he began to move above her. He withdrew and pushed into her, only a little, the movement tiny and controlled, the effect devastating to her senses. She watched him, this man she loved, this man who'd offered his life for hers, as he made love to her. His face was hard and grim, the bird tattoos exotic and foreboding, but his mouth was gentle, and his eyes held an emotion that made her arch up into him.

"Beatrice," he whispered, and began to move faster.

She gripped him, her muscles tightening, her breathing quickening, watching him, waiting. He hitched himself a little higher on her, grinding down, hitting her just there. And she broke. Suddenly, without warning. Gasping and shaking and crying, pressing herself up urgently into him, staring into those ruthless black eyes. Heat crashed through her, seemingly without end.

"Beatrice," he cried. "God! Beatrice!"

And he convulsed above her, shuddering as he flooded her with his seed. Shaking, his black eyes wide and desperate, his mouth twisted as if in agony. He slowly closed his eyes and let his head drop as his great chest heaved for breath.

She stroked his back in little tired circles, her body replete, her mind at rest.

He bent his head and kissed her, his mouth opened wide, his tongue claiming possession. She arched again, helplessly, her nerves still raw.

He lifted his head and looked at her. "I love you, Beatrice. Now and forever. I love you."

She smiled. "And I love you. Now and forever." It was like a new beginning. A new pact.

So she pulled his head down to seal it with a kiss.

"Then he's been condemned," Samuel Hartley said sotto voce nearly a month later.

"Condemned and scheduled to be hanged afore the new year," Reynaud replied equally quietly. The gentlemen stood in a group to one side of his blue sitting room, but the ladies weren't too far away, and they had damnably sharp hearing. The topic wasn't appropriate for the day.

"Serves him right," Reginald St. Aubyn said, not at all quietly. He saw Vale's raised eyebrow and flushed. "Told you I never would've backed the man had I known he'd murdered his brother, let alone was a traitor to the Crown. Good God."

"None of us knew," Munroe growled. "'Tisn't your fault, man."

"Ah." Reginald cleared his throat, looking surprised. "Well, thank you."

Hartley leaned forward to say something else, and Reynaud bit back a smile. In the last month, he'd gotten used to having "Uncle Reggie" about the place, and while he wouldn't call the other man his bosom bow yet, they were getting along rather well. It'd helped that Reggie had quite the knack for managing money, making it grow by leaps and bounds. But then he would've borne with Reggie even if he'd been the most curmudgeonly old man possible. He'd raised Beatrice and she loved him. That was all that mattered in the end.

He glanced to where the ladies were gathered in a knot by one of the settees. Beatrice stood by the others, smiling at something Lady Munroe had said. She wore a pale rose frock tonight, and her hair glowed golden in the candlelight. The Blanchard sapphires sparkled at her neck, but even they were dull next to the bright beauty of her face. Had they been alone, he would've strode over and picked her up, carrying her to his bed so that he might demonstrate again how deep his devotion was. He had a feeling that the urgency of the need to convince her of his love would never pass. He inhaled deeply. But they had guests now, and he wouldn't have Beatrice to himself for several hours yet.

Reynaud glanced to Emeline, sitting in the middle of the settee, as round as an orange. He'd noticed that Hartley cast frequent glances her way, and he had to approve of such uxorious concern for his sister. Lady Munroe—Helen—stood just a little apart, though all the ladies included her in the conversation, and Tante Cristelle sat enthroned in a gilt chair. Lady Vale sat beside Emeline on the settee, ramrod straight, a faint smile about her thin lips.

Feminine laughter drew his eyes to another settee, where Miss Rebecca Hartley sat. Standing stiffly next to her was a young man in simple black clothes, his dark hair clubbed back.

"I think I'll have a new brother-in-law in the coming year," Hartley murmured next to Reynaud.

Reynaud grunted. "Emeline says he was a footman in her household."

"Indeed." Hartley glanced again at his wife. "But O'Hare has spent the last year learning my business in the Colonies. His head for figures is amazing. I've been thinking that should Emeline and I wish to spend a protracted length of time in England, I'd put him in charge of the Boston warehouses."

Reynaud raised his eyebrows. "He looks young for the job."

"He is," Hartley replied. "But in another few years . . ." He shrugged. "Of course, it would help to keep the business in the family."

Reynaud glanced again at the couple by the settee. Miss Hartley's cheeks were a bright pink, and O'Hare hadn't taken his eyes from her face since entering the room. "Then you approve of the match."

"Yes, I do." Hartley's mouth quirked. "Not that my opinion matters. I trust Rebecca to make the right decision in choosing a husband."

A sudden rise in the ladies' chatter made Reynaud

turn his head. Beatrice was leaning forward, placing a package on Emeline's lap.

"What are they up to now?" Hartley wondered next to him.

Reynaud shook his head, feeling that smile returning at Beatrice's excited look. "I haven't the faintest."

"THE GENTLEMEN, THEY are talking about that so 'orrible traitor again," Tante Cristelle commented to no one in particular.

Beatrice glanced over. The gentlemen were all huddled in a corner, and Lord Hasselthorpe was a frequent topic of discussion, but Reynaud looked almost lighthearted tonight. He caught her watching him and gave her a slow wink that made the heat rush into her cheeks. Goodness! Now was not the time to be remembering what he'd done just this morning to her.

Hurriedly she turned to Emeline. "Open it, please."

"There's no need for gifts," Emeline said, but she looked quite pleased nonetheless.

Beatrice had learned in the last month that her sister-in-law was rather nice underneath her formidable exterior. "Actually, it's for Lady Vale and Lady Munroe and me as well. But you'll see. Oh, do open it."

Emeline lifted the box lid. Inside were four bound books, each a different color. One was blue, one yellow, one lavender, and one scarlet.

Emeline glanced up at Beatrice. "What are they?"

Beatrice shook her head. "Look inside one."

Emeline chose the blue and opened it. And then she gasped. "Oh. Oh, my goodness. I'd almost forgotten."

She looked from Melisande to Helen to Beatrice. "How . . . ?"

Tante Cristelle leaned forward. "What is this?"

"It's the fairy-tale book that my nanny used to read to Reynaud and me when we were children. Forgive me." Emeline dabbed at her eyes with her fingertips. "I gave the original book to Melisande to translate."

"And I did," Melisande said in her steady voice. "And when I was done, I gave the translation to Helen to transcribe. She has such an elegant hand."

Helen blushed. "Thank you."

"She gave me back the sheets of papers—she'd made four copies—but for a long while I did not know what to do with them," Melisande said. "When Beatrice married Reynaud, I gave them to her to bind into a book. But I had no idea she'd made four books."

Beatrice smiled. "Each of us worked on it, so I thought each of us should have a book of the fairy tales as a memento."

"Thank you," Emeline said softly. "Thank you, Melisande and Helen, and you as well, Beatrice. This is a wonderful gift." She cradled the blue book against her breast and glanced at the gentlemen. "For so long, all I had were memories of Reynaud, and this book was one of the best. Now I have him back again. I'm so grateful."

Beatrice had to dab at her own eyes. Reynaud was back, and she was grateful as well.

The door to the sitting room opened at that moment, revealing the magnificent form of the butler. "Dinner is served, my lord."

"Ah. Good," Reynaud said. He strode to where Tante

Cristelle sat and bowed to her. "I know 'tisn't the done thing for a gentleman to escort his wife to dinner, but we are still newly wed. Might I have dispensation this once?"

That old lady glared at him with steely pale blue eyes, but then they softened. "Tch. Silly boy. But it is Christmas Day, after all, so I forgive you." She waved her hand at him. "Take your wife. All of you, take your wives. And you"—she crooked a finger at an alarmed Uncle Reggie—"you may escort me!"

Reynaud offered his arm to Beatrice as their guests assembled to be led in to dinner. She placed her fingers on his sleeve, and he tilted his head toward hers. "Have I wished you a Merry Christmas yet, madam?"

"You have," she said. "Several times. But I don't grow weary of hearing it."

"And I'm afraid I'll never grow weary of saying it." His obsidian eyes danced. "Now or in the future. So let me say it once again, the first of many more: Merry Christmas, my love. Merry Christmas, my darling Beatrice."

And he kissed her.

Epilogue

At the Goblin King's awful words, Longsword fell to his knees before him. He drew his magical sword and laid it on the ground at the Goblin King's feet and said, "I will give you my sword, though it means my own death, if you will only let my wife go."

The Goblin King stared, so shocked his orange eyes nearly popped from his head. "You would forfeit your life for this woman?"

"Gladly," was Longsword's simple answer.

The Goblin King turned to Princess Serenity. "And you, you have decided to sacrifice yourself for all eternity for this man?"

"I have already said so," the princess replied.

"ARGH!" the Goblin King cried in frustration, tearing at his green hair. "Then this is True Love—a terrible thing!—for I can have no truck with so powerful a force as True Love." He bent to pick up the sword but hissed as the mere touch of the metal burned his evil flesh. "Bah! Even the sword is tainted by love! This is a most dissatisfactory turn of events!"

And the Goblin King, provoked beyond endurance,

vanished back into the crack in the earth from whence he came.

Princess Serenity came and sank to her knees before her husband, who still knelt in the dust. She took his hands and said, "I do not understand. You hated the Goblin Kingdom; you told me so. Why, then, did you seek to prevent my sacrifice?"

Longsword raised his wife's hands to his lips and kissed them one at a time. "Life without you would be worse than an eternity in the Goblin Kingdom."

"Then you do love me?" she whispered.

"With all my heart," he replied.

Princess Serenity shivered and glanced at the spot where the Goblin King had stood. "Do you think he'll return for us?"

Longsword smiled. "Did you not hear, my sweet? We have a magic so powerful it can defeat the Goblin King himself. It is our love for each other."

And he kissed her.

Don't miss the beginning

of Elizabeth Hoyt's

stunning new series!

Please turn this page

for a preview of

the first book in

the Maiden Lane series,

Wicked Intentions

AVAILABLE IN SUMMER 2010

Chapter One

Once upon a time, in a land forgotten now, there lived a mighty king, feared by all and loved by none. His name was King Lockedheart. . . .

—from *King Lockedheart*

LONDON
FEBRUARY 1742

A woman abroad in St. Giles near midnight was either very foolish or very desperate. Or, as in her own case, Temperance Dews reflected wryly, she was a combination of both.

"'Tis said the Ghost of St. Giles haunts on nights like this," Nell Jones, Temperance's maidservant, said chattily as she skirted a noxious puddle in the narrow alley.

Temperance glanced dubiously at her. Nell had spent three years in a traveling company of actors and sometimes she had a tendency toward melodrama.

"There's no ghost haunting St. Giles," Temperance

replied firmly. The cold winter night was frightening enough without the addition of specters.

"'Course there is." Nell hoisted the sleeping babe in her arms higher. "'E wears a mask and cloak, but 'tis said 'e's disfigured."

"And how would anyone know that if he's masked?" Temperance asked.

They were coming to a turn in the alley and she thought she saw light up ahead. She held her lantern high and gripped the ancient pistol in her other hand a little tighter. The weapon was heavy enough to make her arm ache. She could've brought a sack to carry it in, but that would've defeated its purpose as a deterrent. Though loaded, the pistol held but one shot and to tell the truth, she was somewhat hazy on the actual operation of the weapon.

Still, the pistol looked dangerous and Temperance was grateful for that. The night was black, the wind moaned eerily, bringing the smell of excrement and rotting offal, and the sounds of St. Giles rose about them—voices raised in argument, cries and laughter, and now and again the odd chilling scream. St. Giles was enough to send the most intrepid woman running for her life.

And that was without Nell's conversation.

"'Orribly disfigured," Nell continued, ignoring Temperance's logic. "'Tis said 'is lips and eyelids are clean cut off, so that 'e seems to be grinning at you with 'is great yellow teeth as he comes to pull the guts from your belly."

Temperance wrinkled her nose. "Nell!"

"That's what they say," Nell said virtuously. "Guts

'em and flays the 'ide from their bodies, 'e does. 'Course with the lasses 'e 'as some fun first."

"Well, I don't believe in spirits in any case." Temperance took a breath as they turned the corner into a small, wretched courtyard. Two figures stood at the opposite end, but they scuttled away at their approach. Temperance let out her breath. "Lord, I hate being abroad at night."

Nell patted the infant's back. "Only a half mile more. Then we can put this wee one to bed and send for the wet nurse in the morning."

Temperance bit her lip as they ducked into another alley. "Do you think she'll live until morning?"

But Nell, usually quite free with her opinions, was silent. Temperance peered ahead and hurried her step. The baby looked to be only weeks old and had not yet made a sound since they'd recovered her from the arms of her dead mother. In Temperance's experience a thriving infant was quite loud. Terrible to think that she and Nell might've made this dangerous outing for nought.

But then what choice had there been, really? When she'd received word at the Home for Unfortunate Infants and Foundling Children that a baby was in need of her help it'd still been light. She'd known from bitter experience that if they'd waited 'til morn to retrieve the child, it would either have expired in the night from lack of care or would've already been sold for a beggar's prop. She shuddered. The children bought by beggars were often made more pitiful to elicit sympathy from passersby. An eye might be put out or a limb broken or twisted. No, she'd really had no choice. The baby couldn't wait until morning.

Still, she'd be very happy when they made it back to the home.

They were in a narrow passage now, the tall houses on either side leaning inward ominously. Nell was forced to walk behind or risk brushing the sides of the buildings. A scrawny cat snaked by and then there was a shout very near.

Temperance's steps faltered.

"Someone's up ahead," Nell whispered hoarsely.

They could hear scuffling and then a sudden high scream.

Temperance swallowed. The alley had no side passages. They could either retreat or continue—and to retreat meant another twenty minutes added to their journey.

That decided her. The night was chilly and the cold wasn't good for the babe.

"Stay close to me," she whispered to Nell.

"Like a flea on a dog," Nell muttered.

Temperance squared her shoulders and held the pistol firmly in front of her. Winter, her brother, had said that one need only point it and shoot. That couldn't be too difficult. The light from the lantern spilled before them as she entered another crooked courtyard. Here she froze for just a second, her light illuminating the scene before them like a pantomime on a stage.

A man lay on the ground, bleeding from the head. But that wasn't what froze her—blood and even death were common enough in St. Giles. No, what arrested her was the *second* man. He crouched over the first, his black cloak spread to either side of him like the wings of a great bird of prey. He held a long black walking stick, the end tipped with silver, echoing his hair, which was silver as well. It fell straight and long, glinting in the lantern's light. Though his face was mostly in darkness, she could see his eyes were so blue they nearly glowed. Temperance could feel the weight of the stranger's stare. It was as if he'd physically touched her.

"Lord save and preserve us from evil," Nell murmured, for the first time sounding fearful. "Come away, ma'am. Swiftly!"

Thus urged, Temperance ran across the courtyard and into another passage, leaving the scene behind.

"Who was he, Nell?" She panted as they made their way through the stinking alley. "Do you know?"

The passage let out suddenly into a wider road and Temperance relaxed a little, feeling safer without the walls pressing in.

Nell spat as if to clear a foul taste from her mouth.

Temperance looked at her curiously. "You sounded like you knew that man."

"Knew 'im, no," Nell replied. "But I've seen him about. That was Lord Caire. 'E's best left to 'imself, that one."

"Why?" Temperance asked.

Nell shook her head, pressing her lips firmly together. "I shouldn't be speaking about the likes of 'im to you at all."

Temperance let that cryptic comment go. They were on a better street now—some of the shops had lanterns hanging by the doors, lit by the inhabitants within. Temperance turned one more corner and the foundling home came within sight. Like its neighbors it was a tall brick building of dubious construction. The windows were few and very narrow, the doorway unmarked by any sign. In the fifteen precarious years of the foundling home's existence there had never been a need to advertise.

Abandoned and orphaned children were all too common in St. Giles.

"Home safely," Temperance said as they made the door. She set down the lantern and took out the big iron key hanging by a cord at her waist. "I'm looking forward to a dish of hot tea."

"I'll put this wee one to bed," Nell said as they entered the dingy little hall. It was quite spotlessly clean, but that didn't hide the fallen plaster or the warping of the floorboards.

"Thank you." Temperance removed her cloak and was just hanging it on a peg when a tall male form appeared at the far doorway.

"Temperance."

She swallowed and turned. "Oh! Oh, Winter, I did not know you'd returned."

"Obviously," her younger brother said drily. He nodded to the maidservant. "A good eventide to you, Nell."

"Sir." Nell curtsied and looked nervously between brother and sister. "I'll just see to the, ah, children, shall I?"

And she fled upstairs, leaving Temperance to face Winter's disapproval alone.

Temperance squared her shoulders and moved past her brother. The foundling home was long and narrow, squeezed by the neighboring houses. The small entryway led past a room used for dining and, on occasion, receiving the home's infrequent important visitors. At the back of the house were the kitchens, which Temperance entered now. The children had all had their dinner promptly at five o'clock, but neither she nor her brother had eaten.

"I was just about to make some tea," she said as she went to stir the fire on the hearth. "There's a bit of beef left from yesterday and some new radishes I bought at market this morning."

Behind her Winter sighed. "Temperance."

She hurried to find the kettle. "The bread's a bit stale, but I can toast it if you like."

He was silent and she finally turned and faced the inevitable.

It was worse than she'd feared. Winter's long thin face merely looked sad, which always made her feel terrible. She hated to disappoint him.

"It was still light when we set out," she said in a small voice.

He sighed again, taking off his round black hat to sit at the kitchen table. "Could you not wait for my return, sister?"

Temperance looked at her brother. He was only five and twenty, but he bore himself with the air of a man twice his age. His countenance was lined with weariness, his wide shoulders slumped beneath his ill-fitting black coat, and his long limbs were much too thin. For the last five years he had taught at the tiny daily school attached to the home. The position was wretchedly paid because each pupil was charged only pennies a week. And in addition, since Papa's death last year, Winter had taken over management of the foundling home. Even with her help, the work was overwhelming for one man. Temperance feared for her brother's well-being, but both the foundling home and the tiny day school had been founded by Papa. Winter felt it was his filial duty to keep the two in business.

If only his health did not give out first.

She filled the teakettle from the water jar by the back door to the kitchen. "Had we waited it would've been full dark with no assurance that the babe would still be there." She glanced at him as she placed the kettle over the fire. "Besides, have you not enough work to do?"

Winter frowned. "If I lose my sister think you that I'd be more free of work?"

Temperance looked away guiltily.

Her brother's voice softened. "And that discounts the lifelong sorrow I would feel had anything happened to you this night."

"Nell knew the mother of the baby—a girl of less than fifteen years." Temperance took out the bread and carved it into thin slices. "Besides, I carried the pistol."

"Hmm," Winter said behind her. "And had you been accosted would you have used it?"

"Yes, of course," she said with flat certainty.

"And if the shot misfired?"

She wrinkled her nose. Their father had brought up all her brothers to debate a point finely and that fact could be quite irritating at times.

She carried the bread slices to the fire to toast. "In any case, nothing did happen."

"*This* night." Winter sighed again. "Sister, you must promise me you'll not act so foolishly again."

"Mmm," Temperance mumbled, concentrating on the toast. "How was your day at the school?"

For a moment she thought Winter wouldn't consent to

changing the subject. Then he said, "A good day, I think. The Samuels boy remembered his Latin lesson finally and I did not have to punish any of the boys."

Temperance glanced at him with sympathy. She knew Winter hated to take a switch to a palm, let alone cane a boy's bottom. On the days that Winter had felt he must punish a boy he came home in a black mood.

"I'm glad," she said simply.

He stirred in his chair. "I returned for luncheon, but you were not here."

Temperance took the toast from the fire and placed it on the table. "I must have been taking Mary Found to her new position. I think she'll do quite well there. Her mistress seemed very kind and the woman took only five pounds as payment to apprentice Mary as her maid."

"God willing she'll actually teach the child something so we won't see Mary Found again," Winter muttered.

Temperance poured the hot water into their small teapot and brought it to the table. "You sound cynical, brother."

Winter passed a hand over his brow. "Forgive me. Cynicism is a terrible vice. I shall try to correct my humor."

Temperance sat and silently served her brother, waiting. Something more than her late night adventure was bothering him.

At last he said, "Mr. Wedge visited whilst I ate my luncheon."

Temperance paused, her hand on the teapot. "What did he say?"

"He'll give us only another two weeks and then he'll have the foundling home forcibly vacated."

"Dear God." Temperance stared at the little piece of beef on her plate. It was stringy and hard and from an obscure part of the cow, but she'd been looking forward to it. Now her appetite was suddenly gone. The foundling home's rent was in arrears—they hadn't been able to pay the full rent last month and nothing at all this month.

Perhaps she shouldn't have bought the radishes, Temperance reflected morosely. But the children hadn't had anything but broth and bread for the last week.

"If only Sir Gilpin had remembered our home in his will," Temperance murmured.

Sir Stanley Gilpin had been the patron of the foundling home. A retired merchant who'd managed to make a fortune on the South Sea Company and had been wily enough to withdraw his funds before the notorious bubble burst. Sir Gilpin had been a generous patron while alive, but on his unexpected death six months before the home had been left floundering. They'd limped along, using what money had been saved, but now they were in desperate straits.

"Sir Gilpin was an unusually generous man, it would seem," Winter replied. "I have not been able to find another gentleman so willing to fund a home for the infant poor."

Temperance poked at her beef. "What shall we do?"

"The Lord shall provide," Winter said, rising. "And if He does not, well, then perhaps I can take on private students in the evenings."

"You already work too many hours," Temperance protested. "You hardly have time to sleep as it is."

Winter shrugged. "How can I live with myself if the innocents we protect are thrown into the street?"

Temperance looked down at her plate. She had no answer to that.

"Come." Her brother held out his hand and smiled.

Winter's smiles were so rare, so precious. When he smiled, his entire face lit as if from a flame within, and a dimple appeared on one cheek, making him look boyish, more his true age.

One couldn't help but smile back when Winter smiled, and Temperance did so as she laid her hand in his. "Where will we go?"

"Let us visit our charges," he said as he took a candle and led her to the stairs. "Have you ever noticed that they look quite angelic when asleep?"

Temperance laughed as they climbed the narrow wooden staircase to the next floor. There was a small hall here with three doors leading off it. They peered in the first as Winter held his candle high. Six tiny cots lined the walls of the room. The youngest of the foundlings slept here, two or three to a cot. Nell lay in an adult-sized bed by the door, already asleep.

Winter walked to the cot nearest Nell. Two babes lay there. The first was a boy, red-haired and pink-cheeked, sucking on his fist as he slept. The second child was half the size of the first, her cheeks pale, her eyes hollowed, even in sleep.

"This is the baby you rescued tonight?" Winter asked softly.

Temperance nodded mutely. The little girl looked even more frail next to the thriving baby boy.

But Winter merely touched the baby's hand with a gentle finger. "How do you like the name Mary Hope?"

Temperance swallowed past the thickness in her throat. "'Tis most apt."

Winter nodded and with a last caress for the tiny babe, left the room. The next door led to the boys' dormitory. Four beds held thirteen boys, all below the age of nine—nine was when they were apprenticed out. The boys lay, limbs sprawled, faces flushed in sleep. Winter smiled and pulled a blanket over the three boys nearest the door, tucking in a leg that had escaped the bed.

Temperance sighed. "One would never think that they spent an hour at luncheon, hunting for rats in the alley."

"Mmm," Winter answered as he closed the door softly behind them. "Small boys grow so swiftly to men."

"They do indeed." Temperance opened the last door—the one to the girls' dormitory—and a small face immediately popped off a pillow.

"Did you get 'er, ma'am?" Mary Whitson whispered hoarsely.

She was the eldest of the girls in the foundling home, named for the Whit Sunday morning twelve years before when she'd been discovered on the home's step. Young though Mary Whitson was, Temperance had to sometimes leave her in charge of the other children—as she'd had to tonight.

"Yes, Mary," Temperance whispered back. "Nell and I brought the babe home safely."

"I'm glad." Mary Whitson yawned widely.

"You did well watching the children tonight," Temperance whispered. "Now sleep. A new day will be here soon."

Mary Whitson nodded sleepily and closed her eyes.

Winter picked up a candlestick from a little table by

the door and led the way out of the girls' dormitory. "I shall take your good advice, sister, and bid you good night."

He lit the candlestick from his own and gave it to Temperance.

"Sleep well," she replied. "I think I'll have one more cup of tea before retiring."

"Don't stay up too late," Winter said. He touched her cheek with a finger—much as he had the babe—and turned to mount the stairs.

Temperance watched him go, frowning at how slowly he moved up the stairs. It was past midnight and he would rise again before five of the clock to read, write letters to prospective patrons, and prepare his school lessons for the day. Then he would lead the morning prayers at breakfast, hurry to his job as schoolmaster, work all the morning before taking one hour for a meager luncheon and then work again until after dark. In the evening he heard the girls' lessons and read from the Bible to the older children. Yet when she voiced her worries, Winter would merely raise an eyebrow and inquire who would do the work if not he?

Temperance shook her head. She should be to bed as well—her day started at six of the clock—but these moments by herself in the evening were precious. She'd sacrifice a half hour's sleep to sit by herself with a cup of tea.

So she took her candle back downstairs. Out of habit, she checked to see that the front door was locked and barred. The wind whistled and shook the shutters as she made her way to the kitchen, making the back door rattle. She checked it as well and was relieved to see the back door still barred.

Temperance shivered, glad she was no longer outside on a night like this. She rinsed out the teapot and filled it again. To make a pot of tea with fresh leaves and only for herself was a terrible luxury. Soon she'd have to give this up as well, but tonight she'd enjoy her cup.

Off the kitchen was a tiny room. Its original purpose was forgotten, but it had a small fireplace and Temperance had made it her own private sitting room. Inside was a stuffed chair, much battered, but refurbished with a quilted blanket thrown over the back. A small table and a footstool were there as well—all she needed to sit by herself next to a warm fire.

Humming, Temperance placed her teapot and cup, a small dish of sugar, and the candlestick on an old wooden tray. She picked it up and because both her hands were full, she backed into the door leading to her little sitting room. Which was why she didn't notice until she turned that the sitting room was already occupied.

There, sprawled in her chair like a conjured demon, sat Lord Caire. His silver hair spilled over the shoulders of his black cape, a cocked hat lay on one knee, and his right hand caressed the end of his long ebony walking stick. This close she realized that his hair gave lie to his age. The lines about his startlingly blue eyes were few, his mouth and jaw firm. He couldn't be much above five and thirty.

He inclined his head at her entrance and spoke, his voice deep and smooth and quietly dangerous.

"Good evening, Mrs. Dews."

* * *

SHE STOOD STRAIGHT and tall, this respectable woman who lived in the sewer that was St. Giles. Her eyes had widened at the sight of him, but she made no move to flee. Indeed, finding a strange man in her pathetic sitting room seemed not to frighten her at all.

Interesting.

"I am Lazarus Huntington, Lord Caire," he said.

She blinked. "I know. What are you doing here?"

He tilted his head, studying her. She knew him, yet did not recoil in horror? Yes, she'd do quite well. "I've come to make a proposition to you, Mrs. Dews."

Still no sign of fear, though she eyed the doorway. "You've chosen the wrong woman, my lord. The night is late. Please leave my house."

No fear and no deference to his rank. An interesting woman indeed.

"My proposition is not, er, *illicit* in nature," he drawled. "In fact, it's quite respectable. Or nearly so."

She sighed, looked down at her tray, and then back up at him. "Would you like a cup of tea?"

He almost smiled. Tea? When had he last been offered something so very prosaic by a woman? He couldn't remember.

But he replied gravely enough, "Thank you, no."

She nodded. "Then if you don't mind?"

He waved a hand to indicate permission.

She set the tea tray on the wretched little table and sat on the padded footstool to pour herself a cup. He watched her. She was a monochromatic study. Her dress, bodice, hose, and shoes were all flat black. A fichu tucked in at her severe neckline, an apron, and a cap—no lace or ruffles—were all white. No color marred her aspect, making the lush red of her full lips all the more startling. She wore the clothes of a nun, yet had the mouth of a sybarite.

The contrast was fascinating—and arousing.

"You're a Puritan?" he asked.

She stirred a large lump of sugar into her cup. "No."

"Ah." He was interested in her religious beliefs only as they impacted his own mission.

She took a sip of tea. "How do you know my name?"

He shrugged. "Mrs. Dews and her brother are well known for their good deeds in St. Giles."

"Really?" Her tone was dry. "I was not aware we were so famous beyond the boundaries of St. Giles."

She might look demure, but there were teeth beyond the prim expression. And she was quite right—he would never have heard of her had he not spent the last month stalking the shadows of this poor district.

Stalking fruitlessly, which was why he'd followed her home and sat before this miserable fire now.

"How did you get in?" she asked.

"I believe the back door was unlocked," he replied smoothly.

"No, it wasn't." Her brown eyes met his over her teacup. They were an odd light color, almost golden. "Why are you here, Lord Caire?"

"I wish to hire you, Mrs. Dews," he said softly.

She stiffened and set her teacup down on the tray. "No."

He tilted his head. "You haven't heard the task I wish to hire you for."

She sighed. "It's past midnight, my lord, and I'm not

inclined to games even during the day. Please leave or I shall be forced to call my brother."

He didn't move. "Not a husband?"

"I'm widowed, as I'm sure you already know." She turned to look into the fire, presenting her profile to him.

He stretched his legs in what room there was, his boots nearly in the fire. "You're quite correct, I do know. I also know that you and your brother have not paid the rent on this property."

She said nothing, merely sipping her tea.

"I'll pay handsomely for your time," he murmured.

She looked at him finally, and he saw a flame in those pale eyes. "You think all women can be bought?"

He rubbed his thumb across his chin, considering the question. "Yes, I do, though perhaps not strictly by money. And I do not limit it to women—all men can be bought in one form or another as well. The only trouble is in finding the applicable currency."

She simply stared at him with those odd eyes.

He dropped his hand, resting it on his knee. "You, for instance, Mrs. Dews. I would've thought your currency would be money for your foundling home, but perhaps I'm mistaken. Perhaps I've been fooled by your plain exterior, your reputation as a prim widow. Perhaps you would be better persuaded by influence or knowledge or even the pleasures of the flesh."

"You still haven't said what you want me for."

Though she hadn't moved, hadn't changed expression at all, her voice had a rough edge to it. He caught it only because he had years of experience at the chase. His nostrils flared involuntarily as if the hunter within was trying to scent her. Which of his list had interested her?

"A guide." His eyelids drooped as he pretended to examine his fingernails. "Merely that."

He watched her from under his brows and saw when that lush mouth pursed. "A guide to what?"

"St. Giles."

"Why do you need a guide?"

Ah, this was where it got tricky. "I'm searching for . . . something in St. Giles. I would like to interview some of the inhabitants, but I find my search confounded by my ignorance of the area and people. Hence, a guide."

Her eyes had narrowed as she listened, her fingers tapping against the teacup. "What do you search for?"

He shook his head slowly. "Not unless you agree to be my guide."

"And that is all you want? A guide?"

He nodded, watching her.

She turned to look into the fire as if consulting it. For a moment the only sound in the room was the snap as a piece of coal fell. He waited patiently, caressing the silver head of his cane.

Then she turned to face him fully. "You're right. I'm not tempted by your money. It's a stopgap measure that would only delay our eventual eviction."

He cocked his head, feeling the beat of the pulse beneath his skin, his body's response to her feminine vitality. "What do you want, then, Mrs. Dews?"

She met his gaze levelly. "I want you to introduce me to the wealthy and titled people of London. I want you to help me find a new patron for our foundling home."

Lazarus kept his lips firmly straight, but he felt a surge of triumph as the prim widow ran headlong into his talons.

"Done."

DON'T MISS THESE
SEXY HISTORICALS FROM FOREVER
"Hoyt's writing is almost too good to be true."
—Lisa Kleypas, New York Times bestselling author
ELIZABETH HOYT
To Beguile A Beast
Book Three in The Legend of the Four Soldiers Series
ISBN 978-0-446-40693-2
Knight of Desire
MARGARET MALLORY
All the King's Men
ISBN 978-0-446-55339-1
"One of the best Scottish historical romance authors writing today."
—Midwest Book Review
AMANDA SCOTT
USA TODAY BESTSELLING AUTHOR
TAMED BY A LAIRD
ISBN 978-0-446-54137-4
What happens when a lady desires not one man, but two?
JENNIFER HAYMORE
A Hint of Wicked
ISBN 978-0-446-54029-2